ISBN 978-1-331-71734-8
PIBN 10225477

English
Français
Deutsche
Italiano
Español
Português

www.forgottenbooks.com

Mythology Photography **Fiction**
Fishing Christianity **Art** Cooking
Essays Buddhism Freemasonry
Medicine **Biology** Music **Ancient
Egypt** Evolution Carpentry Physics
Dance Geology **Mathematics** Fitness
Shakespeare **Folklore** Yoga Marketing
Confidence Immortality Biographies
Poetry **Psychology** Witchcraft
Electronics Chemistry History **Law**
Accounting **Philosophy** Anthropology
Alchemy Drama Quantum Mechanics
Atheism Sexual Health **Ancient History**
Entrepreneurship Languages Sport
Paleontology Needlework Islam
Metaphysics Investment Archaeology
Parenting Statistics Criminology
Motivational

IS HE POPENJOY?

A NOVEL

BY

ANTHONY TROLLOPE

FRONTISPIECE BY
WALTER H. EVERETT

VOL. I

NEW YORK
DODD, MEAD & COMPANY
1907

CONTENTS

v

206695

gentlemen who condescend to review us, and who
take up our volumes with a view to business rather
than pleasure, we must be infinite in length and tedium.
But the story must be made intelligible from the
beginning, or the real novel readers will not like it.
The plan of jumping at once into the middle has been
often tried, and sometimes seductively enough for
a chapter or two; but the writer still has to hark
back, and to begin again from the beginning—not
always very comfortably after the abnormal brightness of his few opening pages; and the reader, who
is then involved in some ancient family history, or
long local explanation, feels himself to have been defrauded. It is as though one were asked to eat boiled
mutton after woodcocks, caviare, or maccaroni cheese.
I hold that it is better to have the boiled mutton first,
if boiled mutton there must be.

The story which I have to tell is something in its
nature akin to that of poor Mrs. Jones, who was happy
enough down in Devonshire till that wicked Lieu-
tenant Smith came and persecuted her; not quite
so tragic, perhaps, as it is stained neither by murder
nor madness. But before I can hope to interest readers in the perplexed details of the life of a not unworthy lady, I must do more than remind them that
they do know, or might have known, or should have
known the antecedents of my personages. I must
let them understand how it came to pass that so pretty,
so pert, so gay, so good a girl as Mary Lovelace, without any great fault on her part, married a man so
grim, so gaunt, so sombre, and so old as Lord George
Germain. It will not suffice to say that she had done
so. A hundred and twenty little incidents must be
dribbled into the reader's intelligence, many of them,

let me hope, in such manner that he shall himself be insensible to the process. But unless I make each one of them understood and appreciated by my ingenious, open-hearted, rapid reader—by my reader who will always have his fingers impatiently ready to turn the page—he will, I know, begin to masticate the real kernel of my story with infinite prejudices against Mary Lovelace.

Mary Lovelace was born in a country parsonage; but at the age of fourteen, when her life was in truth beginning, was transferred by her father to the Deanery of Brotherton. Dean Lovelace had been a fortunate man in life. When a poor curate, a man of very humble origin, with none of what we commonly call Church interest, with nothing to recommend him but a handsome person, moderate education, and a quick intellect, he had married a lady with a considerable fortune, whose family had bought for him a living. Here he preached himself into fame. It is not at all to be implied from this that he had not deserved the fame he acquired. He had been active and resolute in his work, holding opinions which, if not peculiar, were at any rate advanced, and never being afraid of the opinions which he held. His bishop had not loved him, nor had he made himself dear to the bench of bishops generally. He had the reputation of having been in early life a sporting parson. He had written a book which had been characterised as tending to infidelity, and had more than once been invited to state dogmatically what was his own belief. He had never quite done so, and then been made a dean. Brotherton, as all the world knows, is a most interesting little city, neither a Manchester nor a Salisbury; full of architectural excellences, given to

literature, and fond of hospitality. The Bishop of
Brotherton—who did not love the Dean—was not a
general favourite, being strict, ascetic, and utterly hostile to all compromises. At first there were certain
hostile passages between him and the new Dean. But
the Dean, who was and is urbanity itself, won the
day, and soon became certainly the most popular man
in Brotherton. His wife's fortune doubled his clerical
income, and he lived in all respects as a dean ought
to live. His wife had died very shortly after his promotion, and he had been left with one only daughter
on whom to lavish his cares and his affection.

Now we must turn for a few lines to the family of
Lord George Germain. Lord George was the brother
of the Marquis of Brotherton, whose family residence
was at Manor Cross, about nine miles from the city.
The wealth of the family of the Germains was not
equal to their rank, and the circumstances of the family
were not made more comfortable by the peculiarities
of the present Marquis. He 'was an idle, self-indul-
gent, ill-conditioned man, who found that it suited
his tastes better to live in Italy, where his means were
ample, than on his own property, where he would
have been comparatively a poor man. And he had a
mother and four sisters, and a brother with whom he
would hardly have known how to deal had he remained
at Manor Cross. As it was, he allowed them to keep the
house, while he simply took the revenue of the estate.
With the Marquis I do not know that it will be necessary to trouble the reader much at present. The old
Marchioness and her daughters lived always at Manor
Cross, in possession of a fine old house in which they
could have entertained half the county, and a magnifi-
cent park—which, however, was let for grazing up to

the garden-gates—and a modest income unequal to the splendour which should have been displayed by the inhabitants of Manor Cross.

And here also lived Lord George Germain, to whom at a very early period of his life had been entrusted the difficult task of living as the head of his family with little or no means for the purpose. When the old Marquis died—very suddenly, and soon after the Dean's coming to Brotherton—the widow had her jointure, some two thousand a year, out of the property, and the younger children had each a small settled sum. That the four ladies—Sarah, Alice, Susanna, and Amelia—should have sixteen thousand pounds among them, did not seem to be so very much amiss to those who knew how poor was the Germain family; but what was Lord George to do with four thousand pounds, and no means of earning a shilling? He had been at Eton, and had taken a degree at Oxford with credit, but had gone into no profession. There was a living in the family, and both father and mother had hoped that he would consent to take orders; but he had declined to do so, and there had seemed to be nothing for him but to come and live at Manor Cross. Then the old Marquis had died, and the elder brother, who had long been abroad, remained abroad. Lord George, who was the youngest of the family, and at that time about five-and-twenty, remained at Manor Cross, and became not only ostensibly but in very truth the managing head of the family.

He was a man whom no one could despise, and in whom few could find much to blame. In the first place he looked his poverty in the face, and told himself that he was a very poor man. His bread he might earn by looking after his mother and sisters, and he knew no other way in which he could do so. He was a just steward, spending nothing to gratify his own whims, acknowledging on all sides that he had nothing of his own, till some began to think that he was almost proud of his poverty. Among the ladies of the family, his mother and sisters, it was of course said that George must marry money. In such a position there is nothing else that the younger son of a marquis can do. But Lord George was a person somewhat difficult of instruction in such a matter. His mother was greatly afraid of him. Among his sisters Lady Sarah alone dared to say much to him; and even to her teaching on the subject he turned a very deaf ear. "Quite so, George," she said; "quite so. No man with a spark of spirit would marry a woman for her money"—and she laid a stress on the word "for"—"but I do not see why a lady who has money should be less fit to be loved than one who has none. Miss Barm is a most charming young woman, of excellent manners, admirably educated, if not absolutely handsome, quite of distinguished appearance, and she has forty thousand pounds. We all liked her when she was here." But there came a very black frown upon Lord George's brow, and then even Lady Sarah did not dare to speak again in favour of Miss Barm.

Then there came a terrible blow. Lord George Germain was in love with his cousin, Miss de Baron! It would be long to tell, and perhaps unnecessary, how that young lady had made herself feared by the ladies of Manor Cross. Her father, a man of birth and fortune, but not perhaps with the best reputation in the world, had married a Germain of the last generation, and lived, when in the country, about twenty miles from Brotherton. He was a good deal on the turf, spent much of his time at card-playing clubs, and was generally known as a fast man. But he paid his way, had never put himself beyond the pale of society, and was, of course, a gentleman. As to Adelaide de Baron, no one doubted her dash, her wit, her grace, or her toilet. Some also gave her credit for beauty; but there were those who said that, though she would behave herself decently at Manor Cross and houses of that class, she could be loud elsewhere. Such was the lady whom Lord George loved, and it may be conceived that this passion was distressing to the ladies of Manor Cross. In the first place, Miss de Baron's fortune was doubtful and could not be large; and then—she certainly was not such a wife as Lady Brotherton and her daughters desired for the one male hope of the family.

But Lord George was very resolute, and for a time it seemed to them all that Miss de Baron—of whom the reader will see much if he go through with our story—was not unwilling to share the poverty of her noble lover. Of Lord George personally something must be said. He was a tall, handsome, dark-browed man, silent generally, and almost gloomy, looking, as such men do, as though he were always revolving deep things in his mind, but revolving in truth things not very deep—how far the money would go, and whether it would be possible to get a new pair of carriage-horses for his mother. Birth and culture had given to him a look of intellect greater than he possessed; but I would not have it thought that he traded on this, or endeavoured to seem other than he was. He was simple, conscientious, absolutely truthful, full of prejudices, and weak-minded. Early in life he had been taught to entertain certain ideas as to religion by those with whom he had lived at college, and had therefore refused to become a clergyman. The bishop of the diocese had attacked him; but though weak, he was obstinate. The Dean and he had become friends, and so he had learned to think himself in advance of the world. But yet he knew himself to be a backward, slow, unappreciative man. He was one who could bear reproach from no one else, but who never praised himself even to himself.

But we must return to his love, which is that which now concerns us. His mother and sisters altogether failed to persuade him. Week after week he went over to Baronscourt, and at last threw himself at Adelaide's feet. This was five years after his father's death, when he was already thirty years old. Miss de Baron, though never a favourite at Manor Cross, knew intimately the history of the family. The present Marquis was over forty, and as yet unmarried;—but then Lord George was absolutely a pauper. In that way she might probably became a marchioness; but then of what use would life be to her, should she be doomed for the next twenty years to live simply as one of the ladies of Manor Cross? She consulted her father, but he seemed to be quite indifferent, merely reminding her that though he would be ready to do everything handsomely for her wedding, she would have no fortune till after his death. She consulted her glass, and told herself that, without self-praise, she must regard herself as the most beautiful woman of her own acquaintance. She consulted her heart, and found that in that direction she need not trouble herself. It would be very nice to be a marchioness, but she certainly was not in love with Lord George. He was handsome, no doubt—very handsome; but she was not sure that she cared much for men being handsome. She liked men that "had some go in them," who were perhaps a little fast, and who sympathised with her own desire for amusement. She could not bring herself to fall in love with Lord George. But then, the rank of a marquis is very high! She told Lord George that she must take time to consider.

When a young lady takes time to consider she has, as a rule, given way; Lord George felt it to be so, and was triumphant. The ladies at Manor Cross thought they saw what was coming, and were despondent. The whole country declared that Lord George was about to marry Miss de Baron. The country feared that they would be very poor; but the recompence would come at last, and the present Marquis was known not to be a marrying man. Lady Sarah was mute with despair. Lady Alice had declared that there was nothing for them but to make the best of it. Lady Susanna, who had high ideas of aristocratic duty, thought that George was forgetting himself. Lady Amelia, who had been snubbed by Miss de Baron, shut herself up and wept. The Marchioness took to her bed. Then, exactly at the same time, two things happened, both of which were felt to be of vital importance at Manor Cross. Miss de Baron wrote a most determined refusal to her lover, and old Mr. Tallowax died. Now old Mr. Tallowax had been Dean Lovelace's father-in-law, and had never had a child but she who had been the Dean's wife.

Lord George did in truth suffer dreadfully. There are men to whom such a disappointment as this causes enduring physical pain—as though they had become suddenly affected with some acute and yet lasting

disease. And there are men, too, who suffer the more
because they cannot conceal the pain. Such a man
was Lord George. He shut himself up for months
at Manor Cross, and would see no one. At first it was
his intention to try again, but very shortly after the
letter to himself came one from Miss de Baron to
Lady Alice, declaring that she was about to be married immediately to one Mr. Houghton; and that closed
the matter. Mr. Houghton's history was well known
to the Manor Cross family. He was a friend of Mr.
de Baron, very rich, almost old enough to be the girl's
father, and a great gambler. But he had a house in
Berkeley Square, kept a stud of horses in Northamp-
tonshire, and was much thought of at Newmarket.
Adelaide de Baron explained to Lady Alice that the
marriage had been made up by her father, whose advice she had thought it her duty to take. The news was
told to Lord George, and then it was found expedient
never to mention further the name of Miss de Baron
within the walls of Manor Cross.

But the death of Mr. Tallowax was also very important. Of late the Dean of Brotherton had become
very intimate at Manor Cross. For some years the
ladies had been a little afraid of him, as they were by
no means given to free opinions. But he made his
way. They were decidedly high; the bishop was no-
toriously low; and thus, in a mild manner, without
malignity on either side, Manor Cross and the Palace
fell out. Their own excellent young clergyman was
snubbed in reference to his church postures, and Lady
Sarah was offended. But the Dean's manners were
perfect. He never trod on anyone's toes. He was
rich, and, as far as birth went, nobody—but he knew
how much was due to the rank of the Germains. In

all matters he obliged them, and had lately made the Deanery very pleasant to Lady Alice—to whom a widowed canon at Brotherton was supposed to be partial. The interest between the Deanery and Manor Cross was quite close; and now Mr. Tallowax had died leaving the greater part of his money to the Dean's daughter.

When a man suffers from disappointed love he requires consolation. Lady Sarah boldy declared her opinion—in female conclave of course—that one pretty girl is as good to a man as another, and might be a great deal better if she were at the same time better mannered and better dowered than the other. Mary Lovelace, when her grandfather died, was only seventeen. Lord George was at that time over thirty. But a man of thirty is still a young man, and a girl of seventeen may be a young woman. If the man be not more than fifteen years older than the woman the difference of age can hardly be regarded as an obstacle. And then Mary was much loved at Manor Cross. She had been a most engaging child, was clever, well-educated, very pretty, with a nice sparkling way, fond of pleasure, no doubt, but not as yet instructed to be fast. And now she would have at once thirty thousand pounds, and in course of time would be her father's heiress.

All the ladies at Manor Cross put their heads together—as did also Mr. Canon Holdenough, who, while these things had been going on, had been accepted by Lady Alice. They fooled Lord George to the top of his bent, smoothing him down softly amidst the pangs of his love, not suggesting Mary Lovelace at first, but still in all things acting in that direction. And they so far succeeded that within twelve months of the marriage of Adelaide de Baron to Mr. Houghton, when Mary Lovelace was not yet nineteen and Lord George was thirty-three, with some few gray hairs on his handsome head, Lord George did go over to the Deanery and offer himself as a husband to Mary Lovelace.

CHAPTER II

"WHAT ought I to do, papa?" The proposition was in the first instance made to Mary through the Dean. Lord George had gone to the father, and the father with many protestations of personal goodwill, had declared that in such a matter he would not attempt to bias his daughter. "That the connection would be personally agreeable to myself, I need hardly say," said the Dean. "For myself I have no objection to raise. But I must leave it to Mary. I can only say that you have my permission to address her." But the first appeal to Mary was made by her father himself, and was so made in conformity with his own advice. Lord George, when he left the Deanery, had thus arranged it, but had been hardly conscious that the Dean had advised such an arrangement. And it may be confessed between ourselves—between me and my readers, who in these introductory chapters may be supposed to be lookng back together over past things—that the Dean was from the first determined that Lord George should be his son-in-law. What son-in-law could he find that would redound more to his personal credit, or better advance his personal comfort. As to his daughter, where could a safer husband be found? And then she might in this way become a marchioness! His own father had kept livery stables at Bath. Her other grandfather had been a candle-maker in the

Borough. "What ought I to do, papa?" Mary asked, when the proposition was first made to her. She of course admired the Germains, and appreciated, at perhaps more than its full value, the notice she had received from them. She had thought Lord George to be the handsomest man she had ever seen. She had heard of his love for Miss de Baron, and had felt for him. She was not as yet old enough to know how dull was the house at Manor Cross, or how little of resource she might find in the companionship of such a man as Lord George. Of her own money she knew almost nothing. Nor as yet had her fortune become as a carcass to the birds. And now, should she decide in Lord George's favour, would she be saved at any rate from that danger.

"You must consult your own feelings, my dear," said her father. She looked up to him in blank dismay. She had as yet no feelings.

"But, papa——"

"Of course, my darling, there is a great deal to be said in favour of such a marriage. The man himself is excellent—in all respects excellent. I do not know that there is a young man of higher principles than Lord George in the whole county."

"He is hardly a young man, papa."

"Not a young man! he is thirty. I hope you do not call that old. I doubt whether men in his position of life should ever marry at an earlier age. He is not rich."

"Would that matter?"

"No; I think not. But of that you must judge. Of course with your fortune you would have a right to expect a richer match. But though he has not money, he has much that money gives. He lives in a large house with noble surroundings. The question is whether you can like him?"

"I don't know, papa." Every word she spoke she uttered hesitatingly. When she had asked whether "that would matter," she had hardly known what she was saying. The thing was so important to her, and yet so entirely mysterious and as yet unconsidered, that she could not collect her thoughts sufficiently for proper answers to her father's sensible but not too delicate inquiries. The only ideas that had really struck her were that he was grand and handsome, but very old.

"If you can love him I think you would be happy," said the Dean. "Of course you must look at it all round. He will probably live to be the Marquis of Brotherton. From all that I hear I do not think that his brother is likely to marry. In that case you would be the Marchioness of Brotherton, and the property, though not great, would then be handsome. In the meanwhile you would be Lady George Germain, and would live at Manor Cross. I should stipulate on your behalf that you should have a house of your own in town, for, at any rate, a portion of the year. Manor Cross is a fine place, but you would find it dull if you were to remain there always. A married woman too should always have some home of her own."

"You want me to do it, papa?"

"Certainly not. I want you to please yourself. If I find that you please yourself by accepting this man, I myself shall be better pleased than if you please yourself by rejecting him; but you shall never know that by my manner. I shall not put you on bread and water, and lock you up in the garret, either if you accept him, or if you reject him." The Dean smiled as he said this, as all the world at Brotherton knew that he had never in his life even scolded his daughter.

"And you, papa?"

"I shall come and see you, and you will come and see me. I shall get on well enough. I have always known that you would leave me soon. I am prepared for that." There was something in this which grated on her feelings. She had, perhaps, taught herself to believe that she was indispensable to her father's happiness. Then after a pause he continued: "Of course you must be ready to see Lord George when he comes again, and you ought to remember, my dear, that marquises do not grow on every hedge."

With great care and cunning workmanship one may almost make a silk purse out of a sow's ear, but not quite. The care which Dean Lovelace had bestowed upon the operation in regard to himself had been very great, and the cunning workmanship was to be seen in every plait and every stitch. But still there was something left of the coarseness of the original material. Of all this poor Mary knew nothing at all; but yet she did not like being told of marquises and hedges where her heart was concerned. She had wanted—had unconsciously wanted—some touch of romance from her father to satisfy the condition in which she found herself. But there was no touch of romance there; and when she was left to herself to work the matter out in her own heart and in her own mind she was unsatisfied.

Two or three days after this Mary received notice that her lover was coming. The Dean had seen him and had absolutely fixed a time. To poor Mary this seemed to be most unromantic, most unpromising. And though she had thought of nothing else since she had first heard of Lord George's intention, though she had lain awake struggling to make up her mind, she had reached no conclusion. It had become quite clear to her that her father was anxious for the marriage, and there was much in it which recommended it to herself. The old elms of the park of Manor Cross were very tempting. She was not indifferent to being called My Lady. Though she had been slightly hurt when told that marquises did not grow on hedges, still she knew that it would be much to be a marchioness. And the man himself was good, and not only good but very handsome. There was a nobility about him beyond that of his family. Those prone to ridicule might perhaps have called him Werter-faced, but to Mary there was a sublimity in this. But then, was she in love with him?

She was a sweet, innocent, ladylike, high-spirited, joyous creature. Those struggles of her father to get rid of the last porcine taint, though not quite successful as to himself, had succeeded thoroughly in regard to her. It comes at last with due care, and the due care had here been taken. She was so nice that middle-aged men wished themselves younger that they might make love to her, or older that they might be privileged to kiss her. Though keenly anxious for amusement, though over head and ears in love with sport and frolic, no unholy thought had ever polluted her mind. That men were men, and that she was a woman, had of course been considered by her. Oh, that it might some day be her privilege to love some man with all her heart and all her strength, some man who, should be, at any rate to her, the very hero of heroes, the cynosure of her world! It was thus that she considered the matter. There could surely

be nothing so glorious as being well in love. And the
one to be thus worshipped must of course become her
husband. Otherwise would her heart be broken, and
perhaps his—and all would be tragedy. But with
tragedy she had no sympathy. The loved one must
become her husband. But the pictures she had made
to herself of him were not at all like Lord George Germain. He was to be fair, with laughing eyes, quick
in repartee, always riding well to hounds. She had
longed to hunt herself, but her father had objected.
He must be sharp enough sometimes to others, though
ever soft to her, with a silken moustache and a dimpled
chin, and perhaps twenty-four years old. Lord George
was dark, his eyes never laughed; he was silent generally, and never went out hunting at all. He was
dignified and tall, very handsome, no doubt—and a
lord. The grand question was that: could she love
him? Could she make another picture, and paint him
as her hero? There were doubtless heroic points in
the sidewave of that coal-black lock—coal-black where
the few gray hairs had not yet shown themselves, in
his great height, and solemn polished manners.

When her lover came, she could only remember that
if she accepted him she would please everybody. The
Dean had taken occasion to assure her that the ladies
at Manor Cross would receive her with open arms.
But on this occasion she did not accept him. She was
very silent, hardly able to speak a word, and almost
sinking out of sight when Lord George endeavoured
to press his suit by taking her hand. But she contrived at last to make him the very answer that Adelaide de Baron had made. She must take time to
think of it. But the answer came from her in a different spirit. She at any rate knew as soon as it

was given that it was her destiny in life to become Lady George Germain. She did not say "Yes" at the moment, only because it is so hard for a girl to tell a man that she will marry him at the first asking! He made his second offer by letter, to which the Dean wrote the reply:

"MY DEAR LORD GEORGE,

"My daughter is gratified by your affection, and flattered by your manner of showing it. A few plain words are perhaps the best. She will be happy to receive you as her future husband, whenever it may suit you to come to the Deanery.

"Yours affectionately,

"HENRY LOVELACE."

Immediately upon this the conduct of Lord George was unexceptionable. He hurried over to Brotherton, and as he clasped his girl in his arms, he told her that he was the happiest man in England. Poor as he was he made her a handsome present, and besought her if she had any mercy, any charity, any love for him, to name an early day. Then came the four ladies from Manor Cross—for Lady Alice had already become Lady Alice Holdenough—and caressed her, and patted her, and petted her, and told her that she should be as welcome as flowers in May. Her father, too, congratulated her with more of enthusiasm, and more also of demonstrated feeling than she had ever before seen him evince. He had been very unwilling, he said, to express any strong opinion of his own. It had always been his desire that his girl should please herself. But now that the thing was settled he could assure her of his thorough satisfaction. It was all that he could

have desired; and now be would be ready at any time
to lay himself down, and be at rest. Had his girl
married a spendthrift lord, even a duke devoted to
pleasure and iniquity, it would have broken his heart.
But he would now confess that the aristocracy of the
country had charms for him; and he was not ashamed
to rejoice that his child should be accepted within their
pale. Then he brushed a real tear from his eyes, and
Mary threw herself into his arms. The tear was real,
and in all that he said there was not an insincere word.
It was to him a very glory of glories that his child
should be in the way of becoming the Marchioness of
Brotherton. It was even a great glory that she should
be Lady George Germain. The Dean never forgot the
livery stable, and owned day and night that God had
been very good to him.

It was soon settled that Mary was to be allowed
three months for preparation, and that the marriage
was to be solemnised in June. Of course she had
much to do in preparing her wedding garments, but
she had before her a much more difficult task than
that, at which she worked most sedulously. It was
now the great business of her life to fall in love with
Lord George. She must get rid of that fair young
man with the silky moustache and the darling dimple.
The sallow, the sublime, and the Werter-faced must
be made to take the place of laughing eyes and pink
cheeks. She did work very hard, and sometimes, as
she thought, successfully. She came to a positive conclusion that he was the handsomest man she ever saw,
and that she certainly liked the few gray hairs. That
his manner was thoroughly noble no one could doubt.
If he were seen merely walking down the street he
would surely be taken for a great man. He was one

of whom, as her husband, she could be always proud; and that she felt to be a great thing. That he would not play lawn tennis, and that he did not care for riding, were points in his character to be regretted. Indeed, though she made some tenderly cautious inquiries, she could not find what were his amusements. She herself was passionately fond of dancing, but he certainly did not dance. He talked to her, when he did talk, chiefly of his family, of his own poverty, of the goodness of his mother and sisters, and of the great regret which they all felt that they should have been deserted by the head of their family.

"He has now been away," said Lord George, "for ten years; but not improbably he may return soon, and then we shall have to leave Manor Cross."

"Leave Manor Cross?"

"Of course we must do so should he come home. The place belongs to him, and we are only there because it has not suited him to reside in England."

This he said with the utmost solemnity, and the statement had been produced by the answer which the Marquis had made to a letter announcing to him his brother's marriage. The Marquis had never been a good correspondent. To the ladies of the house he never wrote at all, though Lady Sarah favoured him with a periodical quarterly letter. To his agent, and less frequently to his brother, he would write curt questions on business, never covering more than one side of a sheet of notepaper, and always signed "Yours, B." To these the inmates of Manor Cross had now become accustomed, and little was thought of them; but on this occasion he had written three or four complete sentences, which had been intended to have, and which did have, a plain meaning. He congratulated his

brother, but begged Lord George to bear in mind that
he himself might not improbably want Manor Cross
for his own purpose before long. If Lord George
thought it would be agreeable, Mr. Knox, the agent,
might have instructions to buy Miss Lovelace a present.
Of this latter offer Lord George took no notice; but
the intimation concerning the house sat gravely on
his mind.

The Dean did exactly as he had said with reference
to the house in town. Of course it was necessary that
there should be arrangements as to money between him
and Lord George, in which he was very frank. Mary's
money was all her own—giving her an income of
nearly £1500 per annum. The Dean was quite of
opinion that this should be left to Lord George's management, but he thought it right as Mary's father to
stipulate that his daughter should have a home of her
own. Then he suggested a small house in town, and
expressed an opinion that his daughter should be allowed to live there six months in the year. The
expense of such a sojourn might be in some degree
shared by himself if Lord George would receive him
for a month or so in the spring. And so the thing
was settled, Lord George pledging himself that the
house should be taken. The arrangement was distasteful to him in many ways, but it did not seem to
be unreasonable, and he could not oppose it. Then
came the letter from the Marquis. Lord George did
not consider himself bound to speak of that letter to
the Dean; but he communicated the threat to Mary.
Mary thought nothing about it, except that her future
brother-in-law must be a very strange man.

During all these three months she strove very hard
to be in love, and sometimes she thought that she had

succeeded. In her little way, she studied the man's character, and did all she could to ingratiate herself with him. Walking seemed to be his chief relaxation, and she was always ready to walk with him. She tried to make herself believe that he was profoundly wise. And then, when she failed in other things, she fell back upon his beauty. Certainly she had never seen a handsomer face, either on a man's shoulders or in a picture. And so they were married.

Now I have finished my introduction—having married my heroine to my hero—and have, I hope, instucted my reader as to those hundred and twenty incidents, of which I spoke—not too tediously. If he will go back and examine, he will find that they are all there. But perhaps it will be better for us both that he should be in quiet possession of them without any such examination.

CHAPTER III

LIFE AT MANOR CROSS

THE married couple passed their honeymoon in Ireland, Lady Brotherton having a brother, an Irish peer, who lent them for a few months his house on the Black-water. The marriage, of course, was celebrated in the cathedral, and equally of course, the officiating clergymen were the Dean and Canon Holdenough. On the day before the marriage, Lord George was astonished to find how rich a man was his father-in-law.

" Mary's fortune is her own," he said; " but I should like to give her something. Perhaps I had better give it to you on her behalf."

Then he shuffled a cheque for a thousand pounds into Lord George's hands. He moreover gave his daughter a hundred pounds in notes on the morning of the wedding, and thus acted the part of the benevolent father and father-in-law to a miracle. It may be acknowledged here that the receipt of the money removed a heavy weight from Lord George's heart. He was himself so poor, and at the same time so scrupulous, that he had lacked funds sufficient for the usual brightness of a wedding tour. He would not take his mother's money, nor lessen his own small patrimony; but now it seemed that wealth was showered on him from the Deanery.

Perhaps a sojourn in Ireland did as well as anything could towards assisting the young wife in her

24

object of falling in love with her husband. He would hardly have been a sympathetic companion in Switzerland or Italy, as he did not care for lakes or mountains. But Ireland was new to him and new to her, and he was glad to have an opportunity of seeing something of a people as to whom so little is really known in England. And at Ballycondra, on the Blackwater, they were justified in feeling a certain interest in the welfare of the tenants around them. There was something to be done, and something of which they could talk. Lord George, who couldn't hunt, and wouldn't dance, and didn't care for mountains, could inquire with some zeal how much wages a peasant might earn, and what he would do with it when earned. It interested him to learn that whereas an English labourer will certainly eat and drink his wages from week to week—so that he could not be trusted to pay any sum half-yearly—an Irish peasant, though he be half starving, will save his money for the rent. And Mary, at his instance, also cared for these things. It was her gift, as with many women, to be able to care for everything. It was, perhaps, her misfortune that she was apt to care too much for many things. The honeymoon in Ireland answered its purpose, and Lady George, when she came back to Manor Cross, almost thought that she had succeeded. She was at any rate able to assure her father that she had been as happy as the day was long, and that he was absolutely—"perfect."

This assurance of perfection the Dean no doubt took at its proper value. He patted his daughter's cheek as she made it, and kissed her, and told her that he did not doubt but that with a little care she might make herself a happy woman. The house in town had already been taken under his auspices, but of course was not to be inhabited yet.

It was a very small but a very pretty little house, in a quaint little street called Munster Court, near Storey's Gate, with a couple of windows looking into St. James's Park. It was now September, and London, for the present, was out of the question. Indeed, it had been arranged that Lord George and his wife should remain at Manor Cross till after Christmas. But the house had to be furnished, and the Dean evinced his full understanding of the duties of a father-in-law in such an emergency. This, indeed, was so much the case that Lord George became a little uneasy. He had the greater part of the thousand pounds left, which he insisted on expending—and thought that that should have sufficed. But the Dean explained, in his most cordial manner—and no man's manner could be more cordial than the Dean's—that Mary's fortune from Mr. Tallowax had been unexpected, that having had but one child he intended to do well by her, and that, therefore, he could now assist in starting her well in life without doing himself a damage. The house in this way was decorated and furnished, and sundry journeys up to London served to brighten the autumn, which might otherwise have been dull and tedious.

At this period of her life two things acting together, and both acting in opposition to her anticipations of life, surprised the young bride not a little. The one was her father's manner of conversation with her, and the other was her husband's. The Dean had never been a stern parent; but he had been a clergyman, and as a clergyman he had inculcated a certain strictness of life—a very modified strictness, indeed, but something more rigid than might have come from him had he been a lawyer or a country gentleman. Mary had learned that he wished her to attend the cathedral services, and to interest herself respecting them, and she had always done so. He had explained to her that, although he kept a horse for her to ride, he, as the Dean of Brotherton, did not wish her to be seen in the hunting field. In her dress, her ornaments, her books, her parties, there had been always something to mark slightly her clerical belongings. She had never chafed against this, because she loved her father and was naturally obedient; but she had felt something perhaps of a soft regret. Now her father, whom she saw very frequently, never spoke to her of any duties. How should her house be furnished? In what way would she lay herself out for London society? What enjoyments of life could she best secure? These seemed to be matters on which he was most intent. It occurred to her that, when speaking to her of the house in London, he never once asked her what church she would attend; and that when she spoke with pleasure of being so near the Abbey, he paid little or no attention to her remark. And then, too, she felt, rather than perceived, that in his counsels to her he almost intimated that she must have a plan of life different from her husband's. There were no such instructions given, but it almost seemed as though this were implied. He took it for granted that her life was to be gay and bright, though he seemed to take it also for granted that Lord George did not wish to be gay and bright.

All this surprised her. But it did not, perhaps, surprise her so much as the serious view of life which her husband from day to day impressed upon her. That

hero of her early dreams, that man with the light hair
and the dimpled chin, whom she had not as yet quite
forgotten, had never scolded her, had never spoken a
serious word to her, and had always been ready to provide her with amusements that never palled. But
Lord George made out a course of reading for her—
so much for the two hours after breakfast, so much
for the hour before dressing—so much for the evening;
and also a table of results to be acquired in three
months—in six months—and so much by the close of
the first year; and even laid down the sum total of
achievements to be produced by a dozen years of such
work! Of course she determined to do as he would
have her do. The great object of her life was to
love him; and, of course, if she really loved him, she
would comply with his wishes. She began her daily
hour of Gibbon, after breakfast, with great zeal. But
there was present to her an idea that if the Gibbon
had come from her father, and the instigations to
amuse herself from her husband, it would have been
better.

These things surprised her; but there was another
matter that vexed her. Before she had been six weeks
at Manor Cross she found that the ladies set themselves up as her tutors. It was not the Marchioness
who offended her so much as her three sisters-in-law.
The one of the family whom she had always liked best
had been also liked best by Mr. Holdenough, and had
gone to live next door to her father in the Close.
Lady Alice, though perhaps a little tiresome, was
always gentle and good-natured. Her mother-in-law
was too much in awe of her own eldest daughter ever
to scold anyone. But Lady Sarah could be very
severe; and Lady Susanna could be very stiff; and

Lady Amelia always re-echoed what her elder sisters said.

Lady Sarah was by far the worst. She was forty years old, and looked as though she were fifty, and wished to be thought sixty. That she was, in truth, very good, no one either at Manor Cross or in Brotherton or in any of the parishes around ever doubted. She knew every poor woman on the estate, and had a finger in the making of almost every petticoat worn. She spent next to nothing on herself, giving away almost all her own little income. She went to church whatever was the weather. She was never idle and never wanted to be amused. The place in the carriage which would naturally have been hers, she had always surrendered to one of her sisters, when there had been five ladies at Manor Cross, and now she surrendered again to her brother's wife. She spent hours daily in the parish school. She was doctor and surgeon to the poor people—never sparing herself. But she was harsh-looking, had a harsh voice, and was dictatorial. The poor people had become used to her, and liked her ways. The women knew that her stitches never gave way, and the men had a wholesome confidence in her medicines, her plasters, and her cookery. But Lady George Germain did not see by what right she was to be made subject to her sister-in-law's jurisdiction.

Church matters did not go quite on all fours at Manor Cross. The ladies, as has before been said, were all high, the Marchioness being the least *exigeante* in that particular, and Lady Amelia the most so. Ritual, indeed, was the one point of interest in Lady Amelia's life. Among them there was assent enough for daily comfort; but Lord George was in this

respect, and in this respect only, a trouble to them.
He never declared himself openly, but it seemed to
them that he did not care much about church at all.
He would generally go of a Sunday morning; but
there was a conviction that he did so chiefly to oblige
his mother. Nothing was ever said of this. There
was probably present to the ladies some feeling, not
uncommon, that religion is not so necessary for men
as for women. But Lady George was a woman.

And Lady George was also the daughter of a clergyman. There was now a double connection between
Manor Cross and the Close at Brotherton. Mr. Canon
Holdenough, who was an older man than the Dean,
and had been longer known in the diocese, was a most
unexceptional clergyman, rather high, leaning towards
the high and dry, very dignified, and quite as big a
man in Brotherton as the Dean himself. The Dean
was, indeed, the Dean; but Mr. Holdenough was uncle
to a baronet, and the Holdenoughs had been Holdenoughs when the Conqueror came. And then he
also had a private income of his own. Now all
this gave to the ladies at Manor Cross a peculiar
right to be great in church matters—so that Lady
Sarah was able to speak with much authority to
Mary when she found that the bride, though a Dean's
daughter, would only go to two services a week, and
and would shirk one of them if the weather gave the
slightest colouring of excuse.

"You used to like the cathedral services," Lady
Sarah said to her, one day, when Mary had declined
to go to the parish church, to sing the praises of St.
Processus.

"That was because they were cathedral services,"
said Mary.

"You mean to say that you attended the House of God because the music was good!" Mary had not thought the subject over sufficiently to be enabled to say that good music is supplied with the object of drawing large congregations, so she only shrugged her shoulders. "I, too, like good music, dear; but I do not think the want of it should keep me from church." Mary again shrugged her shoulders, remembering, as she did so, that her sister-in-law did not know one tune from another. Lady Alice was the only one of the family who had ever studied music.

"Even your papa goes on Saint's days," continued Lady Sarah, conveying a sneer against the Dean by that word "even."

"Papa is Dean. I suppose he has to go."

"He would not go to church, I suppose, unless he approved of going."

The subject then dropped. Lady George had not yet arrived at that sort of snarling home intimacy, which would have justified her in telling Lady Sarah that if she wanted a lesson at all, she would prefer to take it from her husband.

The poor women's petticoats were another source of trouble. Before the autumn was over—by the end of October—when Mary had been two months at Manor Cross, she had been got to acknowledge that ladies living in the country should employ a part of their time in making clothes for the poor people; and she very soon learned to regret the acknowledgment. She was quickly driven into a corner by an assertion from Lady Sarah that, such being the case, the time to be so employed should be defined. She had intended to make something—perhaps an entire petticoat —at some future time. But Lady Sarah was not going

to put up with conduct such as that. Mary had acknowledged her duty. Did she mean to perform it,
or to neglect it? She made one petticoat, and then
gently appealed to her husband. Did not he think
that petticoats could be bought cheaper than they could
be made? He figured it out, and found that his wife
could earn three-halfpence a day by two hours' work;
and even Lady Sarah did not require from her more
than two hours daily. Was it worth while that she
should be made miserable for ninepence a week—less
than £2 a year? Lady George figured it out also, and
offered the exact sum, £1 19s., to Lady Sarah, in order
that she might be let off for the first twelve months.
Then Lady Sarah was full of wrath. Was that the
spirit in which offerings were to be made to the Lord?
Mary was asked, with stern indignation, whether in
bestowing the work of her hands upon the people,
whether in the very fact that she was doing for the
poor that which was distasteful to herself, she did not
recognise the performance of a duty? Mary considered awhile, and then said that she thought a petticoat was a petticoat, and that perhaps the one made
by the regular petticoat-maker would be the best. She
did not allude to the grand doctrine of the division of
labour, nor did she hint that she might be doing more
harm than good by interfering with regular trade, because she had not studied those matters. But that was
the line of her argument. Lady Sarah told her that
her heart in that matter was as hard as a nether mill-
stone. The young wife, not liking this, withdrew; and
again appealed to her husband. His mind was divided
on the subject. He was clearly of opinion that the
petticoat should be obtained in the cheapest market,
but he doubted much about that three-halfpence in

two hours. It might be that his wife could not do
better at present; but experience would come, and
in that case, she would be obtaining experience as
well as earning three-halfpence. And, moreover,
petticoats made at Manor Cross would, he thought,
undoubtedly be better than any that could be bought.
He came, however, to no final decision; and Mary,
finding herself every morning sitting in a great petticoat conclave, hardly had an alternative but to join it.

It was not in any spirit of complaint that she spoke
on the subject to her father as the winter came on.
A certain old Miss Tallowax had come to the Deanery,
and it had been thought proper that Lady George
should spend a day or two there. Miss Tallowax,
also, had money of her own, and even still owned a
share in the business; and the Dean had pointed out,
both to Lord George and his wife, that it would be
well that they should be civil to her. Lord George
was to come on the last day, and dine and sleep at
the Deanery. On this occasion, when the Dean and
his daughter were alone together, she said something
in a playful way about the great petticoat contest.

" Don't you let those old ladies sit upon you," said
the Dean. He smiled as he spoke, but his daughter
well knew, from his tone, that he meant his advice to
be taken seriously.

"Of course, papa, I should like to accommodate
myself to them as much as I can."

" But you can't, my dear. Your manner of life
can't be their manner, nor theirs yours. I should
have thought George would see that."

"He didn't take their part, you know."

"Of course he didn't. As a married woman you
are entitled to have your own way, unless he should

wish it otherwise. I don't want to make this matter
serious; but if it is pressed, tell them that you do
not care to spend your time in that way. They cling
to old fashions. That is natural enough; but it is
absurd to suppose that they should make you as old-
fashioned as themselves."

He had taken the matter up quite seriously, and
had given his daughter advice evidently with the intention that she should profit by it. That which he
had said as to her being a married woman struck her
forcibly. No doubt these ladies at Manor Cross were
her superiors in birth; but she was their brother's
wife, and as a married woman had rights of her
own. A little spirit of rebellion already began to kindle
itself within her bosom; but in it there was nothing
of mutiny against her husband. If he were to desire
her to make petticoats all day, of course she would
make them; but in this contest he had been, as it
were, neutral, and had certainly given her no orders.
She thought a good deal about it while at the Deanery,
and made up her mind that she would sit in the petticoat conclave no longer. It could not be her duty to
pass her time in an employment in which a poor
woman might with difficulty earn sixpence a day.
Surely she might do better with her time than that,
even though she should spend it all in reading Gibbon.

CHAPTER IV

AT THE DEANERY

THERE was a dinner-party at the Deanery during Miss Tallowax's sojourn at Brotherton. Mr. Canon Holdenough and Lady Alice were there. The bishop and his wife had been asked—a ceremony which was gone through once a year—but had been debarred from accepting the invitation by the presence of clerical guests at the Palace. But his lordship's chaplain, Mr. Groschut, was present. Mr. Groschut also held an honorary prebendal stall, and was one of the chapter— a thorn sometimes in the Dean's side. But appearances were well kept up at Brotherton, and no one was more anxious that things should be done in a seemly way than the Dean. Therefore, Mr. Groschut, who was a very low churchman, and had once been a Jew, but who bore a very high character for theological erudition, was asked to the Deanery. There was also one or two other clergymen there, with their wives, and Mr. and Mrs. Houghton. Mrs. Houghton, it will be remembered, was the beautiful woman who had refused to become the wife of Lord George Germain. Before taking this step, the Dean had been careful to learn whether his son-in-law would object to meet the Houghtons. Such objection would have been foolish, as the families had all known each other. Both Mr. de Baron, Mrs. Houghton's father, and Mr. Houghton himself, had been intimate with the late marquis, and had been friends of the present lord before he had quitted the country. A lady when she refuses a gentleman gives no cause of quarrel. All this the Dean understood; and as he himself had known both Mr. Houghton and Mr. de Baron ever since he came to Brotherton, he thought it better that there should be such a meeting. Lord George blushed up to the roots of his hair, and then said that he should be very glad to meet the gentleman and his wife.

The two young brides had known each other as girls, and now met with, at any rate, an appearance of friendship.

"My dear," said Mrs. Houghton, who was about four years the elder, "of course I know all about it, and so do you. You are an heiress, and could afford to please yourself. I had nothing of my own, and should have had to pass all my time at Manor Cross. Are you surprised?"

"Why should I be surprised?" said Lady George, who was, however, very much surprised at this address.

"Well, you know, he is the handsomest man in England. Everybody allows that; and then, such a family—and such possibilities! I was very much flattered. Of course he had not seen you then, or only seen you as a child, or I shouldn't have had a chance. It is a great deal better as it is—isn't it?"

"I think so, certainly."

"I am so glad to hear that you have a house in town. We go up about the first of April, when the hunting is over. Mr. Houghton does not ride much, but he hunts a great deal. We live in Berkeley Square, you know; and I do so hope we shall see ever so much of you."

"I'm sure I hope so, too," said Lady George, who had never, hitherto, been very fond of Miss de Baron, and had entertained a vague idea that she ought to be a little afraid of Mrs. Houghton. But when her father's guest was so civil to her she did not know how to be other than civil in return.

"There is no reason why what has passed should make any awkwardness—is there?"

"No," said Lady George, feeling that she almost blushed at the allusion to so delicate a subject.

"Of course not. Why should there? Lord George will soon get used to me, just as if nothing had happened; and I shall always be ever so fond of him— in a way, you know. There shall be nothing to make you jealous."

"I'm not a bit afraid of that," said Lady George, almost too earnestly.

"You need not be, I'm sure. Not but what I do think he was at one time very—very much attached to me. But it couldn't be. And what's the good of thinking of such a thing when it can't be? I don't pretend to be very virtuous, and I like money. Now Mr. Houghton, at any rate, has got a large income. If I had had your fortune at my own command, I don't say what I might not have done."

Lady George almost felt that she ought to be offended by all this—almost felt that she was disgusted; but, at the same time, she did not quite understand it. Her father had made a point of asking the Houghtons, and had told her that of course she would know the Houghtons up in town. She had an idea that she was very ignorant of the ways of life; but that now it would behove her, as a married woman, to learn those ways. Perhaps the free and easy mode

of talking was the right thing. She did not like being
told by another lady that that other lady would have
married her own husband, only that he was a pauper;
and the offence of all this seemed to be the greater
because it was all so recent. She didn't like being told
that she was not to be jealous, especially when she
remembered that her husband had been desperately in
love with the lady who told her so not many months
ago. But she was not jealous, and was quite sure
she never would be jealous; and, perhaps, it did not
matter. All this had occurred in the drawing-room
before dinner. Then Mr. Houghton came up to her,
telling that he had been commissioned by the Dean
to have the honour of taking her down to dinner.
Having made his little speech, Mr. Houghton retired—
as gentlemen generally do retire when in that position.

"Be as nice as you can to him," said Mrs. Houghton.
"He hasn't much to say for himself, but he isn't half
a bad fellow; and a pretty woman like you can do what
she likes with him."

Lady George, as she went down to dinner, assured
herself that she had no slightest wish to take any
unfair advantage of Mr. Houghton.

Lord George had taken down Miss Tallowax, the
Dean having been very wise in this matter; and Miss
Tallowax was in a seventh heaven of happiness. Miss
Tallowax, though she had made no promises, was
quite prepared to do great things for her noble connections, if her noble connections would treat her
properly. She had already made half-a-dozen wills,
and was quite ready to make another if Lord George
would be civil to her. The Dean was in his heart a
little ashamed of his aunt; but he was man enough
to be able to bear her eccentricities without showing

his vexation, and sufficiently wise to know that more was to be won than lost by the relationship.

"The best woman in the world," he had said to Lord George beforehand, speaking of his aunt; "but, of course, you will remember that she was not brought up as a lady."

Lord George, with stately urbanity, had signified his intention of treating Miss Tallowax with every consideration.

"She has thirty thousand pounds at her own disposal," continued the Dean. "I have never said a word to her about money, but, upon my honour, I think she likes Mary better than anyone else. It's worth bearing in mind, you know."

Lord George smiled again in a stately manner—perhaps showing something of displeasure in his smile. But nevertheless he was well aware that it was worth his while to bear Miss Tallowax and her money in his mind.

"My lord," said Miss Tallowax, "I hope you will allow me to say how much honoured we all feel by Mary's proud position." Lord George bowed and smiled, and led the lady into the Deanery dining-room. Words did not come easily to him, and he hardly knew how to answer the lady. "Of course, it's a great thing for people such as us," continued Miss Tallowax, "to be connected with the family of a marquis." Again Lord George bowed. This was very bad indeed—a great deal worse than he had anticipated from the aunt of so courtly a man as his father-in-law, the Dean. The lady looked to be about sixty, very small, very healthy, with streaky red cheeks, small grey eyes, and a brown front. Then came upon him an idea, that it would be a very long time before the thirty thousand pounds, or .any part of it, would come to him. And then there came to him another idea, that, as he had married the Dean's daughter, it was his duty to behave well to the Dean's aunt, even though the money should never come to him. He therefore told Miss Tallowax that his mother hoped to have the pleasure of seeing her at Manor Cross before she left Brotherton. Miss Tallowax almost got out of her seat, as she curtseyed with her head and shoulders to this proposition.

The Dean was a very good man at the head of his own dinner-table, and the party went off pleasantly, in spite of sundry attempts at clerical pugnacity made by Mr. Groschut. Every man and every beast has his own weapon. The wolf fights with his tooth, the bull with his horn, and Mr. Groschut always fought with his bishop—so taught by inner instinct. The bishop, according to Mr. Groschut, was inclined to think that this and that might be done. That such a change might be advantageously made in reference to certain clerical meetings, and that the hilarity of the diocese might be enhanced by certain evangelical festivities. These remarks were generally addressed to Mr. Canon Holdenough, who made almost no reply to them. But the Dean was on each occasion prepared with some civil answer, which, while it was an answer, would still seem to change the conversation. It was a law in the Close that Bishop Barton should be never allowed to interfere with the affairs of Brotherton cathedral; and if not the bishop, certainly not the bishop's chaplain. Though the Canon and the Dean did not go altogether on all fours in reference to clerical affairs generally, they were both agreed on this point. But the Chaplain, who knew the condition of affairs as well as they did, thought the law a bad law, and was determined to abolish it. "It certainly would be very pleasant, Mr. Holdenough, if we could have such a meeting within the confines of the Close. I don't mean to-day, and I don't mean to-morrow; but we might think of it. The bishop, who has the greatest love for the cathedral services, is very much of that mind."

"I do not know that I care very much for any out-of-door gatherings," said the Canon.

"But why out of doors?" asked the Chaplain.

"Whatever meeting there is in the Close, will, I hope, be held in the Deanery," said the Dean; "but of all meetings, I must say that I like meetings such as this the best. Germain, will you pass the bottle?" When they were alone together he always called his son-in-law George; but in company he always dropped the more familiar name.

Mr. de Baron, Mrs. Houghton's father, liked his joke. "Sporting men," he said, "always go to a meet, and clerical men to a meeting. What's the difference?"

"A good deal, if it is in the colour of the coat," said the Dean.

"The one is always under cover," said the Canon. "The other, I believe, is generally held out of doors."

"There is, I fancy, a considerable resemblance in the energy of those who are brought together," said the Chaplain.

"But clergymen ain't allowed to hunt, are they?" said Mr. Houghton, who, as usual, was a little in the dark as to the subject under consideration.

"What's to prevent them?" asked the Canon, who had never been out hunting in his life, and who cer-

tainly would have advised a young clergyman to
abstain from the sport. But in asking the question
he was enabled to strike a sidelong blow at the
objectionable chaplain, by seeming to question the
bishop's authority.

"Their own conscience, I should hope," said the
Chaplain, solemnly, thereby parrying the blow successfully.

"I am very glad, then," said Mr. Houghton, "that
I didn't go into the Church." To be thought a real
hunting man was the great object of Mr. Houghton's
ambition.

"I am afraid you would hardly have suited us,
Houghton," said the Dean. "Come, shall we go up
to the ladies?"

In the drawing-room, after a little while, Lord
George found himself seated next to Mrs. Houghton
—Adelaide de Baron, as she had been when he had
sighed in vain at her feet. How it had come to pass
that he was sitting there he did not know, but he
was quite sure that it had come to pass by no arrangement contrived by himself. He had looked at
her once since he had been in the room, almost blushing as he did so, and had told himself that she was
certainly very beautiful. He almost thought that she
was more beautiful than his wife; but he knew—
he knew now—that her beauty and her manners were
not as well suited to him as those of the sweet creature
whom he had married. And now he was once more
seated close to her, and it was incumbent on him to
speak to her. "I hope," she said, almost in a whisper,
but still not seeming to whisper, "that we have both
become very happy since we met last."

"I hope so, indeed," said he.

"There cannot, at least, be any doubt as to you, Lord George. I never knew a sweeter young girl than Mary Lovelace; so pretty, so innocent, and so enthusiastic. I am but a poor worldly creature compared to her."

"She is all that you say, Mrs. Houghton." Lord George also was displeased—more thoroughly displeased than had been his wife. But he did not know how to show his displeasure; and though he felt it, he still felt also the old influence of the woman's beauty.

"I am so delighted to have heard that you have got a house in Munster Court. I hope that Lady George and I may be fast friends. Indeed, I won't call her Lady George; for she was Mary to me before we either of us thought of getting husbands for ourselves." This was not strictly true, but of that Lord George could know nothing. "And I do hope —may I hope—that you will call on me?"

"Certainly I will do so."

"It will add so much to the happiness of my life, if you will allow me to feel that all that has come and gone has not broken the friendship between us."

"Certainly not," said Lord George.

The lady had then said all that she had got to say, and changed her position as silently as she had occupied it. There was no abruptness of motion, and yet Lord George saw her talking to her husband at the other side of the room, almost while his own words were still sounding in his own ears. Then he watched her for the next few minutes. Certainly, she was very beautiful. There was no room for comparison, they were so unlike; otherwise, he would have been disposed to say that Adelaide was the

more beautiful. But Adelaide certainly would not
have suited the air of Manor Cross, or have associated
well with Lady Sarah.

On the next day the Marchioness and Ladies Susanna and Amelia drove over to the Deanery in great
state, to call on Miss Tallowax, and to take Lady
George back to Manor Cross. Miss Tallowax enjoyed
the company of the Marchioness greatly. She had
never seen a lady of that rank before. "Only think
how I must feel," she said to her niece, that morning,
"I, that never spoke to any one above a baronet's
lady in my life."

"I don't think you'll find much difference," said
Mary.

"You're used to it. You're one of them yourself.
You're above a baronet's lady—ain't you, my dear?"

"I have hardly looked into all that as yet, aunt."
There must surely have been a little fib in this, or
the Dean's daughter must have been very much unlike other young ladies.

"I suppose I ought to be afraid of you, my dear;
only you are so nice and so pretty. And as for
Lord George, he is quite condescending." Lady
George knew that praise was intended, and therefore
made no objection to the otherwise objectionable
epithet.

The visit of the Marchioness was passed over with
the less disturbance to Miss Tallowax because it
was arranged that she was to be taken over to lunch
at Manor Cross on the following day. Lord George
had said a word, and Lady Sarah had consented,
though, as a rule, Lady Sarah did not like the company of vulgar people. The peasants of the parish,
down to the very poorest of the poor, were her daily

companions. With them she would spend hours, feeling no inconvenience from their language or habits. But she did not like gentlefolk who were not gentle. In days now long gone by, she had only assented to the Dean, because holy orders are supposed to make a gentleman; for she would acknowledge a bishop to be as grand a nobleman as any, though he might have been born the son of a butcher. But nobility and gentry cannot travel backwards, and she had been in doubt about Miss Tallowax. But even with the Lady Sarahs a feeling has made its way which teaches them to know that they must submit to some changes. The thing was to be regretted, but Lady Sarah knew that she was not strong enough to stand quite alone. "You know she is very rich," the Marchioness' had said in a whisper; "and, if Brotherton marries, your poor brother will want it so badly."

"That ought not to make any difference, mamma," said Lady Sarah. Whether it did make any difference or not, Lady Sarah herself probably hardly knew; but she did consent to the asking of Miss Tallowax to lunch at Manor Cross.

CHAPTER V

THE Dean took his aunt over to Manor Cross in his brougham. The Dean's brougham was the neatest carriage in Brotherton, very much more so than the bishop's family carriage. It was, no doubt, generally to be seen with only one horse; and neither the bishop nor Mrs. Barton ever stirred without two; but then one horse is enough for town work, and that one horse could lift his legs and make himself conspicuous in a manner of which the bishop's rather sorry jades knew nothing. On this occasion, as the journey was long, there were two horses—hired; but, nevertheless, the brougham looked very well as it came up the long Manor Cross avenue. Miss Tallowax became rather frightened as she drew near to the scene of her coming grandeur.

"Henry," she said to her nephew, "they will think so little of me."

"My dear aunt," replied the Dean, "in these days a lady who has plenty of money of her own can hold her head up anywhere. The dear old Marchioness will think quite as much of you as you do of her."

What perhaps struck Miss Tallowax most at the first moment was the plainness of the ladies' dresses. She herself was rather gorgeous, in a shot-silk gown, and a fashionable bonnet crowded with flowers. She had been ashamed of the splendour of the article as

46

she put it on, and yet had been ashamed also of her ordinary daily head-gear. But when she saw the Marchioness, and especially when she saw Lady Sarah, who was altogether strange to her, she wished that she had come in her customary black gown. She had heard something about Lady Sarah from her niece, and had conceived an idea that Lady Sarah was the dragon of the family. But when she saw a little woman, looking almost as old as herself—though in truth the one might have been the other's mother—dressed in an old brown merino, with the slightest morsel of white collar to be seen round her neck, she began to hope that the dragon would not be very fierce.

"I hope you like Brotherton, Miss Tallowax," said Lady Sarah. "I think I have heard that you were here once before."

"I like Brotherton very much, my lady." Lady Sarah smiled as graciously as she knew how. "I came when they first made Henry dean, a long time ago now it seems. But he had not then the honour of knowing your mamma or the family."

"It wasn't long before we did know him," said the Marchioness. Then Miss Tallowax turned round and again curtseyed with her head and shoulders.

The Dean at this moment was not in the room, having been withdrawn from the ladies by his son-in-law at the front door; but as luncheon was announced, the two men came in. Lord George gave his arm to his wife's great aunt, and the Dean followed with the Marchioness.

"I really am almost ashamed to walk out before her ladyship," said Miss Tallowax, with a slight attempt at laughing at her own ignorance.

But Lord George rarely laughed at anything, and certainly did not know how to treat pleasantly such a subject as this. "It's quite customary," he said, very gravely.

The lunch was much more tremendous to Miss Tallowax than had been the dinner at the Deanery. Though she was ignorant—ignorant at any rate of the ways of such people as those with whom she was now consorting—she was by no means a stupid old woman. She was soon able to perceive that, in spite of the old merino gown, it was Lady Sarah's spirit that quelled them all. At first there was very little conversation. Lord George did not speak a word. The Marchioness never exerted herself. Poor Mary was cowed and unhappy. The Dean made one or two little efforts, but without much success. Lady Sarah was intent upon her mutton-chop, which she finished to the last shred, turning it over and over in her plate so that it should be economically disposed of, looking at it very closely, because she was short-sighted. But, when the mutton-chop had finally done its duty, she looked up from her plate and gave evident signs that she intended to take upon herself the weight of the conversation. All the subsequent ceremonies of the lunch itself, the little tarts, and the jelly, and the custard pudding, she despised altogether, regarding them as wicked additions. One pudding after dinner she would have allowed, but nothing more of that sort. It might be all very well for parvenu millionaires to have two grand dinners a day, but it could not be necessary that the Germains should live in that way, even when the Dean of Brotherton and his aunt came to lunch with them.

"I hope you like this part of the country, Miss

Tallowax," she said, as soon as she had deposited her
knife and fork over the bone.

"Manor Cross is quite splendid, my lady," said Miss
Tallowax.

"It is an old house, and we shall have great pleasure in showing you what the people call the state-
rooms. We never use them. Of course you know
the house belongs to my brother, and we only live
here because it suits him to stay in Italy."

"That's the young Marquis, my lady?"

"Yes; my elder brother is Marquis of Brotherton,
but I cannot say that he is very young. He is
two years my senior, and ten years older than
George."

"But I think he's not married yet?" asked Miss
Tallowax.

The question was felt to be disagreeable by them
all. Poor Mary could not keep herself from blushing, as she remembered how much to her might depend on this question of her brother-in-law's marriage.
Lord George felt that the old lady was inquiring
what chance there might be that her grandniece
should ever become a marchioness. Old Lady Brotherton, who had always been anxious that her elder
son should marry, felt uncomfortable, as did also the
Dean, conscious that all there must be conscious how
important must be the matter to him.

"No," said Lady Sarah, with stately gravity; "my
elder brother is not yet married. If you would like
to see the rooms, Miss Tallowax, I shall have pleasure
in showing you the way."

The Dean had seen the rooms before, and remained
with the old lady. Lord George, who thought very
much of everything affecting his own family, joined

the party, and Mary felt herself compelled to follow
her husband and her aunt. The two younger sisters
also accompanied Lady Sarah.

"This is the room in which Queen Elizabeth slept,"
said Lady Sarah, entering a large chamber on the
ground floor, in which there was a fourpost bedstead,
almost as high as the ceiling, and looking as though
no human body had profaned it for the last three
centuries.

"Dear me," said Miss Tallowax, almost afraid to
press such sacred boards with her feet. "Queen Elizabeth! Did she really now?"

"Some people say she never did actually come to
Manor Cross at all," said the conscientious Lady
Amelia; "but there is no doubt that the room was
prepared for her."

"Laws!" said Miss Tallowax, who began to be
less afraid of distant royalty now that a doubt was
cast on its absolute presence.

"Examining the evidence as closely as we can,"
said Lady Sarah, with a savage glance at her sister,
"I am inclined to think that she certainly did come.
We know that she was at Brotherton in 1582, and
there exists the letter in which Sir Humphrey Ger-
maine, as he was then, is desired to prepare rooms
for her. I myself have no doubt on the subject."

"After all it does not make much difference," said
Mary.

"I think it makes all the difference in the world,"
said Lady Susanna. "That piece of furniture will
always be sacred to me, because I believe it did once
afford rest and sleep to the gracious majesty of
England."

"It do make a difference, certainly," said Miss

Tallowax, looking at the bed with all her eyes. "Does anybody ever go to bed here now?"

"Nobody, ever," said Lady Sarah. "Now we will go through to the great dining-hall. That's the portrait of the first earl."

"Painted by Kneller," said Lady Amelia proudly.

"Oh, indeed," said Miss Tallowax.

"There is some doubt as to that," said Lady Sarah. "I have found out that Sir Godfrey Kneller was only born in 1648, and as the first earl died a year or two after the Restoration, I don't know that he could have done it."

"It was always said that it was painted by Kneller," said Lady Amelia.

"There has been a mistake, I fear," said Lady Sarah.

"Oh, indeed," said Miss Tallowax, looking up with intense admiration at a very ill-drawn old gentleman in armour. Then they entered the state dining-room or hall, and Miss Tallowax was informed that the room had not been used for any purpose whatever for very many years. "And such a beautiful room!" said Miss Tallowax, with much regret.

"The fact is, I believe, that the chimney smokes horribly," said Lord George.

"I never remember a fire here," said Lady Sarah. "In very cold weather we have a portable stove brought in, just to preserve the furniture. This is called the old ball-room."

"Dear me!" ejaculated Miss Tallowax, looking round at the faded yellow hangings.

"We did have a ball here once," said Lady Amelia, "when Brotherton came of age. I can just remember it."

"Has it never been used since?" asked Mary.

"Never," said Lady Sarah. "Sometimes when it's
rainy we walk up and down for exercise. It is a
fine old house, but I often wish that it were smaller.
I don't think people want rooms of this sort now
as much as they used to do. Perhaps a time may come
when my brother will make Manor Cross gay again,
but it is not very gay now. I think that is all, Miss
Tallowax."

"It's very fine—very fine, indeed," said Miss Tallowax, shivering. Then they all trooped back into the
morning-room which they used for their daily life.

The old lady, when she had got gack into the
brougham with her nephew, the Dean, was able to
express her mind freely. "I wouldn't live in that
house, Henry, not if they was to give it me for
nothing."

"They'd have to give you something to keep it up
with."

"And not then, neither. Of course it's all very
well having a bed that Queen Elizabeth slept in."

"Or didn't sleep in."

"I'd teach myself to believe she did. But, dear
me, that isn't everything. It nearly gave me the horrors to look at it. Room after room—room after room
—and nobody living in any of them."

"People can't live in more than a certain number
of rooms at once, aunt."

"Then what's the use of having them? And don't
you think for the daughters of a Marchioness they
are a little what you'd call—dowdy?"

"They don't go in for dress much."

"Why, my Jemima at home, when the dirty work is
done, is twice smarter than Lady Sarah. And, Henry,
don't you think they're a little hard upon Mary?"

" Hard upon her; how?" The Dean had listened to the old woman's previous criticisms with a smile; but now he was interested and turned sharply round to her. "How, hard?"

"Moping her up there among themselves; and it seemed to me they snubbed her whenever she spoke." The Dean had not wanted his aunt's observation to make him feel this. The tone of every syllable addressed to his girl had caught his ear. He had been pleased to marry her into so good a family. He had been delighted to think that by means of his prosperity in the world his father's granddaughter might probably become a peeress. But he certainly had not intended that even for such a reward as that his daughter should become submissive to the old maids at Manor Cross. Foreseeing something of this he had stipulated that she should have a house of her own in London; but half her time would probably be spent in the country, and with reference to that half of her time it would be necessary that she should be made to understand that as the wife of Lord George she was in no respect inferior to his sisters, and that in some respects she was their superior. "I don't see the good of living in a big house," continued Miss Tallowax, "if all the time everything is to be as dull as dull."

" They are older than she is, you know."

" Poor little dear! I always did say that young folk should have young folk about 'em. Of course it's a great thing for her to have a lord for her husband. But he looks a'most too old himself for such a pretty darling as your Mary."

" He's only thirty-three."

" It's in the looks, I suppose, because he's so grand.

But it's that Lady Sarah puzzles me. It isn't in her looks, and yet she has it all her own way. Well, I liked going there, and I'm glad I've been; but I don't know as I shall ever want to go again." Then there was a silence for some time; but as the brougham was driven into Brotherton Miss Tallowax spoke again. "I don't suppose an old woman like me can ever be of any use, and you'll always be at hand to look after her. But if ever she should want an outing, just to raise her spirits, old as I am, I think I could make it brighter for her than it is there." The Dean took her hand and pressed it, and then there was no more said.

When the brougham was driven away, Lady George took his wife for a walk in the park. She was still struggling hard to be in love with him, never owning failure to herself, and sometimes assuring herself that she had succeeded altogether. Now, when he asked her to come with him, she put on her hat joyfully, and joined her hands over his arm as she walked away with him into the shrubbery.

"She's a wonderful old woman; is not she, George?"

"Not very wonderful."

"Of course you think she's vulgar."

"I didn't say so."

"No; you're too good to say so, because she's papa's aunt. But she's very good. Don't you think she's very good?"

"I daresay she is. I don't know that I run into superlatives quite as much as you do."

"She has brought me such a handsome present. I could not show it you before them all just now, and it only came down from London this morning.

She did not say a word about it before. Look here."
Then she slipped her glove off and showed him a
diamond ring.

"You should not wear that out of doors."

"I only put it on to show you. Wasn't it good of
her? 'Young people of rank ought to wear nice
things,' she said, as she gave it me. Wasn't it an
odd thing for her to say? and yet I understood her."
Lord George frowned, thinking that he also understood the old woman's words, and reminding himself
that the ladies of rank at Manor Cross never did wear
nice things. "Don't you think it was nice?"

"Of course she is entitled to make you a present
if she pleases."

"It pleased me, George."

"I daresay, and as it doesn't displease me all is
well. You, however, have quite sense enough to understand that in this house more is thought of—of—
of—" he would have said blood, but that he did not
wish to hurt her—"more is thought of personal good
conduct than of rings and jewels."

"Rings and jewels, and—personal conduct may go
together; mayn't they?"

"Of course they may."

"And very often do. You won't think my—personal conduct—will be injured because I wear my
aunt's ring?"

When Lord George made his allusion to personal
conduct one of her two hands dropped from his arm,
and now, as she repeated the words, there was a little
sting of sarcasm in her voice.

"I was intending to answer your aunt's opinion
that young people ought to wear nice things. No
doubt there is at present a great rage for rich orna-

ments and costly dress, and it was of these she was
thinking when she spoke of nice things. When I
spoke of personal conduct being more thought of here,
I intended to imply that you had come into a family
not given to rich ornaments and costly dress. My
sisters feel that their position in this world is assured
to them without such outward badges, and wish that
you should share the feeling."

This was a regular sermon, and to Mary's thinking
was very disagreeable, and not at all deserved. Did
her husband really mean to tell her that, because his
sisters chose to dress themselves down in the country
like dowdy old maids, whom the world had deserted,
she was to do the same up in London? The injustice
of this on all sides struck home to her at the moment.
They were old, and she was young. They were plain;
she was pretty. They were poor; she was rich. They
didn't feel any wish to make themselves what she
called "nice." She did feel a very strong wish in
that direction. They were old maids; she was a young
bride. And then what right had they to domineer
over her, and send word to her through her husband
of their wishes as to her manner of dressing? She
said nothing at the moment, but she became red, and
began to feel that she had power within her to rebel
at any rate against her sisters-in-law. There was
silence for a moment or so, and then Lord George
reverted to the subject.

"I hope you can sympathise with my sisters," he
said. He had felt that the hand had been dropped,
and had understood something of the reason.

She wished to rebel against them, but by no means
wished to oppose him. She was aware, as though by
instinct, that her life would be very bad indeed should

she fail to sympathise with him. It was still the all-paramount desire of her heart to be in love with him. But she could not bring herself to say that she sympathised with them in this direct attack that was made on her own mode of thought.

"Of course, they are a little older than I am," she said, hoping to get out of the difficulty.

"And therefore the more entitled to consideration. I think you will own that they must know what is, and what is not, becoming to a lady."

"Do you mean," said she, hardly able to choke a rising sob, "that they—have anything—to find fault with in me?"

"I have said nothing as to finding fault, Mary."

"Do they think that I do not dress as I ought to do?"

"Why should you ask such a question as that?"

"I don't know what else I am to understand, George. Of course I will do anything that you tell me. If you wish me to make any change, I will make it. But I hope they won't send me messages through you."

"I thought you would have been glad to know that they interested themselves about you." In answer to this Mary pouted, but her husband did not see the pout.

"Of course they are anxious that you should become one of them. We are a very united family. I do not speak now of my elder brother, who is in a great measure separated from us, and is of a different nature. But my mother, my sisters, and I have very many opinions in common. We live together, and have the same way of thinking. Our rank is high, and our means are small. But to me blood is much more than wealth. We acknowledge, however, that rank demands many sacrifices, and my sisters endeavor to make those sacrifices conscientiously. A woman more thoroughly devoted to good works than Sarah I have never even read of. If you will believe this, you will understand what they mean, and what I mean, when we say that here at Manor Cross we think more of personal conduct than of rings and jewels. You wish, Mary, to be one of us; do you not?"

She paused for a moment, and then she answered, "I wish to be always one with you."

He almost wanted to be angry at this, but it was impossible. "To be one with me, dearest," he said, "you must be one also with them."

"I cannot love them as I do you, George. That, I am sure, is not the meaning of being married." Then she thought of it all steadily for a minute, and after that made a further speech. "And I don't think I can quite dress like them. I'm sure you would not like it if I did."

As she said this she put her second hand back upon his arm.

He said nothing further on the subject until he had brought her back to the house, walking along by her side almost mute, not quite knowing whether he ought to be offended with her or to take her part. It was true that he would not have liked her to look like Lady Sarah, but he would have liked her to make some approach in that direction, sufficient to show submission. He was already beginning to fear the absence of all control which would befall his young wife in that London life to which she was to be so soon introduced, and was meditating whether he could not induce one of his sisters to accompany them. As to

Sarah he was almost hopeless. Amelia would be of little or no service, though she would be more likely to ingratiate herself with his wife than the others. Susanna was less strong than Sarah and less amiable than Amelia. And then, how would it be if Mary were to declare that she would rather begin the campaign without any of them?

The young wife, as soon as she found herself alone in her own bedroom, sat down and resolved that she would never allow herself to be domineered over by her husband's sisters. She would be submissive to him in all things, but his authority should not be delegated to them.

CHAPTER VI

About the middle of October there came a letter from the Marquis of Brotherton to his brother, which startled them all at Manor Cross very much indeed. In answering Lord George's communication as to the marriage, the Marquis had been mysterious and disagreeable; but then he was always diagreeable, and would on occasions take the trouble to be mysterious also. He had warned his brother that he might himself want the house at Manor Cross; but he had said the same thing frequently during his residence in Italy, being always careful to make his mother and sisters understand that they might have to take themselves away any day at a very short warning. But now the short warning had absolutely come, and had come in such a shape as to upset everything at Manor Cross, and to upset many things at the Brotherton Deanery. The letter was as follows:

"My dear George,

"I am to be married to the Marchesa Luigi. Her name is Catarina Luigi, and she is a widow. As to her age, you can ask her yourself when you see her, if you dare. I haven't dared. I suppose her to be ten years younger than myself. I did not expect that it would be so, but she says now that she would like to live in England. Of course I've always meant to go back myself some day. I don't suppose we shall be there before May, but we must have the house got

60

ready. My mother and the girls had better look out
for a place as soon as they can. Tell my mother of
course I will allow her the rent of Cross Hall, to which
indeed she is entitled. I don't think she would care
to live there, and neither she nor the girls would get
on with my wife.

Yours, B.

"I am waiting to know about getting the house
painted and furnished."

When Lord George received this letter, he showed
it first in privacy to his sister Sarah. As the reader
will have understood, there had never been any close
family affection between the present Marquis and his
brother and sisters; nor had he been a loving son
to his mother. But the family at Manor Cross had
always endeavored to maintain a show of regard for
the head of the family, and the old Marchioness would
no doubt have been delighted had her eldest son come
home and married an English wife. Lady Sarah, in
performing what she had considered to be a family
duty, had written regular despatches to her elder
brother, telling him everything that happened about
the place—despatches which he probably never read.
Now there had come a blow indeed. Lady Sarah read
the letter, and then looked into her brother's face.

"Have you told Mary?." she asked.

"I have told no one."

"It concerns her as much as any of us. Of course,
if he has married, it is right that he should have his
house. We ought to wish that he should live here."

"If he were different from what he is," said Lord
George.

"If she is good it may be that he will become different. It is not the thing, but the manner in which he tells it to us! Did you ever hear her name before?"

"Never."

"What a way he has of mentioning her—about her age," said Lady Sarah, infinitely shocked. "Well, mamma must be told, of course. Why shouldn't we live at Cross Hall? I don't understand what he means about that. Cross Hall belongs to mamma for her life, as much as Manor Cross does to him for his."

Just outside the park gate, at the side of the park farthest away from Brotherton, and therefore placed very much out of the world, there stood a plain substantial house built in the days of Queen Anne, which had now for some generations been the habitation of the dowager of the Brotherton family. When the late Marquis died, this had become for her life the property of the Marchioness; but had been ceded by her to her son, in return for the loan of the big house. The absentee Marquis had made with his mother the best bargain in his power, and had let the dower-house, known as Cross Hall, to a sporting farmer. He now kindly offered to allow his mother to have the rent of her own house, signifying at the same time his wish that all his family should remove themselves out of his way.

"He wishes that we should take ourselves off," said Lord George hoarsely.

"But I do not see why we are to give way to his wishes, George. Where are we to go? Of what use can we be in a strange country? Wherever we are we shall be very poor, but our money will go further here than elsewhere. How are we to get up new interests in life? The land is his, but the poor people belong to us as much as to him. It is unreasonable."

"It is frightfully selfish."

"I for one am not prepared to obey him in this," said Lady Sarah. "Of course mamma will do as she pleases, but I do not see why we should go. He will never live here all the year through."

"He will be sick of it after a month. Will you read the letter to my mother?"

"I will tell her, George. She had better not see the letter, unless she makes a point of it. I will read it again, and then do you keep it. You should tell Mary at once. It is natural that she should have built hopes on the improbability of Brotherton's marriage."

Before noon on that day the news had been disseminated through the house. The old Marchioness, when she first heard of the Italian wife, went into hysterics, and then was partly comforted by reminding herself that all Italians were not necessarily bad. She asked after the letter repeatedly; and at last, when it was found to be impossible to explain to her otherwise what her eldest son meant about the houses, it was shown to her. Then she began to weep afresh.

"Why mayn't we live at Cross Hall, Sarah?" she said.

"Cross Hall belongs to you, mamma, and nothing can hinder you from living there."

"But Augustus says that we are to go away."

The Marchioness was the only one of the family who ever called the Marquis by his Christian name, and she did so only when she was much disturbed.

"No doubt he expresses a wish that we should do so."

"Where are we to go to, and I at my age?"

"I think you should live at Cross Hall."

"But he says that we mayn't. We could never go on there if he wants us to go away."

"Why not, mamma? It is your house as much as this is his. If you will let him understand that when you leave this you mean to go there, he will probably say nothing more about it."

"Mr. Price is living there. I can't make Mr. Price go away directly the painter people come in here. They'll come to-morrow, perhaps, and what am I to do then?"

The matter was discussed throughout the whole day between Lady Sarah and her mother, the former bearing the old woman's plaintive weakness with the utmost patience, and almost succeeding, before the evening came, in inducing her mother to agree to rebel against the tyranny of her son. There were peculiar difficulties and peculiar hardships in the case. The Marquis could turn out all the women of his family at a day's notice. He had only to say to them "Go!" and they must be gone. And he could be rid of them without even saying or writing another word. A host of tradesmen would come, and then of course they must go. But Mr. Price at Cross Hall must have a regular year's notice, and that notice could not now be given till Lady-day next.

"If the worst comes to the worst, mamma, we will go and live in Brotherton for the time. Mr. Holden-ough or the Dean would find some place for us." Then the old lady began to ask how Mary had borne the news; but as yet Lady Sarah had not been able to interest herself personally about Mary.

Lord George was surprised to find how little his

wife was affected by the terrible thunderbolt which
had fallen among them. On him the blow had been
almost as terrible as on his mother. He had taken
a house in town, at the instance of the Dean, and, in
consequence of a promise made before his marriage,
which was sacred to him, but which he regretted. He
would have preferred himself to live the whole year
through at Manor Cross. Though he had not very
much to do there the place was never dull to him.
He liked the association of the big house. He liked
the sombre grandeur of the park. He liked the mag-
istrates' bench, though he rarely spoke a word when
he was there. And he liked the thorough economy
of the life. But as to that house in town, though his
wife's fortune would enable him to live there four or
five months, he knew that he could not stretch the income so as to bear the expense of the entire year. And
yet, what must he do now? If he could abandon the
house in town, then he could join his mother as to
some new country house. But he did not dare to
suggest that the house in town should be abandoned.
He was afraid of the Dean, and afraid, so to say, of
his own promise. The thing had been stipulated, and
he did not know how to go back from the stipulation.

"Going to leave Manor Cross," said Mary, when
she was told. "Dear me; how odd. Where will
they go to?"

It was evident to her husband from the tone of
voice that she regarded her own house in Munster
Court, for it was her own, as her future residence—
as hers and his. In asking where "they" would live,
she spoke of the other ladies of the family. He had
expected that she would have shown some disappointment at the danger to her future position which this

new marriage would produce. But in regard to that she was, he thought, either perfectly indifferent, or else a very good actor. In truth, she was almost indifferent. The idea that she might some day be Lady Brotherton had been something to her, but not much. Her happiness was not nearly as much disturbed by this marriage as it had been by the allusion made to her dress. She herself could hardly understand the terrible gloom which seemed during that evening and the whole of the next day to have fallen on the entire family.

"George, does it make you very unhappy?" she said, whispering to him on the morning of the second day.

"Not that my brother should marry," he said. "God forbid that I, as a younger brother, should wish to debar him from any tittle of what belongs to him. If he would marry well it ought to be a joy to us all."

"Is not this marrying well?"

"What, with a foreigner; with an Italian widow? And then there will, I fear, be great trouble in finding a comfortable home for my mother."

"Amelia says she can go to Cross Hall."

"Amelia does not know what she is talking of. It would be very long before they could get into Cross Hall, even if they can go there at all. It would have to be completely furnished, and there is no money to furnish it."

"Wouldn't your brother——?" Lord George shook his head. "Or papa——?" Lord George again shook his head. "What will they do?"

"If it were not for our house in London we might take a place in the country together," said Lord George.

All the various facts of the proposition now made to her flashed upon Mary's mind at once. Had it been suggested to her, when she was first asked to marry Lord George, that she should live permanently in a country house with his mother and sisters, in a house of which she would not be and could not be the mistress, she would certainly have rejected the offer. And now the tedium of such a life was plainer to her than it would have been then. But, under her father's auspices, a pleasant, gay little house in town had been taken for her, and she had been able to gild the dulness of Manor Cross with the brightness of her future prospects. For four or five months she would be her own mistress, and would be so in London. Her husband would be living on her money, but it would be the delight of her heart that he should be happy while doing so. And all this must be safe and wise, because it was to be done under the advice of her father. Now it was proposed to her that she should abandon all this and live in some smaller, poorer, duller country residence, in which she would be the least of the family instead of the mistress of her own home. She thought of it all for a moment, and then she answered him with a firm voice.

"If you wish to give up the house in London we will do so."

"It would distress you, I fear." When we call on our friends to sacrifice themselves, we generally wish them also to declare that they like being sacrificed.

"I should be disappointed, of course, George."

"And it would be unjust," said he.

"If you wish it I will not say a word against it."

On that afternoon he rode into Brotherton to tell
the tidings to the Dean. Upon whatever they might
among them decide, it was expedient that the Dean
should be at once told of the marriage. Lord George,
as he thought over it all on horseback, found difficulties on every side. He had promised that his wife
should live in town, and he could not go back from
that promise without injustice. He understood the
nature of her lately offered sacrifice, and felt that it
would not liberate his conscience. And then he was
sure that the Dean would be loud against any such
arrangement. The money no doubt was Mary's own
money and, subject to certain settlement, was at Lord
George's immediate disposal; but he would be unable
to endure the Dean's reproaches. He would be unable
also to endure his own, unless—which was so very
improbable—the Dean should encourage him. But
how were things to be arranged? Was he to desert
his mother and sisters in their difficulty? He was
very fond of his wife; but it had never yet occurred to
him that the daughter of Dean Lovelace could be as
important to him as all the ladies of the house of
Germain. His brother purposed to bring his wife to
Manor Cross in May, when he would be up in London.
Where, at that moment, and after what fashion, would
his mother and sisters be living?

The Dean showed his dismay at the marriage plainly
enough.

"That's very bad, George," he said; "very bad
indeed!"

"Of course we don't like her being a foreigner."

"Of course you don't like his marrying at all.
Why should you? You all know enough of him to

be sure that he wouldn't marry the sort of woman you would approve."

"I don't know why my brother should not have married any lady in England."

"At any rate he hasn't. He has married some Italian widow, and it's a misfortune. Poor Mary!"

"I don't think Mary feels it at all."

"She will some day. Girls of her age don't feel that kind of thing at first. So he is going to come over at once. What will your mother do?"

"She has Cross Hall."

"That man Price is there. He will go out, of course?"

"With notice he must go."

"He won't stand about that, if you don't interfere with his land and farm-yard. I know Price. He's not a bad fellow."

"But Brotherton does not want them to go there," said Lord George, almost in a whisper.

"Does not want your mother to live in her own house! Upon my word the Marquis is considerate to you all! He has said that plainly, has he? If I were Lady Brotherton I would not take the slightest heed of what he says. She is not dependent on him. In order that he may be relieved from the bore of being civil to his own family she is to be sent out about the world to look for a home in her old age! You must tell her not to listen for a minute to such a proposition."

Lord George, though he put great trust in his father-in-law, did not quite like hearing his brother spoken of so very freely by a man who was, after all, the son of a tradesman. It seemed to him as though the Dean made himself almost too intimate with the affairs at Manor Cross, and yet he was obliged to go on and tell the Dean everything.

"Even if Price went, there must be some delay in getting the house ready."

"The Marquis surely won't turn your mother out before the spring?"

"Tradesmen will have to come in. And then I don't quite know what we are to do as to the—expense of furnishing the new house. It will cost a couple of thousand pounds, and none of us have ready money." The Dean assumed a very serious face. "Every spoon and fork at Manor Cross, every towel and every sheet belongs to my brother."

"Was not the Cross House ever furnished?"

"Many years ago; in my grandmother's time. My father left money for the purpose, but it was given up to my sister Alice when she married Holdenough." He found himself explaining all the little intricacies of his family to the Dean, because it was necessary that he should hold council with some one. "I was thinking of a furnished house for them elsewhere."

"In London?"

"Certainly not there. My mother would not like it, nor would my sisters. I like the country very much the best myself."

"Not for the whole year?"

"I have never cared to be in London; but, of course, as for Mary and myself that is settled. You would not wish her to give up the house in Munster Court?"

"Certainly not. It would not be fair to her to ask her to live always under the wing of your mother and sisters. She would never learn to be a woman.

She would always be in leading strings. Do you not feel that yourself?"

"I feel that beggars cannot be choosers. My mother's fortune is £2000 a year. As you know, we have only £5000 a piece. There is hardly income enough among us for a house in town and a house in the country."

The Dean paused a moment, and then replied that his daughter's welfare could not be made subordinate to that of the family generally. He then said that if any immediate sum of money were required he would lend it either to the dowager or to Lord George.

Lord George, as he rode home, was angry both with himself and with the Dean. There had been an authority in the Dean's voice which had grated upon his feelings; of course he intended to be as good as his word; but, nevertheless, his wife was his wife and subject to his will; and her fortune had been her own and had not come from the Dean. The Dean took too much upon himself. And yet, with all that, he had consulted the Dean about everything, and had confessed the family poverty. The thing, however, was quite certain to him; he could not get out of the house in town.

During the whole of that day Lady Sarah had been at work with her mother, instigating her to insist on her own rights, and at last she had succeeded.

"What would our life be, mamma," Lady Sarah had said, "if we were removed altogether into a new world. Here we are of some use. People know us, and give us credit for being what we are. We can live after our own fashion, and yet live in accordance with our rank. There is not a man or a woman or a child in the parish whom I do not know. There is not a house in which you would not see Amelia's and Susanna's work. We cannot begin all that over again."

"When I am gone, my dear, you must do so."

"Who can say how much may be done before that sad day shall come to us? He may have taken his Italian wife back again to Italy. Mamma, we ought not to run from our duties."

On the following morning it was settled among them that the dowager should insist on possession of her own house at Cross Hall, and a letter was written to the Marquis, congratulating him of course on his marriage, but informing him at the same time that the family would remain in the parish.

Some few days later, Mr. Knox, the agent for the property, came down from London. He had received the orders of the Marquis, and would be prepared to put workmen into the house as soon as her ladyship would be ready to leave it. But he quite agreed that this could not be done at once. A beginning no doubt might be made while they were still there, but no painting should be commenced or buildings knocked down or put up till March. It was settled at the same time that on the first of March the family should leave the house.

"I hope my son won't be angry," the Marchioness said to Mr. Knox.

"If he be angry, my lady, he will be angry without a cause. But I never knew him to be very angry about anything."

"He always did like to have his own way, Mr. Knox," said the mindful mother.

CHAPTER VII

CROSS HALL GATE

WHILE Mr. Knox was still in the country, negotiations were opened with Mr. Price, the sporting farmer, who, like all sporting farmers, was in truth a very good fellow. He had never been liked by the ladies at Manor Cross, as having ways of his own which were not their ways. He did not go to church as often as they thought he ought to do; and, being a bachelor, stories were told about him which were probably very untrue. A bachelor may live in town without any inquiries as to any of the doings of his life; but if a man live forlorn and unmarried in a country house, he will certainly become the victim of calumny should any woman under sixty ever be seen about his place. It was said also of Mr. Price that sometimes, after hunting, men had been seen to go out of his yard in an uproarious condition. But I hardly think that old Sir Simon Bolt, the master of the hounds, could have liked him so well, or so often have entered his house, had there been much amiss there; and as to the fact of there always being a fox in Cross Hall Holt, which a certain little wood was called about half a mile of the house, no one even doubted that. But there had always been a prejudice against Price at the great house, and in this even Lord George had coincided. But when Mr. Knox went to him and explained to him what was about to happen—that the ladies would be forced, almost before the end of winter, to leave Manor Cross and

73

make way for the Marquis, Mr. Price declared that
he would clear out, bag and baggage, top-boots, spurs,
and brandy-bottles, at a moment's notice. The Prices
of the English world are not, as a rule, deficient in
respect for the marquises and marchionesses. "The
workmen can come in to-morrow," Price said, when
he was told that some preparations would ·be necessary. "A bachelor can shake down anywhere, Mr.
Knox." Now it happened that Cross Hall House
was altogether distinct from the Cross Hall Farm, on
which, indeed, there had been a separate farmhouse,
now only used by labourers. But Mr. Price was a
comfortable man, and, when the house had been vacant, had been able to afford himself the luxury of
living there.

So far the primary difficulties lessened themselves
when they were well looked in the face. And yet
things did not run altogether smoothly. The Marquis
did not condescend to reply to his brother's letter;
but he wrote what was for him a long letter to Mr.
Knox, urging upon the agent the duty of turning
his mother and sisters altogether out of the place.
"We shall be a great deal better friends apart," he
said. "If they remain there we shall see little or
nothing of each other, and it will be very uncomfortable. If they will settle themselves elsewhere, I
will furnish a house for them; but I don't want to
have them at my elbow." Mr. Knox was of course
bound to show this to Lord George, and Lord George
was bound to consult Lady Sarah. Lady Sarah told
her mother something of it, but not all; but she
told it in such a way that the old lady consented
to remain and to brave her eldest son. As for Lady
Sarah herself, in spite of her true Christianity and

real goodness, she did not altogether dislike the fight. Her brother was her brother, and the head of the family, and he had his privileges; but they, too, had their rights, and she was not disposed to submit herself to tyranny. Mr. Knox was therefore obliged to inform the Marquis, in what softest language he could find applicable for the purpose, that the ladies of the family had decided upon removing to the dower-house.

About a month after this there was a meet of the Brotherton Hunt, of which Sir Simon Bolt was the master, at Cross Hall Gate. The grandfather of the present Germains had in the early part of the century either established this special pack, or at any rate become the master of it. Previous to that the hunting probably had been somewhat precarious; but there had been, since his time, a regular Brotherton Hunt associated with a collar and button of its own—a blue collar on a red coat, with B. H. on the buttons— and the thing had been done well. They had four days a week, with an occasional bye, and £2500 were subscribed annually. Sir Simon Bolt had been the master for the last fifteen years, and was so well known that no sporting pen and no sporting tongue in England ever called him more than Sir Simon. Cross Hall Gate, a well-loved meet, was the gate of the big park which opened out upon the road just opposite to Mr. Price's house. It was an old stone structure, with a complicated arch stretching across the gate itself, with a lodge on each side. It lay back in a semicircle from the road, and was very imposing. In old days no doubt the gate was much used, as the direct traffic from London to Brotherton passed that way. But the railway had killed the road; and as the nearer road from the Manor Cross

House to the town came out on the same road much nearer to Brotherton, the two lodges and all the grandeur were very much wasted. But it was a pretty site for a meet when the hounds were seated on their haunches inside the gate, or moving about slowly after the huntsman's horse, and when the horses and carriages were clustered about on the high-road and inside the park. And it was a meet, too, much loved by the riding men. It was always presumed that Manor Cross itself was preserved for foxes, and the hounds were carefully run through the belt of woods. But half an hour did that, and then they went away to Price's Little Holt. On that side there were no more gentlemen's places; there was a gorse-cover or two and sundry little spinnes; but the country was a country for foxes to run and men to ride; and, with this before them, the members of the Brotherton Hunt were pleased to be summoned to Cross Hall Gate.

On such occasions Lord George was always there. He never hunted, and very rarely went to any other meet; but on these occasions he would appear mounted, in black, and would say a few civil words to Sir Simon, and would tell George Scruby, the huntsman, that he had heard that there was a fox among the laurels. George would touch his hat and say in his loud, deep voice: "Hope so, my lord," having no confidence whatever in a Manor Cross fox. Sir Simon would shake hands with him, make a suggestion about the weather, and then get away as soon as possible; for there was no sympathy and no common subject between the men. On this occasion Lady Amelia had driven down Lady Susanna in the pony-carriage, and Lady George was there, mounted, with her father the Dean, longing to be allowed to go away with the hounds, but having been strictly forbidden by her husband to do so. Mr. Price was of course there, as was also Mr. Knox, the agent, who had a little shooting-box down in the country, and kept a horse, and did a little hunting.

There was good opportunity for talking as the hounds were leisurely taken through the loose belt of woods which were by courtesy called the Manor Cross Coverts, and Mr. Price took the occasion of drawing a letter from his pocket and showing it to Mr. Knox.

"The Marquis has written to you!" said the agent in a tone of surprise, the wonder not being that the Marquis should write to Mr. Price, but that he should write to any one.

"Never did such a thing in his life before, and I wish he hadn't now."

Mr. Knox wished it also when he had read the letter. It expressed a very strong desire on the part of the Marquis that Mr. Price should keep the Cross Hall House, saying that it was proper that the house should go with the farm, and intimating the Marquis's wish that Mr. Price should remain as his neighbour. "If you can manage it, I'll make the farm pleasant and profitable to you," said the Marquis.

"He don't say a word about her ladyship," said Price; "but what he wants is just to get rid of 'em all, box and dice."

"That's about it, I suppose," said the agent.

"Then he's come to the wrong shop, that's what he has done, Mr. Knox. I've three more years of my lease of the farm, and after that, out I must go, I dare say."

"There's no knowing what may happen before that, Price."

"If I was to go, I don't know that I need quite starve, Mr. Knox."

"I don't suppose you will."

"I ain't no family, and I don't know as I'm just bound to go by what a lord says, though he is my landlord. I don't know as I don't think more of them ladies than I does of him—him, Mr. Knox." And then Mr. Price used some very strong language indeed. "What right has he to think as I'm going to do his dirty work? You may tell him from me as he may do his own."

"You'll answer him, Price?"

"Not a line. I ain't got nothing to say to him. He knows I'm a-going out of the house; and if he don't you can tell him."

"Where are you going to?"

"Well, I was going to fit up a room or two in the old farmhouse; and, if I had anything like a lease, I wouldn't mind spending three or four hundred pounds there. I was thinking of talking to you about it, Mr. Knox."

"I can't renew the lease without his approval."

"You write and ask him, and mind you tell him that there ain't no doubt at all as to my going out of Cross Hall after Christmas. Then, if he'll make it fourteen years, I'll put the old house up and not ask him for a shilling. As I'm a living sinner, they're on a fox! Who'd have thought of that in the park? That's the old vixen from the Holt, as sure as my name's Price. Them cubs haven't travelled here yet."

So saying, he rode away, and Mr. Knox rode after him, and there was consternation throughout the hunt.

It was so unaccustomed a thing to have to gallop across Manor Cross Park! But the hounds were in full cry, through the laurels, and into the shrubbery, and round the conservatory, close up to the house. Then she got into the kitchen-garden, and back again through the laurels. The butler and the gardener and the housemaid and the scullery-maid were all there to see.

Even Lady Sarah came to the front door, looking very severe, and the old Marchioness gaped out of her own sitting-room window upstairs. Our friend Mary thought it excellent fun, for she was really able to ride to the hounds; and even Lady Amelia became excited as she flogged the pony along the road. Stupid old vixen, who ought to have known better! Price was quite right, for it was she, and the cubs in the Holt were now finally emancipated from all maternal thraldom. She was killed ignominiously in the stoke-hole under the greenhouse—she who had been the mother of four litters, and who had baffled the Brotherton hounds half a dozen times over the cream of the Brotherton country!

"I knew it," said Price, in a melancholy tone, as he held up the head which the huntsman had just dissevered from the body. "She might 'a' done better with herself than come to such a place as this for the last move."

"Is it all over?" asked Lady George.

"That one is pretty nearly all over, miss," said George Scruby, as he threw the fox to the hounds. "My lady, I mean, begging your ladyship's pardon." Someone had prompted him at the moment. "I'm very glad to see your ladyship out, and I hope we'll show you something better before long."

But poor Mary's hunting was over. When George
Scruby and Sir Simon and the hounds went off to
the Holt, she was obliged to remain with her husband
and sisters-in-law.

While this was going on Mr. Knox had found time
to say a word to Lord George about that letter from
the Marquis. "I am afraid," he said, "your brother
is very anxious that Price should remain at Cross
Hall."

"Has he said anything more?"

"Not to me; but to Price he has."

"He has written to Price?"

"Yes, with his own hand, urging him to stay. I
cannot but think it was very wrong." A look of deep
displeasure came across Lord George's face. "I have
thought it right to mention it, because it may be a
question whether her ladyship's health and happiness
may not be best consulted by her leaving the neighbourhood."

"We have considered it all, Mr. Knox, and my
mother is determined to stay. We are very much
obliged to you. We feel that in doing your duty
by my brother you are anxious to be courteous to
us. The hounds have gone on; don't let me keep
you."

Mr. Houghton was of course out. Unless the meets
were very distant from his own place, he was always
out. On this occasion his wife also was there. She
had galloped across the park as quickly as anybody,
and, when the fox was being broken up in the grass
before the hall-door, was sitting close to Lady George.
"You are coming on?" she said, in a whisper.

"I am afraid not," answered Mary.

"Oh, yes; do come. Slip away with me. Nobody'll see you. Get as far as the gate, and then you can see that covert drawn."

"I can't very well. The truth is, they don't want me to hunt."

"They! Who is they? 'They' don't want me to hunt. That is, Mr. Houghton doesn't. But I mean to get out of his way by riding a little forward. I don't see why that is not just as good as staying behind. Mr. Price is going to give me a lead. You know Mr. Price?"

"But he goes everywhere."

"And I mean to go everywhere. What's the good of half doing it? Come along."

But Mary had not even thought of rebellion such as this—did not in her heart approve of it, and was angry with Mrs. Houghton. Nevertheless, when she saw the horsewoman gallop off across the grass towards the gate, she could not help thinking that she would have been just as well able to ride after Mr. Price as her old friend Adelaide de Baron. The Dean did go on, having intimated his purpose of riding on just to see Price's farm.

When the unwonted perturbation was over at Manor Cross, Lord George was obliged to revert again to the tidings he had received from Mr. Knox. He could not keep it to himself. He felt himself obliged to tell it all to Lady Sarah.

"That he should write to such a man as Mr. Price, telling him of his anxiety to banish his own mother from her own house!"

"You did not see the letter?"

"No; but Knox did. They could not very well

show such a letter to me; but Knox says that Price was very indignant, and swore that he would not even answer it."

"I suppose he can afford it, George? It would be very dreadful to ruin him."

"Price is a rich man. And after all, if Price were to do all that Brotherton desires him, he could only keep us out for a year or so. But don't you think you will all be very uncomfortable here. How will my mother feel if she isn't ever allowed to see him? And how will you feel if you find that you never want to see his wife?"

Lady Sarah sat silent for a few minutes before she answered him, and then declared for war. "It is very bad, George; very bad. I can foresee great unhappiness; especially the unhappiness which must come from constant condemnation of one whom we ought to wish to love and approve of before all others. But nothing can be so bad as running away. We ought not to allow anything to drive mamma from her own house, and us from our own duties. I don't think we ought to take any notice of Brotherton's letter to Mr. Price." It was thus decided between them that no further notice should be taken of the Marquis's letter to Mr. Price.

CHAPTER VIII

THERE was great talking about the old vixen as they trotted away to Cross Hall Holt—how it was the same old fox that they hadn't killed in a certain run last January, and how one old farmer was quite sure that this very fox was the one which had taken them that celebrated run to Bamham Moor three years ago, and how she had been the mother of quite a Priam's progeny of cubs. And now that she should have been killed in a stoke-hole! While this was going on a young lady rode up along side of Mr. Price, and said a word to him with her sweetest smile.

"You remember your promise to me, Mr. Price?"

"Surely, Mrs. Houghton. Your nag can jump a few, no doubt."

"Beautifully. Mr. Houghton bought him from Lord Mountfencer. Lady Mountfencer couldn't ride him because he pulls a little. But he's a perfect hunter."

"We shall find him, Mrs. Houghton, to a moral; and do you stick to me. They generally go straight away to Thrupp's larches. You see the little wood. There's an old earth there, but that's stopped. There is only one fence between this and that, a biggish ditch, with a bit of a hedge on this side, but it's nothing to the horses when they're fresh."

"Mine's quite fresh."

"Then they mostly turn to the right for Pugsby; nothing but grass then for four miles ahead."

"And the jumping?"

"All fair. There's one bit of water—Pugsby Brook —that you ought to have as he'll be sure to cross it ever so much above the bridge. But, lord love you, Mrs. Houghton, that horse'll think nothing of the brook."

"Nothing at all, Mr. Price. I like brooks."

"I'm afraid he's not here, Price," said Sir Simon, trotting round the cover towards the whip, who was stationed at the further end.

"Well, Sir Simon, her as we killed came from the Holt, you know," said the farmer, mindful of his reputation for foxes. "You can't eat your cake and have it too, can you, Sir Simon?"

"Ought to be able in a cover like this."

"Well, perhaps we shall. The best lying is down in that corner. I've seen a brace of cubs together there a score of times." Then there was one short, low, dubious bark, and then another a little more confirmed. "That's it, Sir Simon. There's your 'cake.'"

"Good hound, Blazer," cried Sir Simon, recognising the voice of his dog. And many of the pack recognised the well-known sound as plainly as the master, for you might hear the hounds rustling through the covert as they hurried up to certify to the scent which their old leader had found for them. The Holt though thick was small, and a fox had not much chance but by breaking. Once up to covert and once back again the animal went, and then Dick, the watchful whip, holding his hand up to his face, hollooed him away. "Gently, gentlemen," shouted Sir Simon, "let them settle. Now, Mr. Bottomley, if you'll only keep yourself a little steady, you'll find yourself the better for it at the finish." Mr. Bottomley was a young man from London, who was often addressed after this fashion, was always very unhappy for a few minutes, and then again forgot it in his excitement.

"Now, Mr. Price," said Mrs. Houghton in a fever of expectation. She had been dodging backwards and forwards trying to avoid her husband, and yet unwilling to leave the farmer's side.

"Wait a moment, ma'am; wait a moment. Now we're right; here to the left." So saying Mr. Price jumped over a low hedge, and Mrs. Houghton followed him, almost too closely. Mr. Houghton saw it, and didn't follow. He had made his way up, resolved to stop his wife, but she gave him the slip at the last moment. "Now through the gate, ma'am, and then on straight as an arrow for the little wood. I'll give you a lead over the ditch, but don't ride quite so close, ma'am." Then the farmer went away, feeling perhaps that his best chance of keeping clear from his too loving friend was to make the pace so fast that she should not be able quite to catch him. But Lady Mountfencer's nag was fast, too, was fast and had a will of his own. It was not without a cause that Lord Mountfencer had parted with so good a horse out of his stable. "Have a care, ma'am," said Price, as Mrs. Houghton cannoned against him as they both landed over the big ditch; "have a care, or we shall come to grief together. Just see me over before you let him take his jump." It was very good advice, and is very often given; but both ladies and gentlemen, whose hands are a little doubtful, sometimes find themselves unable to follow it. But now they were at Thrupp's larches. George Scruby had led the way, as becomes a huntsman, and a score or more had fol-

lowed him over the big fence. Price had been going
a little to the left, and when they reached the wood
was as forward as any one.

"He won't hang here, Sir Simon," said the farmer,
as the master came up; "he never does."

"He's only a cub," said the master.

"The Holt cubs this time of the year are nigh
as strong as old foxes. Now for Pugsby."

Mrs. Houghton looked round, fearing every moment that her husband would come up. They had
just crossed a road, and wherever there was a road,
there, she thought, he would certainly be.

"Can't we get round the other side, Mr. Price?"
she said.

"You won't be any better nor here."

"But there's Mr. Houghton on the road," she
whispered.

"Oh-h-h!" ejaculated the farmer, just touching
the end of his nose with his finger and moving gently
on through the wood. "Never spoil sport," was the
motto of his life, and to his thinking it was certainly
sport that a young wife should ride to hounds in opposition to an old husband. Mrs. Houghton followed
him, and as they got out on the other side, the fox
was again away. "He ain't making for Pugsby's
after all," said Price to George Scruby.

"He don't know that country yet," said the huntsman. "He'll be back in them Manor Cross woods.
You'll see else."

The park of Manor Cross lay to the left of them,
whereas Pugsby and the desirable grass country away
to Bamham Moor were all to the right. Some men,
mindful of the big brook and knowing the whereabouts
of the bridge, among whom was Mr. Houghton, kept

very much to the right, and were soon out of the run altogether. But the worst of it was that though they were not heading for their good country, still there was the brook, Pugsby Brook, to be taken. Had the fox done as he ought to have done, and made for Pugsby itself, the leap would have been from grass to grass; but now it must be from plough to plough, if taken at all. It need hardly be said that the two things are very different. Sir Simon, when he saw how the land lay, took a lane leading down to the Brotherton road. If the fox was making for the park he must be right in that direction. It is not often that a master of hounds rides for glory, and Sir Simon had long since left all that to younger men. But there were still a dozen riders pressing on, and among them were the farmer and his devoted follower—and a gentleman in black.

Let us give praise where praise is due, and acknowledge that young Bottomley was the first at the brook —and the first over it. As soon as he was beyond Sir Simon's notice he had scurried on across the plough, and being both light and indiscreet, had enjoyed the heartfelt pleasure of passing George Scruby. George, who hated Mr. Bottomley, grunted out his malediction, even though no one could hear him. "He'll soon be at the bottom of that," said George, meaning to imply in horsey phrase that the rider, if he rode over ploughed ground after that fashion, would soon come to the end of his steed's power. But Bottomley, if he could only be seen to jump the big brook before anyone else, would have happiness enough for a month. To have done a thing that he could talk about was the charm that Bottomley found in hunting. Alas, though he rode gallantly at the brook and did get over it, there was not much to talk about; for, unfortunately, he left his horse behind him in the water. The poor beast going with a rush off the plough, came with his neck and shoulders against the opposite bank, and shot his rider well on to the dry land.

"That's about as good as a dead 'un," said George, as he landed a yard or two to the right. This was ill-natured, and the horse, in truth, was not hurt. But a rider, at any rate a young rider, should not take a lead from a huntsman unless he is very sure of himself, of his horse, and of the run of the hounds. The next man over was the gentleman in black, who took it in a stand, and who really seemed to know what he was about. There were some who afterwards asserted that this was the Dean, but the Dean was never heard to boast of the performance.

Mrs. Houghton's horse was going very strong with her. More than once the farmer cautioned her to give him a pull over the plough. And she attempted to obey the order. But the horse was self-willed, and she was light; and in truth the heaviness of the ground would have been nothing to him had he been fairly-well ridden. But she allowed him to rush with her through the mud. As she had never yet had an accident she knew nothing of fear, and she was beyond measure excited. She had been near enough to see that a man fell at the brook, and then she saw also that the huntsman got over, and also the gentleman in black. It seemed to her to be lovely. The tumble did not scare her at all, as others coming after the unfortunate one had succeeded. She was aware that there were three or four other men behind her, and she was determined that they should not pass her.

They should see that she also could jump the river. She had not rid herself of her husband for nothing. Price, as he came near the water, knew that he had plenty to do, and knew also how very close to him the woman was. It was too late now to speak to her again, but he did not fear for his own horse if she would only give him room. He steadied the animal a yard or two from the margin as he came to the headland that ran down the side of the brook, and then took his leap.

But Mrs. Houghton rode as though the whole thing was to be accomplished by a rush, and her horse, true to the manner of horses, insisted on following in the direct track of the one who had led him so far. When he got to the bank he made his effort to jump high, but he had got no footing for a fair spring. On he went, however, and struck Price's horse on the quarter so violently as to upset that animal, as well as himself.

Price, who was a thoroughly good horseman, was knocked off, but got on to the bank as Bottomley had done. The two animals were both in the brook, and when the farmer was able to look round, he saw that the lady was out of sight. He was in the water immediately himself, but before he made the plunge he had resolved that he never again would give a lady a lead till he knew whether she could ride.

Mr. Knox and Dick were soon on the spot, and Mrs. Houghton was extracted. "I'm blessed if she ain't dead," said the whip, pale as death himself. "Hush!" said Mr. Knox; "she's not dead, but I'm afraid she's hurt." Price had come back through the water with the woman in his arms, and the two horses were still floundering about unattended. "It's her shoulder, Mr. Knox," said Price. "The horse has jammed her against the bank under water." During this time her head was drooping, and her eyes were closed, and she was apparently senseless. "Do you look to the horses, Dick; there ain't no reason why they should get their death of cold." By this time there were a dozen men round them, and Dick and others were able to attend to the ill-used nags. "Yes; it's her shoulder," continued Price. "That's out, any way. What the mischief will Mr. Houghton say to me when he comes up?"

There is always a doctor in the field—sent there by some benignity of Providence—who always rides forward enough to be near to accidents, but never so forward as to be in front of them. It has been hinted that this arrangement is professional rather than providential; but the present writer, having given his mind to the investigation of the matter, is inclined to think that it arises from the general fitness of things. All public institutions have, or ought to have, their doctor; but in no institution is the doctor so invariably at hand, just when he is wanted, as in the hunting field. A very skilful young surgeon from Brotherton was on the spot almost as soon as the lady was out of the water, and declared that she had dislocated her shoulder.

What was to be done? Her hat was gone; she had been under the water; she was covered with mud; she was still senseless, and of course she could neither ride nor walk. There were ever so many suggestions. Price thought that she had. better be taken back to Cross Hall, which was about a mile and a half distant. Mr. Knox, who knew the country, told them of a side gate in the Manor Cross wall, which made the great house nearer than the Cross Hall.

They could get her there in a little over a mile. But how to get her there? They must find a door on which to carry her. First a hurdle was suggested, and then Dick was sent galloping up to the house for a carriage. In the meantime she was carried to a labourer's cottage by the roadside on a hurdle, and there the party was joined by Sir Simon and Mr. Houghton.

"It's all your fault," said the husband, coming up to Price as though he meant to strike him with his whip. "Part of it is, no doubt, sir," said Price, looking his assailant full in the face, but almost sobbing as he spoke, "and I'm very unhappy about it." Then the husband went and hung over his wife; but his wife, when she saw him, found it convenient to faint again.

At about two o'clock the *cortège* with the carriage reached the great house. Sir Simon, after expressions of deep sorrow, had of course gone on after his hounds. Mr. Knox, as belonging to Manor Cross, and Price, and, of course, the doctor, with Mr. Houghton and Mr. Houghton's groom, accompanied the carriage. When they got to the door all the ladies were there to receive them. "I don't think we want to see anything more of you," said Mr. Houghton to the farmer. The poor man turned round and went away home alone, feeling himself to be thoroughly disgraced. "After all," he said to himself, "if you come to fault, it was she nigh killed me, not me her. How was I to know she didn't know nothing about it?"

"Now, Mary, I think you'll own that I was right," Lord George said to his wife, as soon as the sufferer had been put quietly to bed.

"Ladies don't always break their arms," said Mary.

"It might have been you as well as Mrs. Houghton."

"As I didn't go, you need not scold me, George."

"But you were discontented because you were prevented," said he, determined to have the last word.

CHAPTER IX

LADY SARAH, who was generally regarded as the arbiter of the very slender hospitalities exercised at Manor Cross, was not at all well pleased at being forced to entertain Mrs. Houghton, whom she especially disliked; but, circumstanced as they were, there was no alternative. She had been put to bed with a dislocated arm, and had already suffered much in having it reduced, before the matter could be even discussed. And then it was of course felt that she could not be turned out of the house. She was not only generally hurt, but she was a cousin also. "We must ask him, mamma," Lady Sarah said. The Marchioness whined piteously. Mr. Houghton's name had always been held in great displeasure by the ladies at Manor Cross. "I don't think we can help it. Mr. Sawyer"—Mr. Sawyer was the very clever young surgeon from Brotherton—"Mr. Sawyer says that she ought not to be removed for, at any rate, a week." The Marchioness groaned. But the evil became less than had been anticipated by Mr. Houghton's refusal. At first he seemed inclined to stay; but after he had seen his wife he declared that, as there was no danger, he would not intrude upon Lady Brotherton, but would, if permitted, ride over and see how his wife was progressing on the morrow. "That is a relief," said Lady Sarah to her mother; and yet Lady Sarah had been almost urgent in assuring Mr. Houghton that they would be delighted to have him.

In spite of her suffering, which must have been real, and her fainting, which had partly been so, Mrs. Houghton had had force enough to tell her husband that he would himself be inexpressibly bored by remaining at Manor Cross, and that his presence would inexpressibly bore "all those dowdy old women," as she called the ladies of the house. "Besides, what's the use?" she said; "I've got to lay here for a certain time. You would not be any good at nursing. You'd only kill yourself with *ennui*. I shall do well enough, and do you go on with your hunting." He had assented; but finding her to be well enough to express her opinion as to the desirability of his absence strongly, thought that she was well enough, also, to be rebuked for her late disobedience. He began, therefore, to say a word. "Oh Jeffrey! are you going to scold me?" she said, "while I am in such a state as this!" and then again she almost fainted. He knew that he was being ill-treated, but knowing also that he could not avoid it, he went away without a further word.

But she was quite cheerful that evening when Lady George came up to give her her dinner. She had begged that it might be so. She had known "dear Mary" so long, and was so warmly attached to her. "Dear Mary" did not dislike the occupation, which was soon found to comprise that of being head-nurse to the invalid. She had never especially loved Adelaide de Baron, and had felt that there was something amiss in her conversation when they had met at the Deanery; but she was brighter than the ladies at Manor Cross, was affectionate in her manner, and was at any rate young. There was an antiquity about everything at Manor Cross, which was already crushing the spirit of the young bride.

"Dear me! this is nice," said Mrs. Houghton, disregarding, apparently, altogether the pain of her shoulder; "I declare, I shall begin to be glad of the accident."

"You shouldn't say that."

"Why not, if I feel it? Doesn't it seem like a thing in a story that I should be brought to Lord George's house, and that he was my lover only quite the other day?" The idea had never occurred to Mary, and now that it was suggested to her, she did not like it. "I wonder when he'll come and see me. It would not make you jealous, I hope."

"Certainly not."

"No, indeed. I think he's quite as much in love with you as ever he was with me. And yet he was very, very·fond of me once. Isn't it odd that men should change so?"

"I suppose you are changed too," said Mary, hardly knowing what to say.

"Well—yes—no. I don't know that I'm changed at all. I never told Lord George that I loved him. And what's more, I never told Mr. Houghton so. I don't pretend to be very virtuous, and of course I married for an income. I like him very well, and I always mean to be good to him; that is, if he lets me have my own way. I'm not going to be scolded, and he need not think so."

"You oughtn't to have gone on to-day, ought you?"

"Why not? If my horse hadn't gone so very quick, and Mr. Price at that moment hadn't gone so very slow,

I shouldn't have come to grief, and nobody would have known anything about it. Wouldn't you like to ride?"

"Yes; I should like it. But are not you exerting yourself too much?"

"I should die if I were made to lie here without speaking to anyone. Just put the pillow a little under me. Now I'm all right. Who do you think was going as well as anybody yesterday? I saw him."

"Who was it?"

"The very Reverend the Dean of Brotherton, my dear."

No!"

But he was. I saw him jump the brook just before I fell into it. What will Mr. Groschut say?"

"I don't think papa cares much what Mr. Groschut says."

"And the bishop?"

"I'm not sure that he cares very much for the bishop either. But I am quite sure that he would not do anything that he thought to be wrong."

"A Dean never does, I suppose."

"My papa never does."

"Nor Lord George, I daresay," said Mrs. Houghton.

"I don't say anything about Lord George. I haven't known him quite so long."

"If you won't speak up for him, I will. I'm quite sure Lord George Germain never in his life did anything that he ought not to do. That's his fault. Don't you like men who do what they ought not to do?"

"No," said Mary, "I don't. Everybody always ought to do what they ought to do. And you ought to go to sleep, and so I shall go away." She knew that it was not all right—that there was something fast, and also something vulgar, about this self-appointed friend of hers. But though Mrs. Houghton was fast, and though she was vulgar, she was a relief to the endless gloom of Manor Cross.

On the next day Mr. Houghton came, explaining to everybody that he had given up his day's hunting for the sake of his wife. But he could say but little, and could do nothing, and he did not remain long. "Don't stay away from the meet another day," his wife said to him; "I shan't get well any the sooner, and I don't like being a drag upon you." Then the husband went away, and did not come for the next two days. On the Sunday he came over in the afternoon and stayed for half an hour, and on the following Tuesday he appeared on his way to the meet in top-boots and a red coat. He was, upon the whole, less troublesome to the Manor Cross people than might have been expected.

Mr. Price came every morning to inquire, and very gracious passages passed between him and the lady. On the Saturday she was up, sitting on a sofa in a dressing-gown, and he was brought in to see her. "It was all my fault, Mr. Price," she said immediately. "I heard what Mr. Houghton said to you; I couldn't speak then, but I was so sorry."

"What a husband says, ma'am, at such a time, goes for nothing."

"What a husband says, Mr. Price, very often does go for nothing." He turned his hat in his hand, and smiled. "If it had not been so all this wouldn't have happened, and I shouldn't have upset you into the water. But, all the same, I hope you'll give me a lead another day, and I'll take great care not to come

so close to you again." This pleased Mr. Price so
much that, as he went home, he swore to himself that
if ever she asked him again he would do just the same
as he had done on the day of the accident.

When Price the farmer had seen her, of course
it became Lord George's duty to pay her his compliments in person. At first he visited her in company
with his wife and Lady Sarah, and the conversation
was very stiff. Lady Sarah was potent enough to
quell even Mrs. Houghton. But later in the afternoon Lord George came back again, his wife being
in the room, and then there was a little more ease.
"You can't think how it grieves me," she said, "to
bring all this trouble upon you." She emphasised
the word "you," as though to show him that she
cared nothing for his mother and sisters.

"It is no trouble to me," said Lord George, bow-
ing low. "I should say that it was a pleasure, were
it not that your presence here is attended with so much
pain to yourself."

"The pain is nothing," said Mrs. Houghton. "I
have hardly thought of it. It is much more than com-
pensated by the renewal of my intimacy with Lady
George Germain." This she said with her very prettiest manner, and he told himself that she was indeed
very pretty.

Lady George—or Mary, as we will still call her,
for simplicity, in spite of her promotion—had become
somewhat afraid of Mrs. Houghton; but now, seeing
her husband's courtesy to her guest, understanding
from his manner that he liked her society, began to
thaw, and to think that she might allow herself
to be intimate with the woman. It did not occur to
her to be in any degree jealous—not, at least, as yet.

In her innocence she did not think it possible that her
husband's heart should be untrue to her, nor did it
occur to her that such a one as Mrs. Houghton could
be preferred to herself. She thought that she knew
herself to be better than Mrs. Houghton, and she
certainly thought herself to be the better looking of
the two.

Mrs. Houghton's beauty, such as it was, depended
mainly on style; on a certain dash and manner which
she had acquired, and which to another woman were
not attractive. Mary knew that she herself was beautiful. She could not but know it. She had been
brought up by all belonging to her with that belief;
and so believing, had taught herself to acknowledge
that no credit was due to herself on that score. Her
beauty now belonged entirely to her husband. There
was nothing more to be done with it, except to maintain her husband's love, and that, for the present, she
did not in the least doubt. She had heard of married
men falling in love with other people's wives, but she
did not in the least bring home the fact to her own
case.

In the course of that afternoon all the ladies of the
family sat for a time with their guest. First came
Lady Sarah and Lady Susanna. Mrs. Houghton,
who saw very well how the land lay, rather snubbed
Lady Sarah. She had nothing to fear from the
dragon of the family. Lady Sarah, in spite of their
cousinship, had called her Mrs. Houghton, and Mrs.
Houghton in return called the other Lady Sarah.
There was to be no intimacy, and she was only received there because of her dislocated shoulder. Let
it be so. Lord George and his wife were coming up
to town, and the intimacy should be there. She cer-

tainly would not wish to repeat her visit to Manor Cross.

"Some ladies do like hunting, and some don't," she said, in answer to a severe remark from Lady Sarah. "I am one of those who do, and I don't think an accident like that has anything to do with it."

"I'can't say I think it an amusement fit for ladies," said Lady Sarah.

"I suppose ladies may do what clergymen do. The Dean jumped over the brook just before me." There was not much of an argument in this, but Mrs. Houghton knew that it would vex Lady Sarah, because of the alliance between the Dean and the Manor Cross family.

"She's a detestable young woman," Lady Sarah said to her mother, "and I can only hope that Mary won't see much of her up in town."

"I don't see how she can, after what there has been between her and George," said the innocent old lady. In spite, however, of this strongly expressed opinion, the old lady made her visit, taking Lady Amelia with her. "I hope, my dear, you find yourself getting better."

"So much better, Lady Brotherton! But I am sorry to have given you all this trouble; but it has been very pleasant to me to be here, and to see Lord George and Mary together. I declare I think hers is the sweetest face I ever looked upon. And she is so much improved. That's what perfect happiness does. I do so like her."

"We love her very dearly," said the Marchioness.

"I am sure you do. And he is so proud of her!" Lady Sarah had said that the woman was detestable, and therefore the Marchioness felt that she ought to detest her. But, had it not been for Lady Sarah, she would have been rather pleased with her guest than otherwise. She did not remain very long, but promised that she would return on the next day.

On the following morning Mr. Houghton came again, staying only a few minutes; and while he was in his wife's sitting-room, both Lord George and Mary found them. As they were all leaving her together, she contrived to say a word to her old love. "Don't desert me all the morning. Come and talk to me a bit. I am well now, though they won't let me move about."

In obedience to this summons, he returned to her when his wife was called upon to attend to the ordinary cloak and petticoat conclave of the other ladies. In regard to these charitable meetings she had partly carried her own way. She had so far thrown off the authority as to make it understood that she was not to be bound by the rules which her sisters-in-law had laid down for their own guidance, but her rebellion had not been complete, and she still gave them a certain number of weekly stitches. Lord George had said nothing of his purpose; but for a full hour before luncheon he was alone with Mrs. Houghton. If a gentleman may call on a lady in her house, surely he may, without scandal, pay her a visit in his own. That a married man should chat for an hour with another man's wife in a country house is not much. Where is the man and where the woman who has not done that, quite as a matter of course? And yet when Lord George knocked at the door there was a feeling on him that he was doing something in which he would not wish to be detected. "This is so good of you," she said. "Do sit down;

and don't run away. Your mother and sisters have been here—so nice of them, you know; but everybody treats me as though I oughtn't to open my mouth for above five minutes at a time. I feel as though I should like to jump the brook again immediately."

"Pray don't do that."

"Well, no; not quite yet. You don't like hunting, I'm afraid?"

"The truth is," said Lord George, "that I've never been able to afford to keep horses."

"Ah, that's a reason. Mr. Houghton, of course, is a rich man; but I don't know anything so little satisfactory in itself as being rich."

"It is comfortable."

"Oh yes, it is comfortable; but so unsatisfactory! Of course Mr. Houghton can keep any number of horses; but what's the use, when he never rides to hounds? Better not have them at all, I think. I am very fond of hunting myself."

"I daresay I should have liked it had it come in my way early in life."

"You speak of yourself as if you were a hundred years old. I know your age exactly. You are just seventeen years younger than Mr. Houghton!" To this Lord George had no reply to make. Of course he had felt that when Miss de Baron had married Mr. Houghton she had married quite an old man. "I wonder whether you were much surprised when you heard that I was engaged to Mr. Houghton?"

"I was, rather."

"Because he is so old?"

"Not that altogether."

"I was surprised myself, and I knew that you would be. But what was I to do?"

"I think you have been very wise," said Lord George.

"Yes, but you think I have been heartless. I can see it in your eyes and hear it in your voice. Perhaps I was heartless—but then I was bound to be wise. A man may have a profession before him. He may do anything. But what has a girl to think of? You say that money is comfortable."

"Certainly it is."

"How is she to get it, if she has not got it of her own, like dear Mary?"

"You do not think that I have blamed you?".

"But even though you have not, yet I must excuse myself to you," she said with energy, bending forward from her sofa towards him. "Do you think that I do not know the difference?"

"What difference?"

"Ah, you shouldn't ask. I may hint at it, but you shouldn't ask. But it wouldn't have done, would it?" Lord George hardly understood what it was that wouldn't have done; but he knew that a reference was being made to his former love by the girl he had loved; and, upon the whole, he rather liked it. The flattery of such intrigues is generally pleasant to men, even when they cannot bring their minds about quick enough to understand all the little ins and outs of the woman's manœuvres. "It is my very nature to be extravagant. Papa has brought me up like that. And yet I had nothing that I could call my own. I had no right to marry any one but a rich man. You said just now you couldn't afford to hunt."

"I never could."

"And I couldn't afford to have a heart. You said just now, too, that money is very comfortable. There was a time when I should have found it very, very comfortable to have had a fortune of my own."

"You have plenty."

She wasn't angry with him, because she had already found out that it is the nature of men to be slow. And she wasn't angry with him, again, because, though he was slow, yet also was he evidently gratified. "Yes," she said, "I have plenty now. I have secured so much. I couldn't have done without a large income; but a large income doesn't make me happy. It's like eating and drinking. One has to eat and drink, but yet one doesn't care very much about it. Perhaps you don't regret hunting very much?"

"Yes, I do, because it enables a man to know his neighbours."

"I know that I regret the thing I couldn't afford."

Then a glimmer of what she meant did come across him, and he blushed. "Things will not always turn out as they are wanted," he said. Then his conscience upbraided him, and he corrected himself. "But, God knows that I have no reason to complain. I have been fortunate."

"Yes, indeed."

"I sometimes think it is better to remember the good things we have than to regret those that are gone."

"That is excellent philosophy, Lord George. And therefore I go out hunting, and break my bones, and fall into rivers, and ride about with such men as Mr. Price. One has to make the best of it, hasn't one? But you, I see, have no regrets."

He paused for a moment, and then found himself driven to make some attempt at gallantry. "I didn't quite say that," he replied.

"You were able to re-establish yourself according to your own tastes. A man can always do so. I was obliged to take whatever came. I think that Mary is so nice."

"I think so too, I can assure you."

"You have been very fortunate to find such a girl; so innocent, so pure, so pretty, and with a fortune too. I wonder how much difference it would have made in your happiness if you had seen her before we had ever been acquainted. I suppose we should never have known each other then."

"Who can say?"

"No; no one can say. For myself, I own that I like it better as it is. I have something to remember that I can be proud of."

"And I something to be ashamed of."

"To be ashamed of!" she said, almost rising in anger.

"That you should have refused me!"

She had got it at last. She had made her fish rise to the fly. "Oh, no," she said, "there can be nothing of that. If I did not tell you plainly then, I tell you plainly now. I should have done very wrong to marry a poor man."

"I ought not to have asked you."

"I don't know how that may be," she said, in a very low voice, looking down to the ground. "Some say that if a man loves he should declare his love, let the circmustances be what they may. I rather think that I agree with them. You at any rate knew that I felt greatly honoured, though the honour was out of my reach." Then there was a pause during which he could find nothing to say. He was trapped by her flattery, but he did not wish to betray his wife

by making love to the woman. He liked her words
and her manner, but he was aware that she was a
thing sacred as being another man's wife. "But it
is all better as it is," she said with a laugh, "and
Mary Lovelace is the happiest girl of her year. I am
so glad you are coming to London, and do so hope
you'll come and see me."

"Certainly I will."

"I mean to be such friends with Mary. There is
no woman I like so much. And then circumstances
have thrown us together, haven't they? and if she
and I are friends, real friends, I shall feel that our
friendship may be continued—yours and mine. I
don't mean that all this accident shall go for nothing.
I wasn't quite clever enough to contrive it; but I am
very glad of it, because it has brought us once more
together, so that we may understand each other.
Good-bye, Lord George. Don't let me keep you longer
now. I wouldn't have Mary jealous, you know."

"I don't think there is the least fear of that," he
said in real displeasure.

"Don't take me up seriously for my little joke,"
she said, as she put out her hand. He took it, and
once more smiled, and then left her.

When she was alone there came a feeling on her
that she had gone through some hard work with only
moderate success; and also a feeling that the game
was hardly worth the candle. She was not in the
least in love with the man, or capable of being in
love with any man. In a certain degree she was
jealous, and felt that she owed Mary Lovelace a turn
for having so speedily won her own rejected lover.
But her jealousy was not strong enough for absolute
malice. She had formed no plot against the happi-

ness of the husband and wife when she came into the house; but the plot made itself, and she liked the excitement. He was heavy, certainly heavy, but he was very handsome, and a lord; and then, too, it was much in her favour that he certainly had once loved her dearly.

Lord George, as he went down to lunch, felt himself to be almost guilty, and hardly did more than creep into the room where his wife and sisters were seated.

"Have you been with Mrs. Houghton?" asked Lady Sarah, in a firm voice.

"Yes, I have been sitting with her for the last half hour," he replied; but he couldn't answer the question without hesitation in his manner. Mary, however, thought nothing about it.

CHAPTER X

THE DEAN AS A SPORTING MAN

In Brotherton the Dean's performance in the run from Cross Hall Holt was almost as much talked of as Mrs. Houghton's accident. There had been rumours of things that he had done in the same line after taking orders, when a young man, of runs that he had ridden, and even of visits which he had made to Newmarket, and other wicked places. But, as far as Brotherton knew, there had been nothing of all this since the Dean had been a dean. Though he was constantly on horseback, he had never been known to do more than perhaps look at a meet, and it was understood through Brotherton generally that he had forbidden his daughter to hunt. But now, no sooner was his daughter married, and the necessity of setting an example to her at an end, than the Dean, with a rosette in his hat—for so the story was told—was after the hounds like a sporting farmer or a mere country gentleman! On the very next day Mr. Groschut told the whole story to the bishop. But Mr. Groschut had not seen the performance, and the bishop affected to disbelieve it.

"I'm afraid, my lord," said the Chaplain, "I'm afraid you'll find it's true."

"If he rides after every pack of dogs in the county, I don't know that I can help it," said the bishop. With this Mr. Groschut was by no means inclined to agree.

A bishop is as much entitled to cause inquiries to be made into the moral conduct of a dean as of any country clergyman in his diocese.

"Suppose he were to take to gambling on the turf," said Mr. Groschut, with much horror expressed in his tone and countenance.

"But riding after a pack of dogs isn't gambling on the turf," said the bishop, who, though he would have liked to possess the power of putting down the Dean, by no means relished the idea of being beaten in an attempt to do so.

And Mr. Canon Holdenough heard of it. "My dear," he said to his wife, "Manor Cross is coming out strong in the sporting way. Not only is Mrs. Houghton laid up there with a broken limb, but your brother's father-in-law took the brush on the same day."

"The Dean!" said Lady Alice.

"So they tell me."

"He was always so particular in not letting Mary ride over a single fence. He would hardly let her go to a meet on horseback."

"Many fathers do what they won't let their daughters do. The Dean has been always giving signs that he would like to break out a little."

"Can they do anything to him?"

"Oh, dear no; not if he was to hunt a pack of hounds himself, as far as I know."

"But I suppose it's wrong, Canon," said the clerical wife.

"Yes, I think it's wrong, because it will scandalise. Everything that gives offence is wrong, unless it be something that is on other grounds expedient. If it be true, we shall hear about it a good deal here, and it will not contribute to brotherly love and friendship among us clergymen."

There was another canon at Brotherton, one Dr. Pountner, a red-faced man, very fond of his dinner, a man of infinite pluck, and much attached to the cathedral, towards the reparation of which he had contributed· liberally. And, having an ear for music, he had done much to raise the character of the choir. Though Dr. Pountner's sermons were supposed to be the worst ever heard from the pulpit of the cathedral, he was, on account of the above good deeds, the most popular clergyman in the city. "So I'm told you've been distinguishing yourself, Mr. Dean," said the Doctor, meeting our friend in the Close.

"Have I done so lately, more than is usual with me?" asked the Dean, who had not hitherto heard of the rumour of his performances.

"I am told that you were so much ahead the other day in the hunting field, that you were unable to give assistance to the poor lady who broke her arm."

"Oh, that's it! If I do anything at all, though I may do it but once in a dozen years, I like to do it well, Dr. Pountner. I wish I thought that you could follow my example, and take a little exercise. It would be very good for you." The Doctor was a heavy man, and hardly walked much beyond the confines of the Close or his own garden. Though a bold man, he was not so ready as the Dean, and had no answer at hand. "Yes," continued our friend, "I did go a mile or two with them, and I enjoyed it amazingly. I wish with all my heart there was no prejudice against clergymen hunting."

"I think it would be an abominable practice," said Dr. Pountner, passing on.

The Dean himself would have thought nothing more about it had there not appeared a few lines on the subject in a weekly newspaper called *The Brotherton Church,* which was held to be a pestilential little rag by all the Close. Deans, canons, and minor canons were all agreed as to this, Dr. Pountner hating *The Brotherton Church* quite as sincerely as did the Dean. *The Brotherton Church* was edited nominally by a certain Mr. Grease, a very pious man who had long striven, but hitherto in vain, to get orders. But it was supposed by many that the paper was chiefly inspired by Mr. Groschut. It was always very laudatory of the bishop. It had distinguished itself by its elaborate opposition to ritual. Its mission was to put down popery in the diocese of Brotherton. It always sneered at the Chapter generally, and very often said severe things of the Dean. On this occasion the paragraph was as follows: " There is a rumour current that Dean Lovelace was out with the Brotherton foxhounds last Wednesday, and that he rode with the pack all the day, leading the field. We do not believe this, but we hope that for the sake of the cathedral and for his own sake, he will condescend to deny the report." On the next Saturday there was another paragraph, with a reply from the Dean: " We have received from the Dean of Brotherton the following startling letter, which we publish without comment. What our opinion on the subject may be our readers will understand."

" Deanery, November, 187—
" SIR,—You have been correctly informed that I was out with the Brotherton foxhounds on Wednesday week last. The other reports which you have

published, and as to which, after publication, you have asked for information, are unfortunately incorrect. I wish I could have done as well as my enemies accuse me of doing.

                              "I am, Sir,
                    "Your humble servant,
                                   "HENRY LOVELACE."
"To the Editor of *The Brotherton Church*."

The Dean's friends were unanimous in blaming him for having taken any notice of the attack. The bishop, who was at heart an honest man and a gentleman, regretted it. All the Chapter were somewhat ashamed of it. The minor canons were agreed that it was below the dignity of a dean. Dr. Pountner, who had not yet forgotten the allusion to his obesity, whispered in some clerical ear that nothing better could be expected out of a stable; and Canon Holdenough, who really liked the Dean in spite of certain differences of opinion, expostulated with him about it.

"I would have let it pass," said the Canon. "Why notice it at all?"

"Because I would not have anyone suppose that I was afraid to notice it. Because I would not have it thought that I had gone out with the hounds and was ashamed of what I had done."

"Nobody who knows you would have thought that."

"I am proud to think that nobody who knows me would. I make as many mistakes as another, and am sorry for them afterwards. But I am never ashamed. I'll tell you what happened, not to justify my hunting, but to justify my letter. I was over at Manor Cross, and I went to the meet, because Mary went. I have not done such a thing before since I came to

Brotherton, because there is—what I will call a feeling against it. When I was there I rode a field or two with them, and I can tell you I enjoyed it."

"I daresay you did."

"Then, very soon after the fox broke, there was that brook at which Mrs. Houghton hurt herself. I happened to jump it, and the thing became talked about because of her accident. After that we came out on the Brotherton road, and I went back to Manor Cross. Do not suppose that I should have been ashamed of myself if I had gone on even half-a-dozen more fields."

"I'm sure you wouldn't."

"The thing in itself is not bad. Nevertheless,—thinking as the world around us does about hunting—a clergyman in my position would be wrong to hunt often. But a man who can feel horror at such a thing as this is a prig in religion. If, as is more likely, a man affects horror, he is a hypocrite. I believe that most clergymen will agree with me in that; but there is no clergyman in the diocese of whose agreement I feel more certain than of yours."

It is the letter, not the hunting, to which I object."

There was an apparent cowardice in refraining from answering such an attack. I am aware, Canon, of a growing feeling of hostility to myself."

"Not in the Chapter?"

"In the diocese. And I know whence it comes, and I think I can understand its cause. Let what will come of it I am not going to knock under. I want to quarrel with no man, and certainly with no clergyman; but I am not going to be frightened out of my own manner of life or my own manner of thinking by fear of a quarrel."

"Nobody doubts your courage; but what is the use of fighting when there is nothing to win? Let that wretched newspaper alone. It is beneath you and me, Dean."

"Very much beneath us, and so is your butler beneath you. But if he asks you a question, you answer him. To tell the truth, I would rather they should call me indiscreet than timid. If I did not feel that it would be really wrong and painful to my friends, I would go out hunting three days next week, to let them know that I am not to be cowed."

There was a good deal said at Manor Cross about the newspaper correspondence, and some condemnation of the Dean expressed by the ladies, who thought that he had lowered himself by addressing a reply to the editor. In the heat of discussion a word or two was spoken by Lady Susanna—who entertained special objections to all things low—which made Mary very angry. "I think papa is at any rate a better judge than you can be," she said. Between sisters as sisters generally are, or even sisters-in-law, this would not be much; but at Manor Cross it was felt to be misconduct. Mary was so much younger than they were! And then she was the grand-daughter of a tradesman! No doubt they all thought that they were willing to admit her among themselves on terms of equality; but then there was a feeling among them that she ought to repay this great goodness by a certain degree of humility and submission. From day to day the young wife strengthened herself in a resolution that she would not be humble and would not be submissive.

Lady Susanna, when she heard the words, drew herself up with an air of offended dignity. "Mary, my dear," said Lady Sarah, "is not that a little unkind?"

"I think it is unkind to say that papa is indiscreet," said the Dean's daughter. "I wonder what you'd think if I were to say a word against dear mamma." She had been specially instructed to call the Marchioness mamma.

"The Dean is not my father-in-law," said Lady Amelia, very proudly, as though in making the suggestion, she begged it to be understood that under no circumstances could such a connection have been possible.

"But he's my papa, and I shall stand up for him; and I do say that he must know more about such things than any lady." Then Lady Susanna got up and marched majestically out of the room.

Lord George was told of this, and found himself obliged to speak to his wife. "I'm afraid there has been something between you and Susanna, dear."

"She abused papa, and I told her papa knew better than she did, and then she walked out of the room."

"I don't suppose she meant to—abuse the Dean."

"She called him names."

"She said he was indiscreet."

"That is calling him names."

"No, my dear, indiscreet is an epithet: and even were it a noun substantive, as a name must be, it could only be one name." It was certainly very hard to fall in love with a man who could talk about epithets so very soon after his marriage; but yet she would go on trying.

"Dear George," she said, "don't you scold me. I will do anything you tell me, but I don't like them

to say hard things of papa. You are not angry with
me for taking papa's part, are you?"

He kissed her, and told her that he was not in
the least angry with her; but nevertheless, he went
on to insinuate, that if she could bring herself to
show something of submission to his sisters, it would
make her own life happier and theirs and his. "I
would do anything I could to make your life happy,"
she said.

CHAPTER XI

TIME went on, and the day arranged for the migration to London came round. After much delicate fencing on one side and the other, this was fixed for the 31st January. The fencing took place between the Dean, acting on behalf of his daughter, and the ladies of the Manor Cross family generally. They, though they conceived themselves to have had many causes of displeasure with Mary, were not the less anxious to keep her at Manor Cross. They would all at any moment have gladly assented to an abandonment of the London house, and had taught themselves to look upon the London house as an allurement of Satan, most unwisely contrived and countenanced by the Dean. And there was no doubt that, as the Dean acted on behalf of his daughter, so did they act on behalf of their brother. He could not himself oppose the London house; but he disliked it and feared it, and now, at last, thoroughly repented himself of it. But it had been a stipulation made at the marriage; and the Dean's money had been spent. The Dean had been profuse with his money, and had shown himself to be a more wealthy man than any one at Manor Cross had suspected. Mary's fortune was no doubt her own; but the furniture had been in a great measure supplied by the Dean, and the Dean had paid the necessary premium on going into the house. Lord George felt it to be impossible to change his mind after all that had been done; but he had been quite willing to postpone the evil day as long as possible.

Lady Susanna was especially full of fears, and, it must be owned, especially inimical to all Mary's wishes. She was the one who had perhaps been most domineering to her brother's wife, and she was certainly the one whose domination Mary resisted with the most settled determination. There was a self-abnegation about Lady Sarah, a down-right goodness, and at the same time an easily-handled magisterial authority, which commanded reverence. After three months of residence at Manor Cross, Mary was willing to acknowledge that Lady Sarah was more than a sister-in-law,—that her nature partook of divine omnipotence, and that it compelled respect, whether given willingly or unwillingly. But to none of the others would her spirit thus humble itself, and especially not to Lady Susanna. Therefore Lady Susanna was hostile, and therefore Lady Susanna was quite sure that Mary would fall into great trouble amidst the pleasures of the metropolis.

"After all," she said to her elder sister, "what is £1500 a year to keep up a house in London?"

"It will only be for a few months," said Lady Sarah.

"Of course she must have a carriage, and then George will find himself altogether in the hands of the Dean. That is what I fear. The Dean has done very well with himself, but he is not a man whom I like to trust altogether."

"He is at any rate generous with his money."

"He is bound to be that, or he could not hold up his head at all. He has nothing else to depend on.

Did you hear what Dr. Pountner said about him the other day? Since that affair with the newspaper, he has gone down very much in the Chapter. I am sure of that."

"I think you are a little hard upon him, Susanna."

"You must feel that he is very wrong about this house in London. Why is a man, because he's married, to be taken away from all his own pursuits. If she could not accommodate herself to his tastes, she should not have accepted him."

"Let us be just," said Lady Sarah.

"Certainly, let us be just," said Lady Amelia, who in these conversations seldom took much part, unless when called upon to support her eldest sister.

"Of course we should be just," said Lady Susanna.

"She did not accept him," said Lady Sarah, "till he had agreed to comply with the Dean's wish that they should spend part of their time in London."

"He was very weak," said Lady Susanna.

"I wish it could have been otherwise," continued Lady Sarah; "but we can hardly suppose that the tastes of a young girl from Brotherton should be the same as ours. I can understand that Mary should find Manor Cross dull."

"Dull!" exclaimed Lady Susanna.

"Dull!" ejaculated Lady Amelia, constrained on this occasion to differ even from her eldest sister. "I can't understand that she should find Manor Cross dull, particularly while she has her husband with her."

"The bargain, at any rate, was made," said Lady Sarah, "before the engagement was settled; and as the money is hers, I do not think we have a right to complain. I am very sorry that it should be so. Her character is very far from being formed, and his tastes are so competely fixed that nothing will change them."

"And then there's that Mrs. Houghton!" said Lady Susanna. Mrs. Houghton had of course left Manor Cross long since; but she had left a most unsatisfactory feeling behind her in the minds of all the Manor Cross ladies. This arose not only from their personal dislike, but from a suspicion, a most agonising suspicion, that their brother was more fond than he should have been of the lady's society. It must be understood that Mary herself knew nothing of this, and was altogether free from such suspicion. But the three sisters, and the Marchioness under their tuition, had decided that it would be very much better that Lord George should see no more of Mrs. Houghton. He was not, they thought, infatuated in such a fashion that he would run to London after her; but, when in London, he would certainly be thrown into her society. "I cannot bear to think of it," continued Lady Susanna. Lady Amelia shook her head. "I think, Sarah, you ought to speak to him seriously. No man has higher ideas of duty than he has; and if he be made to think of it, he will avoid her."

"I have spoken," replied Lady Sarah, almost in a whisper.

"Well!"

"Well!"

"Was he angry?"

"How did he bear it?"

"He was not angry, but he did not bear it very well. He told me that he certainly found her to be attractive, but that he thought he had power enough to keep himself free from any such fault as that. I asked him to promise me not to see her; but he declined to make a promise which he said he might not be able to keep."

" She is a horrid woman, and Mary, I am afraid, likes her," said Lady Susanna. " I know that evil will come of it."

Sundry scenes counter to this were enacted at the Deanery. Mary was in the habit of getting herself taken over to Brotherton more frequently than the ladies liked; but it was impossible that they should openly oppose her visits to her father. On one occasion, early in January, she had got her husband to ride over with her, and was closeted with the Dean while he was away in the city. " Papa," she said, " I almost think that I'll give up the house in Munster Court."

" Give it up! Look here, Mary; you'll have no happiness in life unless you can make up your mind not to allow those old ladies at Manor Cross to sit upon you."

" It is not for their sake. He does not like it, and I would do anything for him."

" That is all very well; and I would be the last to advise you to oppose his wishes if I did not see that the effect would be to make him subject to his sisters' dominion as well as you. Would you like him to be always under their thumb?"

" No, papa; I shouldn't like that."

" It was because I foresaw all this that I stipulated so expressly as I did that you should have a house of your own. Every woman, when she marries, should be emancipated from other domestic control than that of her husband. From the nature of Lord George's family this would have been impossible at Manor Cross, and therefore I insisted on a house

in town. I could do this the more freely because the
wherewithal was to come from us, and not from
them. Do not disturb what I have done."

"I will not go against you, of course, papa."

"And remember always that this is to be done
as much for his sake as for yours. His position has
been very peculiar. He has no property of his own,
and he has lived there with his mother and sisters
till the feminine influences of the house have almost
domineered him. It is your duty to assist in free-
ing him from this." Looking at the matter in the
light now presented to her, Mary began to think that
her father was right. "With a husband there should
at any rate be only one feminine influence," he added,
laughing.

"I shall not overrule him, and I shall not try,"
said Mary, smiling.

"At any rate, do not let other women rule him.
By degrees he will learn to enjoy London society,
and so will you. You will spend half the year at
Manor Cross or the Deanery, and by degrees both
he and you will be emancipated. For myself, I can
conceive nothing more melancholy than would be his
slavery and yours if you were to live throughout the
year with those old women." Then, too, he said
something to her of the satisfaction which she herself would receive from living in London, and told
her that for her, life itself had hardly as yet been
commenced. She received her lessons with thank-
fulness and gratitude, but with something of wonder
that he should so openly recommend to her a manner
of life which she had hitherto been taught to regard
as worldly.

After that no further hint was given to her that

the house in London might yet be abandoned. When riding back with her husband, she had been clever enough to speak of the thing as a fixed certainty; and he had then known that he also must regard it as fixed. "You had better not say anything more about it," he said one day almost angrily to Lady Susanna; and then nothing more had been said about it—to him.

There were other causes of confusion—of terrible confusion—at Manor Cross, of confusion so great that from day to day the Marchioness would declare herself unable to go through the troubles before her. The workmen were already in the big house, preparing for the demolition and reconstruction of everything as soon as she should be gone; and other workmen were already demolishing and reconstructing Cross Hall. The sadness of all this and the weight on the old lady's mind were increased by the fact that no member of the family had received so much even as a message from the Marquis himself since it had been decided that his wishes should not be obeyed. Over and over again the dowager attempted to give way, and suggested that they should all depart and be out of sight. It seemed to her that when a marquis is a marquis he ought to have his own way, though it be never so unreasonable. Was he not the head of the family? But Lady Sarah was resolved, and carried her point. Were they all to be pitched down into some strange corner where they would be no better than other women, incapable of doing good or exercising influence, by the wish of one man who had never done any good anywhere, or used his own influence legitimately? Lady Sarah was no coward, and Lady Sarah stuck to Cross Hall, though in doing so she had very much to endure. "I won't go out, my lady," said Price, "not till the day when her ladyship is ready to come in. I can put up with things, and I'll see as all is done as your ladyship wishes." Price, though he was a sporting farmer, and though men were in the habit of drinking cherry brandy at his house, and though naughty things had been said about him, had in these days become Lady Sarah's prime minister at Cross Hall, and was quite prepared in that capacity to carry on war against the Marquis.

When the day came for the departure of Mary and her husband, a melancholy feeling pervaded the whole household. A cook had been sent up from Brotherton who had lived at Manor Cross many years previously. Lord George took a man who had waited on himself lately at the old house, and Mary had her own maid who had come with her when she married. They had therefore been forced to look for but one strange servant. But this made the feeling the stronger that they would all be strange up in London. This was so strong with Lord George that it almost amounted to fear. He knew that he did not know how to live in London. He belonged to the Carlton, as became a conservative nobleman; but he very rarely entered it, and never felt himself at home when he was there. And Mary, though she had been quite resolved since the conversation with her father that she would be firm about her house, still was not without her own dread. She herself had no personal friends in town—not one but Mrs. Houghton, as to whom she heard nothing but evil words from the ladies around her. There had been an attempt made to get one of the sisters to go up with them for the first month. Lady Sarah had positively refused, almost with indignation. Was it to be supposed that she would desert her mother at so trying a time? Lady Amelia was then asked, and with many regrets declined the invitation. She had not dared to use her own judgment, and Lady Sarah had not cordially advised her to go. Lady Sarah had thought that Lady Susanna would be the most useful. But Lady Susanna was not asked. There were a few words on the subject between Lord George and his wife. Mary, remembering her father's advice, had determined that she would not be sat upon, and had whispered to her husband that Susanna was always severe to her. When, therefore, the time came, they departed from Manor Cross without any protecting spirit.

There was something sad in this, even to Mary. She knew that she was taking her husband away from the life he liked, and that she herself was going to a life as to which she could not even guess whether she would like it or not. But she had the satisfaction of feeling that she was at last going to begin to live as a married woman. Hitherto she had been treated as a child. If there was danger, there was, at any rate, the excitement which danger produces. "I am almost glad that we are going alone, George," she said. "It seems to me that we have never been alone yet."

He wished to be gracious and loving to her, and yet he was not disposed to admit anything which might seem to imply that he had become tired of living with his own family. "It is very nice, but——"

"But what, dear?"

"Of course I am anxious about my mother just at present."

"She is not to move for two months yet."

"No—not to move; but there are so many things to be done."

"You can run down whenever you please."

"That's expensive; but of course it must be done."

"Say that you'll like being with me alone." They had the compartment of the railway carriage all to themselves, and she, as she spoke, leaned against him, inviting him to caress her. "You don't think it a trouble, do you, having to come and live with me?" Of course he was conquered, and said, after his nature, what prettiest things he could to her, assuring her that he would sooner live with her than with anyone in the world, and promising that he would always endeavour to make her happy. She knew that he was doing his best to be a loving husband, and she felt, therefore, that she was bound to be loyal in her endeavours to love him; but at the same time, at the very moment in which she was receiving his words with outward show of satisfied love, her imagination was picturing to her something else which would have been so immeasurably superior, if only it had been possible.

That evening they dined together, alone; and it was the first time that they had even done so, except at an inn. Never before had been imposed on her the duty of seeing that his dinner was prepared for him. There certainly was very little of duty to perform in the matter, for he was a man indifferent as to what he ate, or what he drank. The plainness of the table at Manor Cross had surprised Mary,

after the comparative luxury of the Deanery. All
her lessons at Manor Cross had gone to show that
eating was not a delectation to be held in high esteem.
But still she was careful that everything around him
should be nice. The furniture was new, the glasses
and crockery were new. Few, if any, of the ar-
ticles used, had ever been handled before. All
her bridal presents were there; and no doubt there
was present to her mind the fact that everything in
the house had in truth been given to him by her.
If only she could make the things pleasant! If only
he would allow himself to be taught that nice things
are nice! She hovered around him, touching him
every now and then with her light fingers, moving a
lock of his hair, and then stooping over him and
kissing his brow. It might still be that she would
be able to galvanise him into that lover's vitality, of
which she had dreamed. He never rebuffed her; he
did not scorn her kisses, or fail to smile when his
hair was moved; he answered every word she spoke
to him carefully and courteously; he admired her
pretty things when called upon to admire them. But
through it all, she was quite aware that she had not
galvanised him as yet.

Of course there were books. Every proper preparation had been made for rendering the little house
pleasant. In the evening she took from her shelf
a delicate little volume of poetry, something exquisitely
bound, pretty to look at, and sweet to handle, and
settled herself down to be happy in her own drawing-
room. But she soon looked up from the troubles of
Aurora Leigh to see what her husband was doing.
He was comfortable in his chair, but was busy with
the columns of *The Brothershire Herald*.

"Dear me, George, have you brought that musty old paper up here?"

"Why shouldn't I read the *Herald* here, as well as at Manor Cross?"

"Oh, yes! if you like it."

"Of course I want to know what is being done in the county."

But, when next she looked, the county had certainly faded from his mind, for he was fast asleep.

On that occasion she did not care very much for Aurora Leigh. Her mind was hardly tuned to poetry of that sort. The things around her were too important to allow her mind to indulge itself with foreign cares. And then she found herself looking at the watch. At Manor Cross ten o'clock every night brought all the servants into the drawing-room. First the butler would come and place the chairs, and then the maids, and then the coachman and footman would follow. Lord George read the prayers, and Mary had always thought them to be very tiring. But she now felt that it would almost be a relief if the butler would come in and place the chairs.

CHAPTER XII

MISS MILDMAY AND JACK DE BARON

LADY GEORGE was not left long in her new house without visitors. Early on the day after her arrival, Mrs. Houghton came to her, and began at once, with great volubility, to explain how the land lay, and to suggest how it should be made to lie for the future.

"I am so glad you have come. As soon, you know, as they positively forbade me to get on horseback again this winter, I made up my mind to come to town. What is there to keep me down there if I don't ride! I promised to obey if I was brought here—and to disobey if I was left there. Mr. Houghton goes up and down, you know. It is hard upon him, poor old fellow. But then the other thing would be harder on me. He and papa are together somewhere now arranging about the spring meetings. They have got their stables joined, and I know very well who will have the best of that. A man has to get up very early to see all round papa. But Mr. Houghton is so rich, it doesn't signify. And now, my dear, what are you going to do? and what is Lord George going to do? I am dying to see Lord George. I daresay you are getting a little tired of him by this time."

"Indeed, I'm not."

"You haven't picked up courage enough yet to say so; that's it, my dear. I've brought cards from Mr. Houghton, which means to say that though he

is down somewhere at Newmarket in the flesh he is
to be supposed to have called upon you and Lord
George. And now we want you both to come and
dine with us on Monday. I know Lord George is
particular, and so I've brought a note. You can't
have anything to do yet, and of course you'll come.
Houghton will be back on Sunday, and goes down
again on Tuesday morning. To hear him talk about
it you'd think he was the keenest man in England
across a country. Say that you'll come."

"I'll ask Lord George."

"Fiddle-de-dee. Lord George will be only too delighted to come and see me. I've got such a nice
cousin to introduce to you; not one of the Germain
sort, you know, who are all perhaps a little slow.
This man is Jack de Baron, a nephew of papa's.
He's in the Coldstreams, and I do think you'll like
him. There's nothing on earth he can't do, from
waltzing down to polo. And old Mildmay will be
there, and Guss Mildmay, who is dying in love with
Jack."

"And is Jack dying in love with Guss?"

"Oh, dear no! not a bit. You needn't be afraid.
Jack de Baron has just five hundred a year and his
commission, and must, I should say, be over head
and ears in debt. Miss Mildmay may perhaps have
five thousand for her fortune. Put this and that together and you can hardly see anything comfortable in
the way of matrimony, can you?"

"Then I fear your——Jack is mercenary."

"Mercenary—of course he's mercenary. That is to
say, he doesn't want to go to destruction quite at
one leap. But he's awfully fond of falling in love,

and when he is in love he'll do almost anything—
except marry."

"Then, if I were you, I shouldn't ask——Guss to
meet him."

"She can fight her own battles, and wouldn't thank
me at all if I were to fight them for her after that
fashion.   There'll be nobody else except Houghton's
sister, Hetta.   You never met Hetta Houghton?"

"I've heard of her."

"I should think so. 'Not to know her'—I forget
the words; but if you don't know Hetta Houghton
you're just nowhere.   She has lots of money, and lives
all alone, and says whatever comes uppermost, and
does what she pleases.   She goes everywhere, and
is up to everything.   I always made up my mind I
wouldn't be an old maid, but I declare I envy Hetta
Houghton.   But then she'd be nothing unless she
had money.   There'll be eight of us, and at this
time of the year we dine at half-past seven, sharp.
Can I take you anywhere?   The carriage can come
back with you."

"Thank you, no.   I am going to pick Lord George
up at the Carlton at four."

"How nice!   I wonder how long you'll go on pick-
ing up Lord George at the Carlton."

She could only suppose, when her friend was
gone, that this was the right kind of thing.   No
doubt Lady Susanna had warned her against Mrs.
Houghton, but then she was not disposed to take
Lady Susanna's warnings on any subject.   Her father
had known that she intended to know the woman;
and her father, though he had cautioned her very
often as to the old women at Manor Cross, as he

called them, had never spoken a word of caution to
her as to Mrs. Houghton. And her husband was
well aware of the intended intimacy.

She picked up her husband, and rather liked being
kept waiting a few minutes at the club-door in her
brougham. Then they went together to look at the
new picture, which was being exhibited by gas-light
in Bond Street, and she began to feel that the pleasures
of London were delightful.

"Don't you think those two old priests are magnifi-
cent?" she said, pressing on his arm, in the obscurity
of the darkened chamber.

"I don't know that I care much about old priests,"
said Lord George.

"But the heads are so fine."

"I daresay. Sacerdotal pictures never please me.
Didn't you say you wanted to go to Swan and Ed-
gar's?" He would not sympathise with her about
pictures, but perhaps she would be able to find out
his taste at last.

He seemed quite well satisfied to dine with the
Houghtons, and did, in fact, call at the house before
that day came round. "I was in Berkeley Square
this morning," he said one day, "but I didn't find
anyone."

"Nobody ever is at home, I suppose," she said.
"Look here. There have been Lady Brabazon, and
Mrs. Patmore Green, and Mrs. Montacute Jones. Who
is Mrs. Montacute Jones?"

"I never heard of her."

"Dear me; how very odd. I daresay it was kind
of her to come. And yesterday the Countess of Care
called. Is not she some relative?"

"She is my mother's first cousin."

"And then there was dear old Miss Tallowax. And I wasn't at home to see one of them."

"No one I suppose ever is at home in London, unless they fix a day for seeing people."

Lady George, having been specially asked to come "sharp" to her friend's dinner-party, arrived with her husband exactly at the hour named, and found no one in the drawing-room. In a few minutes Mrs. Houghton hurried in, apologising. "It's all Mr. Houghton's fault indeed, Lord George. He was to have been in town yesterday, but would stay down and hunt to-day. Of course the train was late, and of course he was so tired that he couldn't dress without going to sleep first." As nobody else came for a quarter of an hour Mrs. Houghton had an opportunity of explaining some things. "Has Mrs. Montacute Jones called? I suppose you were out of your wits to find out who she was. She's a very old friend of papa's, and I asked her to call. She gives awfully swell parties, and has no end of money. She was one of the Montacutes of Montacute, and so she sticks her own name on to her husband's. He's alive, I believe, but he never shows. I think she keeps him somewhere down in Wales."

"How odd!"

"It is a little queer, but, when you come to know her, you'll find it will make no difference. She's the ugliest old woman in London, but I'd be as ugly as she is to have her diamonds."

"I wouldn't," said Mary.

"Your husband cares about your appearance," said Mrs. Houghton, turning her eyes upon Lord George. He simpered and looked pleased, and did not seem to be at all disgusted by their friend's slang, and

yet had his wife talked of "awfully swell" parties,
he would, she was well aware, have rebuked her
seriously.

Miss Houghton—Hetta Houghton—was the first to
arrive, and she somewhat startled Mary by the gorgeous glories of her dress, though Mrs. Houghton
afterwards averred that she wasn't "a patch upon
Mrs. Montacute Jones." But Miss Houghton was a
lady, and though over forty years of age, was still
handsome.

"Been hunting to-day, has he?" she said. "Well,
if he likes it, I shan't complain. But I thought he
liked his ease too well to travel fifty miles up to
town after riding about all day."

"Of course he's knocked up, and at his age it's
quite absurd," said the young wife. "But Hetta, I
want you to know my particular friend, Lady George
Germain. Lord George, if he'll allow me to say so,
is a cousin, though I'm afraid we have to go back
to Noah to make it out."

"Your great-grandmother was my great-grandmother's sister. That's not so very far off."

"When you get to grandmothers no fellow can
understand it, can they, Mary?" Then came Mr. and
Miss Mildmay. He was a grey-haired old gentleman,
rather short and rather fat, and she looked to be
just such another girl as Mrs. Houghton herself had
been, though blessed with more regular beauty. She
was certainly handsome, but she carried with her that
wearied air of being nearly worn out by the toil
of searching for a husband which comes upon some
young women after the fourth or fifth year of their
labours. Fortune had been very hard upon Augusta
Mildmay. Early in her career she had fallen in love,

while abroad, with an Italian nobleman, and had immediately been carried off home by her anxious parents. Then in London she had fallen in love again with an English nobleman, an eldest son, with wealth of his own. Nothing could be more proper, and the young man had fallen also in love with her. All her friends were beginning to hate her with virulence, so lucky had she been, when, on a sudden, the young lord told her that the match would not please his father and mother, and that therefore there must be an end of it. What was there to be done? All London had talked of it, all London must know the utter failure. Nothing more cruel, more barefaced, more unjust, had ever been perpetrated. A few years since all the Mildmays in England, one after another, would have had a shot at the young nobleman. But in these days there seems to be nothing for a girl to do but to bear it and try again. So Augusta Mildmay bore it and did try again; tried very often again. And now she was in love with Jack de Baron. The worst of Guss Mildmay was that, after it all, she had a heart, and would like the young men—would like them, or perhaps dislike them, equally to her disadvantage. Old gentlemen, such as was Mr. Houghton, had been willing to condone all her faults, and all her loves, and to take her as she was. But, when the moment came, she would not have her Houghton, and then she was in the market again. Now a young woman entering the world cannot make a greater mistake than not to know her own line, or, knowing it, not to stick to it. Those who are thus weak are sure to fall between two stools. If a girl chooses to have a heart, let her marry the man of her heart, and take her mutton-chops and bread and cheese, her stuff gown

and her six children, as they may come. But if she
can decide that such horrors are horrid to her, and
that they must at any cost be avoided, then let her
take her Houghton when he comes, and not hark back
upon feelings and fancies, upon liking and loving,
upon youth and age. If a girl has money and beauty
too, of course she can pick and choose. Guss Mildmay had no money to speak of, but she had beauty
enough to win either a working barrister or a rich
old sinner. She was quite able to fall in love with
the one and flirt with the other at the same time;
but, when the moment for decision came, she could
not bring herself to put up with either. At present
she was in real truth in love with Jack de Baron, and
had brought herself to think that if Jack would ask
her, she would risk everything. But were he to do
so, which was not probable, she would immediately
begin to calculate what could be done by Jack's moderate income and her own small fortune. She and
Mrs. Houghton kissed each other affectionately, being
at the present moment close in each other's confi-
dences, and then she was introduced to Lady George.
"Adelaide hasn't a chance," was Miss Mildmay's first
thought as she looked at the young wife.

Then came Jack de Baron. Mary was much interested in seeing a man of whom she had heard so
striking an account, and for the love of whom she
had been told that a girl was almost dying. Of
course all that was to be taken with many grains of
salt, but still the fact of the love and the attractive
excellence of the man had been impressed upon her.
She declared to herself at once that his appearance
was very much in his favour, and a fancy passed across
her mind that he was somewhat like that ideal man

of whom she herself had dreamed, ever so many years
ago as it seemed to her now, before she had made
up her mind that she would change her ideal and
accept Lord George Germain.   He was about the
middle height, light-haired, broad-shouldered, with a
pleasant smiling mouth and well-formed nose; but,
above all, he had about him that pleasure-loving look,
that appearance of taking things jauntily, and of en-
joying life, which she in her young girlhood had
regarded as being absolutely essential to a pleasant
lover.   There are men whose very eyes glance business, whose every word imports care, who step as
though their shoulders were weighted with thought-
fulness, who breathe solicitude, and who seem to think
that all the things of life are too serious for smiles.
Lord George was such a man, though he had in truth
very little business to do.   And then there are men
who are always playfellows with their friends, who
—even should misfortune be upon them—still smile
and make the best of it, who come across one like
sunbeams, and who, even when tears are falling, produce the tints of a rainbow.   Such a one Mary Lovelace had perhaps seen in her childhood, and had then
dreamed of him.   Such a one was Jack de Baron, at
any rate to the eye.

And such a one in truth he was.   Of course the
world had spoiled him.   He was in the Guards.   He
was fond of pleasure.   He was fairly well off in regard to all his own wants, for his cousin had simply
imagined those debts with which ladies are apt to
believe that young men of pleasure must be overwhelmed.   He had gradually taught himself to think
that his own luxuries and his own comforts should
in his own estimation be paramount to everything.

He was not naturally selfish, but his life had almost
necessarily engendered selfishness. Marrying had
come to be looked upon as an evil—as had old age
—not of course an unavoidable evil, but one into
which a man will probably fall sooner or later. To
put off marriage as long as possible, and when it
could no longer be put off to marry money, was a
part of his creed. In the meantime the great delight
of his life came from women's society. He neither
gambled nor drank. He hunted and fished, and shot
deer and grouse, and occasionally drove a coach to
Windsor. But little love affairs, flirtation, and intrigues, which were never intended to be guilty, but
which now and again had brought him into some trouble, gave its charm to his life. On such occasions he
would, too, at times, be very badly in love, assuring
himself sometimes with absolute heroism that he would
never again see this married woman, or declaring to
himself in moments of self-sacrificial grandness that
he would at once marry that unmarried girl. And
then, when he had escaped from some special trouble,
he would take to his regiment for a month, swearing
to himself that for the next year he would see no
women besides his aunts and his grandmother. When
making this resolution he might have added his cousin
Adelaide. They were close friends, but between them
there had never been the slightest spark of a flirtation.

In spite of all his little troubles Captain de Baron
was a very popular man. There was a theory abroad
about him that he always behaved like a gentleman,
and that his troubles were misfortunes rather than
faults. Ladies always liked him, and his society was
agreeable to men because he was neither selfish nor

loud. He talked only a little, but still enough not to
be thought dull. He never bragged or bullied or
bounced. He didn't want to shoot more deer or
catch more salmon than another man. He never cut
a fellow down in the hunting-field. He never bor-
rowed money, but would sometimes lend it when a
reason was given. He was probably as ignorant as
an owl of anything really pertaining to literature,
but he did not display his ignorance. He was regarded by all who knew him as one of the most
fortunate of men. He regarded himself as being very
far from blessed, knowing that there must come a
speedy end to the things which he only half enjoyed,
and feeling partly ashamed of himself in that he had
found for himself no better part.

"Jack," said Mrs. Houghton, "I can't blow you
up for being late, because Mr. Houghton has not
yet condescended to show himself. Let me introduce
you to Lady George Germain." Then he smiled in
his peculiar way, and Mary thought his face the most
beautiful she had ever seen. "Lord George Germain, who allows me to call him my cousin, though
he isn't as near as you are. My sister-in-law, you
know." Jack shook hands with the old lady in his
most cordial manner. "I think you have seen Mr.
Mildmay before, and Miss Mildmay." Mary could
not but look at the greeting between the two, and she
saw that Miss Mildmay almost turned up her nose
at him. She was quite sure that Mrs. Houghton had
been wrong about the love. There had surely only
been a pretence of love. But Mrs. Houghton had
been right, and Mary had not yet learned to read
correctly the signs which men and women hang out.

At last Mr. Houghton came down. "Upon my

word," said his wife, "I wonder you ain't ashamed
to show yourself."

"Who says I'm not ashamed? I'm very much
ashamed. But how can I help it if the trains won't
keep their time? We were hunting all day to-day
—nothing very good, Lord George, but on the trot
from eleven to four. That tires a fellow, you know.
And the worst of it is I've got to do it again on
Wednesday, Thursday, and Saturday."

"Is there a necessity?" asked Lord George.

"When a man begins that kind of thing he must
go through with it. Hunting is like women. It's
a jealous sport. Lady George, may I take you down
to dinner? I am so sorry to have kept you waiting."

CHAPTER XIII

Mr. Houghton took Lady George down to dinner; but Jack de Baron sat on his left hand. Next to him was Augusta Mildmay, who had been consigned to his care. Then came Lord George, sitting opposite to his host at a round table, with Mrs. Houghton at his right hand. Mrs. Mildmay and Miss Hetta Houghton filled up the vacant places. To all this a great deal of attention had been given by the hostess. She had not wished to throw her cousin Jack and Miss Mildmay together. She would probably have said to a confidential friend that "there had been enough of all that." In her way she liked Guss Mildmay, but Guss was not good enough to marry her cousin. Guss herself must know that such a marriage was impossible. She had on an occasion said a word or two to Guss upon the subject. She had thought that a little flirtation between Jack and her other friend Lady George might put things right; and she had thought, too—or perhaps felt rather than thought—that Lord George had emancipated himself from the thraldom of his late love rather too quickly. Mary was a dear girl. She was quite prepared to make Mary her friend, being in truth somewhat sick of the ill-humours and disappointments of Guss Mildmay; but it might be as well that Mary should be a little checked in her triumph. She herself had been obliged to put up with old Mr. Houghton. She never for a moment told herself that she had done wrong, but of course she required compensation. When she was manœuvring she never lost sight of her manœuvres. She had had all this in her mind when she made up her little dinner-party. She had had it all in her mind when she arranged the seats. She didn't want to sit next to Jack herself, because Jack would have talked to her to the exclusion of Lord George, so she placed herself between Lord George and Mr. Mildmay. It had been necessary that Mr. Mildmay should take Miss Houghton down to dinner, and therefore she could not separate Guss from Jack de Baron. Anybody who understands dinner-parties will see it all at a glance. But she was convinced that Jack would devote himself to Lady George at his left hand; and so he did.

"Just come up to town, haven't you?" said Jack.

"Only last week."

"This is the nicest time in the year for London, unless you do a deal of hunting; then it's a grind."

"I never hunt at all; Lord George won't let me."

"I wish someone wouldn't let me. It would save me a deal of money, and a great deal of misery. It's all a delusion and a snare. You never get a run nowadays."

"Do you think so? I'd rather hunt than do anything."

"That's because you are not let to do it; the perversity of human nature, you know! The only thing I'm not allowed to do is to marry, and it's the only thing I care for."

"Who prevents it, Captain de Baron?"

"There's a new order come out from the Horse Guards yesterday. No one under a field officer is to marry unless he has got two thousand a year."

"Marrying is cheaper than hunting."

"Of course, Lady George, you may buy your horses cheap or dear, and you may do the same with your wives. You may have a cheap wife who doesn't care for dress, and likes to sit at home and read good books."

"That's just what I do."

"But then they're apt to go wrong and get out of order."

"How do you mean? I shan't get out of order, I hope."

"The wheels become rusty, don't you think? and then they won't go as they ought. They scold and turn up their noses. What I want to find is perfect beauty, devoted affection, and fifty thousand."

"How modest you are."

In all this badinage there was not much to make a rival angry; but Miss Mildmay, who heard a word or two now and then, was angry. He was talking to a pretty woman about marriage and money, and of course that amounted to flirtation. Lord George, on the other hand, now and then said a word to her; but he was never given to saying many words, and his attention was nearly monopolised by his hostess. She had heard the last sentence, and determined to join the conversation.

"If you had the fifty thousand, Captain de Baron," she said, "I think you would manage to do without the beauty and the devoted affection."

"That's ill-natured, Miss Mildmay, though it may be true. Beggars can't be choosers. But you've known me a long time, and I think it's unkind that you should run me down with a new acquaintance. Suppose I was to say something bad of you?"

"You can say whatever you please, Captain de Baron."

"There is nothing bad to say, of course, except that you are always down on a poor fellow in distress. Don't you think it's a grand thing to be good-natured, Lady George?"

"Indeed I do. It's almost better than being virtuous."

"Ten to one. I don't see the good of virtue myself. It always makes people stingy and cross and ill-mannered. I think one should always promise to do everything that is asked. Nobody would be fool enough to expect you to keep your word afterwards, and you'd give a lot of pleasure."

"I think promises ought to be kept, Captain de Baron."

"I can't agree to that. That's bondage, and it puts an embargo on the pleasant way of living that I like. I hate all kind of strictness and duty and self-denying and that kind of thing. It's rubbish. Don't you think so?"

"I suppose one has to do one's duty."

"I don't see it. I never do mine."

"Suppose there were a battle to fight."

"I should get invalided at once. I made up my mind to that long ago. Fancy the trouble of it. And when they shoot you they don't shoot you dead, but knock half your face away, or something of that sort. Luckily we live in an island, and haven't much fighting to do. If we hadn't lived in an island I should never have gone into the army."

This was not flirting certainly. It was all sheer nonsense—words without any meaning in them. But Mary liked it. She decidedly would not have liked it had it ever occurred to her that the man was flirting with her. It was the very childishness of the thing that pleased her—the contrast to conversation at Manor Cross, where no childish word was ever spoken. And though she was by no means prepared to flirt with Captain de Baron, still she found in him something of the realisation of her dreams. There was the combination of manliness, playfulness, good looks, and good humour which she had pictured to herself. To sit well-dressed in a well-lighted room and have nonsense talked to her suited her better than a petticoat conclave. And she knew of no harm in it. Her father encouraged her to be gay, and altogether discouraged petticoat conclaves. So she smiled her sweetest on Captain de Baron, and replied to his nonsense with other nonsense, and was satisfied.

But Guss Mildmay was very much dissatisfied, both as to the amusement of the present moment and as to the conduct of Captain de Baron generally. She knew London life well, whereas Lady George did not know it at all; and she considered that this was flirtation. She may have been right in any accusation which she made in her heart against the man, but she was quite wrong in considering Lady George to be a flirt. She had, however, grievances of her own —great grievances. It was not only that the man was attentive to someone else, but that he was not attentive to her. He and she had had many passages in life together, and he owed it to her at any rate not to appear to neglect her. And then what a stick was that other man on the other side of her—that young woman's husband! During the greater part of the dinner she was sitting speechless—not only loverless, but manless. It is not what one suffers that kills

one, but what one knows that other people see that
one suffers.

There was not very much conversation between
Lord George and Mrs. Houghton at dinner. Perhaps
she spoke as much to Mr. Mildmay as to him; for
she was a good hostess, understanding and performing her duty. But what she did say to him she said
very graciously, making allusion to further intimacy
between herself and Mary, flattering his vanity by
little speeches as to Manor Cross, always seeming
to imply that she felt hourly the misfortune of having been forced to decline the honour of such an
alliance as had been offered to her. He was, in truth,
as innocent as his wife, except in this, that he would
not have wished her to hear all that Mrs. Houghton
said to him, whereas Mary would have had not the
slightest objection to his hearing all the nonsense
between her and Captain de Baron.

The ladies sat a long time after dinner, and when
they went Mrs. Houghton asked her husband to come
up in ten minutes. They did not remain much longer,
but during those ten minutes Guss Mildmay said
something of her wrongs to her friend, and Lady
George heard some news from Miss Houghton. Miss
Houghton had got Lady George on to a sofa, and
was talking to her about Brotherton and Manor Cross.
"So the Marquis is coming," she said. "I knew the
Marquis years ago, when we used to be staying with
the De Barons—Adelaide's father and mother. She
was alive then, and the Marquis used to come over
there. So he has married?"

"Yes; an Italian."

"I did not think he would ever marry. It makes
a difference to you, does it not?"

"I don't think of such things."

"You will not like him, for he is the very opposite to Lord George."

"I don't know that I shall ever even see him. I don't think he wants to see any of us."

"I daresay not. He used to be very handsome, and very fond of ladies' society, but I think the most selfish human being I ever knew in my life. That is a complaint that years do not cure. He and I were great friends once."

"Did you quarrel?"

"Oh, dear, no! I had rather a large fortune of my own, and there was a time in which he was, perhaps, a little in want of money. But they had to build a town on his property in Staffordshire, and you see that did instead."

"Did instead!" said Lady George, altogether in the dark.

"There was suddenly a great increase to his income, and, of course, that altered his view. I am bound to say that he was very explicit. He could be so without suffering himself, or understanding that anyone else would suffer. I tell you because you are one of the family, and would, no doubt, hear it all some day through Adelaide. I had a great escape."

"And he a great misfortune," said Mary civilly.

"I think he had, to tell you the truth. I am good-tempered, long-suffering, and have a certain grain of sagacity that might have been useful to him. Have you heard about this Italian lady?"

"Only that she is an Italian lady."

"He is about my age. If I remember rightly there is hardly a month or two between us. She is three or four years older."

"You knew her, then?"

"I know of her. I have been curious enough to inquire, which is, I daresay, more than anybody has done at Manor Cross."

"And is she so old?"

"And a widow. They have been married, you know, over twelve months; nearly two years, I believe."

"Surely not; we heard of it only since our own marriage."

"Exactly; but the Marquis was always fond of a little mystery. It was the news of your marriage that made him hint at the possibility of such a thing; and he did not tell the fact till he had made up his mind to come home. I do not know that he has told all now."

"What else is there?"

"She has a baby—a boy." Mary felt that the colour flew to her cheeks; but she knew that it did so not from any disappointment of her own, not because these tidings were in truth a blow to her, but because others—this lady, for instance—would think that she suffered.

"I am afraid it is so," said Miss Houghton.

"She may have twenty, for what I care," said Mary, recovering herself.

"I think Lord George ought to know."

"Of course I shall tell him what you told me. I am sorry that he is not nice, that's all. I should have liked a brother-in-law that I could have loved. And I wish he had married an English woman. I think English women are best for English men."

"I think so too, I am afraid you will none of you like the lady. She cannot speak a word of English.

Of course you will use my name in telling Lord George. I heard it all from a friend of mine who is married to one of the secretaries at the Embassy." Then the gentlemen came in, and Mary began to be in a hurry to get away that she might tell this news to her husband.

In the meantime Guss Mildmay made her complaints, deep but not loud. She and Mrs. Houghton had been very intimate as girls, knew each other's secrets, and understood each other's characters. "Why did you have him to such a party as this?" said Guss.

"I told you he was coming."

"But you didn't tell me about that young woman. You put him next to her on purpose to annoy me."

"That's nonsense. You know as well as I do that nothing can come of it. You must drop it, and you'd better do it at once. You don't want to be known as the girl who is dying for the love of a man she can't marry. That's not your *métier*."

"That's my own affair. If I choose to stick to him, you at least ought not to cross me."

"But he won't stick to you. Of course he's my cousin, and I don't see why he's to be supposed never to say a word to anyone else, when it's quite understood that you're not going to have one another. What's the good of being a dog in the manger?"

"Adelaide, you never had any heart!"

"Of course not; or, if I had, I knew how to get the better of so troublesome an appendage. I hate hearing about hearts. If he'd take you to-morrow you wouldn't marry him."

"Yes, I would."

"I don't believe it. I don't think you'd be so

wicked. Where would you live, and how? How long
would it be before you hated each other? Hearts!
As if hearts weren't just like anything else which
either you can or you cannot afford yourself. Do
you think I couldn't go and fall in love to-morrow,
and think it the best fun in the world? Of course
it's nice to have a fellow like Jack, always ready to
spoon, and always sending one things, and riding
with one, and all that. I don't know any young
woman in London that would like it better than I
should. But I can't afford it, my dear, and so I don't
do it."

"It seems to me you are going to do it with your
old lover?"

"Dear Lord George! I swear it's only to bring
Mary down a peg, because she is so proud of her
nobleman. And then he is handsome! But, my dear,
I've pleased myself. I have got a house over my
head, and a carriage to sit in, and servants to wait
on me, and I've settled myself. Do you do likewise,
and you shall have your Lord George, or Jack de
Baron, if he pleases; only don't go too far with
him."

"Adelaide," said the other, "I'm not good, but
you're downright bad." Mrs. Houghton only laughed,
as she got up from her seat to welcome the gentlemen
as they entered the room.

Mary, as soon as the door of the brougham had
been closed upon her and her husband, began to tell
her story. "What do you think Miss Houghton has
told me?" Lord George, of course, could have no
thoughts about it, and did not at first very much care
what the story might have been. "She says that
your brother was married ever so long ago."

"I don't believe it," said Lord George, suddenly and angrily.

"A year before we were married, I mean."

"I don't believe it."

"And she says that they have a son."

"What!"

"That there is a baby—a boy. She has heard it all from some friend of hers at Rome."

"It can't be true."

"She said that I had better tell you. Does it make you unhappy, George?" To this he made no immediate answer. "What can it matter whether he was married two months ago or two years? It does not make me unhappy." As she said this, she locked herself close into his arm.

"Why should he deceive us? That would make me unhappy. If he had married in a proper way and had a family, here in England, of course I should have been glad. I should have been loyal to him as I am to the others. But if this be true, of course it will make me unhappy. I do not believe it. It is some gossip."

"I could not but tell you."

"It is some jealousy. There was a time when they said that Brotherton meant to marry her."

"What difference could it make to her? Of course we all know that he is married. I hope it won't make you unhappy, George?" But Lord George was unhappy, or at any rate was moody, and would talk no more then on that subject or any other. But in truth the matter rested on his mind all the night.

CHAPTER XIV

"ARE WE TO CALL HIM POPENJOY?"

THE news which he had heard did afflict Lord George very much. A day of two after the dinner-party in Berkeley Square he found Mr. Knox, his brother's agent, and learned from him that Miss. Houghton's story was substantially true. The Marquis had informed his man of business that an heir had been born to him, but had not communicated the fact to any one of the family! This omission, in such a family, was, to Lord George's thinking, so great a crime on the part of his brother, as to make him doubt whether he could ever again have fraternal relations with a man who so little knew his duty. When Mr. Knox showed him the letter his brow became very black. He did not often forget himself— was not often so carried away by any feeling as to be in danger of doing so. But on this occasion even he was so moved as to be unable to control his words. "An Italian brat? Who is to say how it was born?"

"The Marquis, my lord, would not do anything like that," said Mr. Knox, very seriously.

Then Lord George was ashamed of himself, and blushed up to the roots of his hair. He had hardly himself known what he had meant. But he mistrusted an Italian widow, because she was an Italian, and because she was a widow, and he mistrusted the whole connection, because there had been in it none of that honourable openness which should, he thought,

characterise all family doings in such a family as
that of the Germains. "I don't know of what kind
you mean," he said, shuffling, and knowing that he
shuffled. "I don't suppose my brother would do anything really wrong. But it's a blot to the family—
a terrible blot."

"She is a lady of good family—a Marchese," said
Mr. Knox.

"An Italian Marchese!" said Lord George, with
that infinite contempt which an English nobleman has
for foreign nobility not of the highest order.

He had learnt that Miss Houghton's story was
true, and was certainly very unhappy. It was not
at all that he had pictured to himself the glory of
being himself the Marquis of Brotherton after his
brother's death; nor was it only the disappointment
which he felt as to any possible son of his own,
though on that side he did feel the blow. The re-
flection which perplexed him most was the consciousness that he must quarrel with his brother, and that
after such a quarrel he would become nobody in the
world. And then, added to this, was the sense of
family disgrace. He would have been quite content
with his position had he been left master of the house
at Manor Cross, even without any of his brother's
income to maintain the house. But now he would
only be his wife's husband, the Dean's son-in-law,
living on their money, and compelled by circumstances
to adapt himself to them. He almost thought that
had he known that he would be turned out of Manor
Cross, he would not have married. And then, in
spite of his disclaimer to Mr. Knox, he was already
suspicious of some foul practice. An heir to the
title and property, to all the family honours of the

Germains, had suddenly burst upon him, twelve months—for aught that he knew, two or three years —after the child's birth! Nobody had been informed when the child was born, or in what circumstances —except that the mother was an Italian widow! What evidence on which an Englishman might rely could possibly be forthcoming from such a country as Italy! Poor Lord George, who was himself as honest as the sun, was prepared to believe all evil things of people of whom he knew nothing! Should his brother die—and his brother's health was bad— what steps should he take? Would it be for him to accept this Italian brat as the heir to everything, or must he ruin himself by a pernicious lawsuit? Looking forward he saw nothing but misery and disgrace; and he saw, also, unavoidable difficulties with which he knew himself to be incapable to cope. "It is true," he said to his wife very gloomily, when he first met her after his interview with Mr. Knox.

"What Miss Houghton said? I felt sure it was true, directly she told me."

"I don't know why you should have felt sure, merely on her word, as to a thing so monstrous as this is. You don't seem to see that it concerns yourself."

"No; I don't. It doesn't concern me at all, except as it makes you unhappy." Then there was a pause for a moment, during which she crept close up to him, in a manner that had now become usual with her. "Why do you think I married you?" she said. He was too unhappy to answer her pleasantly—too much touched by her sweetness to answer her unpleasantly; and so he said nothing. "Certainly not with any hope that I might become Marchioness of Brotherton. Whatever may have made me do such a thing, I can assure you that that had nothing to do with it."

"Can't you look forward? Don't you suppose that you may have a son?" Then she buried her face upon his shoulder. "And if so, would it not be better that a child so born should be the heir, than some Italian baby, of whom no one knows anything?"

"If you are unhappy, George, I shall be unhappy. But for myself I will not affect to care anything. I don't want to be a Marchioness. I only want to see you without a frown on your brow. To tell the truth, if you didn't mind it, I should care nothing about your brother and his doings. I would make a joke of this Marchese, who, Miss Houghton says, is a puckered-faced old woman. Miss Houghton seems to care a great deal more about it than I do."

"It cannot be a subject for a joke." He was almost angry at the idea of the wife of the head of the family being made a matter of laughter. That she should be reprobated, hated—cursed, if necessary—was within the limits of family dignity; but not that she should become a joke to those with whom she had unfortunately connected herself. When he had finished speaking to her she could not but feel that he was displeased, and could not but feel also the injustice of such displeasure. Of course she had her own little share in the general disappointments. But she had striven before him to make nothing of it, in order that he might be quite sure that she had married him, not with any idea to rank or wealth, but for himself alone. She had made light of the family misfortune, in order that he might be relieved. And yet he was angry with her! This was unreasonable. How much had she done for him! Was she not striving every hour of her life to love him, and, at any rate, to comfort him with the conviction that he was loved? Was she not constant in her assurance to herself that her whole life should be devoted to him? And yet he was surly to her simply because his brother had disgraced himself! When she was left alone she sat down and cried, and then consoled herself by remembering that her father was coming to her.

It had been arranged that the last days of February should be spent by Lord George with his mother and sisters at Cross Hall, and that the Dean should run up to town for a week. Lord George went down to Brotherton by a morning train, and the Dean came up on the same afternoon. But the going and coming were so fixed that the two men met at the Deanery. Lord George had determined that he would speak fully to the Dean respecting his brother. He was always conscious of the Dean's low birth, remembering with some slight discomfort the stable-keeper and the tallow-chandler; and he was a little inclined to resent what he thought to be a disposition on the part of the Dean to domineer. But still the Dean was a practical, sagacious man, in whom he could trust; and the assistance of such a friend was necessary to him. Circumstances had bound him to the Dean, and he was a man not prone to bind himself to many men. He wanted and yet feared the confidence of friendship. He lunched with the Dean, and then told his story. "You know," he said, "that my brother is married?"

"Of course, we all heard that."

"He was married more than twelve months before he informed us that he was going to be married."

"No!"

"It was so."

"Do you mean, then, that he told you a falsehood?"

"His letter to me. was very strange, though I did not think much of it at the time. He said 'I am to be married'—naming no day."

"That certainly was a falsehood, as, at that time, he was married."

"I do not know that harsh words will do any good."

"Nor I. But it is best, George, that you and I should be quite plain in our words to each other. Placed as he was, and as you were, he was bound to tell you of his marriage as soon as he knew it himself. You had waited till he was between forty and fifty, and, of course, he must feel that what you would do would depend materially upon what he did."

"It didn't at all."

"And then, having omitted to do his duty, he screens his fault by a——positive misstatement, when his intended return home makes further concealment impossible."

"All that, however, is of little moment," said Lord George, who could not but see that the Dean was already complaining that he had been left without information which he ought to have possessed when he was giving his daughter to a probable heir to the title. "There is more than that."

"What more?"

"He had a son born more than twelve months since."

"Who says so?" exclaimed the Dean, jumping up from his chair.

"I heard it first—or rather Mary did—in common conversation, from an old friend. I then learned the truth from Knox. Though he had told none of us, he had told Knox."

"And Knox has known it all through?"

"No, only lately. But he knows it now. Knox supposes that they are coming home so that the people about may be reconciled to the idea of his having an heir. There will be less trouble, he thinks, if the boy comes now, than if he were never heard of till he was ten or fifteen years old, or perhaps till after my brother's death."

"There may be trouble enough still," said the Dean, almost with a gasp.

The Dean, it was clear, did not believe in the boy. Lord George remembered that he himself had expressed disbelief, and that Mr. Knox had almost rebuked him. "I have now told you all the facts," said Lord George, "and have told them as soon as I knew them."

"You are as true as the sun," said the Dean, putting his hand on his son-in-law's shoulder. "You will be honest. But you must not trust in the honesty of others. Poor Mary!"

"She does not feel it in the least; will not even interest herself about it."

"She will feel it some day. She is no more than a child now. I feel it, George; I feel it; and you ought to feel it."

"I feel his ill-treatment of myself."

"What—in not telling you? That is probably no more than a small part of a wide scheme. We must find out the truth of all this."

"I don't know what there is to find out," said Lord George hoarsely.

"Nor do I; but I do feel that there must be something. Think of your brother's position and standing—on his past life and his present character. This is no time now for being mealy-mouthed. When such a man as he appears suddenly with a foreign woman and a foreign child, and announces one as his wife and the other as his heir, having never reported the existence of one or of the other, it is time that some inquiry should be made. I, at any rate, shall make inquiry. I shall think myself bound to do so on behalf of Mary." Then they parted as confidential friends do part, but each with some feeling antagonistic to the other. The Dean, though he had from his heart acknowledged that Lord George was as honest as the sun, still felt himself to be aggrieved by the Germain family, and doubted whether his son-in-law would be urgent enough and constant in hostility to his own brother. He feared that Lord George would be weak, feeling, as regarded himself, that he would fight till he had spent his last penny, as long as there was a chance that, by fighting, a grandson of his own might be made Marquis of Brotherton. He, at any rate, understood his own heart in the matter, and knew what it was that he wanted. But Lord George, though he had found himself compelled to tell everything to the Dean, still dreaded the Dean. It was not in accordance with his principles that he should be leagued against his brother with such a

man as Dean Lovelace, and he could see that the
Dean was thinking of his own possible grandchildren,
whereas he himself was thinking only of the family of
Germain.

He found his mother and sister at the small house
—the house at which Farmer Price was living only
a month or two since. No doubt it was the recognised dower-house, but nevertheless there was still
about it a flavour of Farmer Price. A considerable
sum of money had been spent upon it, which had
come from a sacrifice of a small part of the capital
belonging to the three sisters, with an understanding
that it should be repaid out of the old lady's income.
But no one, except the old lady herself, anticipated
such repayment. All this had created trouble and
grief, and the family, which was never gay, was now
more sombre than ever.

When the further news was told to Lady Sarah
it almost crushed her. "A child!" she said in a
horror-stricken whisper, turning quite pale, and looking as though the crack of doom were coming at
once. "Do you believe it?" Then her brother explained the grounds he had for believing it. "And
that it was born in wedlock twelve months before
the fact was announced to us?"

"It has never been announced to us," said Lord
George.

"What are we to do? is my mother to be told?
She ought to know at once; and yet how can we
tell her? What shall you do about the Dean?"

"He knows."

"You told him?"

"Yes; I thought it best."

"Well—perhaps. And yet it is terrible that any

man so distant from us should have our secrets in
his keeping."

"As Mary's father, I thought it right that he should
know."

"I have always liked the Dean personally," said
Lady Sarah. "There is a manliness about him which
has recommended him, and having a full hand he
knows how to open it. But he isn't—he isn't
quite——"

"No; he isn't quite——," said Lord George, also
hesitating to pronounce the word which was understood by both of them.

"You must tell my mother, or I must. It will be
wrong to withhold it. If you like, I will tell Susanna
and Amelia."

"I think you had better tell my mother," said Lord
George; "she will take it more easily from you. And
then, if she breaks down, you can control her better." That Lady Sarah should have the doing of any
difficult piece of work was almost a matter of course.
She did tell the tale to her mother, and her mother
did break down. The Marchioness, when she found
that an Italian baby had been born twelve months
before the time which she had been made to believe
was the date of the marriage, took at once to her
bed. What a mass of horrors was coming on them!
Was she to go and see a woman who had had a baby
under such circumstances? Or was her own eldest
son, the very, very Marquis of Brotherton, to be there
with his wife, and was she not to go and see them?
Through it all her indignation against her son had
not been hot as had been theirs against their brother.
He was her eldest son—the very Marquis—and ought
to be allowed to do almost anything he pleased. Had

it not been impossible for her to rebel against Lady
Sarah she would have obeyed her son in that matter
of the house. And, even now, it was not against her
son that her heart was bitter, but against the woman
who, being an Italian, and having been married, if
married, without the knowledge of the family, presumed to say that her child was legitimate. Had
her eldest son brought over with him to the halls of
his ancestors an Italian mistress, that would, of course,
have been very bad, but it would not have been so
bad as this. Nothing could be so bad as this. "Are
we to call him Popenjoy?" she asked with a gurgling
voice from amidst the bed-clothes. Now the eldest son
of the Marquis of Brotherton would, as a matter of
course, be Lord Popenjoy, if legitimate. "Certainly
we must," said Lady Sarah, authoritatively, "unless
the marriage should be disproved."

"Poor dear little thing," said the Marchioness, beginning to feel some pity for the odious stranger as
soon as she was told that he really was to be called
Popenjoy. Then the Ladies Susanna and Amelia
were informed, and the feeling became general throughout the household that the world must be near its
end. What were they all to do when he should
come? That was the great question. He had begun
by declaring that he did not want to see any of them.
He had endeavoured to drive them away from the
neighbourhood, and had declared that neither his
mother nor his sisters would "get on" with his wife.
All the ladies at Cross Hall had a very strong opinion
that this would turn out to be true, but still they could
not bear to think that they should be living as it were
next door to the head of the family, and never see
him. A feeling began to creep over all of them, ex-

cept Lady Sarah, that it would have been better for them to have obeyed the head of the family and gone elsewhere. But it was too late now. The decision had been made, and they must remain.

Lady Sarah, however, never gave way for a minute. "George," she said very solemnly, "I have thought a great deal about this, and I do not mean to let him trample upon us."

"It is all very sad," said Lord George.

"Yes, indeed. If I know myself, I think I should be the last person to attribute evil motives to my elder brother, or to stand in his way in aught that he might wish to do in regard to the family. I know all that is due to him. But there is a point beyond which even that feeling cannot carry me. He has disgraced himself." Lord George shook his head. "And he is doing all he can to bring disgrace upon us. It has always been my wish that he should marry."

"Of course, of course."

"It is always desirable that the eldest son should marry. The heir to the property then knows that he is the heir, and is brought up to understand his duties. Though he had married a foreigner, much as I should regret it, I should be prepared to receive her as a sister; it is for him to please himself; but in marrying a foreigner he is more specially bound to let it be known to all the world, and to have everything substantiated, than if he had married an English girl in her own parish church. As it is, we must call on her because he says that she is his wife. But I shall tell him that he is acting very wrongly by us all, especially by you, and most especially by his own child, if he does not take care that such evidence of his marriage is forthcoming as shall satisfy all the world."

"He won't listen to you."

"I think I can make him, as far as that goes; at any rate I do not mean to be afraid of him. Nor must you."

"I hardly know whether I will even see him."

"Yes, you must see him. If we are to be expelled from 'the family house, let it be his doing, and not ours. We have to take care, George, that we do not make a single false step. We must be courteous to him, but above all we must not be afraid of him."

In the meantime the Dean went up to London, meaning to spend a week with his daughter in her new house. They had both intended that this should be a period of great joy to them. Plans had been made as to the theatres and one or two parties, which were almost as exciting to the Dean as to his daughter. It was quite understood by both of them that the Dean up in London was to be a man of pleasure, rather than a clergyman. He had no purpose of preaching either at St. Paul's or the Abbey. He was going to attend no Curates' Aid Society or Sons of the Clergy. He intended to forget Mr. Groschut, to ignore Dr. Pountney, and have a good time. That had been his intention, at least till he saw Lord George at the Deanery. But now there were serious thoughts in his mind. When he arrived Mary had for the time got nearly rid of the incubus of the Italian Marchioness with her baby. She was all smiles as she kissed him. But he could not keep himself from the great subject.

"This is terrible news, my darling," he said at once.

"Do you think so, papa?"

"Certainly I do."

"I don't see why Lord Brotherton should not have a son and heir as well as anybody else."

"He is quite entitled to have a son and heir—one may almost say more entitled than anyone else, seeing that he has got so much to leave to him—but on that very account he is more bound than anyone else to let all the world feel sure that his declared son and heir is absolutely his son and heir."

"He couldn't be so vile as that, papa!"

"God forbid that I should say that he could! It may be that he considers himself married, though the marriage would not be valid here. Maybe he is married, and that yet the child is not legitimate." Mary could not but blush as her father spoke to her thus plainly. "All we do know is that he wrote to his own brother declaring that he was about to be married twelve months after the birth of the child whom he now expects us to recognise as the heir to the title. I for one am not prepared to accept his word without evidence, and I shall have no scruple in letting him know that such evidence will be wanted."

CHAPTER XV

"DROP IT"

FOR ten or twelve days after the little dinner in Berkeley Square Guss Mildmay bore her misfortunes without further spoken complaint. During all that time, though they were both in London, she never saw Jack de Baron, and she knew that in not seeing her he was neglecting her. But for so long she bore it. It is generally supposed that young ladies have to bear such sorrow without loud complaint; but Guss was more thoroughly emancipated than are some young ladies, and when moved was wont to speak her mind. At last, when she herself was only on foot with her father, she saw Jack de Baron riding with Lady George. It is quite true that she also saw, riding behind them, her perfidious friend, Mrs. Houghton, and a gentleman whom at that time she did not know to be Lady George's father. This was early in March, when equestrians in the Park are not numerous. Guss stood for a moment looking at them, and Jack de Baron took off his hat. But Jack did not stop, and went on talking with that pleasant vivacity which she, poor girl, knew so well and valued so highly. Lady George liked it too, though she could hardly have given any reason for liking it, for to tell the truth, there was not often much pith in Jack's conversation.

On the following morning Captain de Baron, who had lodgings in Charles Street, close to the Guard's

Club, had a letter brought to him before he was out of bed. The letter was from Guss Mildmay, and he knew the handwriting well. He had received many notes from her, though none so interesting on the whole as was this letter. It was written, certainly, with a swift pen, and, but that he knew her writing well, would in parts have been hardly legible.

"I think you are treating me very badly. I tell you openly and fairly. It is neither gentlemanlike or high spirited, as you know that I have no one to take my part but myself. If you mean to cut me, say so, and let me understand it at once. You have taken up now with that young married woman just because you know it will make me angry. I don't believe for a moment that you really care for such a baby-faced chit as that. I have met her too, and I know that she hasn't a word to say for herself. Do you mean to come and see me? I expect to hear from you, letting me know when you will come. I do not intend to be thrown over for her or anyone. I believe it is mostly Adelaide's doing, who doesn't like to think that you should really care for anyone. You know very well what my feelings are, and what sacrifice I am ready to make. And you know what you have told me of yourself. I shall be at home all this afternoon. Papa, of course, will go to his club at three. Aunt Julia has an afternoon meeting at the Institute for the distribution of prizes among the Rights-of-Women young men, and I have told her positively that I won't go. Nobody else will be admitted. Do come and at any rate let us have it out. This state of things will kill me, though, of course, you don't mind that. "G.

"I shall think you a coward if you don't come. Oh Jack, do come!"

She had begun like a lion, but had ended like a lamb; and such was the nature of every thought she had respecting him. She was full of indignation. She assured herself hourly that such treachery as his deserved death. She longed for a return of the old times—thirty years since—and for some old-fashioned brother, so that Jack might be shot at and have a pistol bullet in his heart. And yet she told herself as often that she could not live without him. Where should she find another Jack after her recklessness in letting all the world know that this man was her Jack? She hardly wanted to marry him, knowing full well the nature of the life which would then be before her. Jack had told her often that if forced to do that he must give up the army and go and live in——. He had named Dantzic as having the least alluring sound of any place he knew. To her it would be best that things should go on just as they were now till something should turn up. But that she should be enthralled and Jack free was not to be borne. She begrudged him no other pleasure. She was willing that he should hunt, gamble, eat, drink, smoke, and be ever so wicked, if that were his taste; but not that he should be seen making himself agreeable to another young woman. It might be that their position was unfortunate, but of that misfortune she had by far the heavier share. She could not eat, drink, smoke, gamble, hunt, and be generally wicked. Surely he might bear it if she could.

Jack, when he had read the letter, tossed it on to the counterpane, and rolled himself again in bed. It was not as yet much after nine, and he need not decide for an hour or two whether he would accept the invitation or not. But the letter bothered him and he could not sleep. She told him that if he did not come he would be a coward, and he felt that she had told him the truth. He did not want to see her—not because he was tired of her, for in her softer humours she was always pleasant to him, but because he had a clear insight into the misery of the whole connection. When the idea of marrying her suggested itself, he always regarded it as being tantamount to suicide. Were he to be persuaded to such a step he would simply be blowing his own brains out because someone else asked him to do so. He had explained all this to her at various times when suggesting Dantzic, and she had agreed with him. Then, at that point, his common sense had been better than hers, and his feeling really higher. " That being so," he had said, " it is certainly for your advantage that we should part." But this to her had been as though he were striving to break his own chains, and was indifferent as to her misery. " I can take care of myself," she had answered him. But he knew that she could not take care of herself. Had she not been most unwise, most imprudent, she would have seen the wisdom of letting the intimacy of their acquaintance drop without any further explanation. But she was most unwise. Nevertheless, when she accused him of cowardice, must he not go?

He breakfasted uncomfortably, trying to put off the consideration, and then uncomfortably sauntered down to the Guard House, at St. James's. He had no intention of writing, and was therefore not compelled to make up his mind till the hour named for the appointment should actually have come. He thought for awhile that he would write her a long letter, full of good sense; explaining to her that it was impossible that they should be useful to each other, and that he found himself compelled, by his regard for her, to recommend that their peculiar intimacy should be brought to an end. But he knew that such a letter would go for nothing with her—that she would regard it simply as an excuse on his part. They two had tacitly agreed not to be bound by common sense—not to be wise. Such tacit agreements are common enough between men, between women, and between men and women. What! a sermon from you! No indeed; not that. Jack felt all this—felt that he could not preach without laying himself open to ridicule. When the time came he made up his mind that he must go. Of course it was very bad for her. The servants would all know it. Everybody would know it. She was throwing away every chance she had of doing well for herself. But what was he to do? She told him that he would be a coward, and he at any rate could not bear that.

Mr. Mildmay lived in a small house in Green Street, very near the Park, but still a modest, unassuming, cheap little house. Jack de Baron knew the way to it well, and was there not above a quarter of an hour after the appointed time. "So Aunt Ju has gone to the Rights of Women, has she?" he said, after his first greeting. He might have kissed her if he would, but he didn't. He had made up his mind about that. And so had she. She was ready for him, whether he should kiss her or not—ready to accept either greeting, as though it was just that which she had expected.

" Oh yes; she is going to make a speech herself."

" But why do they give prizes to young men?"

" Because the young men have stood up for the old women. Why don't you go and get a prize?"

" I had to be here instead."

" Had to be here, sir?"

" Yes, Guss; had to be here! Isn't that about it? When you tell me to come, and tell me that I am a coward if I don't come, of course I am here."

" And now you are here, what have you got to say for yourself?" This she attempted to say easily and jauntily.

" Not a word."

" Then I don't see what is the use of coming."

" Nor I either. What would you have me say?"

" I would have you—I would have you——" And then there was something like a sob. It was quite real. " I would have you tell me—that you—love me."

" Have I not told you so a score of times, and what has come of it?"

" But is it true?"

" Come, Guss, this is simple folly. You know it is true; and you know, also, that there is no good to be got from such truth."

" If you loved me, you would like—to—see me."

" No, I shouldn't; no, I don't; unless it could lead to something. There was a little fun to be had when we could spoon together—when I hardly knew how to ask for it, and you hardly knew how to grant it; when it was a little shooting bud, and had to be nursed by smiles and pretty speeches. But there are only three things it can come to now. Two are impossible, and therefore there is the other."

"What are the three?"

"We might get married."

"Well?"

"One of the three I shall not tell you. And we might—make up our minds to forget it all. Do what the people call 'part.' That is what I suggest."

"So that you may spend your time in riding about with Lady George Germain?"

"That is nonsense, Guss. Lady George Germain I have seen three times, and she talks only about her husband; a pretty little woman more absolutely in love I never came across."

"Pretty little fool!"

"Very likely. I have nothing to say against that. Only, when you have no heavier stone to throw against me than Lady George Germain, really you are badly off for weapons."

"I have stones enough, if I chose to throw them. Oh, Jack!"

"What more is there to be said?"

"Have you had enough of me, already, Jack?"

"I should not have had half enough of you if either you or I had fifty thousand pounds."

"If I had them I would give them all to you."

"And I to you. That goes without telling. But as neither of us have got the money, what are we to do? I know what we had better not do. We had better not make each other unhappy by what people call recriminations."

"I don't suppose that anything I say can affect your happiness."

"Yes, it does; very much. It makes me think of deep rivers and high columns; of express trains and prussic acid. Well as we have known each other, you have never found out how unfortunately soft I am."

"Very soft!"

"I am. This troubles me so that I ride over awfully big places, thinking that I might, perhaps, be lucky enough to break my neck."

"What must I feel, who have no way of amusing myself at all?"

"Drop it. I know it is a hard thing for me to say. I know it will sound heartless. But I am bound to say so. It is for your sake. I can't hurt myself. It does me no harm that everybody knows that I am philandering after you; but it is the very deuce for you." She was silent for a moment. Then he said again, emphatically, "Drop it."

"I can't drop it," she said, through her tears.

"Then what are we to do?" As he asked this question, he approached her and put his arm round her waist. This he did in momentary vacillating mercy—not because of the charm of the thing to himself, but through his own inability not to give her some token of affection.

"Marry," she said, in a whisper.

"And go and live at Dantzic for the rest of our lives!" He did not speak these words, but such was the exclamation which he at once made internally to himself. If he had resolved on anything, he had resolved that he would not marry her. One might sacrifice one's self, he had said to himself, if one could do her any good; but what's the use of sacrificing both? He withdrew his arm from her, and stood a yard apart from her, looking into her face.

"That would be so horrible to you!" she said.

"It would be horrible to have nothing to eat."

"We should have seven hundred and fifty pounds a year," said Guss, who had made her calculations very narrowly.

"Well, yes; and no doubt we could get enough to eat at such a place as Dantzic."

"Dantzic! you always laugh at me when I speak seriously."

"Or Lubeck, if you like it better; or Leipsig. I shouldn't care the least in the world where we went. I know a chap who lives in Minorca, because he has not got any money. We might go to Minorca, only the mosquitos would eat you up."

"Will you do it? I will if you will." They were standing now three yards apart, and Guss was looking terrible things. She did not endeavour to be soft, but had made up her mind as to the one step that must be taken. She would not lose him. They need not be married immediately. Something might turn up before any date was fixed for their marriage. If she could only bind him by an absolute promise that he would marry her some day! "I will if you will," she said again, after waiting a second or two for his answer. Then he shook his head. "You will not, after all that you have said to me?" He shook his head again. "Then, Jack de Baron, you are perjured, and no gentleman."

"Dear Guss, I can bear that. It is not true, you know, as I have never made you any promise which I am not ready to keep; but still I can bear it."

"No promise! Have you not sworn that you loved me?"

"A thousand times."

"And what does that mean from a gentleman to a lady?"

"It ought to mean matrimony and all that kind of thing, but it never did mean it with us. You know how it all began."

"I know what it has come to, and that you owe it to me as a gentleman to let me decide whether I am able to encounter such a life or not. Though it were absolute destruction, you ought to face it if I bid you."

"If it were destruction for myself only—perhaps yes. But though you have so little regard for my happiness, I still have some for yours. It is not to be done. You and I have had our little game, as I said before, and now we had better put the rackets down and go and rest ourselves."

"What rest? Oh, Jack—what rest is there?"

"Try somebody else."

"Can you tell me to do that!"

"Certainly I can. Look at my cousin Adelaide."

"Your cousin Adelaide never cared for any human being in her life except herself. She had no punishment to suffer as I have. Oh, Jack! I do so love you." Then she rushed at him, and fell upon his bosom and wept.

He knew that this would come, and he felt that, upon the whole, this was the worst part of the performance. He could bear her anger or her sullenness with fortitude, but her lachrymose caresses were insupportable. He held her, however, in his arms, and gazed at himself in the pier glass most uncomfortably over her shoulder. "Oh, Jack," she said, "oh, Jack—what is to come next?" His face became somewhat more lugubrious than before, but he said not a word. "I cannot lose you altogether. There is no one else in the wide world that I care for.

Papa thinks of nothing but his whist. Aunt Ju, with
her 'Rights of Women,' is an old fool."

"Just so," said Jack, still holding her, and still looking very wretched.

"What shall I do if you leave me?"

"Pick up someone that has a little money. I
know it sounds bad and mercenary, and all that, but
in our way of life there is nothing else to be done.
We can't marry like the ploughboy and milkmaid?"

"I could."

"And would be the first to find out your mistake afterwards. It's all very well saying that Adelaide hasn't got a heart. I daresay she has as much
heart as you or me."

"As you—as you."

"Very well. Of course you have a sort of pleasure in abusing me. But she has known what she
could do, and what she could not. Every year as she
grows older she will become more comfortable. Houghton is very good to her, and she has lots of money to
spend. If that's heartlessness there's a good deal to
be said for it." Then he gently disembarrassed himself of her arms, and placed her on a sofa.

"And this is to be the end?"

"Well—I think so really." She thumped her hand
upon the neck of the sofa as a sign of her anger. "Of
course we shall always be friends?"

"Never!" she almost screamed.

"We'd better. People will talk less about it, you
know."

"I don't care what people talk. If they knew the
truth, no one would ever speak to you again."

"Good-bye, Guss." She shook her head as he had
shaken his before. "Say a word to a fellow." Again

she shook her head. He attempted to take her hand, but she withdrew it. Then he stood for perhaps a minute looking at her, but she did not move. "Good-bye, Guss," he said again; and then he left the room.

When he got into the street he congratulated himself. He had undergone many such scenes before, but none which seemed so likely to bring the matter to an end. He was rather proud of his own conduct, thinking that he had been at the same time both tender and wise. He had not given way in the least, and had yet been explicit in assuring her of his affection. He felt now that he would go and hunt on the morrow without any desire to break his neck over the baron's fences. Surely the thing was done now for ever and ever! Then he thought how it would have been with him at this moment had he in any transient weakness told her that he would marry her. But he had been firm, and could now walk along with a light heart.

She, as soon as he had left her, got up, and taking the cushion off the sofa, threw it to the farther end of the room. Having so relieved herself, she walked up to her own chamber.

CHAPTER XVI

ALL IS FISH THAT COMES TO HIS NET

THE Dean's week up in London during the absence
of Lord George was gay enough; but through it all
and over it all there was that cloud of seriousness
which had been produced by the last news from Italy.
He rode with his daughter, dined out in great state
at Mrs. Montacute Jones's, talked to Mr. Houghton
about Newmarket and the next Derby, had a little
flirtation of his own with Hetta Houghton,—into
which he contrived to introduce a few serious words
about the Marquis—and was merry enough; but, to
his daughter's surprise, he never for a moment ceased
to be impressed with the importance of the Italian
woman and her baby. "What does it signify, papa?"
she said.

"Not signify!"

"Of course it was to be expected that the Marquis
should marry. Why should he not marry as well as
his younger brother?"

"In the first place, he is very much older."

"As to that, men marry at any age. Look at Mr.
Houghton." The Dean only smiled. "Do you know,
papa, I don't think one ought to trouble about such
things."

"That's nonsense, my dear. Men, and women too,
ought to look after their own interests. It is the only
way in which progress can be made in the world. Of
course you are not to covet what belongs to others.

178

You will make yourself very unhappy if you do. If Lord Brotherton's marriage were all fair and above board, nobody would say a word; but, as it has not been so, it will be our duty to find out the truth. If you should have a son, do not you think that you would turn every stone before you would have him defrauded of his rights?"

"I shouldn't think anyone would defraud him."

"But if this child be—anything else than what he pretends to be, there will be fraud. The Germains, though they think as I do, are frightened and superstitious. They are afraid of this imbecile who is coming over; but they shall find that if they do not move in the matter, I will. I want nothing that belongs to another; but while I have a hand and tongue with which to protect myself, or a purse—which is better than either—no one shall take from me what belongs to me." All this seemed to Mary to be pagan teaching, and it surprised her much as coming from her father. But she was beginning to find out that she, as a married woman, was supposed to be now fit for other teaching than had been administered to her as a child. She had been cautioned in her father's house against the pomps and vanities of this wicked world, and could remember the paternal, almost divine expression of the Dean's face as the lesson was taught. But now it seemed to her that the pomps and vanities were spoken of in a very different way. The divine expression was altogether gone, and that which remained, though in looking at her it was always pleasant, was hardly paternal.

Miss Mildmay—Aunt Ju as she was called—and Guss Mildmay came and called, and, as it happened, the Dean was in the drawing-room when they came.

They were known to be friends of Mrs. Houghton's
who had been in Brothershire, and were therefore in
some degree connected even with the Dean. Guss
began at once about the new Marchioness and the
baby; and the Dean, though he did not of course speak
to Guss Mildmay as he had done to his own daughter,
still sneered at the mother and her child. In the
meantime Aunt Ju was enlisting poor Mary. "I should
be so proud if you would come with me to the Institute,
Lady George."

"I am sure I should be delighted. But what
Institute?"

"Don't you know?—in the Marylebone Road—for
relieving females from their disabilities."

"Do you mean Rights of Women? I don't think
papa likes that," said Mary, looking at her father.

"You haven't got to mind what papa likes and dislikes any more," said the Dean, laughing. "Whether
you go in for the rights or wrongs of women is past
my caring for now. Lord George must look after
that."

"I am sure Lord George could not object to your
going to the Marylebone Institute," said Aunt Ju.
"Lady Selina Protest is there every week, and
Baroness Banmann, the delegate from Bavaria, is
coming next Friday."

"You'd find the Disabilities awfully dull, Lady
George," said Guss.

"Everybody is not so flighty as you are, my dear.
Some people do sometimes think of serious things.
And the Institute is not called the Disabilities."

"What is it all about?" said Mary.

"Only to empower women to take their own equal
places in the world—places equal to those occupied

by men," said Aunt Ju eloquently. "Why should one-half of the world be ruled by the *ipse dixit* of the of the other?"

"Or fed by their labours?" said the Dean.

"That is just what we are not. There are one million one hundred and thirty-three thousand five hundred females in England——"

"You had better go and hear it all at the Disabilities, Lady George," said Guss. Lady George said that she would like to go for once, and so that matter was settled.

While Aunt Ju was pouring out the violence of her doctrine upon the Dean, whom she contrived to catch in a corner just before she left the house, Guss Mildmay had a little conversation on her own part with Lady George. "Captain de Baron," she said, "is an old friend of yours, I suppose." She, however, had known very well that Jack had never seen Lady George till within the last month.

"No, indeed; I never saw him till the other day."

"I thought you seemed so intimate. And then the Houghtons and the De Barons and the Germains are all Brothershire people."

"I knew Mrs. Houghton's father, of course, a little; but I never saw Captain de Baron." This she said rather seriously, remembering what Mrs. Houghton had said to her of the love affair between this young lady and the Captain in question.

"I thought you seemed to know him the other night, and I saw you riding with him."

"He was with his cousin Adelaide, not with us."

"I don't think he cares much for Adelaide. Do you like him?"

"Yes, I do; very much. He seems to be so gay."

"Yes, he is gay. He's a horrid flirt, you know."

"I didn't know; and what is more, I don't care."

"So many girls have said that about Captain de Baron; but they have cared afterwards."

"But I am not a girl, Miss Mildmay," said Mary, colouring, offended and resolved at once that she would have no intimacy and as little acquaintance as possible with Guss Mildmay.

"You are so much younger than so many of us that are girls," said Guss, thinking to get out of the little difficulty in that way. "And then it's all fish that comes to his net." She hardly knew what she was saying, but was anxious to raise some feeling that should prevent any increased intimacy between her own lover and Lady George. It was nothing to her whether or no she offended Lady George Germain. If she could do her work without sinning against good taste, well; but if not, then good taste must go to the wall. Good taste certainly had gone to the wall.

"Upon my word, I can hardly understand you!" Then Lady George turned away to her father. "Well, papa, has Miss Mildmay persuaded you to come to the Institute with me?"

"I am afraid I should hardly be admitted, after what I have just said."

"Indeed you shall be admitted, Mr. Dean," said the old woman. "We are quite of the Church's way of thinking, that no sinner is too hardened for repentance."

"I am afraid the day of grace has not come yet," said the Dean.

"Papa," said Lady George, as soon as her visitors were gone, "do you know that I particularly dislike that younger Miss Mildmay?"

"Is she worth being particularly disliked so rapidly?"

"She says nasty, impudent things. I can't quite explain what she said." And again Lady George blushed.

"People in society now do give themselves strange liberty—women I think more than men. You shouldn't mind it."

"Not mind it?"

"Not mind it so as to worry yourself. If a pert young woman like that says anything to annoy you, put her down at the time, and then think no more about it. Of course you need not make a friend of her."

"That I certainly shall not do."

On the Sunday after this Lady George dined again with her father at Mr. Houghton's house, the dinner having been made up especially for the Dean. On this occasion the Mildmays were not there; but Captain de Baron was one of the guests. But then he was Mrs. Houghton's cousin, and had the run of the house on all occasions. Again, there was no great party: Mrs. Montacute Jones was there, and Hetta—Miss Houghton, that is, whom all the world called Hetta— and Mrs. Houghton's father, who happened to be up in town. Again Lady George found herself sitting between her host and Jack de Baron, and again she thought Jack a very agreeable companion. The idea of being in any way afraid of him did not enter into her mind. Those horrid words which Guss Mildmay had said to her—as to all being fish for his net—had no effect of that nature. She assured herself that she knew herself too well to allow anything of that kind to influence her. That she, Lady George Germain, the daughter of the Dean of Brotherton, a married woman, should be afraid of any man, afraid of any too close intimacy! The idea was horrible and disgusting to her. So that when Jack proposed to join her and her father in the Park on the next afternoon, she said that she would be delighted; and when he told her absurd stories of his regimental duties, and described his brother officers, who probably did not exist as described by him, and then went on to hunting legends in Buckinghamshire she laughed at everything he said, and was very merry.

"Don't you like Jack?" Mrs. Houghton said to her in the drawing-room.

"Yes, I do; very much. He's just what Jack ought to be."

"I don't know about that. I suppose Jack ought to go to church twice on Sundays, and give half what he has to the poor, just as well as John."

"Perhaps he does. But Jack is bound to be amusing, while John need not have a word to say for himself."

"You know he's my pet friend. We are almost like brother and sister, and therefore I need not be afraid of him."

"Afraid of him! Why should anybody be afraid of him?"

"I am sure you needn't. But Jack has done mischief in his time. Perhaps he's not the sort of man that would ever touch your fancy." Again Lady George blushed, but on this occasion she had nothing to say. She did not want to quarrel with Mrs. Houghton, and the suggestion that she could possibly love any other man than her husband had not now been made in so undisguised a manner as before.

"I thought he was engaged to Miss Mildmay," said Lady George.

"Oh, dear, no; nothing of the kind. It is impossible, as neither of them has anything to speak of. When does Lord George come back?"

"To-morrow."

"Mind that he comes to see me soon. I do so long to hear what he'll say about his new sister-in-law. I had made up my mind that I should have to koto to you before long as a real live marchioness."

"You'll never have to do that."

"Not if this child is a real Lord Popenjoy. But I have my hopes still, my dear."

Soon after that Hetta Houghton reverted to the all-important subject. "You have found out that what I told you was true, Lady George?"

"Oh, yes—all true."

"I wonder what the Dowager thinks about it."

"My husband is with his mother. She thinks, I suppose, just what we all think, that it would have been better if he had told everybody of his marriage sooner."

"A great deal better."

"I don't know whether, after all, it will make a great deal of difference. Lady Brotherton—the Dowager I mean—is so thoroughly English in all her ways that she never could have got on very well with an Italian daughter-in-law."

"The question is whether, when a man springs a wife and family on his relations in that way, everything can be taken for granted. Suppose a man had been ever so many years in Kamptschatka, and had then come back with a Kamptschatkean female,

calling her his wife, would everybody take it as all
gospel?"

"I suppose so."

"Do you? I think not. In the first place it might
be difficult for an Englishman to get himself married in that country according to English laws, and
in the next, when there, he would hardly wish to
do so."

"Italy is not Kamptschatka, Miss Houghton."

"Certainly not; and it isn't England. People are
talking about it a great deal, and seem to think
that the Italian lady oughtn't to have a walk over."

Miss Houghton had heard a good deal about races
from her brother, and the phrase she had used was
quite an everyday word to her. Lady George did
not understand it, but felt that Miss Houghton was
talking very freely about a very delicate matter. And
she remembered at the same time what had been
the aspirations of the lady's earlier life, and put down
a good deal of what was said to personal jealousy.
"Papa," she said, as she went home, "it seems to
me that people here talk a great deal about one's
private concerns."

"You mean about Lord Brotherton's marriage?"

"That among other things."

"Of course they will talk about that. It is hardly
to be considered private. And I don't know but
what the more it is talked about the better for us.
It is felt to be a public scandal, and that feeling may
help us."

"Oh, papa, I wish you wouldn't think that we
wanted any help."

"We want the truth, my dear, and we must have
it."

On the next day they met Jack de Baron in the
Park. They had not been long together before the
Dean saw an old friend on the footpath, and stopped
to speak to him. Mary would have stayed, too, had
not her horse displayed an inclination to go on, and
that she had felt herself unwilling to make an effort
in the matter. As she rode on with Captain de
Baron she remembered all that had been said by
Guss Mildmay and Mrs. Houghton, and remembered
also her own decision that nothing of that kind could
matter to her. It was an understood thing that ladies
and gentlemen when riding should fall into this kind
of intercourse. Her father was with her, and it would
be absurd that she should be afraid to be a minute
or two out of his sight. "I ought to have been hunting," said Jack; "but there was frost last night,
and I do hate going down and being told that the
ground is as hard as brickbats at the kennels, while
men are ploughing all over the country. And now
it's a delicious spring day."

"You didn't like getting up, Captain de Baron,"
she said.

"Perhaps there's something in that. Don't you
think getting up is a mistake? My idea of a perfect
world is one where nobody would ever have to get
up."

"I shouldn't at all like always to lie in bed."

"But there might be some sort of arrangement
to do away with the nuisance. See what a good time
the dogs have."

"Now Captain de Baron, would you like to be
a dog?" This she said, turning round and looking
him full in the face.

"Your dog, I would." At that moment, just over

his horse's withers, she saw the face of Guss Mildmay who was leaning on her father's arm. Guss
bowed to her, and she was obliged to return the
salute. Jack de Baron turned his face to the path,
and, seeing the lady, raised his hat. "Are you two
friends?" he asked.

"Not particularly."

"I wish you were. But, of course, I have no
right to wish in such a matter as that." Lady George
felt that she wished that Guss Mildmay had not seen
her riding in the Park on that day with Jack de
Baron.

CHAPTER XVII

THE DISABILITIES

It had been arranged that on Friday evening Lady George should call for Aunt Ju in Green Street, and that they should go together to the Institute in the Marylebone Road. The real and full name of The College, as some ladies delighted to call it, was, though somewhat lengthy, placarded in big letters on a long black board on the front of the building, and was as follows: "Rights of Women Institute; established for the Relief of the Disabilities of Females." By friendly tongues to friendly ears "The College" or "The Institute" was the pleasant name used; but the irreverent public was apt to speak of the building generally as the "Female Disabilities." And the title was made even shorter. Omnibuses were desired to stop at the "Disabilities"; and it had become notorious that it was just a mile from King's Cross to the "Disabilities." There had been serious thoughts among those who were dominant in the Institute of taking down the big board and dropping the word. But then a change of a name implies such a confession of failure! It had on the whole been thought better to maintain the courage of the opinion which had first made the mistake. "So you're going to the Disabilities, are you?" Mrs. Houghton had said to Lady George.

"I'm to be taken by old Miss Mildmay."

"Oh, yes; Aunt Ju is a sort of first-class priestess

189

among them. Don't let them bind you over to belong to them. Don't go in for it." Lady George
had declared it to be very improbable that she should
go in for it, but had adhered to her determination
of visiting the Institute.

She called in Green Street fearing that she should
see Guss Mildmay, whom she had determined to keep
at arm's distance as well as her friendship with Mrs.
Houghton would permit; but Aunt Ju was ready for
her in the passage. "I forgot to tell you that we
ought to be a little early, as I have to take the chair.
I daresay we shall do very well," she added, "if the
man drives fast. But the thing is so important! One
doesn't like to be flurried when one gets up to make
the preliminary address." The only public meetings
at which Mary had ever been present had appertained
to certain lectures at Brotherton, at which her father
or some other clerical dignity had presided, and she
could not as yet understand that such a duty should
be performed by a woman. She muttered something
expressing a hope that all would go right. "I've
got to introduce the Baroness, you know."

"Introduce the Baroness?"

"The Baroness Banmann. Haven't you seen the
bill of the evening? The Baroness is going to address the meeting on the propriety of patronising
female artists, especially in regard to architecture.
A combined college of female architects is to be established in Posen and Chicago, and why should we
not have a branch in London, which is the centre of
the world?"

"Would a woman have to build a house?" asked
Lady George.

"She would draw the plans, and devise the proportions, and—and—do the æsthetic part of it. An architect doesn't carry bricks on his back, my dear."

"But he walks over planks, I suppose?"

"And so could I walk over a plank; why not as well as a man? But you will hear what the Baroness says. The worst is that I am a little afraid of her English."

"She's a foreigner, of course. How will she manage?"

"Her English is perfect, but I am afraid of her pronunciation. However, we shall see." They had now arrived at the building, and Lady George followed the old lady in with the crowd. But when once inside the door they turned to a small passage on the left, which conducted those in authority to the august room preparatory to the platform. It is here that bashful speakers try to remember their first sentences, and that lecturers, proud of their prominence, receive the homage of the officers of the Institute. Aunt Ju, who on this occasion was second in glory, made her way in among the crowd and welcomed the Baroness, who had just arrived. The Baroness was a very stout woman, about fifty, with a double chin, a considerable moustache, a low, broad forehead, and bright, round, black eyes, very far apart. When introduced to Lady George, she declared that she had great honour in accepting the re-cog-nition. She had a stout roll of paper in her hand, and was dressed in a black stuff gown, with a cloth jacket buttoned up to neck, which hardly gave to her copious bust that appearance of manly firmness which the occasion almost required. But the virile collars budding out over it perhaps supplied what was wanting. Lady George looked at her to see if she was trembling.

How, thought Lady George, would it have been with
herself if she had been called upon to address a French
audience in French? But as far as she could ·judge
from experience, the Baroness was quite at her ease.
Then she was introduced by Aunt Ju to Lady Selina
Protest, who was a very little woman with spectacles
—of a most severe aspect. " I hope, Lady George,
that you mean to put your shoulder to the wheel,"
said Lady Selina. " I am only here as a stranger,"
said Lady George. Lady Selina did not believe in
strangers, and passed on very severely. There was
no time for further ceremonies, as a bald-headed old
gentleman, who seemed to act as chief usher, informed Aunt Ju that it was time for her to take the
Baroness on to the platform. Aunt Ju led the way,
puffing a little, for she had been somewhat hurried
on the stairs, and was not as yet quite used to the
thing—but still with a proudly prominent step. The
Baroness waddled after her, apparently quite indifferent to the occasion. Then followed Lady Selina
—and Lady George, the bald-headed gentleman telling her where to place herself. She had never been
on a platform before, and it seemed as though the
crowd of people below was looking specially at her.
As she sat down at the right hand of the Baroness,
who was of course at the right hand of the chairwoman, the bald-headed gentleman introduced her to
her other neighbour, Miss Doctor Olivia Q. Fleabody,
from Vermont. There was so much of the name,
and it all sounded so strange to the ears of Lady
George, that she could remember very little of it,
but she was conscious that her new acquaintance was
a miss and a doctor. She looked timidly round, and
saw what` would have been a pretty face, had it not

been marred by a pinched look of studious severity and a pair of glass spectacles, of which the glasses shone in a disagreeable manner. There are spectacles which are so much more spectacles than other spectacles that they make the beholder feel that there is before him a pair of spectacles carrying a face, rather than a face carrying a pair of spectacles. So it was with the spectacles of Olivia Q. Fleabody. She was very thin, and the jacket and collars were quite successful. Sitting in the front row she displayed her feet—and it may also be said her trousers—for the tunic which she wore came down hardly below the knees. Lady George's inquiring mind instantly began to ask itself what the lady had done with her petticoats. "This is a great occasion," said Dr. Fleabody, speaking almost out loud, and with a very strong nasal twang.

Lady George looked at the chair before she answered, feeling that she would not dare to speak a word if Aunt Ju were already on her legs; but Aunt Ju was taking advantage of the commotion which was still going on among those who were looking for seats, to get her breath, and therefore she could whisper a reply. "I suppose it is," she said.

"If it were not that I have wedded myself in a peculiar manner to the prophylactick and therapeutick sciences, I would certainly now put my foot down firmly in the cause of architecture. I hope to have an opportunity of saying a few words on the subject myself before this interesting session shall have closed." Lady George looked at her again, and thought that this enthusiastic hybrid who was addressing her could not be more than twenty-four years old.

But Aunt Ju was soon on her legs. It did not

seem to Lady George that Aunt Ju enjoyed the moment now that it was come. She looked hot, and
puffed once or twice before she spoke. But she had
studied her few words so long, and had made so
sure of them, that she could not go very far wrong.
She assured her audience that the Baroness Banmann, whose name had only to be mentioned to be
honoured both throughout Europe and America, had,
at great personal inconvenience, come all the way
from Bavaria to give them the advantage of her vast
experience on the present occasion. Like a good
chairwoman, she took none of the bread out of the
Baroness's mouth—as we have occasionally known
to be done on such occasions—but confined herself
to ecstatic praises of the German lady. All these
the Baroness bore without a quiver, and, when Aunt
Ju sat down, she stepped on to the rostrum of the
evening amidst the plaudits of the room, with a confidence which, to Lady George, was miraculous. Then
Aunt Ju took her seat, and was able for the next
hour and a half to occupy her arm-chair with gratify-
ing *fainéant* dignity.

The Baroness, to tell the truth, waddled rather
than stepped to the rostrum. She swung herself
heavily about as she went sideways; but it was manifest to all eyes that she was not in the least ashamed
of her waddling. She undid her manuscript on the
desk, and flattened it down all over with her great
fat hand, rolling her head about as she looked around,
and then gave a grunt before she began. During
this time the audience was applauding her loudly,
and it was evident that she did not intend to lose a
breath of their incense by any hurry on her own
part. At last the voices and the hands and the feet

were silent. Then she gave a last roll to her head and a last pat to the papers, and began. "De manifest infairiority of de tyrant saix——." Those first words, spoken in a very loud voice, came clearly home to Lady George's ear, though they were uttered with a most un-English accent. The Baroness paused before she completed her first sentence, and then there was renewed applause. Lady George could remark that the bald-headed old gentleman behind and a cadaverous youth, who was near to him, were particularly energetic in stamping on the ground. Indeed it seemed that the men were specially charmed with this commencement of the Baroness's oration. It was so good that she repeated it with, perhaps, even a louder shout. "De manifest infairiority of de tyrant saix——." Lady George, with considerable trouble, was able to follow the first sentence or two, which went to assert that the inferiority of man to woman in all work was quite as conspicuous as his rapacity and tyranny in taking to himself all the wages. The Baroness, though addressing a mixed audience, seemed to have no hesitation in speaking of man generally as a foul worm who ought to be put down and kept under, and merely allowed to be the father of children. But after a minute or two Lady George found that she could not understand two words consecutively, although she was close to the lecturer. The Baroness, as she became heated, threw out her words quicker and more quickly, till it became almost impossible to know in what language they were spoken. By degrees our friend became aware that the subject of architecture had been reached, and then she caught a word or two as the Baroness declared that the science was "adaapted

only to de æstetic and comprehensive intelligence of
the famale mind." But the audience applauded
throughout as though every word reached them; and
when from time to time the Baroness wiped her brows
with a very large handkerchief, they shook the building with their appreciation of her energy. Then
came a loud rolling sentence, with the old words
as an audible termination—"de manifest infairiority
of de tyrant saix!" As she said this she waved
her handkerchief in the air and almost threw herself
over the desk. "She is very great to-night—very
great indeed," whispered Miss Doctor Olivia Q. Fleabody to Lady George. Lady George was afraid to
ask her neighbour whether she understood one word
out of ten that were being spoken.

Great as the Baroness was, Lady George became
very tired of it all. The chair was hard and the room
was full of dust, and she could not get up. It was
worse than the longest and the worst sermon she had
ever heard. It seemed to her at last that there was
no reason why the Baroness should not go on forever. The woman liked it, and the people applauded
her. The poor victim had made up her mind that
there was no hope of cessation, and in doing so was
very nearly asleep, when, on a sudden, the Baroness
had finished and had thrown herself violently back
into her chair. "Baroness, believe me," said Dr.
Fleabody, stretching across Lady George, "it is the
greatest treat I ever had in my life." The Baroness
hardly condescended to answer the compliment. She
was at this moment so great a woman, at this moment
so immeasurably the greatest human being at any rate
in London, that it did not become her to acknowledge
single compliments. She had worked hard and was

very hot, but still she had sufficient presence of mind to remember her demeanour.

When the tumult was a little subsided, Lady Selina Protest got up to move a vote of thanks. She was sitting on the left-hand side of the chair, and rose so silently that Lady George had at first thought the affair was all over, and that they might go away. Alas, alas! there was more to be borne yet! Lady Selina spoke with a clear but low voice, and, though she was quite audible, and an earl's sister, did not evoke any enthusiasm. She declared that the thanks of every woman in England were due to the Baroness for her exertions, and of every man who wished to be regarded as the friend of women. But Lady Selina was very quiet, making no gesture, and was, indeed, somewhat flat. When she sat down no notice whatever was taken of her. Then very quickly, before Lady George had time to look about her, the Doctor was on her feet. It was her task to second the vote of thanks, but she was far too experienced an occupant of platforms to waste her precious occasion simply on so poor a task. She began by declaring that never in her life had a duty been assigned to her more consonant to her taste than that of seconding a vote of thanks to a woman so eminent, so humanitarian, and at the same time so essentially a female as the Baroness Banmann. Lady George, who knew nothing about speaking, felt at once that here was a speaker who could at any rate make herself audible and intelligible. Then the Doctor broke away into the general subject, with special allusions to the special matter of female architecture, and went on for twenty minutes without dropping a word. There was a moment in which she had almost made Lady George think that women ought to build houses. Her dislike to the American twang had vanished, and she was almost sorry when Miss Doctor Fleabody resumed her seat.

But it was after that—after the Baroness had occupied another ten minutes in thanking the British public for the thanks that had been given to herself—that the supreme emotion of the evening came to Lady George. Again she had thought, when the Baroness a second time rolled back to her chair, that the time for departure had come. Many in the hall, indeed, were already going, and she could not quite understand why no one on the platform had as yet moved. Then came that bald-headed old gentleman to her, to her very self, and suggested to her that she—she, Lady George Germain, who the other day was Mary Lovelace, the Brotherton girl—should stand up and make a speech! "There is to be a vote of thanks to Miss Mildmay as chairwoman," said the bald-headed old man, "and we hope, Lady George, that you will favour us with a few words."

Her heart utterly gave way and the blood flew into her cheeks, and she thoroughly repented of having come to this dreadful place. She knew that she could not do it, though the world were to depend upon it; but she did not know whether the bald-headed old gentleman might not have the right of insisting on it. And then all the people were looking at her as the horrible old man was pressing his request over her shoulder. "Oh," she said, "no, I can't. Pray don't. Indeed I can't—and I won't." The idea had come upon her that it was necessary that she should be very absolute. The old man retired meekly, and himself made the speech in honour of Aunt Ju.

As they were going away Lady George found that she was to have the honour of conveying the Baroness to her lodgings in Conduit Street. This was all very well, as there was room for three in the brougham, and she was not ill-pleased to hear the ecstacies of Aunt Ju about the lecture. Aunt Ju declared that she had agreed with every word that had been uttered. Aunt Ju thought that the cause was flourishing. Aunt Ju was of opinion that women in England would before long be able to sit in Parliament and practise in the Law Courts. Aunt Ju was thoroughly in earnest; but the Baroness had expended her energy in the lecture, and was more inclined to talk about persons. Lady George was surprised to hear her say that this young man was a very handsome young man, and that old man a very nice old man. She was almost in love with Mr. Spuffin, the bald-headed gentleman usher; and, when she was particular in asking whether Mr. Spuffin was married, Lady George could hardly think that this was the woman who had been so eloquent on the " infairiority of de tyrant saix."

But it was not till Aunt Ju had been dropped in Green Street, and the conversation fell upon Lady George herself, that the difficulty began. " You no speak?" asked the Baroness.

" What, in public? Not for the world!"

" You wrong dere. Noting so easy. Say just as you please, only say it vera loud. And alvays abuse somebody or someting. You s'ould try."

" I would sooner die," said Lady George. " Indeed, I should be dead before I could utter a word. Isn't it odd how that lady Doctor could speak like that."

"De American young woman! Dey have de impudence of—of—everything you please; but it come to noting."

"But she spoke well."

"Dear me, no; noting at all. Dere was noting but vords, vords, vords. Tank you; here I am. Mind you come again, and you shall learn to speak."

Lady George, as she was driven home, was lost in her ability to understand it all. She had thought that the Doctor spoke the best of all, and now she was told that it was nothing. She did not yet understand that even people so great as female orators, so nobly humanitarian as the Baroness Banmann, can be jealous of the greatness of others.

CHAPTER XVIII

LORD GEORGE UP IN LONDON

LORD GEORGE returned to town the day after the lecture, and was not altogether pleased that his wife should have gone to the Disabilities. She thought, indeed, that he did not seem to be in a humour to be pleased with anything. . His mind was thoroughly disturbed by the coming of his brother, and perplexed with the idea that something must be done, though he knew not what. And he was pervaded by a feeling that in the present emergency it behoved him to watch his own steps, and more especially those of his wife. An anonymous letter had reached Lady Sarah, signed, "A Friend of the Family," in which it was stated that the Marquis of Brotherton had allied himself to the highest blood that Italy knew, marrying into a family that had been noble before English nobility had existed, whereas his brother had married the granddaughter of a stable-keeper and a tallow-chandler. This letter had, of course, been shown to Lord George; and, though he and his sisters agreed in looking upon it as an emanation from their enemy, the new Marchioness, it still gave them to understand that she, if attacked, ' would be prepared to attack again. And Lord George was open to attack on the side indicated. He was, on the whole, satisfied with his wife. She was ladylike, soft, pretty, well-mannered, and good to him. But her grandfathers had been stable-keepers and

tallow-chandlers. Therefore it was specially impera-
tive that she should be kept from injurious influences.
Lady Selina Protest and Aunt Ju, who were both
well-born, might take liberties; but not so his wife.
"I don't think that was a very nice place to go to,
Mary."

"It wasn't nice at all, but it was very funny. I
never saw such a vulgar creature as the Baroness,
throwing herself about and wiping her face."

"Why should you go and see a vulgar creature
throw herself about and wipe her face."

"Why should anybody do it? One likes to see
what is going on, I suppose. The woman's vulgarity
could not hurt me, George."

"It could do you no good."

"Lady Selina Protest was there, and I went with
Miss Mildmay."

"Two old maids who have gone crazy about
Women's Rights because nobody has married them.
The whole thing is distasteful to me, and I hope you
will not go there again."

"That I certainly shall not, because it is very dull,"
said Mary.

"I hope also that, independently of that, my request would be enough."

"Certainly it would, George; but I don't know why
you should be so cross to me."

"I don't think that I have been cross; but I am
anxious, specially anxious. There are reasons why
I have to be very anxious in regard to you, and
why you have to be yourself more particular than
others."

"What reasons?" She asked this with a look of
bewildered astonishment. He was not prepared to

answer the question, and shuffled out of it, muttering some further words as to the peculiar difficulty of their position. Then he kissed her and left her, telling her that all would be well if she would be careful.

If she would be careful! All would be well if she would be careful! Why should there be need of more care on her part than on that of others? She knew that all this had reference in some way to that troublesome lady and troublesome baby who were about to be brought home; but she could not conceive how her conduct could be specially concerned. It was a sorrow to her that her husband should allow himself to be ruffled about the matter at all. It was a sorrow also that her father should do so. As to herself, she had an idea that if Providence chose to make her a Marchioness, Providence ought to be allowed to do it without any interference on her part. But it would be a double sorrow if she were told that she mustn't do this and mustn't do that because there was before her a dim prospect of being seated in a certain high place which was claimed and occupied by another person. And she was aware, too, that her husband had in very truth scolded her. The ladies at Manor Cross had scolded her before, but he had never done so. She had got away from Manor Cross, and had borne the scolding because the prospect of escape had been before her. But it would be very bad indeed if her husband should take to scold her. Then she thought that if Jack de Baron were married he would never scold his wife.

The Dean had not yet gone home, and in her discomfort she had recourse to him. She did not intend to complain of her husband to her father. Had any such idea occurred to her, she would have stamped it out at once, knowing that such a course would be both unloyal and unwise. But her father was so pleasant with her, so easy to be talked to, so easy to be understood, whereas her husband was almost mysterious—at any rate, gloomy and dark.

"Papa," she said, "what does George mean by saying that I ought to be more particular than other people?"

"Does he say so?"

"Yes; and he didn't like my going with that old woman to hear the other women. He says that I ought not to do it though anybody else might."

"I think you misunderstood him."

"No I didn't, papa."

"Then you had better imagine that he was tired with his journey, or that his stomach was a little out of order. Don't fret about such things, and, whatever you do, make the best of your husband."

"But how am I to know where I may go and where I mayn't? Am I to ask him everything first?"

"Don't be a child, whatever you do. You will soon find out what pleases him and what doesn't, and, if you manage well, what you do will please him. Whatever his manner may be, he is soft-hearted and affectionate."

"I know that, papa."

"If he says a cross word now and again, just let it go by. You should not suppose that words always mean what they seem to mean. I knew a man who used to tell his wife ever so often that he wished she were dead."

"Good heavens, papa!"

"Whenever he said so she always put a little magnesia into his beer, and things went on as comfortably as possible. Never magnify things, even to yourself. I don't suppose Lord George wants magnesia as yet, but you will understand what I mean." She said that she did; but she had not, in truth, quite comprehended the lesson as yet, nor could her father as yet teach it to her in plainer language.

On that same afternoon Lord George called in Berkeley Square and saw Mrs. Houghton. At this time the whole circle of people who were in any way connected with the Germain family, or who by the circumstances of their lives were brought within the pale of the Germain influence, were agog with the marriage of the Marquis. The newspapers had already announced the probable return of the Marquis and the coming of a new Marchioness and a new Lord Popenjoy. Occasion had been taken to give some details of the Germain family, and public allusion had even been made to the marriage of Lord George. These are days in which, should your wife's grandfather have ever been insolvent, some newspaper, in its catering for the public, will think it proper to recall the fact. The Dean's parentage had been alluded to, and the late Tallowax will, and the Tallowax property generally. It had also been declared that the Marchesa Luigi—now the present Marchioness—had been born an Orsini; and also, in another paper, the other fact (?) that she had been divorced from her late husband. This had already been denied by Mr. Knox, who had received a telegram from Florence ordering such denial to be made. It may, therefore, be conceived that the Germains were at this moment the subject of much conversation, and it may be understood that Mrs. Houghton, who considered herself to be on very con-

fidential terms with Lord George, should, as they were
alone, ask a few questions and express a little
sympathy.

"How does the dear Marchioness like the new
house?" she asked.

"It is tolerably comfortable."

"That Price is a darling, Lord George; I've known
him ever so long. And, of course, it is the dower-
house."

"It was the suddenness that disturbed my mother."

"Of course; and then the whole of it must have
gone against the grain with her. You bear it like
an angel."

"For myself, I don't know that I have anything
to bear."

"The whole thing is so dreadful. There are you
and your dear wife—everything just as it ought to
be—idolised by your mother, looked up to by the
whole country, the very man whom we wish to see
the head of such a family."

"Don't talk in that way, Mrs. Houghton."

"I know it is very distant; but still, I do feel
near enough related to you all to be justified in
being proud, and also to be justified in being ashamed.
What will they do about calling upon her?"

"My brother will, of course, come to my mother
first. Then Lady Sarah and one of her sisters will
go over. After that he will bring his wife to Cross
Hall if he pleases."

"I am so glad it is all settled; it is so much better.
But you know, Lord George—I must say it to you
as I would to my own brother, because my regard for
you is the same—I shall never think that that woman
is really his wife."

Lord George frowned heavily, but did not speak. "And I shall never think that that child is really Lord Popenjoy."

Neither did Lord George, in his heart of hearts believe that the Italian woman was a true Marchioness or the little child a true Lord Popenjoy; but he had confessed to himself that he had no adequate reason for such disbelief, and had perceived that it would become him to keep his opinion to himself. The Dean had been explicit with him, and that very explicitness had seemed to impose silence on himself. To his mother he had not whispered an idea of a suspicion. With his sisters he had been reticent, though he knew that Lady Sarah, at any rate, had her suspicions. But now an open expression of the accusation from so dear a friend as Mrs. Houghton —from the Adelaide de Baron whom he had so dearly loved—gratified him and almost tempted him into confidence. He had frowned at first, because his own family was to him so august that he could not but frown when anyone ventured to speak of it. Even crowned princes are driven to relax themselves on occasions, and Lord George Germain felt that he would almost like, just for once, to talk about his brothers and sisters as though they were Smiths and Joneses.

"It is very hard to know what to think," he said.

Mrs. Houghton at once saw that the field was open to her. She had ventured a good deal, and, knowing the man, had felt the danger of doing so; but she was satisfied now that she might say almost anything.

"But one is bound to think, isn't one? Don't you feel that? It is for the whole family that you have to act."

"What is to be done? I can't go and look up evidence."

"But a paid agent can. Think of Mary. Think of Mary's child—if she should have one." As she said this she looked rather anxiously into his face, being desirous of receiving an answer to a question which she did not quite dare to ask.

"Of course there's all that," he said, not answering the question.

"I can only just remember him, though papa knew him so well. But I suppose he has lived abroad till he has ceased to think and feel like an Englishman. Could anyone believe that a Marquis of Brotherton would have married a wife long enough ago to have a son over twelve months old, and never to have said a word about it to his brother or mother? I don't believe it."

"I don't know what to believe," said Lord George.

"And then to write in such a way about the house! Of course I hear it talked of by people who won't speak before you; but you ought to know."

"What do people say?"

"Everybody thinks that there is some fraud. There is old Mrs. Montacute Jones—I don't know anybody who knows everything better than she does—and she was saying that you would be driven by your duty to investigate the matter. 'I daresay he'd prefer to do nothing,' she said, 'but he must.' I felt that to be so true! Then Mr. Mildmay, who is so very quiet, said that there would be a lawsuit. Papa absolutely laughed at the idea of the boy being Lord Popenjoy, though he was always on good terms with your brother. Mr. Houghton says that nobody in society will give the child the name. Of course he's not very bright, but on matters like that he does know what he's talking about. When I hear all this I feel it a great deal, Lord George."

"I know what a friend you are."

"Indeed I am. I think very often what I might have been, but could not be; and, though I am not jealous of the happiness and honours of another, I am anxious for your happiness and your honours." He was sitting near her, on a chair facing the fire, while she was leaning back on the sofa. He went on staring at the hot coals, flattered, in some sort elate, but very disturbed. The old feeling was coming back upon him. She was not as pretty as his wife, but she was, he thought, more attractive, had more to say for herself, was more of a woman. She could pour herself into his heart and understand his feelings, whereas Mary did not sympathise with him at all in this great family trouble. But then Mary was, of course, his wife, and this woman was the wife of another man. He would be the last man in the world—so he would have told himself could he have spoken to himself on the subject—to bring disgrace on himself and misery on other people by declaring his love to another man's wife. He was the last man to do an injury to the girl whom he had made his own wife! But he liked being with his old love, and felt anxious to say a word to her that should have in it something just a little beyond the ordinary tenderness of friendship. The proper word, however, did not come to him at that moment. In such moments the proper word very often will not come. "You are not angry with me for saying so?" she asked.

"How can I be angry?"

"I don't think that there can have been such friendship as there was between you and me, and that it should fade and die away, unless there be some quarrel. You have not quarrelled with me?"

"Quarrelled with you? Never!"

"And you did love me once?" She at any rate knew how to find the tender words that were required for her purpose.

"Indeed I did."

"It did not last very long; did it, Lord George?"

"It was you that—that—— it was you that stopped it."

"Yes, it was I that stopped it. Perhaps I found it easier to—stop than I had expected. But it was all for the best. It must have been stopped. What could our lives have been? I was telling a friend of mine the other day, a lady, that there are people who cannot afford to wear hearts inside them. If I had jumped at your offer—and there was a moment when I would have done so——"

"Was there?"

"Indeed there was, George." The "George" didn't quite mean as much as it might have meant between others, because they were cousins. "But, if I had, the joint home of us all must have been in Mr. Price's farmhouse."

"It isn't a farmhouse."

"You know what I mean. But I want you to believe that I thought of you quite as much as of myself—more than of myself. I should at any rate have had brilliant hopes before me. I could understand what it would be to be the Marchioness of Brotherton. I could have borne much for years to think that at some future day I might hang on your arm in London *salons* as your wife. I had an ambition which now can never be gratified. I, too, can look on this picture and on that. But I had to decide for you as well as for myself, and I did decide that it was not for your welfare nor for your honour nor for your happiness to marry a woman who could not help you in the world." She was now leaning forward and almost touching his arm.

"I think sometimes that those most nearly concerned hardly know what a woman may have to endure because she is not selfish."

How could any man stand this? There are words which a man cannot resist from a woman, even though he knows them to be false. Lord George, though he did not quite believe that all these words were sincere, did think that there was a touch of sincerity about them—an opinion which the reader probably will not share with Lord George. "Have you suffered?" he said, putting out his hand to her and taking hers.

"Suffered!" she exclaimed, drawing away her hand, and sitting bolt upright and shaking her head. "Do you think that I am a fool, not to know! Do you suppose that I am blind and deaf? When I said that I was one of those who could not afford to wear a heart, did you imagine that I had been able to get rid of the article? No; it is here still," and she put her hand upon her side. "It is here still, and very troublesome I find it. I suppose the time will come when it will die away. They say that every plant will fade if it be shut in from the light, and never opened to the rains of heaven."

"Alas! alas!" he said. "I did not know that you would feel like that."

"Of course I feel. I have had something to do
with my life, and I have done this with it! Two
men have honoured me with their choice, and out
of the two I have chosen—Mr. Houghton. I comfort
myself by telling myself that I did right;—and I did
do right. But the comfort is not very comforting."
Still he sat looking at the fire. He knew that it was
open to him to get up and swear to her that she
still had his heart. She could not be angry with
him as she had said as much to himself. And he
almost believed at the moment that it was so. He
was quite alive to the attraction of the wickedness,
though, having a conscience, he was aware that the
wickedness should, if possible, be eschewed. There
is no romance in loving one's own wife. The knowledge that it is a duty deadens the pleasure. "I did
not mean to say all this," she exclaimed at last,
sobbing.

"Adelaide!" he said.

"Do you love me? You may love me without
anything wrong."

"Indeed I do." Then there was an embrace, and
after that he hurried away, almost without another
word.

CHAPTER XIX

"AFTER all, he's very dreary!" It was this that Adelaide Houghton spoke to herself as soon as Lord George had left her. No doubt the whole work of the interview had fallen on to her shoulders. He had at last been talked into saying that he loved her, and had then run away frightened by the unusual importance and tragic significance of his own words. "After all, he's very dreary!"

Mrs. Houghton wanted excitement. She probably did like Lord George as well as she liked anyone. Undoubtedly she would have married him had he been able to maintain her as she liked to be maintained. But, as he had been unable, she had taken Mr. Houghton without a notion on her part of making even an attempt to love him. When she said that she could not afford to wear a heart—and she had said so to various friends and acquaintances—she did entertain an idea that circumstances had used her cruelly, that she had absolutely been forced to marry a stupid old man, and that therefore some little freedom was due to her as a compensation. Lord George was Lord George, and might possibly some day be a marquis. He was at any rate a handsome man, and he had owed allegiance to her before he had transferred his homage to that rich little chit, Mary Lovelace. She was incapable of much passion, but she did feel that she owed it to herself to have some revenge on Mary Lovelace. The game as it stood had charms sufficient to induce her to go on with it; and yet, after all, he was dreary.

Such was the lady's feeling when she was left alone; but Lord George went away from the meeting almost overcome by the excitement of the occasion. To him the matter was of such stirring moment that he could not go home, could not even go to his club. He was so moved by his various feelings that he could only walk by himself and consider things. To her that final embrace had meant very little. What did it signify? He had taken her in his arms and kissed her forehead. It might have been her lips had he so pleased. But to him it had seemed to mean very much indeed. There was a luxury in it which almost intoxicated him, and a horror in it which almost quelled him. That she should so love him as to be actually subdued by her love could not but charm him. He had none of that strength which arms a man against flatterers; none of that experience which strengthens a man against female cajolery. It was to him very serious and very solemn. There might, perhaps, have been exaggeration in her mode of describing her feelings, but there could be no doubt in this—that he had held her in his arms and that she was another man's wife.

The wickedness of the thing was more wicked to him than the charm of it was charming. It was dreadful to him to think that he had done a thing of which he would have to be ashamed if the knowledge of it were brought to his wife's ears. That he should have to own himself to have been wrong to her would tear him to pieces! That he should lord it over her as a real husband, was necessary to

his happiness, and how can a man be a real lord
over a woman when he has had to confess his fault
to her, and to beg her to forgive him? A wife's
position with her husband may be almost improved
by such asking for pardon. It will enhance his tenderness. But the man is so lowered that neither of
them can ever forget the degradation. And, though
it might never come to that, though this terrible passion might be concealed from her, still it was a
grievance to him and a disgrace that he should have
anything to conceal. It was a stain in his own eyes
on his own nobility, a slur upon his escutcheon, a
taint in his hitherto unslobbered honesty; and then
the sin of it—the sin of it! To him it already sat
heavy on his conscience. In his ear, even now,
sounded that commandment which he weekly prayed
that he might be permitted to keep. While with her
there was hardly left a remembrance of the kiss which
he had imprinted on her brow, his lips were still
burning with the fever. Should he make up his mind,
now at once, that he would never, never see her again?
Should he resolve that he would write to her a moving tragic letter—not a love-letter—in which he would
set forth the horrors of unhallowed love, and tell her
that there must be a gulf between them, over which
neither must pass till age should have tamed their
passions! As he walked across the Park he meditated
what would be the fitting words for such a letter, and
almost determined that it should be written. Did
he not owe his first duty to his wife? and was he
not bound for her sake to take such a step? Then,
as he wandered alone in Kensington Gardens—for
it had taken him many steps, and occupied much
time to think of it all—there came upon him an idea

that perhaps the lady would not receive the letter in the proper spirit. Some idea occurred to him of the ridicule which would befall him should the lady at last tell him that he had really exaggerated matters. And then the letter might be shown to others. He did love the lady. With grief and shame and a stricken conscience he owned to himself that he loved her. But he could not quite trust her. And so, as he walked down towards the Albert Memorial, he made up his mind that he would not write the letter. But he also made up his mind—he thought that he made up his mind—that he would go no more alone to Berkeley Square.

As he walked on he suddenly came upon his wife walking with Captain de Baron, and he was immediately struck by the idea that his wife ought not to be walking in Kensington Gardens with Captain de Baron. The idea was so strong as altogether to expel from his mind for the moment all remembrance of Mrs. Houghton. He had been unhappy before because he was conscious that he was illtreating his wife, but now he was almost more disturbed because it seemed to him to be possible that his wife was illtreating him. He had left her but a few minutes ago—he thought of it now as being but a few minutes since—telling her with almost his last word that she was specially bound, more bound than other women, to mind her own conduct—and here she was walking in Kensington Gardens with a man whom all the world called Jack de Baron! As he approached them his brow became clouded, and she could see that it was so. She could not but fear that her companion would see it also. Lord George was thinking how to address them, and had already determined on tucking his wife under his own arm and carrying her off before he saw that a very little way behind them the Dean was walking with—Adelaide Houghton herself. Though he had been more than an hour wandering about the Park he could not understand that the lady whom he had left in her own house so recently, in apparently so great a state of agitation, should be there also, in her best bonnet and quite calm. He had no words immediately at command, but she was as voluble as ever.

"Doesn't this seem odd?" she said. "Why, it is not ten minutes since you left me in Berkeley Square. I wonder what made you cóme here?"

"What made you come?"

"Jack brought me here. If it were not for Jack I should never walk or ride or do anything, except sit in a stupid carriage. And just at the gate of the gardens we met the Dean and Lady George."

This was very simple and straightforward. There could be no doubt of the truth of it all. Lady George had come out with her father and nothing could be more as it ought to be. As to "Jack" and the lady, he did not, at any rate as yet, feel himself justified in being angry at that arrangement. But nevertheless he was disturbed. His wife had been laughing when he first saw her, and Jack had been talking, and they had seemed to be very happy together. The Dean no doubt was there; but still the fact remained that Jack had been laughing and talking with his wife. He almost doubted whether his wife ought, under any circumstances, to laugh in Kensington Gardens. And then the Dean was so indiscreet! He, Lord George, could not of course forbid his wife to walk with her father; but the Dean

had no idea that any real looking after was necessary for anybody. He at once gave his arm to his
wife, but in two minutes she had dropped it. They
were on the steps of the Albert Memorial, and it
was perhaps natural that she should do so. But he
hovered close to her as they were looking at the fig-
ures, and was uneasy. "I think it's the prettist thing
in London," said the Dean, "one of the prettiest things
in the world."

"Don't you find it very cold?" said Lord George,
who did not at the present moment care very much
for the fine arts.

"We have been walking quick," said Mrs. Houghton, "and have enjoyed it." The Dean with the two
others had now passed round one of the corners.
"I wonder," she went on, "I do wonder how it has
come to pass that we should be brought together
again so soon!"

"We both happened to come the same way," said
Lord George, who was still thinking of his wife.

"Yes; that must have been it. Though is it not
a strange coincidence? My mind has been so flurried
that I was glad to get out into the fresh air. When
shall I see you again?" He couldn't bring himself
to say—never. There would have been a mock-tragic
element about the single word which even he felt.
And yet, here on the steps of the monument, there
was hardly an opportunity for him to explain at
length the propriety of their both agreeing to be
severed. "You wish to see me, don't you?" she asked.

"I hardly know what to say."

"But you love me!" She was now close to him,
and there was no one else near enough to interfere.
She was pressing close up to him, and he was sadly

ashamed of himself. And yet he did love her. He thought that she had never looked so well as at the present moment. "Say that you love me," she said, stamping her foot almost imperiously.

"You know I do, but——"

"But what?"

"I had better come to you again and tell you all." The words were no sooner out of his mouth than he remembered that he had resolved that he would never go to her again. But yet, after what had passed, something must be done. He had also made up his mind that he wouldn't write. He had quite made up his mind about that. The words that are written remain. It would perhaps be better that he should go to her and tell her everything.

"Of course you will come again," she said. "What is it ails you? You are unhappy because she is here with my cousin Jack?" It was intolerable to him that anyone should suspect him of jealousy. "Jack has a way of getting intimate with people, but it means nothing." It was dreadful to him that an allusion should be made to the possibility of anybody "meaning anything" with his wife.

Just at this moment Jack's voice was heard coming back round the corner, and also the laughter of the Dean. Captain de Baron had been describing the persons represented on the base of the monument, and had done so after some fashion of his own that had infinitely amused not only Lady George, but her father also. "You ought to be appointed Guide to the Memorial," said the Dean.

"If Lady George will give me a testimonial, no doubt I might get it, Dean," said Jack.

"I don't think you know anything about any of

them," said Lady George. "I'm sure you've told me wrong about two. You're the last man in the world that ought to be a guide to anything."

"Will you come and be guide, and I'll just sweep the steps?"

Lord George heard the last words, and allowed himself to be annoyed at them, though he felt them to be innocent. He knew that his wife was having a game of pleasant play, like a child with a pleasant playfellow. But then he was not satisfied that his wife should play like a child, and certainly not with such a playfellow. He doubted whether his wife ought to allow playful intimacy from any man. Marriage was to him a very serious thing. Was he not prepared to give up a real passion because he had made this other woman his wife? In thinking over all this his mind was not very logical, but he did feel that he was justified in exacting particularly strict conduct from her because he was going to make Mrs. Houghton understand that they two, though they loved each other, must part. If he could sacrifice so much for his wife, surely she might sacrifice something for him.

They returned all together to Hyde Park Corner, and then they separated. Jack went away towards Berkeley Square with his cousin; the Dean got himself taken in a cab to his club; and Lord George walked his wife down Constitution Hill towards their own home. He felt it to be necessary that he should say something to his wife; but, at the same time, was specially anxious that he should give her no cause to suspect him of jealousy. Nor was he jealous, in the ordinary sense of the word. He did not suppose for a moment that his wife was in love with

Jack de Baron, or Jack with his wife. But he did think that whereas she had very little to say to her own husband, she had a great deal to say to Jack. And he was sensible, also, of a certain unbecomingness in such amusement on her part. She had to struggle upwards, so as to be able to sustain properly the position and dignity of Lady George Germain and the possible dignity of the Marchioness of Brotherton. She ought not to want playfellows. If she would really have learned the names of all those artists on the base of the Memorial, as she might so easily have done, there would have been something in it. A lady ought to know, at any rate, the names of such men. But she had allowed this Jack to make a joke of it all, and had rather liked the joke. And the Dean had laughed loud—more like the son of a stable-keeper than a Dean. Lord George was almost more angry with the Dean than with his wife. The Dean, when at Brotherton, did maintain a certain amount of dignity; but here, up in London, he seemed to be intent only on "having a good time," like some schoolboy out on a holiday.

"Were you not a little loud when you were on the steps of the Memorial?" he said.

"I hope not, George; not too loud."

"A lady should never be in the least loud, nor for the matter of that would a gentleman either, if he knew what he was about."

She walked on a little way, leaning on his arm in silence, considering whether he meant anything by what he was saying, and how much he meant. She felt almost sure that he did mean something disagreeable, and that he was scolding her. "I don't quite know what you mean by loud, George. We were talking, and of course wanted to make each other hear. I believe with some people loud means—vulgar. I hope you didn't mean that."

He certainly would not tell his wife that she was vulgar. "There is," he said, "a manner of talking which leads people on to—to—being boisterous."

"Boisterous, George! Was I boisterous?"

"I think your father was a little."

She felt herself blush beneath her veil as she answered: "Of course, if you tell me anything about myself, I will endeavour to do as you tell me; but, as for papa, I am sure he knows how to behave himself. I don't think he ought to be found fault with because he likes to amuse himself."

"And that Captain de Baron was very loud," said Lord George, conscious that, though his ground might be weak in reference to the Dean, he could say what he pleased about Jack de Baron.

"Young men do laugh and talk, don't they, George?"

"What they do in their barracks, or when they are together, is nothing to you or me. What such a one may do when he is in company with my wife is very much to me, and ought to be very much to you."

"George," she said, again pausing for a moment, "do you mean to tell me that I have misbehaved myself? Because, if so, speak it out at once."

"My dear, that is a foolish question for you to ask. I have said nothing about misbehaviour, and you ought, at any rate, to wait till I have done so. I should be very sorry to use such a word, and do not think that I shall ever have occasion. But surely you will admit that there may be practices, and man-

ners, and customs on which I am at liberty to speak
to you. I am older than you."

"Husbands, of course, are older than their wives,
but wives generally know what they are about quite
as well as their husbands."

"Mary, that isn't the proper way to take what
I say. You have a very peculiar place to fill in the
world—a place for which your early life could not
give you the very fittest training."

"Then why did you put me there?"

"Because of my love, and also because I had no
doubt whatever as to your becoming fit. There is
a levity which is often pretty and becoming in a girl,
in which a married woman in some ranks of life
may, perhaps, innocently indulge, but which is not
appropriate to higher positions."

"This is all because I laughed when Captain de
Baron mispronounced the men's names. I don't know
anything peculiar in my position. One would suppose that I was going to be made a sort of female
bishop, or to sit all my life as a chairwoman, like
that Miss Mildmay. Of course I laugh when things
are said that make me laugh. And as for Captain de
Baron, I think he is very nice. Papa likes him, and
he is always at the Houghtons', and I cannot agree
that he was loud and vulgar, or boisterous, because he
made a few innocent jokes in Kensington Gardens."

He perceived now, for the first time since he had
known her, that she had a temper of her own, which
he might find some difficulty in controlling. She had
endured gently enough his first allusions to herself,
but had risen up in wrath against him from the moment he had spoken disparagingly of her father. At
the moment he had nothing further to say. He had

used what eloquence there was in him, what words
he had collected together, and then walked home in
silence. But his mind was full of the matter; and,
though he made no further allusion on that day,
or for some subsequent days either to this conversation or to his wife's conduct in the Park, he had it
always in his mind. He must be the master, and in
order that he might be master the Dean must be as
little as possible in the house. And that intimacy
with Jack de Baron must be crushed—if only that she
might be taught that he intended to be master.

Two or three days passed by, and during those
two or three days he did not go to Berkeley Square.

CHAPTER XX

In the middle of the next week the Dean went back to Brotherton. Before starting he had an interview with Lord George which was not altogether pleasant; but otherwise he had thoroughly enjoyed his visit. On the day on which he started he asked his host what inquiries he intended to set on foot in reference to the validity of the Italian marriage and the legitimacy of the Italian baby. Now Lord George had himself in the first instance consulted the Dean on this very subject, and was therefore not entitled to be angry at having it again mentioned; but, nevertheless, he resented the question as an interference. " I think," he replied, " that at present nothing had better be said upon the subject."

" I cannot agree with you there, George."

" Then I am afraid I must ask you to be silent without agreeing with me."

The Dean felt this to be intentionally uncivil. They two were in a boat together. The injury to be done, if there were an injury, would affect the wife as much as the husband. The baby which might some day be born, and which might be robbed of his inheritance, would be as much the grandchild of the Dean of Brotherton as of the old Marquis. And then perhaps there was present to the Dean some unacknowledged feeling that he was paying and would have to pay for the boat. Much as he revered the rank, he was not disposed to be snubbed by his son-in-law, because his son-in-law was a nobleman. "You mean to tell me that I am to hold my tongue," he said angrily.

"For the present I think we had both better do so."

"That may be, as regards any discussion of the matter with outsiders. I am not at all disposed to act apart from you on a subject of such importance to us both. If you tell me that you are advised this way or that, I should not, without very strong ground, put myself in opposition to that advice; but I do expect that you will let me know what is being done."

"Nothing is being done."

"And also that you will not finally determine on doing nothing without consulting me." Lord George drew himself up and bowed, but made no further reply; and then the two parted, the Dean resolving that he would be in town again before long, and Lord George resolving that the Dean should spend as little time as possible in his house. Now, there had been an undertaking, after a sort, made by the Dean —a compact with his daughter, contracted in a jocose fashion—which in the existing circumstances was like to prove troublesome. There had been a question of expenditure when the house was furnished— whether there should or should not be a carriage kept. Lord George had expressed an opinion that their joint means would not suffice to keep a carriage. Then the Dean had told his daughter that he would allow her £300 a year for her own expenses, to include the brougham—for it was to be no more than a brougham —during the six months they would be in London, and that he would regard this as his subscription

towards the household. Such a mode of being generous to his own child was pretty enough. Of course
the Dean would be a welcome visitor. Equally, of
course, a son-in-law may take any amount of money
from a father-in-law as a portion of his wife's fortune.
Lord George, though he had suffered some inward
qualms, had found nothing in the arrangement to
which he could object while his friendship with the
Deanery was close and pleasant. But now, as the
Dean took his departure, and as Mary, while embracing her father, said something of his being soon back,
Lord George remembered the compact with inward
grief, and wished there had been no brougham.

In the meantime he had not been to Berkeley
Square; nor was he at all sure that he would go
there. A distant day had been named, before that
exciting interview in the square, on which the
Houghtons were to dine in Munster Court. The
Mildmays were also to be there, and Mrs. Montacute
Jones, and old Lord Parachute, Lord George's uncle.
That would be a party, and there would be no danger
of a scene then. He had almost determined that, in
spite of his promise, he would not go to Berkeley
Square before the dinner. But Mrs. Houghton was
not of the same mind. A promise on such a subject
was a sacred thing, and therefore she wrote the following note to Lord George at his club. The secrecy
which some correspondence requires certainly tends
to make a club a convenient arrangement. "Why
don't you come as you said you would?—A." In
olden times, fifteen or twenty years ago, when tele-
graph wires were still young, and messages were confined to diplomatic secrets, horse-racing, and the rise
and fall of stocks, lovers used to indulge in rapturous

them," said Lady George. "I'm sure you've told
me wrong about two. You're the last man in the
world that ought to be a guide to anything."

"Will you come and be guide, and I'll just sweep
the steps?"

Lord George heard the last words, and allowed himself to be annoyed at them, though he felt them to
be innocent. He knew that his wife was having a
game of pleasant play, like a child with a pleasant
playfellow. But then he was not satisfied that his
wife should play like a child, and certainly not with
such a playfellow. He doubted whether his wife ought
to allow playful intimacy from any man. Marriage
was to him a very serious thing. Was he not prepared to give up a real passion because he had made
this other woman his wife? In thinking over all
this his mind was not very logical, but he did feel
that he was justified in exacting particularly strict
conduct from her because he was going to make Mrs.
Houghton understand that they two, though they loved
each other, must part. If he could sacrifice so much
for his wife, surely she might sacrifice something for
him.

They returned all together to Hyde Park Corner,
and then they separated. Jack went away towards
Berkeley Square with his cousin; the Dean got himself taken in a cab to his club; and Lord George
walked his wife down Constitution Hill towards their
own home. He felt it to be necessary that he should
say something to his wife; but, at the same time,
was specially anxious that he should give her no cause
to suspect him of jealousy. Nor was he jealous, in
the ordinary sense of the word. He did not suppose for a moment that his wife was in love with

Jack de Baron, or Jack with his wife. But he did think that whereas she had very little to say to her own husband, she had a great deal to say to Jack. And he was sensible, also, of a certain unbecomingness in such amusement on her part. She had to struggle upwards, so as to be able to sustain properly the position and dignity of Lady George Germain and the possible diginty of the Marchioness of Brotherton. She ought not to want playfellows. If she would really have learned the names of all those artists on the base of the Memorial, as she might so easily have done, there would have been something in it. A lady ought to know, at any rate, the names of such men. But she had allowed this Jack to make a joke of it all, and had rather liked the joke. And the Dean had laughed loud—more like the son of a stable-keeper than a Dean. Lord George was almost more angry with the Dean than with his wife. The Dean, when at Brotherton, did maintain a certain amount of dignity; but here, up in London, he seemed to be intent only on "having a good time," like some schoolboy out on a holiday.

"Were you not a little loud when you were on the steps of the Memorial?" he said.

"I hope not, George; not too loud."

"A lady should never be in the least loud, nor for the matter of that would a gentleman either, if he knew what he was about."

She walked on a little way, leaning on his arm in silence, considering whether he meant anything by what he was saying, and how much he meant. She felt almost sure that he did mean something disagreeable, and that he was scolding her. "I don't quite know what you mean by loud, George. We were on the floor, feeling that, had he been master of the occasion, he would have got rid of it less awkwardly. "I shouldn't wonder if Mary were to be here by-and-by. There was a sort of engagement that she and Jack de Baron were to come and play bagatelle in the back drawing-room; but Jack never comes if he says he will, and I daresay she has forgotten all about it."

He found that his purpose was altogether upset. In the first place, he could hardly begin about her unfortunate passion when she received him just as though he were an ordinary acquaintance; and then the whole tenor of his mind was altered by this allusion to Jack de Baron. Had it come to this, that he could not get through a day without having Jack de Baron thrown at his head? He had from the first been averse to living in London; but this was much worse than he had expected. Was it to be endured that his wife should make appointments to play bagatelle with Jack de Baron by way of passing her time? "I had heard nothing about it," he said with gloomy, truthful significance. It was impossible for him to lie even by a glance of his eye or a tone of his voice. He told it all at once; how unwilling he was that his wife should come out on purpose to meet this man, and how little able he felt himself to prevent it.

"Of course, dear Mary has to amuse herself," said the lady, answering the man's look rather than his words. "And why should she not?"

"I don't know that bagatelle is a very improving occupation."

"Or Jack a very improving companion, perhaps. But I can tell you, George, that there are more dangerous companions than poor Jack. And then, Mary, who is the sweetest, dearest young woman I know, is not impulsive in that way. She is such a very child. I don't suppose she understands what passion means. She has the gaiety of a lark, and the innocence. She is always soaring upwards, which is so beautiful."

"I don't know that there is much soaring upwards in bagatelle."

"Nor in Jack de Baron, perhaps. But we must take all that as we find it. Of course Mary will have to amuse herself. She will never live such a life as your sisters live at Manor Cross. The word that best describes her disposition is—gay. But she is not mischievous."

"I hope not."

"Nor is she—passionate. You know what I mean." He did know what she meant, and was lost in amazement at finding that one woman, in talking of another, never contemplated the idea that passion could exist in a wife for her husband. He was to regard himself as safe, not because his wife loved himself, but because it was not necessary to her nature to be in love with anyone! "You need not be afraid," she went on to say. "I know Jack *au fond*. He tells me everything; and should there be anything to fear, I will let you know at once."

But what had all this to do with the momentous occasion which had brought him to Berkeley Square? He was almost beginning to be sore at heart because she had not thrown herself into his arms. There was no repetition of that "But you do love me?" which had been so very alarming, but at the same time so very exciting, on the steps of the Albert

Memorial. And then there seemed to be a proba-
bility that the words which he had composed with so
much care at his club would be altogether wasted.
He owed it to himself to do or to say something, to
allude in some way to his love and hers. He could
not allow himself to be brought there in a flurry
of excitement, and there to sit till it was time for him
to go, just as though it were an ordinary morning
visit. "You bade me come," he said, "and so I
came."

"Yes, I did bid you come. I would always have
you come."

"That can hardly be; can it?"

"My idea of a friend—of a man friend, I mean,
and a real friend—is someone to whom I can say
everything, who will do everything for me, who will
come if I bid him, and will like to stay and talk to
me just as long as I will let him; who will tell me
everything, and as to whom I may be sure that he
likes me better than anybody else in the world, though
he perhaps doesn't tell me so above once a month.
And then in return——"

"Well, what in return?"

"I should think a good deal about him, you know;
but I shouldn't want always to be telling him that
I was thinking about him. He ought to be contented
with knowing how much he was to me. I suppose
that would not suffice for you?"

Lord George was disposed to think that it would
suffice, and that the whole matter was now being
represented to him in a very different light than
that in which he had hitherto regarded it. The word
"friend" softened down so many asperities! With
such a word in his mind he need not continually

scare himself with the decalogue. All the pleasure might be there, and the horrors altogether omitted. There would, indeed, be no occasion for his eloquence; but he had already become conscious that at this interview his eloquence could not be used. She had given everything so different a turn! "Why not suffice for me?" he said. "Only this—that all I did for my friend I should expect her to do for me."

"But that is unreasonable. Who doesn't see that in the world at large men have the best of it almost in everything. The husband is not only justified in being a tyrant, but becomes contemptible if he is not so. A man has his pockets full of money; a woman is supposed to take what he gives her. A man has all manner of amusements."

"What amusements have I?"

"You can come to me."

"Yes, I can do that."

"I cannot go to you. But when you come to me —if I am to believe that I am really your friend— then I am to be the tyrant of the moment. Is it not so? Do you think you would find me a hard tyrant? I own to you freely that there is nothing in the world I like so much as your society. Do I not earn by that a right to some obedience from you, to some special observance?"

All this was so different from what he had expected, and so much more pleasant! As far as he could look into it and think of it at the pressure of the moment he did not see any reason why it should not be as she proposed. There was clearly no need for those prepared words. There had been one embrace—an embrace that was objectionable because, had either his wife seen it or Mr. Houghton, he would have been

forced to own himself wrong; but that had come from
sudden impulse, and need not be repeated. This that
was now proposed to him was friendship, and not love.
"You shall have all observance," he said with his
sweetest smile.

"And as to obedience? But you are a man, and
therefore must not be pressed too hard. And now
I may tell you what is the only thing that can make
me happy, and the absence of which would make me
miserable."

"What thing?"

"Your society." He blushed up to his eyes as he
heard this. "Now that, I think, is a very pretty
speech, and I expect something equally pretty from
you." He was much embarrassed, but was at the
moment delivered from his embarrassment by the
entrance of his wife. "Here she is," said Mrs.
Houghton, getting up from her chair. "We have
been just talking about you, my dear. If you have
come for bagatelle, you must play with Lord George,
for Jack de Baron isn't here."

"But I haven't come for bagatelle."

"So much the better, for I doubt whether Lord
George would be very good at it. I have been made
to play so much that I hate the very sound of the
balls."

"I didn't expect to find you here," said Mary, turning to her husband.

"Nor I you, till Mrs. Houghton said that you were
coming."

After that there was nothing of interest in their
conversation. Jack did not come, and after a few
minutes Lord George proposed to his wife that they
should return home together. Of course she assented,

and as soon as they were in the brougham made a
little playful attack upon him. "You are becoming
fond of Berkeley Square, I think."

"Mrs. Houghton is a friend of mine, and I am
fond of my friends," he said gravely.

"Oh, of course."

"You went there to play that game with Captain
de Baron."

"No, I didn't! I did nothing of the kind."

"Were you not there by appointment?"

"I told her that I should probably call. We were
to have gone to some shop together, only it seems
she has changed her mind. Why do you tell me that
I had gone there to play some game with Captain de
Baron?"

"Bagatelle."

"Bagatelle, or anything else! It isn't true. I
have played bagatelle with Captain de Baron, and I
daresay I may again. Why shouldn't I?"

"And if so, would probably make some appointment
to play with him?"

"Why not?"

"That was all I said. What I suggested you had
done is what you declare you will do."

"But I had done nothing of the kind. I know very
well, from the tone of your voice, that you meant
to scold me. You implied that I had done something
wrong. If I had done it, it wouldn't be wrong, as
far as I know. But your scolding me about it when
I hadn't done it at all is very hard to bear."

"I didn't scold you."

"Yes you did, George. I understand your voice
and your look. If you mean to forbid me to play
bagatelle with Captain de Baron, or Captain any-

body else, or to talk with Mr. This, or to laugh with Major That, tell me so at once. If I know what you want, I will do it. But I must say that I shall feel it very, very hard, if I cannot take care of myself in such matters as that. If you are going to be jealous, I shall wish that I were dead."

Then she burst out crying; and he, though he would not quite own that he had been wrong, was forced to do so practically by little acts of immediate tenderness.

CHAPTER XXI

THE MARQUIS COMES HOME

Some little time after the middle of April, when the hunting was all over, and Mr. Price had sunk down into his summer insignificance, there came half-a-dozen telegrams to Manor Cross, from Italy, from Mr. Knox, and from a certain managing tradesman in London to say that the Marquis was coming a fortnight sooner than he had expected. Everything was at sixes and sevens. Everything was in a ferment. Everybody about Manor Cross seemed to think that the world was coming to an end. But none of these telegrams were addressed to any of the Germain family, and the last people in the county who heard of this homeward rush of the Marquis were the ladies at Cross Hall, and they heard it from Lord George, upon whom Mr. Knox called in London; supposing, however, when he did call that Lord George had already received full information on the subject. Lord George's letter to Lady Sarah was full of dismay, full of horror. "As he has not taken the trouble to communicate his intentions to me, I shall not go down to receive him." "You will know how to deal with the matter, and will, I am sure, support our mother in this terrible trial." "I think that the child should, at any rate, at first be acknowledged by you all as Lord Popenjoy." "We have to regard, in the first place the honour of the family. No remissness on his part should induce us to forget for a moment what is due to the title, the property and the name." The letter was very long, and was full of sententious instructions, such as the above. But the purport of it was to tell the ladies at Cross Hall that they must go through the first burden of receiving the Marquis without any assistance from himself.

The Dean heard of the reported arrival some days before the family did so. It was rumoured in Brotherton, and the rumour reached the Deanery. But he thought that there was nothing that he could do on the spur of the moment. He perfectly understood the condition of Lord George's mind, and perceived that it would not be expedient for him to interfere quite on the first moment. As soon as the Marquis should have settled himself in his house of course he would call; and when the Marquis had settled himself, and when the world had begun to recognise the fact that the Marquis, with his Italian Marchioness, and his little Italian, so-called Popenjoy, were living at Manor Cross, then—if he saw his way—the Dean would bestir himself.

And so the Marquis arrived. He reached the Brotherton station with his wife, a baby, a lady's maid, a nurse, a valet, a cook, and a courier, about three o'clock in the afternoon; and the whole crowd of them were carried off in their carriages to Manor Cross. A great many of the inhabitants of Brotherton were there to see, for this coming of the Marquis had been talked of far and wide. He himself took no notice of the gathering people—was perhaps unaware that there was any gathering. He and his wife got into one carriage; the nurse, the lady's-maid, and the baby into a second; the valet, and courier, and cook into a third. The world of Brotherton saw them, and the world of

Brotherton observed that the lady was very old and very ugly. Why on earth could he have married such a woman as that, and then have brought her home! That was the exclamation which was made by Brotherton in general.

It was soon ascertained by everyone about Manor Cross that the Marchioness could not speak a word of English, nor could any of the newly-imported servants do so, with the exception of the courier, who was supposed to understand all languages. There was, therefore, an absolutely divided household. It had been thought better that the old family housekeeper, Mrs. Toff, should remain in possession. Through a long life she had been devoted to the old marchioness and to the ladies of the family generally; but she would have been useless at their new home, and there was an idea that Manor Cross could not be maintained without her. It might also be expedient to have a friend in the enemy's camp. Other English servants had been provided—a butler, two footmen, a coachman, and the necessary house-maids and kitchenmaids. It had been stated that the Marquis would bring his own cook. There were, therefore, at once two parties, at the head of one of which was Mrs. Toff, and at the head of the other the courier —who remained, none of the English people knew why.

For the first three days the Marchioness showed herself to no one. It was understood that the fatigues of the journey had oppressed her, and that she chose to confine herself to two or three rooms upstairs, which had been prepared for her. Mrs. Toff, strictly obeying orders which had come from Cross Hall, sent up her duty, and begged to know whether she should wait

upon "my lady." My lady sent down word that she
didn't want to see Mrs. Toff. These messages had to
be filtered through the courier, who was specially odious
to Mrs. Toff. His lordship was almost as closely se-
cluded as her ladyship. He did, indeed, go out to the
stables, wrapped up in furs, and found fault with everything he saw there. And he had himself driven round
the park. But he did not get up on any of these days till
noon, and took all his meals by himself. The English servants averred that during the whole of this
time he never once saw the Marchioness or the baby;
but then the English servants could not very well have
known what he saw or what he did not see.

But this was very certain, that during those three
days he did not go to Cross Hall, or see anyone of
his own family. Mrs. Toff, in the gloaming of the
evening, on the third day, hurried across the park to
see the young ladies, as she still called them. Mrs.
Toff thought that it was all very dreadful. She didn't
know what was being done in those apartments. She
had never set her eyes upon the baby. She didn't
feel sure that there was any baby at all, though John
—John was one of the English servants—had seen a
bundle come into the house. Wouldn't it be natural
and right that any real child should be carried out
to take the air? "And then all manner of messes
were," said Mrs. Toff, "prepared up in the closed
room." Mrs. Toff didn't believe in anything, except
that everything was going to perdition. The Marchioness was intent on asking after the health and appearance of her son, but Mrs. Toff declared that she
hadn't been allowed to catch a sight of " my lord."
Mrs. Toff's account was altogether very lachrymose.
She spoke of the Marquis, of course, with the utmost

respect. But she was sufficiently intimate with the ladies to treat the baby and its mother with all the scorn of an unturned nose. Nor was the name of Popenjoy once heard from her lips.

But what were the ladies to do? On the evening of the third day Lady Sarah wrote to her brother George, begging him to come down to them. "The matter was so serious that he was," said Lady Sarah, "bound to lend the strength of his presence to his mother and sisters." But on the fourth morning Lady Sarah sent over a note to her brother the Marquis.

"DEAR BROTHERTON,—We hope that you and your wife and little boy have arrived well, and have found things comfortable. Mamma is most anxious to see you—as of course we all are. Will you not come over to us to-day? I daresay my sister-in-law may be too fatigued to come out as yet. I need not tell you that we are very anxious to see your little Popenjoy.   "Your affectionate sister,
                "SARAH GERMAIN."

It may be seen from this that the ladies contemplated peace, if peace were possible. But in truth, the nature of the letter, though not the words, had been dictated by the Marchioness. She was intent upon seeing her son, and anxious to acknowledge her grandchild. Lady Sarah had felt her position to be very difficult, but had perceived that no temporary acceptance by them of the child would at all injure her brother George's claim, should Lord George set up a claim; and so, in deference to the old lady, the peaceful letter was sent off, with directions to the messenger to wait for an answer. The messenger came back with tidings that his lordship was in bed. Then there was another consultation. The Marquis, though in bed, had of course read the letter. Had he felt at all as a son and a brother ought to feel, he would have sent some reply to such a message. It must be, they felt, that he intended to live there and utterly ignore his mother and sisters. What should they do then? How should they be able to live? The Marchioness surrendered herself to a paroxysm of weeping, bitterly blaming those who had not allowed her to go away and hide herself in some distant obscurity. Her son, her eldest son, had cast her off because she had disobeyed his orders!

"His orders!" said Lady Sarah, in scorn, almost in wrath against her mother. "What right has he to give orders either to you or us? He has forgotten himself and is only worthy to be forgotten." Just as she spoke the Manor Cross phaeton, with the Manor Cross ponies, was driven up to the door, and Lady Amelia, who went to the window, declared that Brotherton himself was in the carriage.

"Oh, my son; my darling son!" said the Marchioness, throwing up her arms.

It really was the Marquis. It seemed to the ladies to be a very long time indeed before he got into the room, so leisurely was he in divesting himself of his furs and comforters. During this time the Marchioness would have rushed into the hall had not Lady Sarah prevented her. The old lady was quite overcome with emotion, and prepared to lie at the feet of her eldest son, if he would only extend to her the slightest sign of affection.

"So, here you all are," he said, as he entered the room. "It isn't much of a house for you, but you would have it so." He was of course forced to kiss his mother, but the kiss was not very fervent in its nature. To each of his sisters he merely extended his hand. This Amelia received with *empressement;* for, after all, severe though he was, nevertheless he was the head of the family. Susanna measured the pressure which he gave, and returned back to him the exact weight. Lady Sarah made a little speech.

"We are very glad to see you, Brotherton. You have been away a long time."

"A deuced long time."

"I hope your wife is well; and the little boy. When will she wish that we should go and see her?" The Marchioness during this time had got possession of his left hand, and from her seat was gazing up into his face. He was a very handsome man, but pale, worn, thin, and apparently unhealthy. He was very like Lord George, but smaller in feature, and wanting full four inches of his brother's height. Lord George's hair was already becoming gray at the sides. That of the Marquis, who was ten years older, was perfectly black; but his lordship's valet had probably more to do with that than nature. He wore an exquisite moustache, but in other respects was close shaved. He was dressed with great care, and had fur even on the collar of his frock-coat, so much did he fear the inclemency of his native climate.

"She doesn't speak a word of English, you know," he said, answering his sister's question.

"We might manage to get on in French," said Lady Sarah.

"She doesn't speak a word of French either. She never was out of Italy till now. You had better not trouble yourselves about her."

This was dreadful to them all. It was monstrous to them that there should be a Marchioness of Brotherton, a sister-in-law, living close to them, whom they were to acknowledge to be the reigning Marchioness, and that they should not be allowed to see her. It was not that they anticipated pleasure from her acquaintance. It was not that they were anxious to welcome such a new relation. This marriage, if it were a marriage, was a terrible blow to them. It would have been infinitely better for them all that, having such a wife, he should have kept her in Italy. But, as she was here in England, as she was to be acknowledged—as far as they knew at present—it was a fearful thing that she should be living close to them and not be seen by them. For some moments after his last announcement they were stricken dumb. He was standing with his back to the fire, looking at his boots. The Marchioness was the first to speak.

"We may see Popenjoy!" she exclaimed through her sobs.

"I suppose he can be brought down, if you care about it."

"Of course we care about," said Lady Amelia.

"They tell me he is not strong, and I don't suppose they'll let him come out such weather as this. You'll have to wait. I don't think anybody ought to stir out in this weather. It doesn't suit me, I know. Such an abominable place as it is I never saw in my life. There is not a room in the house that is not enough to make a man blow his brains out."

Lady Sarah could not stand this, nor did she think it right to put up with the insolence of his manner generally. "If so," she said, "it is a pity that you came away from Italy."

He turned sharply round and looked at her for an instant before he answered. And as he did so she remembered the peculiar tyranny of his eyes—the tyranny to which, when a boy, he had ever endeavoured to make her subject, and all others around him. Others had become subject because he was the Lord Popenjoy of the day, and would be the future Marquis; but she, though recognising his right to be first in everything, had ever rebelled against his usurpation of unauthorised power. He, too, remembered all this, and almost snarled at her with his eyes. "I suppose I might stay if I liked, or come back if I liked, without asking you," he said.

"Certainly."

"But you are the same as ever you were."

"Oh, Brotherton," said the Marchioness, "do not quarrel with us directly you have come back."

"You may be quite sure, mother, that I shall not take the trouble to quarrel with anyone. It takes two for that work. If I wanted to quarrel with her or you I have cause enough."

"I know of none," said Lady Sarah.

"I explained to you my wishes about this house, and you disregarded them altogether." The old lady looked up at her eldest daughter as though to say, "There—that was your sin." "I knew what was better for you and better for me. It is impossible that there should be pleasant intercourse between you and my wife, and I recommended you to go elsewhere. If you had done so I would have taken care that you were comfortable." Again the Marchioness looked at Lady Sarah with bitter reproaches in her eyes.

"What interest in life would we have had in a distant home?" said Lady Sarah.

"Why not you as well as other people?"

"Because, unlike other people, we have become devoted to one spot. The property belongs to you."

"I hope so."

"But the obligations of the property have been, at any rate, as near to us as to you. Society, I suppose, may be found in a new place, but we do not care much for society."

"Then it would have been so much the easier."

"But it would have been impossible for us to find new duties."

"Nonsense," said the Marquis; "humbug; d——d trash."

"If you cannot speak otherwise than like that before your mother, Brotherton, I think you had better leave her," said Lady Sarah, bravely.

"Don't, Sarah—don't!" said the Marchioness.

"It is trash, and nonsense, and humbug. I told you that you were better away, and you determined to stay. I knew what was best for you, but you chose to be obstinate. I have not the slightest doubt as to who did it."

"We were all of the same mind," said Lady Susanna. "Alice said it would be quite cruel that mamma should be moved." Alice was now the wife of Canon Holdenough.

"It would have been very bad for us all to go away," said Lady Amelia.

"George was altogether against it," said Lady Susanna.

"And the Dean," said Lady Amelia, indiscreetly.

"The Dean!" exclaimed the Marquis. "Do you mean to say that that stable-boy has been consulted about my affairs? I should have thought that not one of you would have spoken to George after he had disgraced himself by such a marriage."

"There was no need to consult anyone," said Lady Sarah. "And we do not think George's marriage at all disgraceful."

"Mary is a very nice young person," said the Marchioness.

"I daresay. Whether she is nice or not is very little to me. She has got some fortune, and I suppose that was what he wanted. As you are all of you fixed here now, and seem to have spent a lot of money, I suppose you will have to remain. You have turned my tenant out——"

"Mr. Price was quite willing to go," said Lady Susanna.

"I daresay. I trust he may be as willing to give up the land when his lease is out. I have been told that he is a sporting friend of the Dean's. It seems to me that you have, all of you, got into a nice mess here by yourselves. All I want you to understand is that I cannot now trouble myself about you."

"You don't mean to give us up," said the afflicted mother. "You'll come and see me sometimes, won't you?"

"Certainly not, if I am to be insulted by my sister."

"I have insulted no one," said Lady Sarah haughtily.

"It was no insult to tell me that I ought to have stayed in Italy, and not have come to my own house!"

"Sarah, you ought not to have said that," exclaimed the Marchioness.

"He complained that everything here was uncomfortable, and therefore I said it. He knows that I did not speak of his return in any other sense. Since

he settled himself abroad there has not been a day on
which I have not wished that he would come back to
his own house and his own duties. If he will treat us
properly, no one will treat him with higher consideration than I. But we have our own rights as well as
he, and are as well able to guard them."

"Sarah can preach as well as ever," he said.

"Oh! my children—oh! my children!" sobbed the
old lady.

"I have had enough of this. I knew what it would
be when you wrote to me to come to you." Then he
took up his hat, as though he were going.

"And am I to see nothing more of you?" asked his
mother.

"I will come to you, mother—once a week if you
wish it. Every Sunday afternoon will be as good a
time as any other. But I will not come unless I
am assured of the absence of Lady Sarah. I will not
subject myself to her insolence, nor put myself in the
way of being annoyed by a ballyragging quarrel."

"I and my sisters are always at church on Sunday
afternoon," said Lady Sarah.

In this way the matter was arranged, and then the
Marquis took himself off. For some time after he
left the room the Marchioness sat in silence, sobbing
now and again, and then burying her face in her handkerchief. "I wish we had gone away when he told
us," she said at last.

"No, mamma," said her eldest daughter. "No—
certainly no. Even though all this is very miserable,
it is not so bad as running away in order that we
might be out of his way. No good can ever be got
by yielding in what is wrong to anyone. This is
your house; and as yours it is ours."

"Oh, yes."

"And here we can do something to justify our lives. We have a work appointed to us which we are able to perform. What will his wife do for the people here? Why are we not to say our prayers in the church which we all know and love? Why are we to leave Alice—and Mary? Why should he, because he is the eldest of us—he, who for so many years has deserted the place—why is he to tell us where to live, and where not to live? He is rich, and we are poor, but we have never been pensioners on his bounty. The park, I suppose, is now closed to us; but I am prepared to live here in defiance of him." This she said walking up and down the room as she spoke, and she said it with so much energy that she absolutely carried her sisters with her and again partly convinced her mother.

CHAPTER XXII

THE MARQUIS AMONG HIS FRIENDS

THERE was, of course, much perturbation of mind at Brotherton as as to what should be done on this occasion of the Marquis's return. Mr. Knox had been consulted by persons in the town, and had given it as his opinion that nothing should be done. Some of the tradesmen and a few of the tenants living nearest to the town had suggested a triumphal entry—green boughs, a bonfire, and fireworks. This idea, however, did not prevail long. The Marquis of Brotherton was clearly not a man to be received with green boughs and bonfires. All that soon died away. But there remained what may be called the private difficulty. Many in Brotherton and around Brotherton had of course known the man when he was young, and could hardly bring themselves to take no notice of his return. One or two drove over and simply left their cards. The bishop asked to see him, and was told that he was out. Dr. Pountner did see him, catching him at his own hall door; but the interview was very short, and not particularly pleasant. "Dr. Pountner. Well; I do remember you, certainly. But we have all grown older, you know."

"I came," said the Doctor, with a face redder than ever, "to pay my respects to your lordship, and to leave my card for your wife."

"We are much obliged to you—very much obliged.

Unfortunately we are both invalids." Then the Doctor, who had not got out of his carriage, was driven home again. The Doctor had been a great many years at Brotherton, and had known the old Marquis well.

"I don't know what you and Holdenough will make of him," the Doctor said to the Dean. "I suppose you will both be driven into some communion with him. I shan't try it again."

The Dean and Canon Holdenough had been in consultation on the subject, and had agreed that they would each of them act as though the Marquis had been like any other gentleman, and his wife like any other newly-married lady. They were both now connected with the family, and even bound to act on the presumption that there would be family friendship. The Dean went on his errand first, and the Dean was admitted into his sitting-room. This happened a day or two after the scene at Cross Hall.

"I don't know that I should have troubled you so soon," said the Dean, "had not your brother married my daughter." The Dean had thought over the matter carefully, making up his mind how far he would be courteous to the man, and where he would make a stand if it were necessary that he should make a stand at all. And he had determined that he would ask after the new Lady Brotherton, and speak of the child as Lord Popenjoy, the presumption being that a man is married when he says so himself, and that his child is legitimate when declared to be so. His present acknowledgment would not bar any future proceedings.

"There has been a good deal of marrying and giving in marriage since I have been away," replied the Marquis.

"Yes, indeed. There has been your brother, your sister, and last, not least, yourself."

"I was not thinking of myself. I meant among you here. The Church seems to carry everything before it."

It seemed to the Dean, who was sufficiently mindful of his daughter's fortune, and who knew to a penny what was the very liberal income of Canon Holdenough, that in these marriages the Church had at least given as much as it had got. "The Church holds its own," said the Dean, "and I hope that it always will. May I venture to express a hope that the Marchioness is well."

"Not very well."

"I am sorry for that. Shall I not have the pleasure of seeing her to-day?"

The Marquis looked as though he were almost astounded at the impudence of the proposition; but he replied to it by the excuse that he had made before. "Unless you speak Italian I'm afraid you would not get on very well with her."

"She will not find that I have the Tuscan tongue or the Roman mouth, but I have enough of the language to make myself perhaps intelligible to her ladyship."

"We will postpone it for the present, if you please, Mr. Dean."

There was an insolence declared in the man's manner, and almost declared in his words, which made the Dean at once determine that he would never again ask after the new Marchioness, and that he would make no allusion whatever to the son. A man may say that his wife is too unwell to receive strangers without implying that the wish to see her should not

have been expressed. The visitor bowed, and then
the two men both sat silent for some moments. "You
have not seen your brother since you have been back?"
the Dean said at last.

"I have not seen him. I don't know where he is,
or anything about him."

"They live in London—in Munster Court."

"Very likely. He didn't consult me about his marriage, and I don't know anything about his concerns."

"He told you of it—before it took place."

"Very likely—though I do not exactly see how that
concerns you and me."

"You must be aware that he is married to—my
daughter."

"Quite so."

"That would, generally, be supposed to give a
common interest."

"Ah! I daresay. You feel it so, no doubt. I
am glad that you are satisfied by an alliance with my
family. You are anxious for me to profess that it is
reciprocal."

"I am anxious for nothing of the kind," said
the Dean, jumping up from his chair. "I have
nothing to get and nothing to lose by the alliance.
The usual courtesies of life are pleasant to me."

"I wish that you would use them on the present
occasion by being a little quieter."

"You brother has married a lady, and my daughter
has married a gentleman."

"Yes; George is a great ass—in some respects
the greatest ass I know; but he is a gentleman. Perhaps if you have anything else that you wish to
say you will do me the honour of sitting down."

The Dean was so angry that he did not know how

to contain himself. The Marquis had snubbed him
for coming. He had then justified his visit by an
allusion to the connection between them, and the Marquis had replied to this by hinting that though a Dean
might think it a very fine thing to have his daughter
married into the family of a marquis, the marquis
probably would not look at it in the same light. And
yet what was the truth? Whence had come the money
which had made the marriage possible? In the
bargain between them which party had had the best
of it? He was conscious that it would not become
him to allude to the money, but his feeling on the
subject was very strong. "My lord," he said, "I do
not know that there is anything to be gained by my
sitting down again."

"Perhaps not. I daresay you know best."

"I came here intent on what I considered to be
a courtesy due to your lordship. I am sorry that my
visit has been mistaken."

"I don't see that there is anything to make a fuss
about."

"It shall not be repeated, my lord." And so he left
the room.

Why on earth had the man come back to England,
bringing a foreign woman and an Italian brat home
with him, if he intended to make the place too hot to
hold him by insulting everybody around him? This
was the first question the Dean asked himself, when
he found himself outside the house. And what could
the man hope to gain by such insolence? Instead of
taking the road through the park back to Brotherton,
he went on to Cross Hall. He was desirous of learning what were the impressions, and what the intentions, of the ladies there. Did this madman mean to

quarrel with his mother and sisters as well as with his other neighbours? He did not as yet know what intercourse there had been between the two houses, since the Marquis had been at Manor Cross. And in going to Cross Hall in the midst of all these troubles he was no doubt actuated in part by a determination to show himself to be one of the family. If they would accept his aid, no one would be more loyal than he to these ladies. But he would not be laid aside. If anything unjust were intended, if any fraud was to be executed, the person most to be injured would be that hitherto unborn grandson of his for whose advent he was so anxious. He had been very free with his money, but he meant to have his money's worth.

At Cross Hall he found Canon Holdenough's wife and the Canon. At the moment of his entrance old Lady Brotherton was talking to the clergyman, and Lady Alice was closeted in a corner with her sister Sarah. " I would advise you to go just as though you had heard nothing from us," Lady Sarah had said. " Of course he would be readier to quarrel with me than with anyone. For mamma's sake I would go away for a time if I had anywhere to go to."

" Come to us," Lady Alice had said. But Lady Sarah had declared that she would be as much in the way at Brotherton as at Cross Hall, and had then gone on to explain that it was Lady Alice's duty to call on her sister-in-law, and that she must do so —facing the consequences, whatever they might be.

" Of course mamma could not go till he had been here," Lady Sarah added; " and now he has told mamma not to go at all. But that is nothing to you."

" I have just come from the house," said the Dean.

"Did you see him?" asked the old woman with awe.

"Yes; I saw him."

"Well!"

"I must say that he was not very civil to me, and that I suppose I have seen all of him that I shall see."

"It is only his manner," said her ladyship.

"An unfortunate manner, surely."

"Poor Brotherton!"

Then the Canon said a word. "Of course, no one wants to trouble him. I can speak at least for myself. I do not—certainly. I have requested her ladyship to ask him whether he would wish me to call or not. If he says that he does, I shall expect him to receive me cordially. If he does not—there's an end of it."

"I hope you won't all of you turn against him," said the Marchioness.

"Turn against him!" repeated the Dean. "I do not suppose that there is anyone who would not be both kind and courteous to him, if he would accept kindness and courtesy. It grieves me to make you unhappy, Marchioness, but I am bound to let you know that he treated me very badly."

From that moment the Marchioness made up her mind that the Dean was no friend of the family, and that he was, after all, vulgar and disagreeable. She undertook, however, to inquire from her son on next Sunday whether he would wish to be called upon by his brother-in-law, the Canon.

On the following day Lady Alice went alone to Manor Cross—being the first lady who had gone to the door since the new arrivals—and asked for Lady Brotherton.

The courier came to the door and said "Not at

home," in a foreign accent, just as the words might
have been said to any chance caller in London.

Then Lady Alice asked the man to tell her brother
that she was there.

"Not at home, miladi," said the man, in the same
tone.

At that moment Mrs. Toff came running through
the long hall to the carriage-door. The house was
built round a quadrangle, and all the ground-floor of
the front and of one of the sides consisted of halls,
passages, and a billiard-room. Mrs. Toff must have
been watching very closely or she could hardly have
known that Lady Alice was there. She came out and
stood beside the carriage, and leaning in, whispered
her fears and unhappinesses.

"Oh my lady, I'm afraid it's very bad! I haven't
set eyes on the the—the—his wife, my lady, yet; nor
the little boy."

"Are they in now, Mrs. Toff?"

"Of course they're in. They never go out. He
goes about all the afternoon in a dressing-gown,
smoking bits of paper, and she lies in bed or gets up
and doesn't do—nothing at all, as far as I can see,
Lady Alice. But as for being in, of course they're in;
they're always in."

Lady Alice, however, feeling that she had done her
duty, and not wishing to take the place by storm, had
herself driven back to Brotherton.

On the following Sunday afternoon the Marquis
came, according to his promise, and found his mother
alone.

"The fact is, mother," he said, "you have got a
regular Church set around you during the last year
or two, and I will have nothing to do with them. I

never cared much for Brotherton Close, and now I
like it less than ever."

The Marchioness moaned and looked up into his
face imploringly. She was anxious to say something
in defence, at any rate, of her daughter's marriage,
but specially anxious to say nothing that should anger
him. Of course he was unreasonable, but according
to her lights, he being the Marquis, had a right to
be unreasonable.

"The Dean came to me the other day," continued
he, "and I could see at a glance that he meant to be
quite at home in the house, if I didn't put him down."

"You'll see Mr. Holdenough, won't you? Mr.
Holdenough is a very gentlemanlike man, and the
Holdenoughs were always quite county people. You
used to like Alice."

"If you ask me, I think she has been a fool at her
age to go and marry an old parson. As for receiving
him, I shan't receive anybody—in the way of entertaining them. I haven't come home for that purpose.
My child will have to live here when he is a man."

"God bless him!" said the Marchioness.

"Or at any rate his property will be here. They
tell me that it will be well that he should be used
to this damnable climate early in life. He will have
to go to school here, and all that. So I have brought
him, though I hate the place."

"It is so nice to have you back, Brotherton."

"I don't know about its being nice. I don't find
much niceness in it. Had I not got myself married
I should never have come back. But it's as well that
you all should know that there is an heir."

"God bless him!" said the Marchioness, again.
"But don't you think we ought to see him?"

"See him? Why?" He asked the question sharply, and looked at her with that savageness in his eyes which all the family remembered so well, and which she specially feared.

That question of the legitimacy of the boy had never been distinctly discussed at Cross Hall, and the suspicious hints on the subject which had passed between the sisters, the allusions to this and the other possibility which had escaped them, had been kept as far as possible from their mother. They had remarked among themselves that it was very odd that the marriage should have been concealed, and almost more than odd that an heir to the title should have been born without any announcement of such a birth. A dread of some evil mystery had filled their thoughts, and shown itself in their words and looks to each other. And, though they had been very anxious to keep this from their mother, something had crept through which had revealed a suspicion of the suspicion even to her. She, dear old lady, had resolved upon no line of conduct in the matter. She had conceived no project of rebelling against her eldest daughter, or of being untrue to her youngest son. But now that she was alone with her eldest son, with the real undoubted Marquis, with him who would certainly be to her more than all the world beside if he would only allow it, there did come into her head an idea that she would put him on his guard.

"Because—because——"

"Because what? Speak out, mother."

"Because, perhaps, they'll say that—that——"

"What will they say?"

"If they don't see him, they may think he isn't Popenjoy at all."

"Oh, they'll think that, will they? How will seeing help them?"

"It would be so nice to have him here, if it's only for a little," said the Marchioness.

"So that's it," he said, after a long pause. "That's George's game, and the Dean's; I can understand."

"No, no, no; not George," said the unhappy mother.

"And Sarah, I daresay, is in a boat with them. I don't wonder that they should choose to remain here and watch me."

"I am sure George has never thought of such a thing."

"George will think as his father-in-law bids him. George was never very good at thinking for himself. So you fancy they'll be more likely to accept the boy if they see him."

"Seeing is believing, Brotherton."

"There's something in that, to be sure. Perhaps they don't think I've got a wife at all, because they haven't seen her."

"Oh, yes; they believe that."

"How kind of them. Well, mother, you've let the cat out of the bag."

"Don't tell them that I said so."

"No; I won't tell. Nor am I very much surprised. I thought how it would be when I didn't announce it all in the old-fashioned way. It's lucky that I have the certificate proof of the date of my marriage, isn't it?"

"It's all right, of course. I never doubted it, Brotherton."

"But all the others did. I knew there was something up when George wasn't at home to meet me."

"He is coming."

"He may stay away if he likes it. I don't want him. He won't have the courage to tell me up to my face that he doesn't intend to acknowledge my boy. He's too great a coward for that."

"I'm sure it's not George, Brotherton."

"Who. is it, then?"

"Perhaps it's the Dean."

"D—— his impudence. How on earth among you could you let George marry the daughter of a low-bred ruffian like that—a man that never ought to have been allowed to put his foot inside the house?"

"She had such a very nice fortune! And then he wanted to marry that scheming girl, Adelaide de Baron—without a penny."

"The De Barons, at any rate, are gentlefolk. If the Dean meddles with me, he shall find that he has got the wrong sow by the ear. If he puts his foot in the park again I'll have him warned off as a trespasser."

"But you'll see Mr. Holdenough?"

"I don't want to see anybody. I mean to hold my own, and do as I please with my own, and live as I like, and toady no one. What can I have in common with an old parson like that?"

"You'll let me see Popenjoy, Brotherton?"

"Yes," he said, pausing a moment before he answered her. "He shall be brought here, and you shall see him. But mind, mother, I shall expect you to tell me all that you hear."

"Indeed I will."

"You will not rebel against me, I suppose."

"Oh, no; my son, my son!" Then she fell upon his neck, and he suffered it for a minute, thinking it wise to make sure of one ally in that house.

CHAPTER XXIII

THE MARQUIS SEES HIS BROTHER

WHEN Lord George was summoned down to Manor Cross, or rather to Cross Hall, he did not dare not to go. Lady Sarah had told him that it was his duty, and he could not deny the assertion. But he was very angry with his brother, and did not in the least wish to see him. Nor did he think that by seeing him he could in any degree render easier that horrible task which would, sooner or later, be imposed upon him, of testing the legitimacy of his brother's child. And there were other reasons which made him unwilling to leave London. He did not like to be away from his young wife. She was, of course, a matron now, and entitled to be left alone, according to the laws of the world; but then she was so childish, and so fond of playing bagatelle with Jack de Baron! He had never had occasion to find fault with her; not to say words to her which he himself would regard as fault-finding words, though she had complained more than once of his scolding her. He would caution her, beg her to be grave, ask her to read heavy books, and try to impress her with the solemnity of married life. In this way he would quell her spirits for a few hours. Then she would burst out again, and there would be Jack de Baron and the bagatelle. In all these sorrows he solaced himself by asking advice from Mrs. Houghton. By degrees he told Mrs. Houghton almost everything. The reader may remember that there had been a moment in which he had resolved that he would not again go to Berkeley Square. But all that was very much altered now. He was there almost every day, and consulted the lady about everything. She had induced him even to talk quite openly about this Italian boy, to express his suspicions, and to allude to most distressing duties which might be incumbent on him. She strenuously advised him to take nothing for granted. If the marquisate was to be had by careful scrutiny she was quite of opinion that it should not be lost by careless confidence. This sort of friendship was very pleasant to him, and especially so because he could tell himself that there was nothing wicked in it. No doubt her hand would be in his sometimes for a moment, and once or twice his arm had almost found its way round her waist. But these had been small deviations, which he had taken care to check. No doubt it had occurred to him once or twice that she had not been careful to check them. But this, when he thought of it maturely, he attributed to innocence.

It was at last, by her advice, that he begged that one of his sisters might come up to town, as a companion to Mary during his absence at Cross Hall. This counsel she had given to him after assuring him half-a-dozen times that there was nothing to fear. He had named Amelia, Mary having at once agreed to the arrangement, on condition that the younger of the three sisters should be invited. The letter was of course written to Lady Sarah. All· such letters always were written to Lady Sarah. Lady Sarah had answered, saying that Susanna would take the place destined for Amelia. Now Susanna, of all the Germain family, was the one whom Mary disliked the most. But there was no help for it. She thought it hard, but she was not strong enough in her own position to say that she would not have Susanna, because Susanna had not been asked.

"I think Lady Susanna will be the best," said Lord George, "because she has so much strength of character."

"Strength of character! You speak as if you were going away for three years, and were leaving me in the midst of danger. You'll be back in five days, I suppose. I really think I could have got on without Susanna's—strength of character!" This was her revenge; but, all the same, Lady Susanna came.

"She is as good as gold," said Lord George, who was himself as weak as water. "She is as good as gold; but there is a young man comes here whom I don't care for her to see too often." This was what he said to Lady Susanna.

"Oh, indeed! Who is he?"

"Captain de Baron. You are not to suppose that she cares a straw about him."

"Oh, no; I am sure there can be nothing of that," said Lady Susanna, feeling herself to be as energetic as Cerberus, and as many-eyed as Argus.

"You must take care of yourself now, Master Jack," Mrs. Houghton said to her cousin. "A duenna has been sent for."

"Duennas always go to sleep, don't they; and take tips; and are generally open to reason?"

"Oh, heavens! Fancy tipping Lady Susanna! I should think that she never slept in her life with both eyes at the same time, and that she thinks in her heart that every man who says a civil word ought to have his tongue cut out."

"I wonder how she'd take it if I were to say a civil word to herself?"

"You can try; but as far as Madame is concerned, you had better wait till Monsieur is back again."

Lord George, having left his wife in the hands of Lady Susanna, went down to Brotherton and on to Cross Hall. He arrived on the Saturday after that first Sunday visit paid by the Marquis to his mother. The early part of the past week had been very blank down in those parts. No further personal attempts had been made to intrude upon the Manor Cross mysteries. The Dean had not been seen again, even at Cross Hall.

Mr. Holdenough had made no attempt after the reception—or rather non-reception—awarded to his wife. Old Mr. de Baron had driven over, and had seen the Marquis, but nothing more than that fact was known at Cross Hall. He had been there for about an hour, and as far as Mrs. Toff knew, the Marquis had been very civil to him. But Mr. de Baron, though a cousin, was not by any means one of the Germain party. Then, on Saturday there had been an affair. Mrs. Toff had come to the Hall, boiling over with the importance of her communication, and stating that she had been—turned out of the house. She, who had presided over everything material at Manor cross for more than thirty years, from the family pictures down to the kitchen utensils, had been absolutely desired to—walk herself off. The message had been given to her by that accursed courier, and she had then insisted on seeing the Marquis. "My lord," she said, "only laughed at her." "Mrs. Toff," he had said, "you are my mother's servant, and my sisters'. You had better go and live with them." She had then hinted at the shortness of the notice given her, upon which he had offered her anything she chose to ask in the way of wages, and board wages. "But I wouldn't take a penny, my lady; only just what was due up to the very day." As Mrs. Toff was a great deal too old a servant to be really turned away, and as she merely migrated from Manor Cross to Cross Hall, she did not injure herself much by refusing the offers made to her.

It must be held that the Marquis was justified in getting rid of Mrs. Toff. Mrs. Toff was, in truth, a spy in his camp, and of course his own people were soon aware of that fact. Her almost daily journeys to Cross Hall were known, and it was remembered, both by the Marquis and his wife, that this old woman, who had never been allowed to see the child, but who had known all the preceding generation as children, could not but be an enemy. Of course it was patent to all the servants, and to everyone connected with the two houses, that there was war. Of course, the Marquis, having an old woman acting spy in his stronghold, got rid of her. But justice would shortly have required that the other old woman, who was acting spy in the other stronghold, should be turned out also. But the Marchioness, who had promised to tell everything to her son, could not very well be offered wages and be made to go.

In the midst of the ferment occasioned by this last piece of work Lord George reached Cross Hall. He had driven through the park, that way being nearly as short as the high-road, and had left word at the house that he would call on the following

morning, immediately after morning church. This
he did, in consequence of a resolution which he made
to act on his own judgment. A terrible crisis was
coming, in which it would not be becoming that he
should submit himself either to his eldest sister or
to the Dean. He had talked the matter over fully
with Mrs. Houghton, and Mrs. Houghton had suggested that he should call on his way out to the
Hall.

The ladies had at first to justify their request
that he should come to them, and there was a difficulty in doing this, as he was received in presence
of their mother. Lady Sarah had not probably told
herself that the Marchioness was a spy, but she had
perceived that it would not be wise to discuss everything openly in her mother's presence. "It is quite
right that you should see him," said Lady Sarah.

"Quite right," said the old lady.

"Had he sent me even a message I should have
been here, of course," said the brother. "He passed
through London, and I would have met him there,
had he not kept everything concealed."

"He isn't like anybody else, you know. You mustn't
quarrel with him. He is the head of the family. If
we quarrel with him, what will become of us?"

"What will become of him if everybody falls off
from him. That's what I'm thinking of," said Lady
Sarah.

Soon after this all the horrors that had taken place
—horrors which could not be intrusted to a letter—
were narrated to him. The Marquis had insulted Dr.
Pountner, he had not returned the bishop's visit, he
had treated the Dean with violent insolence, and he
had refused to receive his brother-in-law, Mr. Hold-

enough, though the Holdenoughs had always moved
in county society! He had declared that none of his
relatives were to be introduced to his wife. He had
not as yet allowed the so-called Popenjoy to be seen.
He had said none of them were to trouble him at
Manor Cross, and had explained his purpose of only
coming to the Hall when he knew that his sister Sarah
was away. "I think he must be mad," said the
younger brother.

"It is what comes of living in a godless country
like Italy," said Lady Amelia.

"It is what comes of utterly disregarding duty,"
said Lady Sarah.

But what was to be done? The Marquis had declared his purpose of doing what he liked with his
own, and certainly none of them could hinder him.
If he chose to shut himself and his wife up at the
big house, he must do so. It was very bad, but it
was clear that they could not interfere with his eccentricities. How was anybody to interfere? Of
course there was present in the mind of each of
them a feeling that this woman might not be his
wife, or that the child might not be legitimate. But
they did not like, with open words among themselves, to accuse their brother of so great a crime.
"I don't see what there is to be done," said Lord
George.

The church was in the park, not very far from the
house, but nearer to the gate leading to Brotherton.
On that Sunday morning the Marchioness and her
youngest daughter went there in the carriage, and
in doing so had to pass the front doors. The previous
Sunday had been cold, and this was the first time
that the Marchioness had seen Manor Cross since her

son had been there. "Oh, dear! if I could only go in and see the dear child!" she said.

"You know you can't, mamma," said Amelia.

"It is all Sarah's fault, because she would quarrel with him."

After church the ladies returned in the carriage, and Lord George went to the house according to his appointment. He was shown into a small parlour, and in about half-an-hour's time luncheon was brought to him. He then asked whether his brother was coming. The servant went away, promising to inquire, but did not return. He was cross, and would eat no lunch; but after awhile rang the bell loudly, and again asked the same question. The servant again went away and did not return. He had just made up his mind to leave the house and never return to it, when the courier, of whom he had heard, came to usher him into his brother's room. "You seem to be in a deuce of a hurry, George," said the Marquis, without getting out of his chair. "You forget that people don't get up at the same hour all the world over."

"It's half-past two now."

"Very likely; but I don't know that there is any law to make a man dress himself before that hour."

"The servant might have given me a message."

"Don't make a row now you are here, old fellow. When I found you were in the house I got down as fast as I could. I suppose your time isn't so very precious."

Lord George had come there determined not to quarrel if he could help it. He had very nearly quarrelled already. Every word that his brother said was in truth an insult—being, as they were, the first

words spoken after so long an interval. They were
intended to be insolent, probably intended to drive
him away. But if anything was to be gained by the
interview he must not allow himself to be driven
away. He had a duty to perform—a great duty. He
was the last man in England to suspect a fictitious
heir—would at any rate be the last to hint at such
an iniquity without the strongest ground. Who is to
be true to a brother if not a brother? Who is to support the honour of a great family if not its own
scions? Who is to abstain from wasting the wealth
and honour of another, if not he who has the nearest
chance of possessing them? And yet who could be
so manifestly bound as he to take care that no sur-
reptitious head was imposed upon the family. This
little child was either the real Popenjoy, a boy to
be held by him as of all boys the most sacred, to the
promotion of whose welfare all his own energies
would be due—or else a brat so abnormously distasteful and abominable as to demand from him an
undying enmity, till the child's wicked pretensions
should be laid at rest. There was something very
serious in it, very tragic—something which demanded
that he should lay aside all common anger, and put
up with many insults on behalf of the cause which he
had in hand.

"Of course I could wait," said he; "only I thought
that perhaps the man would have told me."

"The fact is, George, we are rather a divided
house here. Some of us talk Italian and some English. I am the only common interpreter in the house,
and I find it a bore."

"I daresay it is troublesome."

"And what can I do for you now you're here?"

Do for him! Lord George didn't want his brother to do anything for him. "Live decently, like an English nobleman, and do not outrage your family." That would have been the only true answer he could have made to such a question.

"I thought you would wish to see me after your return," he said.

"It's rather lately thought of; but, however, let that pass. So you've got a wife for yourself."

"As you have done also."

"Just so. I have got a wife, too. Mine has come from one of the oldest and noblest families in Christendom."

"Mine is the granddaughter of a livery-stable keeper," said Lord George, with a touch of real grandeur; "and, thank God, I can be proud of her in any society in England."

"I daresay! particularly as she had some money."

"Yes; she had money. I could have hardly married without. But when you see her I think you will not be ashamed of her as your sister-in-law."

"Ah! She lives in London, and I am just at present down here."

"She is the daughter of the Dean of Brotherton."

"So I have heard. They used to make gentlemen deans."

After this there was a pause, Lord George finding it difficult to go on with the conversation without a quarrel.

"To tell you the truth, George, I will not willingly see anything more of your Dean. He came here and insulted me. He got up and blustered about the room because I wouldn't thank him for the honour he had done our family by his alliance. If you please, George,

we'll understand that the less said about the Dean
the better. You see I haven't any of the money out
of the stable-yard."

"My wife's money didn't come out of a stable-
yard. It came from a wax-chandler's shop," said
Lord George, jumping up, just as the Dean had done.
There was something in the man's manner worse even
than his words, which he found it almost impossible
to bear. But he seated himself again as his brother
sat looking at him with a bitter smile upon his face.
"I don't suppose," he said, "you can wish to annoy
me."

"Certainly not. But I wish that the truth should
be understood between us."

"Am I to be allowed to pay my respects to your
wife?" said Lord George boldly.

"I think, you know, that we have gone so far
apart in our marriages that there is nothing to be
gained by it. Besides, you couldn't speak to her—
nor she to you."

"May I be permitted to see—Popenjoy?"

The Marquis paused a moment, and then rang the
bell.

"I don't know what good it will do you, but if
he can be made fit he shall be brought down."

The courier entered the room and received certain
orders in Italian. After that there was considerable
delay, during which an Italian servant brought the
Marquis a cup of chocolate and a cake. He pushed
a newspaper over to his brother, and, as he was drinking his chocolate, lighted a cigarette. In this way
there was a delay of over an hour, and then there
entered the room an Italian nurse with a little boy
who seemed to Lord George to be nearly two years

old. The child was carried in by the woman, but Lord George thought that he was big enough to have walked. He was dressed up with many ribbons, and was altogether as gay as apparel could make him. But he was an ugly, swarthy little boy, with great black eyes, small cheeks, and a high forehead—very unlike such a Popenjoy as Lord George would have liked to have seen. Lord George got up and stood over him, and leaning down kissed the high forehead. " My poor little darling," he said.

" As for being poor," said the Marquis, " I hope not. As to being a darling, I should think it doubtful. If you've done with him, she can take him away, you know." Lord George had done with him, and so he was taken away. " Seeing is believing, you know," said the Marquis; " that's the only good of it." Lord George said to himself that in this case seeing was not believing.

At this moment the open carriage came round to the door. " If you like to get up behind," said the Marquis, " I can take you back to Cross Hall, as I am going to see my mother. Perhaps you'll remember that I wish to be alone with her." Lord George then expressed his preference for walking, " Just as you please. I want to say a word. Of course I took it very ill of you all when you insisted on keeping Cross Hall in opposition to my wishes. No doubt they acted on your advice."

" Partly so."

" Exactly; yours and Sarah's. You can't expect me to forget it, George—that's all." Then he walked out of the room among the servants, giving his brother no opportunity for further reply.

CHAPTER XXIV

THE MARQUIS GOES INTO BROTHERTON

THE poor dear old Marchioness must have had some feeling that she was regarded as a spy. She had promised to tell everything to her eldest son, and though she had really nothing to tell, though the Marquis did in truth know all that there was as yet to know, still there grew up at Cross Hall a sort of severance between the unhappy old lady and her children. This showed itself in no diminution of affectionate attention; in no intentional change of manner; but there was a reticence about the Marquis and Popenjoy which even she perceived, and there crept into her mind a feeling that Mrs. Toff was on her guard against her—so that on two occasions she almost snubbed Mrs. Toff. "I never see'd him, my lady; what more can I say?" said Mrs. Toff. "Toff, I don't believe you wanted to see your master's son and heir!" said the Marchioness. Then Mrs. Toff pursed up her lips, and compressed her nose, and half-closed her eyes, and the Marchioness was sure that Mrs. Toff did not believe in Popenjoy.

No one but Lord George had seen Popenjoy. To no eyes but his had the august baby been displayed. Of course many questions had been asked, especially by the old lady, but the answers to them had not been satisfactory. "Dark, is he?" asked the Marchioness. Lord George replied that the child was very swarthy. "Dear me! That isn't like the Germains. The Ger-

mains were never light, but they're not swarthy. Did
he talk at all?"   "Not a word."   "Did he play
about?"   "Never was out of the nurse's arms."
"Dear me! Was he like Brotherton?"   "I don't
think I am a judge of likenesses."   "He's a healthy
child?"   "I can't say. He seemed to be a good deal
done up with finery."   Then the Marchioness declared
that her younger son showed an unnatural indifference
to the heir of the family. It was manifest that she
intended to accept the new Popenjoy, and to ally
herself with no party base enough to entertain any
suspicion.

These examinations respecting the baby went on
for the three first days of the week. It was Lord
George's intention to return to town on the Saturday, and it seemed to them all to be necessary that
something should be arranged before that. Lady
Sarah thought that direct application should be made
to her brother for proof of his marriage and for a
copy of the register of the birth of his child. She
quite admitted that he would resent such application
with the bitterest enmity. But that, she thought, must
be endured. She argued that nothing could be done
more friendly to the child than this. If all was right
the inquiry which circumstances certainly demanded
would be made while he could not feel it. If no such
proof were adduced now there would certainly be
trouble, misery, and perhaps ruin in coming years.
If the necessary evidence were forthcoming, then no
one would wish to interfere further. There might
be ill blood on their brother's part, but there would
be none on theirs. Neither Lord George nor their
younger sister gainsaid this altogether. Neither of
them denied the necessity of inquiry. But they de-

sired to temporise; and then how was the inquiry to
be made? Who was to bell the cat? And how should
they go on when the Marquis refused to take any
heed of them—as, of course, he would do? Lady
Sarah saw at once that they must employ a lawyer—
but what lawyer? Old Mr. Stokes, the family attorney, was the only lawyer they knew. But Mr. Stokes
was Lord Brotherton's lawyer, and would hardly consent to be employed against his own client. Lady
Sarah suggested that Mr. Stokes might be induced
to explain to the Marquis that these inquiries should
be made for his, the Marquis's, own benefit. But
Lord George felt that this was impossible. It was
evident that Lord George would be afraid to ask Mr.
Stokes to undertake the work.

At last it came to be understood among them that
they must have some friend to act with them. There
could be no doubt who that friend should be. "As to
interfering," said Lady Sarah, speaking of the Dean,
"he will interfere, whether we ask him to or not.
His daughter is as much affected as anybody, and if
I understand him he is not the man to see any interest
of his own injured by want of care." Lord George
shook his head, but yielded. He greatly disliked the
idea of putting himself into the Dean's hands—of becoming a creature of the Dean's. He felt the Dean
to be stronger than himself, endowed with higher
spirit and more confident hopes. But he also felt
that the Dean was—the son of a stable-keeper.
Though he had professed to his brother that he could
own the fact without shame, still he was ashamed.
It was not the Dean's parentage that troubled him
so much as a consciousness of some defect, perhaps
only of the absence of some quality, which had been

caused by that parentage. The man looked like a gentleman, but still there was a smell of the stable. Feeling this, rather than knowing it, Lord George resisted for awhile the idea of joining forces with the Dean; but when it was suggested to him as an alternative that he himself must go to Mr. Stokes and explain his suspicions in the lawyer's room, then he agreed that, as a first step, he would consult the Dean. The Dean, no doubt, would have his own lawyer, who would not care a fig for the Marquis.

It was thought by them at Cross Hall that the Dean would come over to them, knowing that his son-in-law was in the country; but the Dean did not come, probably waiting for the same compliment from Lord George. On the Friday Lord George rode into Brotherton early, and was at the Deanery by eleven o'clock.

"I thought I should see you," said the Dean, in his pleasantest manner. "Of course, I heard from Mary that you were down here. Well, what do you think of it all?"

"It is not pleasant."

"If you mean your brother, I am bound to say that he is very unpleasant. Of course you have seen him?"

"Yes, I have seen him."

"And her ladyship?"

"No. He said that as I did not speak Italian it would be no good."

"And he seemed to think," said the Dean, "that as I do speak Italian it would be dangerous. Nobody has seen her then?"

"Nobody."

"That promises well! And the little lord?"

"He was brought down to me."

"That was gracious! Well, what of him; did he look like a Popenjoy?"

"He is a nasty little black thing."

"I shouldn't wonder."

"And looks—— Well, I don't want to abuse the poor child, and God knows, if he is what he pretends to be, I would do anything to serve him."

"That's just it, George," said the Dean, very seriously—seriously, and with his kindest manner, being quite disposed to make himself agreeable to Lord George if Lord George would be agreeable to him. "That's just it. If we were certified as to that, what would we not do for the child in spite of the father's brutality? There is no dishonesty on our side, George. You know of me, and I know of you, that if every tittle of the evidence of that child's birth were in the keeping of either of us, so that it could be destroyed on the moment, it should be made as public as the winds of heaven to-morrow, so that it was true evidence. If he be what he pretends to be, who would interfere with him? But if he be not?"

"Any suspicion of that kind is unworthy of us, except on very strong ground."

"True. But, if there be very strong ground, it is equally true that such suspicion is our duty. Look at the case. When was it that he told you that he was going to be married? About six months since, as far as my memory goes."

"He said, 'I am to be married.'"

"That is speaking in the future tense; and now he claims to have been married two or three years ago. Has he ever attempted to explain this?"

"He has not said a word about it. He is quite unwilling to talk about himself."

"I daresay. But a man in such circumstances must be made to talk about himself. You and I are so placed that, if we did not make him talk about himself, we ought to be made to make him do so. He may be deceitful if he pleases. He may tell you and me fibs without end; and he may give us much trouble by doing so. Such trouble is the evil consequence of having liars in the world." Lord George winced at the rough word as applied by inference to his own brother. "But liars themselves are always troubled by their own lies. If he chooses to tell you that on a certain day he is about to be married, and afterwards springs a two-year-old child upon you as legitimate, you are bound to think that there is some deceit. You cannot keep yourself from knowing that there is falsehood; and, if falsehood, then probably fraud. Is it likely that a man with such privileges, and such property ensured to a legitimate son, would allow the birth of such a child to be slurred over without due notice of it? You say that suspicion on our part without strong ground would be unworthy of us. I agree with you. But I ask you whether the grounds are not so strong as to force us to suspect. Come," he continued, as Lord George did not answer at once; "let us be open to each other, knowing as each does that the other means to do what is right. Do not you suspect?"

"I do," said Lord George.

"And so do I. And I mean to learn the truth."

"But how?"

"That is for us to consider; but of one thing I am quite sure. I am quite certain that we must not allow ourselves to be afraid of your brother. To speak the truth, as it must be spoken, he is a bully, George."

"I would rather you would not abuse him, sir."

"Speak ill of him, I must. His character is bad, and I have to speak of it. He is a bully. He set himself to work to put me down when I did myself the honour to call on him, because he felt that my connection with you would probably make me an enemy to him. I intend that he shall know that he cannot put me down. He is undoubtedly Lord Brotherton. He is the owner of a wide property. He has many privileges and much power, with which I cannot interfere. But there is a limit to them. If he have a legitimate son, those privileges will be that son's property; but he has to show to the world that that son is legitimate. When a man marries before all the world, in his own house, and a child is born to him as I may say openly, the proofs are there of themselves. No bringing up of evidence is necessary. The thing is simple, and there is no suspicion and no inquiry. But he has done the reverse of this, and now flatters himself that he can cow those who are concerned by a domineering manner. He must be made to feel that this will not prevail."

"Sarah thinks that he should be invited to produce the necessary certificates."

Lord George, when he dropped his sister's title in speaking of her to the Dean, must have determined that very familiar intercourse with the Dean was a necessity.

"Lady Sarah is always right. That should be the first step. But will you invite him to do so? How shall the matter be broken to him?"

"She thinks a lawyer should do it."

"It must be done either by you or by a lawyer." Lord George looked very blank. "Of course, if the matter were left in my hands—if I had to do it— I should not do it personally. The question is, whether you might not in the first instance write to him?"

"He would not notice it."

"Very likely not. Then we must employ a lawyer." The matter was altogether so distasteful to Lord George that more than once during the interview he almost made up his mind that he would withdraw altogether from the work, and at any rate appear to take it for granted that the child was a real heir, an undoubted Popenjoy. But then, as often, the Dean showed him that he could not so withdraw himself.

"You will be driven," said the Dean, "to express your belief, whatever it may be; and, if you think that there has been foul play, you cannot deny that you think so."

It was at last decided that Lord George should write a letter to his brother, giving all the grounds, not of his own suspicion, but which the world at large would have for suspecting; and earnestly imploring that proper evidence as to his brother's marriage and as to the child's birth, might be produced. Then, if this letter should not be attended to, a lawyer should be employed. The Dean named his own lawyer, Mr. Battle, of Lincoln's Inn Fields. Lord George, having once yielded, found it convenient to yield throughout. Towards the end of the interview the Dean suggested that he would "throw a few words together," or, in other language, write the letter which his son-in-law would have to sign. This suggestion was also accepted by Lord George.

The two men were together for a couple of hours, and then, after lunch, went out together into the town. Each felt that he was now more closely bound to the other than ever. The Dean was thoroughly pleased that it should be so. He intended his son-in-law to be the Marquis, and, being sanguine as well as pugnacious, looked forward to seeing that time himself. Such a man as the Marquis would probably die early, whereas he himself was full of health. There was nothing he would not do to make Lord George's life pleasant, if only Lord George would be pleasant to him, and submissive. But Lord George himself was laden with many regrets. He had formed a conspiracy against the head of his own family, and his brother-conspirator was the son of a stable-keeper. It might be also that he was conspiring against his own legitimate nephew; and, if so, the conspiracy would of course fail, and he would be stigmatised forever among the Germains as the most sordid and vile of the name.

The Dean's house was in the Close, joined on to the cathedral, a covered stone pathway running between the two. The nearest way from the Deanery to the High Street was through the cathedral, the transept of which could be entered by crossing the passage. The Dean and his son-in-law on this occasion went through the building to the west entrance, and there stood for a few minutes in the street while the Dean spoke to men who were engaged on certain repairs of the fabric. In doing this they all went out into the middle of the wide street in order that they might look up at the work which was being done. While they were there, suddenly an open carriage, with a postilion, came upon them unawares, and they had to retreat out of the way. As they did so they perceived that Lord Brotherton was in the carriage, enveloped in furs, and that a lady, more closely enveloped even than himself, was by his side. It was evident to them that he had recognised them. Indeed he had been in the act of raising his hand to greet his brother when he saw the Dean. They both bowed to him, while the Dean, who had the readier mind, raised his hat to the lady. But the Marquis steadily ignored them.

"That's your sister-in-law," said the Dean.

"Perhaps so."

"There is no other lady here with whom he could be driving. I am pretty sure that it is the first time that either of them have been in Brotherton."

"I wonder whether he saw us."

"Of course he saw us. He cut me from fixed purpose, and you because I was with you. I shall not disturb him by any further recognition." Then they went on about their business, and in the afternoon, when the Dean had thrown his few words together, Lord George rode back to Cross Hall. "Let the letter be sent at once, but date it from London." These were the last words the Dean said to him.

It was the Marquis and his wife. All Brotherton heard the news. She had absolutely called at a certain shop, and the Marquis had condescended to be her interpreter. All Brotherton was now sure that there was a new Marchioness, a fact as to which a great part of Brotherton had hitherto entertained doubts. And it seemed that this act of condescension in stopping at a Brotherton shop was so much appreciated that all the former faults of the Marquis were to be condoned on that account. If only Popenjoy

could be taken to a Brotherton pastry-cook, and be
got to eat a Brotherton bun, the Marquis would become the most popular man in the neighbourhood, and
the undoubted progenitor of a long line of marquises
to come. A little kindness after continued cruelty
will always win a dog's heart; some say, also a
woman's. It certainly seemed to be the way to win
Brotherton.

CHAPTER XXV

LADY SUSANNA IN LONDON

IN spite of the caution which he had received from his friend and cousin Mrs. Houghton, Jack de Baron did go to Munster Court during the absence of Lord George, and there did encounter Lady Susanna. And Mrs. Houghton herself, though she had given such excellent advice, accompanied him. She was of course anxious to see Lady Susanna, who had always especially disliked her; and Jack himself was desirous of making the acquaintance of a lady who had been, he was assured, sent up to town on purpose to protect the young wife from his wiles. Both Mrs. Houghton and Jack had become very intimate in Munster Court, and there was nothing strange in their dropping in together, even before lunch. Jack was of course introduced to Lady Susanna. The two ladies grimaced at each other, each knowing the other's feeling towards herself. Mary, having suspected that Lady Susanna had been sent for in reference to this special friend, determined on being specially gracious to Jack. She had already, since Lady Susanna's arrival, told that lady that she was able to manage her own little affairs. Lady Susanna had said an unfortunate word as to the unnecessary expense of four wax candles when they two were sitting alone in the drawing-room. Lady George had said that it was pretty. Lady Susanna had expostulated gravely, and then Lady George had spoken out. "Dear

Susanna, do let me manage my own little affairs."
Of course the words had rankled, and of course the
love which the ladies bore to each other had not been
increased. Lady George was now quite resolved to
show dear Susanna that she was not afraid of her
duenna.

"We thought we'd venture to see if you'd give us
lunch," said Mrs. Houghton.

"Delightful!" exclaimed Lady George. "There's
nothing to eat; but you won't mind that."

"Not in the least," said Jack. "I always think
the best lunch in the world is a bit of the servants'
dinner. It's always the best meat, and the best
cooked, and the hottest served."

There was plenty of lunch from whatsoever source
it came, and the three young people were very merry.
Perhaps they were a little noisy. Perhaps there was
a little innocent slang in their conversation. Ladies
do sometimes talk slang and perhaps the slang was
encouraged for the special edification of Lady Susanna. But slang was never talked at Manor Cross
or Cross Hall, and was odious to Lady Susanna.
When Lady George declared that some offending
old lady ought to be "jumped upon," Lady Susanna
winced visibly. When Jack told Lady George that
"she was the woman to do it," Lady Susanna shivered almost audibly. "Is anything the matter?" asked
Lady George, perhaps not quite innocently.

It seemed to Lady Susanna that these visitors were
never going away, and yet this was the very man
as to whom her brother had cautioned her! And
what an odious man he was—in Lady Susanna's
estimation! A puppy—an absolute puppy! Good-
looking, impudent, familiar, with a light visage, and

continually smiling! All those little gifts, which made him so pleasant to Lady George, were stains and blemishes in the eyes of Lady Susanna. To her thinking, a man—at any rate a gentleman—should be tall, dark, grave, and given to silence rather than to much talk. This Jack chattered about everything, and hardly opened his mouth without speaking slang. About half-past three, when they had been chattering in the drawing-room for an hour, after having chattered over their lunch for a previous hour, Mrs. Houghton made a most alarming proposition. "Let us all go to Berkeley Square and play bagatelle."

"By all means," said Jack. "Lady George, you owe me two new hats already."

Playing bagatelle for new hats! Lady Susanna felt that if ever there could come a time in which interference would be necessary that time had come now. She had resolved that she would be patient; that she should not come down as an offended deity upon Lady George, unless some sufficient crisis should justify such action. But now surely, if ever, she must interpose. Playing at bagatelle with Jack de Baron for new hats, and she with the prospect before her of being Marchioness of Brotherton! "It's only one," said Lady George gaily, "and I daresay I'll win that back to-day. Will you come, Susanna?"

"Certainly not," said Lady Susanna, very grimly. They all looked at her, and Jack de Baron raised his eyebrows, and sat for a moment motionless. Lady Susanna knew that Jack de Baron was intending to ridicule her. Then she remembered that should this perverse young woman insist upon going to Mrs. Houghton's house with so objectionable a companion, her duty to her brother demanded that she also should go. "I mean," said Lady Susanna, "that I had rather not go."

"Why not?" asked Mary.

"I do not think that playing bagatelle for new hats is—is—the best employment in the world either for a lady or for a gentleman." The words were hardly out of her mouth before she herself felt that they were overstrained and more than even this occasion demanded.

"Then we will only play for gloves," said Mary. Mary was not a woman to bear with impunity such an assault as had been made on her.

"Perhaps you will not mind giving it up till George comes back," said Lord George's sister.

"I shall mind very much. I will go up and get ready. You can do as you please." So Mary left the room, and Lady Susanna followed her.

"She means to have her own way," said Jack, when he was alone with his cousin. "She is not at all what I took her to be," said Mrs. Houghton. "The fact is, one cannot know what a girl is as long as a girl is a girl. It is only when she's married that she begins to speak out." Jack hardly agreed with this, thinking that some girls he had known had learned to speak out before they were married.

They all went out together to walk across the parks to Berkeley Square, orders being left that the brougham should follow them later in the afternoon. Lady Susanna had at last resolved that she also would go. The very fact of her entering Mrs. Houghton's house was disagreeable to her; but she felt that duty called her. And, after all, when they got to Berkeley Square no bagatelle was played at all. But the bagatelle would almost have been better than what occurred. A small parcel was lying on the table which was found to contain a pack of pictured cards made for the telling of fortunes, and which some acquaintance had sent to Mrs. Houghton. With these they began telling each other's fortunes, and it seemed to Lady Susanna that they were all as free with lovers and sweethearts as though the two ladies had been housemaids instead of being the wives of steady, well-born husbands. "That's a dark man, with evil designs, a wicked tongue, and no money," said Mrs. Houghton, as a combination of cards lay in Lady George's lap. "Jack, the lady with light hair is only flirting with you. She doesn't care for you one bit."

"I daresay not," said Jack.

"And yet she'll trouble you awfully. Lady Susanna, will you have your fortune told?"

"No," said Lady Susanna, very shortly.

This went on for an hour before the brougham came, during the latter half of which Lady Susanna sat without once opening her lips. If any play could have been childish, it was this play; but to her it was horrible. And then they all sat so near together, and that man was allowed to put cards into her brother's wife's hand and to take them out just as though they had been brother and sister, or play-fellows all their days. And then, as they were going down to the brougham, the odious man got Lady George aside and whispered to her for two minutes. Lady Susanna did not hear a word of their whispers, but knew that they were devilish. And so she would have thought if she had heard them. "You're going to catch it, Lady George," Jack had said. "There's somebody else will catch something if she makes herself disagreeable," Lady George had answered. "I wish I could be invisible and hear it," had been Jack's last words.

"My dear Mary," said Lady Susanna, as soon as they were seated, "you are very young."

"That's a fault that will mend of itself."

"Too quickly, as you will soon find; but in the meantime, as you are a married woman, should you not be careful to guard against the indiscretions of youth?"

"Well, yes; I suppose I ought," said Mary, after a moment of mock consideration. "But then if I were unmarried I ought to do just the same. It's a kind of thing that is a matter of course without talking about it." She had firmly made up her mind that she would submit in no degree to Lady Susanna, and take from her no scolding. Indeed, she had come to a firm resolve long since that she would be scolded by no one but her husband—and by him as little as possible. Now she was angry with him because he had sent this woman to watch her, and was determined that he should know that, though she would submit to him, she would not submit to his sister. The moment for asserting herself had now come.

"A young married woman," said the duenna, "owes it to her husband to be peculiarly careful. She has his happiness and his honour in her hands."

"And he has hers. It seems to me that all these things are matters of course."

"They should be, certainly," said Lady Susanna, hardly knowing how to go on with her work; a little afraid of her companion, but still very intent. "But it will sometimes happen that a young person does not quite know what is right and what is wrong."

"And sometimes it happens that old people don't know. There was Major Jones had his wife taken away from him the other day by the Court because he was always beating her, and he was fifty. I read all about it in the papers. I think the old people are just as bad as the young."

Lady Susanna felt that her reproaches were being cut off from her, and that she must rush at once against the citadel if she meant to take it. "Do you think that playing bagatelle is—nice?"

"Yes, I do; very nice."

"Do you think George would like your playing with Captain de Baron?"

"Why not with Captain de Baron?" said Mary, turning round upon her assailant with absolute ferocity.

"I don't think he would like it. And then that fortune-telling! If you will believe me, Mary, it was very improper."

"I will not believe anything of the kind. Improper! a joke about a lot of picture-cards!"

"It was all about love and lovers," said Lady Susanna, not quite knowing how to express herself, but still sure that she was right.

"Oh, what a mind you must have, Susanna, to pick wrong out of that! All about love and lovers! So are books and songs and plays at the theatre. I suppose you didn't understand that it was intended as a burlesque on fortune telling?"

"And I am quite sure George wouldn't like the kind of slang you were talking with Captain de Baron at lunch."

"If George does not like anything he had better tell me so, and not depute you to do it for him. If he tells me to do anything I shall do it. If you tell me I shall pay no attention to it whatever. You are here as my guest, and not as my governess; and I think your interference very impertinent." This was strong language—so strong that Lady Susanna found it impossible to continue the conversation at that moment. Nothing, indeed, was said between them during the whole afternoon, or at dinner, or in the evening—till Lady Susanna had taken up her candlestick.

There had been that most clearly declared of all war which is shown by absolute silence. But Lady Susanna, as she was retiring to rest, thought it might be wise to make a little effort after peace. She did not at all mean to go back from what charges she had made. She had no idea of owning herself to be wrong. But perhaps she could throw a little oil upon the waters. "Of course," she said, "I should not have spoken as I have done but for my great love for George and my regard for you."

"As far as I am concerned, I think it a mistaken regard," said Mary. "Of course I shall tell George; but even to him I shall say that I will not endure any authority but his own."

"Will you hear me?"

"No, not on this subject. You have accused me of behaving improperly—with that man."

"I do think," began Lady Susanna, not knowing how to pick her words in this emergency, fearing to be too strong, and at the same time conscious that weakness would be folly, "I do think that anything like—like—like flirting is so very bad!"

"Susanna," said Lady George, with a start as she heard the odious words, "as far as I can help it,

I will never speak to you again." There certainly had been no oil thrown upon the waters as yet.

The next day was passed almost in absolute silence. It was the Friday, and each of them knew that Lord George would be home on the morrow. The interval was so short that nothing could be gained by writing to him. Each had her own story to tell, and each must wait till he should be there to hear it. Mary with a most distant civility went through her work of hostess. Lady Susanna made one or two little efforts to subdue her; but, failing, soon gave up the endeavour. In the afternoon Aunt Ju called with her niece, but their conversation did not lessen the breach. Then Lady Susanna went out alone in the brougham; but that had been arranged beforehand. They ate their dinner in silence, in silence read their books, and met in silence at the breakfast-table. At three o'clock Lord George came home, and then Mary, running downstairs, took him with her into the drawing-room. There was one embrace, and then she began. "George," she said, "you must never have Susanna here again."

"Why?" said he.

"She has insulted me. She has said things so nasty that I cannot repeat them, even to you. She has accused me to my face—of flirting. I won't bear it from her. If you said it, it would kill me; but of course you can say what you please. But she shall not scold me, and tell me that I am this and that, because I am not as solemn as she is, George. Do you believe that I have ever—flirted?" She was so impetuous that he had been quite unable to stop her. "Did you mean that she should behave to me like that?"

" This is very bad," he said.

" What is very bad? Is it not bad that she should say such things to me as that? Are you going to take her part against me?"

" Dearest Mary, you seem to be excited."

" Of course I am excited. Would you wish me to have such things as that said to me, and not to be excited? You are not going to take part against me?"

" I have not heard her yet."

" Will you believe her against me? Will she be able to make you believe that I have—flirted? If so, then it is all over."

" What is all over?"

" Oh, George, why did you marry me, if you cannot trust me?"

" Who says that I do not trust you? I suppose the truth is you have been a little—flighty."

" Been what? I suppose you mean the same thing. I have talked and laughed, and been amused, if that means being flighty. She thinks it wicked to laugh, and calls it slang if every word doesn't come out of the grammar. You had better go and hear her, since you will say nothing more to me."

Lord George thought so, too; but he stayed for a few moments in the dining-room, during which he stooped over his wife, who had thrown herself into an arm-chair, and kissed her. As he did so, she merely shook her head, but made no response to his caress. Then he slowly strode away, and went upstairs into the drawing-room.

What took place there need not be recorded at length. Lady Susanna did not try to be mischievous. She spoke much of Mary's youth, and expressed a strong opinion that Captain de Baron was not a fit companion for her. She was very urgent against the use of slang, and said almost harder things of Mrs. Houghton than she did of Jack. She never had meant to imply that Mary had allowed improper attention from the gentleman, but that Mary, being young, had not known what attentions were proper and what improper. To Lady Susanna the whole matter was so serious that she altogether dropped the personal quarrel. " Of course, George," she said, " young people do not like to be told; but it has to be done. And I must say that Mary likes it as little as any person that I have ever known."

This multiplicity of troubles falling together on to the poor man's back almost crushed him. He had returned to town full of that terrible letter which he had pledged himself to write; but the letter was already driven out of his head for the time. It was essentially necessary that he should compose this domestic trouble, and of course he returned to his wife. Equally of course, after a little time, she prevailed. He had to tell her that he was sure that she never flirted. He had to say that she did not talk slang. He had to protest that the fortune-telling cards were absolutely innocent. Then she condescended to say that she would for the present be civil to Susanna, but even while saying that she protested that she would never again have her sister-in-law as a guest in the house.

" You don't know, George, even yet, all that she said to me, or in what sort of way she behaved."

CHAPTER XXVI

THE DEAN RETURNS TO TOWN

"Do you mean to say that you have any objection to my being acquainted with Captain de Baron?" This question Mary asked her husband on the Monday after his return. On that day Lady Susanna went back to Brothershire, having somewhat hurried her return in consequence of the uncomfortable state of things in Munster Court. They had all gone to church together on the intermediate Sunday, and Lady Susanna had done her best to conciliate her sister-in-law. But she was ignorant of the world, and did not know how bitter to a young married woman is such interference as that of which she had been guilty. She could not understand the amount of offence which was rankling in Mary's bosom. It had not consisted only in the words spoken, but her looks in the man's presence had conveyed the same accusation, so that it could be seen and understood by the man himself. Mary, with an effort, had gone on with her play, determined that no one should suppose her to be cowed by her grand sister-in-law; but through it all she had resolved always to look upon Lady Susanna as an enemy. She had already abandoned her threat of not speaking to her own guest; but nothing that Lady Susanna could say, nothing that Lord George could say, softened her heart in the least. The woman had told her that she was a flirt, had declared that what she did and said was improper. The woman had come there as a spy, and the woman should never be her friend. In these circumstances Lord George found it impossible not to refer to the unfortunate subject again, and in doing so caused the above question to be asked. "Do you mean to say that you have any objection to my being acquainted with Captain de Baron?" She looked at him with so much eagerness in her eyes as she spoke that he knew that much at any rate of his present comfort might depend on the answer which he made.

He certainly did object to her being acquainted with Jack de Baron. He did not at all like Jack de Baron. In spite of what he had found himself obliged to say, in order that she might be comforted on his first arrival, he did not like slang, and he did not like fortune-telling cards or bagatelle. His sympathies in these matters were all with his sister. He did like spending his own time with Mrs. Houghton, but it was dreadful to him to think that his wife should be spending hers with Jack de Baron. Nevertheless he could not tell her so.

"No," he said, "I have no particular objection."

"Of course, if you had, I would never see him again. But it would be very dreadful. He would have to be told that you were—jealous."

"I am not in the least jealous," said he angrily. "You should not use such a word."

"Certainly I should not have to use it, but for the disturbance which your sister has caused. But after all that has been said, there must be some understanding. I like Captain de Baron very much, as I daresay you like other ladies. Why not?"

"I have never suspected anything."

"But Susanna did. Of course you don't like all
this, George. I don't like it. I have been so miserable that I have almost cried my eyes out. But
if people will make mischief, what is one to do?
The only thing is not to have the mischief-maker any
more."

The worst of this was, to him, that she was so
manifestly getting the better of him! When he had
married her, not yet nine months since, she had been
a little girl, altogether in his hands, not pretending
to any self-action, and anxious to be guided in everything by him. His only fear had been that she might
be too slow in learning that self-assertion which is
necessary from a married woman to the world at
large. But now she had made very great progress
in the lesson, not only as regarded the world at large,
but as regarded himself also. As for his family—
the grandeur of his family—she clearly had no reverence for that. Lady Susanna, though generally
held to be very awful, had been no more to her than
any other Susan. He almost wished that he had
told her that he did object to Jack de Baron. There
would have been a scene, of course; and she, not
improbably, might have told her father. That at
present would have been doubly disagreeable, as it
was incumbent upon him to stand well with the Dean,
just at this time. There was this battle to be fought
with his brother, and he felt that he could not fight
it without the Dean.

Having given his sanction to Jack de Baron, he
went away to his club to write his letter. This
writing really amounted to no more than copying
the Dean's words, which he had carried in his pocket

ever since he had left the Deanery, and the Dean's words were as follows:

"Munster Court, 26th April, 187—.

"MY DEAR BROTHERTON.—I am compelled to write to you under very disagreeable circumstances, and to do so on a subject which I would willingly avoid if a sense of duty would permit me to be silent.

"You will remember that you wrote to me in October last, telling me that you were about to be married. 'I am to be married to the Marchesa Luigi' were your words. Up to that moment we had heard nothing of the lady or of any arrangement as to a marriage. When I told you of my own intended marriage a few months before that, you merely said in answer that you might probably soon want the house at Manor Cross yourself. It now seems that when you told us of your intended marriage you had already been married over two years, and that, when I told you of mine, you had a son over twelve months old—a fact which I might certainly expect that you would communicate to me at such time.

"I beg to assure you that I am now urged to write by no suspicions of my own; but I know that if things are left to go on as they are now, suspicions will arise at a future time. I write altogether in the interests of your son and heir; and for his sake I beseech you to put at once into the hands of your own lawyer absolute evidence of the date of your marriage, of its legality, and of the birth of your son. It will also be expedient that my lawyer shall see the evidence in your lawyer's hands. If you were to die as matters are now, it would be imperative on me to take steps which would seem to be hostile to

Popenjoy's interest. I think you must yourself feel that this would be so. And yet nothing would be farther from my wish. If we were both to die, the difficulty would be still greater, as in that case proceedings would have to be taken by more distant members of the family.

"I trust you will believe me when I say that my only object is to have the matter satisfactorily settled.   "Your affectionate brother,
                              "GEORGE GERMAIN."

When the Marquis received this letter he was not in the least astonished by it. Lord George had told his sister Sarah that it was to be written, and had even discussed with her the Dean's words. Lady Sarah had thought that, as the Dean was a sagacious man, his exact words had better be used. And then Lady Amelia had been told, Lady Amelia having asked various questions on the subject. Lady Amelia had of course known that her brother would discuss the matter with the Dean, and had begged that she might not be treated as a stranger. Everything had not been told to Lady Amelia, nor had Lady Amelia told all that she had heard to her mother. But the Marchioness had known enough, and had communicated enough to her son to save him from any great astonishment when he got his brother's letter. Of course he had known that some steps would be taken.

He answered the letter at once.

"MY DEAR BROTHER," he said,—"I don't think it necessary to let you know the reasons which induced me to keep my marriage private awhile. You rush at conclusions very fast in thinking that because a

marriage is private, therefore it is illegal. I am glad
that you have no suspicions of your own, and beg
to assure you I don't care whether you have or not.
Whenever you or anybody else may want to try the
case, you, or he, or they will find that I have taken
care that there is plenty of evidence. I didn't know
that you had a lawyer. I only hope he won't run
you into much expense in finding a mare's nest.

"Yours truly, "B."

This was not in itself satisfactory; but, such as
it was, it did for a time make Lord George believe
that Popenjoy was Popenjoy. It was certainly true
of him that he wished Popenjoy to be Popenjoy. No
personal longing for the title or property made him
in his heart disloyal to his brother or his family. And
then the trouble and expense and anxieties of such
a contest were so terrible to his imagination that he
rejoiced when he thought that they might be avoided.
But there was the Dean. The Dean must be satisfied
as well as he, and he felt that the Dean would not
be satisfied. According to agreement he sent a copy
of his brother's letter down to the Dean, and added
the assurance of his own belief that the marriage
had been a marriage, that the heir was an heir, and
that further steps would be useless. It need hardly
be said that the Dean was not satisfied. Before dinner on the following day the Dean was in Munster
Court. "Oh, papa," exclaimed Mary, "I am so glad
to see you." Could it be anything about Captain de
Baron that had brought him up? If so, of course she
would tell him everything. "What brought you up
so suddenly? Why didn't you write? George is at
the club, I suppose." George was really in Berkeley

Square at that moment. "Oh, yes; he will be home
to dinner. Is there anything wrong at Manor Cross,
papa?" Her father was so pleasant in his manner
to her, that she perceived at once that he had not
come up in reference to Captain de Baron. No complaint of her behaviour on that score had as yet
reached him. "Where's your portmanteau, papa?"

"I've got a bed at the hotel in Suffolk Street. I
shall only be here one night, or at the most two;
and, as I had to come suddenly, I wouldn't trouble
you."

"Oh, papa, that's very bad of you."

This she said with that genuine tone which begets
confidence. The Dean was very anxious that his
daughter should in truth be fond of his company. In the
game which he intended to play her co-operation and
her influence over her husband would be very necessary to him. She must be a Lovelace rather than
a Germain till she should blaze forth as the presiding
genius of the Germain family. That Lord George
should become tired of him and a little afraid of him
he knew could not be avoided; but to her he must,
if possible, be a pleasant genius, never accompanied
in her mind by ideas of parental severity or clerical
heaviness. "I should weary you out if I came too
often and come so suddenly," he said, laughing.

"But what has brought you, papa?"

"The Marquis, my dear, who, it seems to me, will,
for some time to come, have a considerable influence
on my doings."

"The Marquis!"

He had made up his mind that she should know everything. If her husband did not tell her, he would.
"Yes, the Marquis. Perhaps I ought to say the

Marchioness, only that I am unwilling to give that title to a lady who I think very probably has no right to it."

" Is all that coming up already?"

" The longer it is postponed the greater will be the trouble to all parties. It cannot be endured that a man in his position should tell us that his son is legitimate when that son was born more than a year before he had declared himself about to marry, and that he should then refuse to furnish us with any evidence."

" Have you asked him?" Mary, as she made the suggestion, was herself horror-stricken at the awfulness of the occasion.

" George has asked him."

" And what has the Marquis done?"

" Sent him back a jeering reply. He has a way of jeering which he thinks will carry everything before it. When I called upon him he jeered at me. But he'll have to learn that he cannot jeer you out of your rights."

" I wish you would not think about my rights, papa."

" Your rights will probably be the rights of some-one else."

" I know, papa; but still——"

" It has to be done, and George quite agrees with me. The letter which he did write to his brother was arranged between us. Lady Sarah is quite of the same accord, and Lady Susanna——"

" Oh, papa, I do so hate Susanna." This she said with all her eloquence.

" I daresay she can make herself unpleasant."

" I have told George that she shall not come here again as a guest."

"What did she do?"

"I cannot bring myself to tell you what it was that she said. I told George, of course. She is a nasty, evil-minded creature—suspecting everything."

"I hope there has been nothing disagreeable."

"It was very disagreeable, indeed, while George was away. Of course I did not care so much when he came back." The Dean, who had been almost frightened, was reassured when he learned that there had been no quarrel between the husband and wife. Soon afterwards Lord George came in, and was astonished to find that his letter had brought up the Dean so quickly. No discussion took place till after dinner, but then the Dean was very perspicuous, and at the same time very authoritative. It was in vain that Lord George asked what they could do, and declared that the evil troubles which must probably arise would all rest on his brother's head. "But we must prevent such troubles, let them rest where they will," said the Dean.

"I don't see what we can do."

"Nor do I, because we are not lawyers. A lawyer will tell us at once. It will probably be our duty to send a commissioner out to Italy to make inquiry."

"I shouldn't like to do that about my brother."

"Of course your brother should be told; or rather everything should be told to your brother's lawyer, so that he might be advised what steps he ought to take. We would do nothing secretly—nothing of which anyone could say that we ought to be ashamed." The Dean proposed that they should both go to his attorney, Mr. Battle, on the following day; but this step seemed to Lord George to be such an absolute declaration of war that he begged for another day's delay; and it was at last arranged that he himself should on that intervening day call on Mr. Stokes, the Germain family lawyer. The Marquis, with one of his jeers, had told his brother that, being a younger brother, he was not entitled to have a lawyer. But in truth Lord George had had very much more to do with Mr. Stokes than the Marquis. All the concerns of the family had been managed by Mr. Stokes. The Marquis probably meant to insinuate that the family bill, which was made out perhaps once every three years, was charged against his account. Lord George did call on Mr. Stokes, and found Mr. Stokes very little disposed to give him any opinion. Mr. Stokes was an honest man who disliked trouble of this kind. He freely admitted that there was ground for inquiry, but did not think that he himself was the man who ought to make it. He would certainly communicate with the Marquis, should Lord George think it expedient to employ any other lawyer, and should that lawyer apply to him. In the meantime he thought that immediate inquiry would be a little precipitate. The Marquis might probably himself take steps to put the matter on a proper footing. He was civil, gracious, almost subservient; but he had no comfort to give and no advice to offer, and, like all attorneys, he was in favour of delay. " Of course, Lord George, you must remember that I am your brother's lawyer, and may .in this matter be called upon to act as his confidential adviser." All this Lord George repeated that evening to the Dean, and the Dean merely said that it had been a matter of course.

Early on the next morning the Dean and Lord George went together to Mr. Battle's chambers. Lord

George felt that he was being driven by his father-in-law; but he felt also that he could not help himself. Mr. Battle, who had chambers in Lincoln's Inn, was a very different man from Mr. Stokes, who carried on his business in a private house at the West End, who prepared wills and marriage settlements for gentlefolk, and who had, in fact, very little to do with law. Mr. Battle was an enterprising man, with whom the Dean's first acquaintance had arisen through the Tallowaxes and the stable interests—a very clever man, and perhaps a little sharp. But an attorney ought to be sharp, and it is not to be understood that Mr. Battle descended to sharp practice. But he was a solicitor with whom the old-fashioned Mr. Stokeses would not find themselves in accord. He was a handsome burly man, nearly sixty years of age, with grey hair and clean shorn face, with bright green eyes, and a well-formed nose and mouth—a prepossessing man, till something restless about the eyes would at last catch the attention and a little change the judgment.

The Dean told him the story, and during the telling he sat looking very pleasant, with a smile on his face, rubbing his two hands together. All the points were made. The letter of the Marquis, in which he told his brother that he was to be married, was shown to him. The concealment of the birth of the boy till the father had made up his mind to come home was urged. The absurdity of his behaviour since he had been at home was described. The singularity of his conduct in allowing none of his family to become acquainted with his wife was pointed out. This was done by the Dean rather than by Lord George, and Lord George, as he heard it all, almost regarded the Dean as his enemy. At last he burst out in his own defence. "Of course you will understand, Mr. Battle, that our only object is to have the thing proved, so that hereafter there may be no trouble."

"Just so, my lord."

"We do not want to oppose my brother, or to injure his child."

"We want to get at the truth," said the Dean.

"Just so."

"Where there is concealment there must be suspicion," urged the Dean.

"No doubt."

"But everything must be done quite openly," said Lord George. "I would not have a step taken without the knowledge of Mr. Stokes. If Mr. Stokes would do it himself on my brother's behalf it would be so much the better."

"That is hardly probable," said the Dean.

"Not at all probable," said Mr. Battle.

"I couldn't be a party to an adverse suit," said Lord George.

"There is no ground for any suit at all," said the lawyer. "We cannot bring an action against the Marquis because he chooses to call the lady he lives with a Marchioness, or because he calls an infant Lord Popenjoy. Your brother's conduct may be ill-judged. From what you tell me, I think it is. But it is not criminal."

"Then nothing need be done," said Lord George.

"A great deal may be done. Inquiry may be made now which might hereafter be impossible." Then he begged that he might have a week to consider the matter, and requested that the two gentlemen would call upon him again.

CHAPTER XXVII

THE BARONESS BANMANN AGAIN

A day or two after the meeting at Mr. Battle's office there came to Lord George a letter from that gentleman suggesting that, as the Dean had undertaken to come up to London again, and as he, Mr. Battle, might not be ready with his advice at the end of a week, that day fortnight might be fixed. To Lord George this delay was agreeable rather than otherwise, as he was not specially anxious for the return of his father-in-law, nor was he longing for action in this question as to his brother's heir. But the Dean, when the lawyer's letter reached him, was certain that Mr. Battle did not seem to lose the time simply in thinking over the matter. Some preliminary inquiry would now be made, even though no positive instructions had been given. He did not at all regret this, but was sure that Lord George would be very angry if he knew it. He wrote back to say that he would be in Munster Court on the evening before the day appointed.

It was now May, and London was bright with all the exotic gaiety of the season. The Park was crowded with riders at one, and was almost impassable at six. Dress was outvying dress, and equipage equipage. Men and women, but principally women, seemed to be intent on finding out new ways of scattering money. Tradesmen, no doubt, knew much of

defaulters, and heads of families might find themselves pressed for means; but to the outside West-end
eye looking at the outside West-end world it seemed
as though wealth was unlimited and money a drug.
To those who had known the thing for years, to
young ladies who were now entering on their seventh or eighth campaign, there was a feeling of business about it all which, though it buoyed them up by
its excitement, robbed amusement of most of its pleasure. A ball cannot be very agreeable in which you
may not dance with the man you like and are not
asked by the man you want; at which you are forced
to make a note that that full-blown hope is futile,
and that this little bud will surely never come to
flower. And then the toil of smiles, the pretence at
flirtation, the long-continued assumption of fictitious
character, the making of oneself bright to the bright,
solemn to the solemn, and romantic to the romantic,
is work too hard for enjoyment. But our heroine
had no such work to do. She was very much admired and could thoroughly enjoy the admiration. She
had no task to perform. She was not carrying out
her profession by midnight labours. Who shall say
whether now and again a soft impalpable regret—a
regret not recognised as such—may not have stolen
across her mind, telling her that if she had seen
all this before she was married instead of afterwards,
she might have found a brighter lot for herself? If
it were so, the only enduring effect of such a feeling
was a renewal of that oft-made resolution that she
would be in love with her husband. The ladies whom
she knew had generally their carriages and riding
horses. She had only a brougham, and had that
kept for her by the generosity of her father. The

Dean, when coming to town, had brought with him
the horse which she used to ride, and wished that
it should remain. But Lord George, with a husband's solicitude, and perhaps with something of a
poor man's proper dislike to expensive habits, had
refused his permission. She soon, too, learned to
know the true sheen of diamonds, the luxury of pearls,
and the richness of rubies; whereas she herself wore
only the little ornaments which had come from the
Deanery. And as she danced in spacious rooms and
dined in noble halls, and was *fêted* on grand stair-
cases, she remembered what a little place was the
little house in Munster Court, and that she was to
stay there only for a few weeks more before she was
taken to the heavy dulness of Cross Hall. But still
she always came back to that old resolution. She
was so flattered, so courted, so petted and made
much of, that she could not but feel that had all this
world been opened to her sooner her destiny would
probably have been different; but then it might have
been different, and very much less happy. She still
told herself that she was sure that Lord George was
all that he ought to be.

Two or three things did tease her certainly. She
was very fond of balls, but she soon found that Lord
George disliked them as much, and when present
was always anxious to get home. She was a married woman, and it was open to her to go alone; but
that she did not like, nor would he allow it. Sometimes she joined herself to other parties. Mrs.
Houghton was always ready to be her companion,
and old Mrs. Montacute Jones, who went everywhere,
had taken a great liking to her. But there were
two antagonistic forces, her husband and herself, and

of course she had to yield to the stronger force. The thing might be managed occasionally—and the occasion was no doubt much the pleasanter because it had to be so managed—but there was always the feeling that these bright glimpses of Paradise, these entrances into Elysium, were not free to her as to other ladies. And then one day, or rather one night, there came a great sorrow—a sorrow which robbed these terrestrial Paradises of half their brightness and more than half their joy. One evening he told her that he did not like her to waltz. "Why?" she innocently asked. They were in the brougham, going home, and she had been supremely happy at Mrs. Montacute Jones's house. Lord George said that he could hardly explain the reason. He made rather a long speech, in which he asked her whether she was not aware that many married women did not waltz. "No," said she. "That is, of course, when they get old they don't." "I am sure," said he, "that when I say I do not like it, that will be enough." "Quite enough," she answered, "to prevent my doing it, though not enough to satisfy me why it should not be done." He said no more to her on the occasion, and so the matter was considered to be settled. Then she remembered that her very last waltz had been with Jack de Baron. Could it be that he was jealous? She was well aware that she took great delight in waltzing with Captain de Baron because he waltzed so well. But now that pleasure was over, and for ever! Was it that her husband disliked waltzing, or that he disliked Jack de Baron?

A few days after this Lady George was surprised by a visit from the Baroness Banmann, the lady whom she had been taken to hear at the Disabilities.

Since that memorable evening she had seen Aunt Ju
more than once, and had asked how the cause of the
female architects was progressing; but she had never
again met the Baroness. Aunt Ju had apparently
been disturbed by these questions. She had made no
further effort to make Lady George a proselyte by
renewed attendance at the Rights of Women Institute,
and had seemed almost anxious to avoid the subject.
As Lady George's acquaintance with the Baroness
had been owing altogether to Aunt Ju she was
now surprised that the German lady should call upon
her.

. The German lady began a story with great impetuosity—with so much impetuosity that poor Mary
could not understand half that was said to her. But
she did learn that the Baroness had in her own estimation been very ill-treated, and that the ill-treatment
had come mainly from the hands of Aunt Ju and Lady
Selina Protest. And it appeared at length that the
Baroness claimed to have been brought over from
Bavaria with a promise that she should have the
exclusive privilege of using the hall of the Disabilities
on certain evenings, but that this privilege was now
denied to her. The Disabilities seemed to prefer her
younger rival, Miss Doctor Olivia Q. Fleabody, whom
Mary now learned to be a person of no good repute
whatever, and by no means fit to address the masses
of Marylebone. But what did the Baroness want of
her? What with the female lecturer's lack of English pronunciation, what with her impetuosity, and
with Mary's own innocence on the matter, it was some
time before the younger lady did understand what the
elder lady required. At last eight tickets were brought
out of her pocket, on looking at which Mary began to

understand that the Baroness had established a rival Disabilities, very near the other, in Lisson Grove; and then at last, but very gradually, she further understood that these were front-row tickets, and were supposed to be worth half-a-crown each. But it was not till after that, till further explanation had been made which must, she feared, have been very painful to the Baroness, that she began to perceive that she was expected to pay for the eight tickets on the moment. She had a sovereign in her pocket, and was quite willing to sacrifice it; but she hardly knew how to hand the coin bodily to a Baroness. When she did do so, the Baroness very well knew how to put it into her pocket. "You will like to keep the entire eight?" asked the Baroness. Mary thought that four might perhaps suffice for her own wants; whereupon the Baroness re-pocketed four, but of course did not return the change.

But even then the Baroness had not completed her task. Aunt Ju had evidently been false and treacherous, but might still be won back to loyal honesty. So much Mary gradually perceived to be the drift of the lady's mind. Lady Selina was hopeless. Lady Selina, whom the Baroness intended to drag before all the judges in England, would do nothing fair or honest; but Aunt Ju might yet be won. Would Lady George go with the Baroness to Aunt Ju? The servant had unfortunately just announced the brougham as being at the door. "Ah," said the Baroness, "it vould be ten minutes, and vould be my salvation." Lady George did not at all want to go to the house in Green Street. She had no great desire to push her acquaintance with Aunt Ju, she particularly disliked the younger Miss Mildmay, and she felt that she had no business to interfere in this matter. But there is nothing which requires so much experience to attain as the power of refusing. Almost before she had made up her mind whether she would refuse or not the Baroness was in the brougham with her, and the coachman had been desired to take them to Green Street. Throughout the whole distance the Baroness was voluble and unintelligible; but Lady George could hear the names of Selina Protest and Olivia Q. Fleabody through the thunder of the lady's loud complaints.

Yes, Miss Mildmay was at home. Lady George gave her name to the servant, and also especially requested that the Baroness Banmann might be first announced. She had thought it over in the brougham, and had determined that if possible it should appear that the Baroness had brought her. Twice she repeated the name to the servant. When they reached the drawing-room only the younger Miss Mildmay was present. She sent the servant to her aunt, and received her two visitors very demurely. With the Baroness, of whom probably she had heard quite enough, she had no sympathies; and with Lady George she had her own special ground of quarrel. Five or six very long minutes passed during which little or nothing was said. The Baroness did not wish to expend her eloquence on an unprofitable young lady, and Lady George could find no subject for small talk. At last the door was opened and the servant invited the Baroness to go downstairs. The Baroness had perhaps been unfortunate, for at this very time Lady Selina Protest was down in the dining-room discussing the affairs of the Institute with Aunt Ju. There was a little difficulty in making the lady understand what was required of her, but after awhile she did follow the servant down to the dining-room.

Lady George, as soon as the door was closed, felt that the blood rushed to her face. She was conscious at the moment that Captain de Baron had been the girl's lover, and there were some who said that it was because of her that he had deserted the girl. The girl had already said words to her on the subject which had been very hard to bear. She had constantly told herself that in this matter she was quite innocent—that her friendship with Jack was simple, pure friendship, that she liked him because he laughed and talked and treated the world lightly; that she rarely saw him except in the presence of his cousin, and that everything was as it ought to be. And yet, when she found herself alone with this Miss Mildmay, she was suffused with blushes, and uneasy. She felt that she ought to make some excuse for her visit. "I hope," she said, "that your aunt will understand that I brought the lady here only because she insisted on being brought." Miss Mildmay bowed. "She came to me, and I really couldn't quite understand what she had to say. But the brougham was there, and she would get into it. I am afraid there has been some quarrel."

"I don't think that matters at all," said Miss Mildmay.

"Only your aunt might think it so impertinent of me! She took me to that Institute once, you know."

"I don't know anything about the Institute. As for the German woman, she is an impostor, but it doesn't matter. There are three of them there now, and they can have it out together."

Lady George didn't understand whether her com-

panion meant to blame her for coming, but was quite
sure, from the tone of the girl's voice and the look
of her eyes, that she meant to be uncivil.

"I am surprised," continued Miss Mildmay, "that
you should come to this house at all."

"I hope your aunt will not think——"

"Never mind my aunt. The house is more my
house than my aunt's. After what you have done
to me——"

"What have I done to you?" She could not help
asking the question, and yet she well knew the nature
of the accusation. And she could not stop the rushing of the tell-tale blood.

Augusta Mildmay was blushing too, but the blush
on her face consisted in two red spots beneath the
eyes. The determination to say what she was going
to say had come upon her suddenly. She had not
thought that she was about to meet her rival. She
had planned nothing; but now she was determined.

"What have you done?" she said. "You know
very well what you have done. Do you mean to tell
me that you had never heard of anything between me
and Captain de Baron. Will you dare to tell me
that? Why don't you answer me, Lady George Germain?"

This was a question which she did not wish to
answer, and one that did not at all appertain to
herself—which did not require any answer for the
clearing of herself; but yet it was now asked in such
a manner that she could not save herself from
answering it.

"I think I did hear that you and he—knew each
other."

"Knew each other! Don't be so mealy-mouthed.

I don't mean to be mealy-mouthed, I can tell you. You knew all about it. Adelaide has told you. You knew that we were engaged."

"No," exclaimed Lady George; "she never told me that."

"She did. I know she did. She confessed to me that she had told you so."

"But what if she had?"

"Of course he is nothing to you," said the young lady with a sneer.

"Nothing at all—nothing on earth. How dare you ask such a question? If Captain de Baron is engaged, I can't make him keep his engagements."

"You can make him break them."

"That is not true. I can make him do nothing of the kind. You have no right to talk to me in this way, Miss Mildmay."

"Then I shall do it without a right. You have come between me and all my happiness."

"You cannot know that I am a married woman," said Lady George, speaking half in innocence and half in anger, almost out of breath with confusion, "or you wouldn't speak like that."

"Psha!" exclaimed Miss Mildmay. "It is nothing to me whether you are married or single. I care nothing though you have twenty lovers, if you do not interfere with me."

"It is a falsehood," said Lady George, who was now standing. "I have no lover. It is a wicked falsehood."

"I care nothing for wickedness or falseness either. Will you promise me if I hold my tongue that you will have nothing further to say to Captain de Baron?"

"No; I will promise nothing. I should be ashamed
of myself to make such a promise."

"Then I shall go to Lord George. I do not want
to make mischief, but I am not going to be treated
in this way. How would you like it? When I tell
you that the man is engaged to me why cannot you
leave him alone?"

"I do leave him alone," said Mary, stamping her
foot.

"You do everything you can to cheat me of him.
I shall tell Lord George."

"You may tell whom you like," said Mary, rushing
to the bell-handle and pulling it with all her might.
"You have insulted me, and I will never speak to
you again." Then she burst out crying, and hurried
to the door. "Will you—get me—my—carriage?"
she said to the man through her sobs. As she descended the stairs she remembered that she had
brought the German baroness with her, and that the
German baroness would probably expect to be taken
away again. But when she reached the hall the door
of the dining-room burst open, and the German
baroness appeared. It was evident that two scenes
had been going on in the same house at the same
moment. Through the door the Baroness came first,
waving her hands above her head. Behind her was
Aunt Ju, advancing with imploring gesture. And
behind Aunt Ju might be seen Lady Selina Protest
standing in mute dignity.

"It is all a got-up cheating and a fraud," said the
Baroness; "and I vill have justice—English justice."

The servant was standing with the front door open,
and the Baroness went straight into Lady George's
brougham, as though it had been her own.

"Oh, Lady George," said Aunt Ju, "what are you to do with her?"

But Lady George was so taken up with her own trouble that she could hardly think of the other matter. She had to say something.

"Perhaps I had better go with her. Good-bye." And then she followed the Baroness.

"I did not tink dere was such robbery with ladies," said the Baroness.

But the footman was asking for directions for the coachman. Whither was he to go?

"I do not care," said the Baroness.

Lady George asked her in a whisper whether she would be taken home.

"Anywhere," said the Baroness.

In the meantime the footman was still standing, and Aunt Ju could be seen in the hall through the open door of the house. During the whole time our poor Mary's heart was crushed by the accusations which had been made against her upstairs.

"Home," said Mary in despair. To have the Baroness in Munster Court would be dreadful; but anything was better than standing in Green Street with the servant at the carriage window.

Then the Baroness began her story. Lady Selina Protest had utterly refused to do her justice, and Aunt Ju was weak enough to be domineered by Lady Selina. That, as far as Mary understood anything about it, was the gist of the story. But she did not try to understand anything about it. During the drive her mind was intent on forming some plan by which she might be able to get rid of her companion without asking her into her house. She had paid her sovereign, and surely the Baroness had no right to de-

mand more of her. When she reached Munster Court
her plan was in some sort framed. "And now,
madam," she said, "where shall I tell my servant to
take you?" The Baroness looked very suppliant.
"If you vas not busy I should so like just one half-
hour of conversation." Mary nearly yielded. For a
moment she hesitated as though she were going to
put up her hand and help the lady out. But then the
memory of her own unhappiness steeled her heart,
and the feeling grew strong within her that this nasty
woman was imposing on her—and she refused. "I
am afraid, madam," she said, "that my time is altogether occupied." "Then let him take me to 10,
Alexandria Row, Maida Vale," said the Baroness,
throwing herself sulkily back into the carriage. Lady
George gave the direction to the astounded coachman
—for Maida Vale was a long way off—and succeeded
in reaching her own drawing-room alone.

What was she to do? The only course in which
there seemed to be safety was in telling all to her
husband. If she did not, it would probably be told
by the cruel lips of that odious woman. But yet, how
was she to tell it? It was not as though everything
in this matter was quite pleasant between her and
him. Lady Susanna had accused her of flirting with
the man, and that she had told to him. And in her
heart of hearts she believed that the waltzing had
been stopped because she had waltzed with Jack de
Baron. Nothing could be more unjust, nothing more
cruel; but still there were the facts. And then the
sympathy between her and her husband was so im-
perfect. She was ever trying to be in love with him,
but had never yet succeeded in telling even herself
that she had succeeded.

CHAPTER XXVIII

"WHAT MATTER IF SHE DOES?"

ABOUT noon on the day after the occurrences related in the last chapter Lady George owned to herself that she was a most unfortunate young woman. Her husband had gone out, and she had not as yet told him anything of what that odious Augusta Mildmay had said to her. She had made various little attempts, but had not known how to go on with them. She had begun by giving him her history of the Baroness, and he had scolded her for giving the woman a sovereign and for taking the woman about London in her carriage. It is very difficult to ask in a fitting way for the sympathies and co-operation of one who is scolding you. And Mary in this matter wanted almost more than sympathy and co-operation. Nothing short of the fullest manifestation of affectionate confidence would suffice to comfort her; and, desiring this, she had been afraid to mention Captain de Baron's name. She thought of the waltzing, thought of Susanna, and was cowardly. So the time slipped away from her, and when he left her on the following morning her story had not been told. He was no sooner gone than she felt that if it were to be told at all it should have been told at once.

Was it possible that that venomous girl should really go to her husband with such a complaint? She knew well enough, or at any rate thought that she knew, that there had never been an engagement be-

tween the girl and Jack de Baron. She had heard
it all over and over again from Adelaide Houghton,
and had even herself been present at some joke on
the subject between Adelaide and Jack. There was an
idea that Jack was being pursued, and Mrs. Houghton
had not scrupled to speak of it before him. Mary had
not admired her friend's taste, and had on such occasions thought well of Jack because he had simply
disowned any consciousness of such a state of things.
But all this had made Mary sure that there was not
and that there never had been any engagement; and
yet the wretched woman, in her futile and frantic
endeavours to force the man to marry her, was not
ashamed to make so gross an attack as this!

If it hadn't been for Lady Susanna and those
wretched fortune-telling cards, and that one last waltz,
there would be nothing in it; but as it was, there
might be so much! She had begun to fear that her
husband's mind was suspicious—that he was prone to
believe that things were going badly. Before her
marriage, when she had in truth known him not at all,
her father had given her some counsels in his light,
airy way, which, however, had sunk deep into her mind,
and which she had endeavoured to follow to the letter.
He had said not a word to her as to her conduct to
other men. It would not be natural that a father
should do so. But he had told her how to behave
to her husband. Men, he had assured her, were to be
won by such comforts as he described. A wife should
provide that a man's dinner was such as he liked to
eat, his bed such as he liked to lie on, his clothes
arranged as he liked to wear them, and the household hours fixed to suit his convenience. She should
learn and indulge his habits, should suit herself to

him in external things of life, and could thus win from
him a liking and a reverence which would wear better
than the feeling generally called love, and would at
last give the woman her proper influence. The Dean
had meant to teach his child how she was to rule her
husband, but of course had been too wise to speak of
dominion. Mary, declaring to herself that the feeling generally called love should exist as well as the
liking and the reverence, had laboured hard to win
it all from her husband in accordance with her father's
teachings; but it had seemed to her that her labour
was wasted. Lord George did not in the least care
what he ate. He evidently had no opinion at all about
the bed; and as to his clothes, seemed to receive no
accession of comfort by having one wife and her
maid, instead of three sisters and their maid and old
Mrs. Toff to look after them. He had no habits which
she could indulge. She had looked about for the
weak point in his armour, but had not found it. It
seemed to her that she had no influence over him
whatever. She was of course aware that they lived
upon her fortune; but she was aware also that he
knew that it was so, and that the consciousness made
him unhappy. She could not, therefore, even endeavour to minister to his comfort by surrounding him
with pretty things. All expenditure was grievous to
him. The only matter in which she had failed to
give way to any expressed wish had been in that important matter of their town residence; and, as to
that, she had in fact had no power of yielding. It
had been of such moment as to have been settled for
her by previous contract. But, she had often thought
whether, in her endeavour to force herself to be in
love with him, she would not persistently demand that

Munster Court should be abandoned, and that all the pleasures of her own life should be sacrificed.

Now, for a day or two, she heartily wished that she had done so. She liked her house; she liked her brougham; she liked the gaieties of her life; and in a certain way she liked Jack de Baron; but they were all to her as nothing when compared to her duty and her sense of the obligations which she owed to her husband. Playful and childish as she was, all this was very serious to her; perhaps the more serious because she was playful and childish. She had not experience enough to know how small some things are, and how few are the evils which cannot be surmounted. It seemed to her that if Miss Mildmay were at this moment to bring the horrid charge against her, it might too probably lead to the crash of ruin and the horrors of despair. And yet, through it all, she had a proud feeling of her own innocence, and a consciousness that she would speak out very loudly should her husband hint to her that he believed the accusation.

Her father would now be in London in a day or two, and on this occasion would again be staying in Munster Court. At last she made up her mind that she would tell everything to him. It was not, perhaps, the wisest resolution to which she could have come. A married woman should not usually teach herself to lean on her parents instead of her husband, and certainly not on her father. It is in this way that divided households are made. But she had no other real friend of whom she could ask a question. She liked Mrs. Houghton, but, as to such a matter as this, distrusted her altogether. She liked Miss Houghton, her friend's aunt, but did not know her well enough for such service as this. She had neither brother nor sister of her own, and her husband's brothers and sisters were certainly out of the question. Old Mrs. Montacute Jones had taken a great fancy to her, and she almost thought that she could have asked Mrs. Jones for advice; but she had no connection with Mrs. Jones, and did not dare to do it. Therefore she resolved to tell everything to her father.

On the evening before her father came to town there was another ball at Mrs. Montacute Jones's. This old lady, who had no one belonging to her but an invisible old husband, was the gayest of the gay among the gay people of London. On this occasion Mary was to have gone with Lady Brabazon, who was related to the Germains, and Lord George had arranged an escape for himself. They were to drive out together, and when she went to her ball he would go to bed. But in the course of the afternoon she told him that she was writing to Lady Brabazon to decline.

"Why won't you go?" said he.

"I don't care about it."

"If you mean that you won't go without me, of course I will go."

"It isn't that exactly. Of course it is nicer if you go; though I wouldn't take you if you don't like it. But——"

"But what, dear?"

"I think I'd rather not to-night. I don't know that I am quite strong enough." Then he didn't say another word to press her—only begging that she would not go to the dinner either if she were not well. But she was quite well, and she did go to the dinner.

Again she had meant to tell him why she would not go to Mrs. Jones's ball, but had been unable. Jack de Baron would be there, and would want to know why

she would not waltz. And Adelaide Houghton would
tease her about it, very likely before him. She had
always waltzed with him, and could not now refuse
without some reason. So she gave up her ball, sending word to say that she was not very well. "I
shouldn't at all wonder if he has kept her at home
because he's afraid of you," said Mrs. Houghton to
her cousin.

Late in the following afternoon, before her husband had come home from his club, she told her father
the whole story of her interview with Miss Mildmay.
"What a tiger," he said, when he had heard it. "I
have heard of women like that before, but I have never
believed in them."

"You don't think she will tell him?"

"What matter if she does? What astonishes me
most is that a woman should be so unwomanly as to
fight for a man in such a way as that. It is the sort
of thing that men used to do. 'You must give up
your claim to that lady or else you must fight me.'
Now she comes forward and says that she will fight
you."

"But, papa, I have no claim."

"Nor probably has she?"

"No; I'm sure she has not. But what does that
matter? The horrid thing is that she should say all
this to me. I told her that she couldn't know that I
was married."

"She merely wanted to make herself disagreeable.
If one comes across disagreeable people one has to
bear with it. I suppose she was jealous. She has
seen you dancing or perhaps talking with the man."

"Oh, yes."

"And in her anger she wanted to fly at someone."

"It is not her I care about, papa."

"What then?"

"If she were to tell George."

"What if she did? You do not mean to say that he would believe her? You do not think that he is jealous?"

She began to perceive that she could not get any available counsel from her father unless she could tell him everything. She must explain to him what evil Lady Susanna had already done; how her sister-in-law had acted as duenna, and had dared to express a suspicion about this very man. And she must tell him that Lord George had desired her not to waltz, and had done so, as she believed, because he had seen her waltzing with Jack de Baron. But all this seemed to her to be impossible. There was nothing which she would not be glad that he knew, if only he could be made to know it all truly. But she did not think that she could tell him what had really happened; and were she to do so, there would be horrid doubts on his mind. "You do not mean to say that he is given to that sort of thing?" asked the Dean, again with a look of anger.

"Oh, no; at least I hope not. Susanna did try to make mischief."

"The d—— she did," said the Dean. Mary almost jumped in her chair, she was so much startled by such a word from her father's mouth. "If he's fool enough to listen to that old cat, he'll make himself a miserable and a contemptible man. Did she say anything to him about this very man?"

"She said something very unpleasant to me, and of course I told George."

"Well?"

"He was all that was kind. He declared that he had no objection to make Captain de Baron at all. I am sure there was no reason why he should."

"Tush!" exclaimed the Dean, as though any assurance or even any notice of the matter in that direction were quite unnecessary. "And there was an end of that?"

"I think he is a little inclined to be—to be——"

"To be what? You had better tell it all out, Mary."

"Perhaps what you would call strict. He told me not to waltz any more the other day."

"He's a fool," said the Dean, angrily.

"Oh, no, papa; don't say that. Of course he has a right to think as he likes, and of course I am bound to do as he says."

"He has no experience—no knowledge of the world. Perhaps one of the last things which a man learns is to understand innocence when he sees it." The word innocence was so pleasant to her that she put out her hand and touched his knee. "Take no notice of what that angry woman said to you. Above all, do not drop your acquaintance with this gentleman. You should be too proud to be influenced in any way by such scandal."

"But if she were to speak to George?"

"She will hardly dare. But if she does, that is no affair of yours. You can have nothing to do with it till he shall speak to you."

"You would not tell him?"

"No; I should not even think about it. She is below your notice. If it should be the case that she dares to speak to him, and that he should be weak enough to be moved by what such a creature can say to him, you will, I am sure, have dignity enough to hold your own with him. Tell him that you think too much of his honour, as well as of your own, to make it necessary for him to trouble himself. But he will know that himself, and if he does speak to you, he will only speak in pity for her." All this he said slowly and seriously, looking as she had sometimes seen him look when preaching in the cathedral. And she believed him now as she always believed him then, and was in a great measure comforted.

But she could not but be surprised that her father should so absolutely refuse to entertain the idea that any intimacy between herself and Captain De Baron should be injurious. It gratified her that it should be so, but nevertheless she was surprised. She had endeavoured to examine the question by her own lights, but had failed in answering it. She knew well enough that she liked the man. She had discovered in him the realisation of those early dreams. His society was in every respect pleasant to her. He was full of playfulness, and yet always gentle. He was not very clever, but clever enough. She had made the mistake in life—or rather others had made it for her—of taking herself too soon from her playthings, and devoting herself to the stern reality of a husband. She understood something of this, and liked to think that she might amuse herself innocently with such a one as Jack de Baron. She was sure that she did not love him—that there was no danger of her loving him; and she was quite confident also that he did not love her. But yet—yet there had been a doubt on her mind. Innocent as it all was, there might be cause of offence to her husband. It was this thought that had made her sometimes long to be taken away from London and be immured amidst the dulness of Cross

Hall. But of such dangers and of such fears her father saw nothing. Her father simply bade her to maintain her own dignity and have her own way. Perhaps her father was right.

On the next day the Dean and his son-in-law went, according to appointment, to Mr. Battle. Mr. Battle received them with his usual bland courtesy and listened attentively to whatever the two gentlemen had to say. Lawyers who know their business always allow their clients to run out their stories even when knowing that the words so spoken are wasted words. It is the quickest way of arriving at their desired result. Lord George had a good deal to say, because his mind was full of the conviction that he would not for worlds put an obstacle in the way of his brother's heir, if he could be made sure that the child was the heir. He wished for such certainty, and cursed the heavy chance that had laid so grievous a duty on his shoulders. When he had done, Mr. Battle began. " I think, Lord George, that I have learned most of the particulars."

Lord George started back in his chair. " What particulars? " said the Dean.

" The Marchioness's late husband—for she doubtless is his lordship's wife—was a lunatic."

" A lunatic! " said Lord George.

" We do not quite know when he died, but we believe it was about a month or two before the date at which his lordship wrote home to say that he was about to be married."

" Then that child cannot be Lord Popenjoy," said the Dean with exultation.

" That's going a little too fast, Mr. Dean. There may have been a divorce."

"There is no such thing in Roman Catholic countries," said the Dean. "Certainly not in Italy."

"I do not quite know," said the lawyer. "Of course we are as yet very much in the dark. I should not wonder if we found that there had been two marriages. All this is what we have got to find out. The lady certainly lived in great intimacy with your brother before her first husband died."

"How do you know anything about it?" asked Lord George.

"I happened to have heard the name of the Marchese Luigi, and I knew where to apply for information."

"We did not mean that any inquiry should be made so suddenly," said Lord George angrily.

"It was for the best," said the Dean.

"Certainly for the best," said the unruffled lawyer. "I would now recommend that I may be commissioned to send out my own confidential clerk to learn all the circumstances of the case; and that I should inform Mr. Stokes that I am going to do so, on your instructions, Lord George." Lord George shivered. "I think we should even offer to give his lordship time to send an agent with my clerk if he pleases to do so, or to send one separately at the same time, or to take any other step that he may please. It is clearly your duty, my lord, to have the inquiry made."

"Your manifest duty," said the Dean, unable to restrain his triumph.

Lord George pleaded for delay, and before he left the lawyer's chambers almost quarrelled with his father-in-law; but before he did leave them he had given the necessary instructions.

CHAPTER XXIX

MR. HOUGHTON WANTS A GLASS OF SHERRY

LORD GEORGE, when he got out of the lawyer's office with his father-in-law, expressed himself as being very angry at what had been done. While discussing the matter within, in the presence of Mr. Battle, he had been unable to withstand the united energies of the Dean and the lawyer, but, nevertheless, even while he had yielded, he had felt that he was being driven.

"I don't think he was at all justified in making any inquiry," he said, as soon as he found himself in the square.

"My dear George," replied the Dean, "the quicker this can be done the better."

"An agent should only act in accordance with his instructions."

"Without disputing that, my dear fellow, I cannot but say that I am glad to have learned so much."

"And I am very sorry."

"We both mean the same thing, George."

"I don't think we do," said Lord George, who was determined to be angry.

"You are sorry that it should be so—and so am I." The triumph which had sat in the Dean's eye when he heard the news in the lawyer's chambers almost belied this latter assertion. "But I certainly am glad to be on the track as soon as possible, if there is a track which it is our duty to follow."

"I didn't like that man at all," said Lord George.

"I neither like him nor dislike him; but I believe him to be honest, and I know him to be clever. He will find out the truth for us."

"And when it turns out that Brotherton was legally married to the woman, what will the world think of me then?"

"The world will think that you have done your duty. There can be no question about it, George. Whether it be agreeable or disagreeable, it must be done. Could you have brought yourself to have thrown the burden of doing this upon your own child, perhaps some five-and-twenty years hence, when it may be done so much easier now by yourself?"

"I have no child," said Lord George.

"But you will have." The Dean, as he said this, could not keep himself from looking too closely into his son-in-law's face. He was most anxious for the birth of that grandson who was to be made a marquis by his own energies.

"God knows. Who can say?"

"At any rate, there is that child at Manor Cross. If he be not the legitimate heir, is it not better for him that the matter should be settled now than when he may have lived twenty years in expectation of the title and property?" The Dean said much more than this, urging the propriety of what had been done, but he did not succeed in quieting Lord George's mind.

That same day the Dean told the whole story to his daughter, perhaps in his eagerness adding something to what he had heard from the lawyer. "Divorces in Roman Catholic countries," he said, "are quite impossible. I believe they are never granted, except for State purposes. There may be some new civil law, but I don't think it; and then, if the man was an acknowledged lunatic, it must have been impossible."

"But how could the Marquis be so foolish, papa?"

"Ah, that is what we do not understand. But it will come out. You may be sure it will all come out. Why did he come home to England and bring them with him? And why just at this time? Why did he not communicate his first marriage? and if not that, why the second? He probably did not intend at first to put his child forward as Lord Popenjoy, but has become subsequently bold. The woman, perhaps, has gradually learned the facts, and insisted on making the claim for her child. She may gradually have become stronger than he. He may have thought that by coming here and declaring the boy to be his heir, he would put down suspicion by the very boldness of his assertion. Who can say? But these are the facts, and they are sufficient to justify us in demanding that everything shall be brought to light." Then for the first time he asked her what immediate hope there was that Lord George might have an heir. She tried to laugh, then blushed; then wept a tear or two, and muttered something which he failed to hear. "There is time enough for all that, Mary," he said, with his pleasant smile, and then left her.

Lord George did not return home till late in the afternoon. He went first to Mrs. Houghton's house, and told her nearly everything. But he told it in such a way as to make her understand that his strongest feeling at the present moment was one of anger against the Dean.

"Of course, George," she said, for she always called him George now, "the Dean will try to have it all his own way."

"I am almost sorry that I ever mentioned my brother's name to him?"

"She, I suppose, is ambitious," said Mrs. Houghton. "She" was intended to signify Mary.

"No. To do Mary justice, it is not her fault. I don't think she cares for it."

"I daresay she would like to be a Marchioness as well as anyone else. I know I should."

"You might have been," he said, looking tenderly into her face.

"I wonder how I should have borne all this? You say that she is indifferent. I should have been so anxious on your behalf—to see you installed in your rights!"

"I have no rights. There is my brother."

"Yes; but as the heir. She has none of the feeling about you that I have, George." Then she put out her hand to him, which he took and held. "I begin to think that I was wrong. I begin to know that I was wrong. We could have lived, at any rate."

"It is too late," he said, still holding her hand.

"Yes; it is too late. I wonder whether you will ever understand the sort of struggle which I had to go through, and the feeling of duty which overcame me at last? Where should we have lived?"

"At Cross Hall, I suppose."

"And if there had been children, how should we have brought them up?" She did not blush as she asked the question, but he did. "And yet I wish that I had been braver. I think I should have suited you better than she."

"She is as good as gold," he said, moved by a certain loyalty which, though it was not sufficient absolutely to protect her from wrong, was too strong to endure to hear her reproached.

"Do not tell me of her goodness," said Mrs. Houghton, jumping up from her seat. "I do not want to hear of her goodness. Tell me of my goodness. Does she love you as I do? Does she make you the hero of her thoughts? She has no idea of any hero. She would think more of Jack de Baron whirling round the room with her than of your position in the world, or of his, or even of her own." He winced visibly when he heard Jack de Baron's name. "You need not be afraid," she continued; "for though she is, as you say, as good as gold, she knows nothing about love. She took you when you came because it suited the ambition of the Dean—as she would have taken anything else that he provided for her."

"I believe she loves me," he said, having in his heart of hearts, at the moment, much more solicitude in regard to his absent wife than to the woman who was close to his feet and was flattering him to the top of her bent.

"And her love, such as it is, is sufficient for you?"

"She is my wife."

"Yes; because I allowed it; because I thought it wrong to subject your future life to the poverty which I should have brought with me. Do you think there was no sacrifice then?"

"But Adelaide; it is so."

"Yes, it is so. But what does it all mean? The time is gone by when men, or women either, were too qualmish and too queasy to admit the truth even to themselves. Of course you are married, and so am I; but marriage does not alter the heart. I did not cease to love you because I would not marry you. You could not cease to love me merely because I refused you. When I acknowledged to myself that Mr. Houghton's income was necessary to me, I did not become enamoured of him. Nor, I suppose, did you when you found the same as to Miss Lovelace's money."

Upon this he also jumped up from his seat, and stood before her. "I will not have even you say that I married my wife for her money."

"How was it, then, George? I am not blaming you for doing what I did as well as you."

"I should blame myself. I should feel myself to be degraded."

"Why so? It seems to me that I am bolder than you. I can look the cruelties of the world in the face, and declare openly how I will meet them. I did marry Mr. Houghton for his money, and of course he knew it. Is it to be supposed that he or any human being could have thought that I married him for love? I make his house comfortable for him as far as I can, and am civil to his friends, and look my best at his table. I hope he is satisfied with his bargain; but I cannot do more. I cannot wear him in my heart. Nor, George, do I believe that you in your heart can ever wear Mary Lovelace!" But he did—only that he thought that he had space there for two, and that in giving habitation to this second love he was adding at any rate to the excitements of his life. "Tell me, George," said the woman, laying her hand upon his breast, "is it she or I that have a home there?"

"I will not say that I do not love my wife," he said.

"No; you are afraid. The formalities of the world are so much more to you than to me! Sit down, George. Oh, George!" Then she was on her knees at his feet, hiding her face upon her hands, while his arms were almost necessarily thrown over her and embracing. The lady was convulsed with sobs, and he was thinking how it would be with him and her should the door be opened and some pair of eyes see them as they were. But her ears were sharp in spite of her sobs. There was the fall of a foot on the stairs which she heard long before it reached him, and, in a moment, she was in her chair. He looked at her, and there was no trace of a tear. "It's Houghton," she said, putting her finger up to her mouth with almost a comic gesture. There was a smile in her eyes, and a little mockery of fear in the trembling of her hand and the motion of her lips. To him it seemed to be tragic enough. He had to assume to this gentleman whom he had been injuring a cordial, friendly manner—and thus to lie to him. He had to make pretences, and at a moment's notice to feign himself something very different from what he was. Had the man come a little more quickly, had the husband caught him with the wife at his knees, nothing could have saved him and his own wife from utter misery. So he felt it to be, and the feeling almost overwhelmed him. His heart palpitated with emotion as the wronged husband's hand was on the door. She, the while, was as thoroughly composed as a stage heroine. But she had flattered him and pretended to love him, and it did not occur to him that he ought to be angry with her. "Who would ever think of seeing you at this time of day?" said Mrs. Houghton.

"Well, no; I'm going back to the club in a few minutes. I had to come up to Piccadilly to have my hair cut!"

"Your hair cut!"

"Honour bright! Nothing upsets me so much as having my hair cut. I'm going to ring for a glass of sherry. By-the-bye, Lord George, a good many of them are talking at the club about young Popenjoy."

"What are they saying?" Lord George felt that he must open his mouth, but did not wish to talk to this man, and especially did not wish to talk about his own affairs.

"Of course I know nothing about it; but surely the way Brotherton has come back is very odd. I used to be very fond of your brother, you know. There was nobody her father used to swear by so much as him. But, by George, I don't know what to make of it now. Nobody has seen the Marchioness."

"I have not seen her," said Lord George; "but she is there all the same for that."

"Nobody doubts that she's there. She's there, safe enough. And the boy is there, too. We're all quite sure of that. But you know the Marquis of Brotherton is somebody."

"I hope so," said Lord George.

"And when he brings his wife home people will expect—will expect to know something about it—eh?" All this was said with an intention of taking Lord George's part in a question which was already becoming one of interest to the public. It was hinted here and there that there was a "screw loose" about this young Popenjoy, who had just been brought from Italy, and that Lord George would have to look to it. Of course they who were connected with Brothershire were more prone to talk of it than others, and Mr. Houghton, who had heard and said a good deal about it, thought that he was only being civil to Lord George in seeming to take part against the Marquis.

But Lord George felt it to be matter of offence that
any outsider should venture to talk about his family.
"If people would only confine themselves to sub-
jects with which they are acquainted, it would be very
much better," he said; and then almost immediately
took his leave.

"That's all regular nonsense, you know," Mr.
Houghton said, as soon as he was alone with his wife.
"Of course people are talking about it. Your father
says that Brotherton must be mad."

"That's no reason why you should come and tell
Lord George what people say. You never have any
tact."

"Of course I'm wrong; I always am," said the husband, swallowing his glass of sherry and then taking
his departure.

Lord George was now in a very uneasy state of
mind. He intended to be cautious—had intended even
to be virtuous and self-denying; and yet, in spite of
his intentions, he had fallen into such a condition of
things with Mr. Houghton's wife, that were the truth
to be known, he would be open to most injurious proceedings. To him the love affair with another man's
wife was more embarrassing even than pleasant. Its
charm did not suffice to lighten for him the burden of
the wickedness. He had certain inklings of complaint
in his own mind against his own wife, but he felt
that his own hands should be perfectly clean before
he could deal with those inklings magisterially and
maritally. How would he look were she to turn upon
him and ask him as to his own conduct with Adelaide
Houghton? And then, into what a sea of trouble had
he not already fallen in this matter of his brother's
marriage? His first immediate duty was that of writ-

ing to his elder sister, and he expressed himself to her in strong language. After telling her all that he had heard from the lawyer, he spoke of himself and of the Dean. "It will make me very unhappy," he wrote. "Do you remember what Hamlet says?

> "Oh cursed spite,
> That ever I was born to set it right.

I feel like that altogether. I want to get nothing by it. No man ever less begrudged to his elder brother than I do all that belongs to him. Though he has himself treated me badly, I would support him in anything for the sake of the family. At this moment I most heartily wish that the child may be Lord Popenjoy. The matter will destroy all my happiness perhaps for the next ten years—perhaps for ever. And I cannot but think that the Dean has interfered in a most unjustifiable manner. He drives me on, so that I almost feel that I shall be forced to quarrel with him. With him it is manifestly personal ambition, and not duty." There was much more of it in the same strain, but at the time an acknowledgment that he had now instructed the Dean's lawyer to make the inquiry.

Lady Sarah's answer was perhaps more judicious; and as it was shorter it shall be given entire.

"Cross Hall, May 10, 187—.

"MY DEAR GEORGE,—Of course it is a sad thing to us all that this terrible inquiry should be forced upon us; and more grievous to you than to us, as you must take the active part in it. But this is a manifest duty, and duties are seldom altogether pleasant. All that you say as to yourself—which I know to be absolutely true—must at any rate make your conscience clear in the matter. It is not for your sake nor for our sake that this is to be done, but for the sake of the family at large, and to prevent the necessity of future lawsuits which would be ruinous to the property. If the child be legitimate, let that, in God's name, be proclaimed so loud that no one shall hereafter be able to cast a doubt upon the fact. To us it must be matter of deepest sorrow that our brother's child and the future head of our family should have been born under circumstances which, at the best, must still be disgraceful. But, although that is so, it will be equally our duty to acknowledge his rights to the full, if they be his rights. Though the son of the widow of a lunatic foreigner, still if the law says that he is Brotherton's heir, it is for us to render the difficulties in his way as light as possible. But that we may do so, we must know what he is.

"Of course you find the Dean to be pushing and perhaps a little vulgar. No doubt with him the chief feeling is one of personal ambition. But in his way he is wise, and I do not know that in this matter he has done anything which had better have been left undone. He believes that the child is not legitimate; and so in my heart do I.

"You must remember that my dear mother is altogether on Brotherton's side. The feeling that there should be an heir is so much to her, and the certainty that the boy is at any rate her grandson, that she cannot endure that a doubt should be expressed. Of course this does not tend to make our life pleasant down here. Poor dear mamma. Of course we do all we can to comfort her.

"Your affectionate sister,

"SARAH GERMAIN."

CHAPTER XXX

A week had passed away and nothing had as yet been heard from the Marquis, nor had Mr. Battle's confidential clerk as yet taken his departure for Italy, when Mrs. Montacute Jones called one day in Munster Court. Lady George had not seen her new old friend since the night of the ball to which she had not gone, but had received more than one note respecting her absence on that occasion and various other little matters. Why did not Lady George come and lunch; and why did not Lady George come and drive? Lady George was a little afraid that there was a conspiracy about her in reference to Captain de Baron, and that Mrs. Montacute Jones was one of the conspirators. If so, Adelaide Houghton was certainly another. It had been very pleasant. When she examined herself about this man, as she endeavoured to do, she declared that it had been as innocent as pleasant. She did not really believe that either Adelaide Houghton or Mrs. Montacute Jones had intended to do mischief. Mischief, such as the alienation of her own affections from her husband, she regarded as quite out of the question. She would not even admit to herself that it was possible that she should fall into such a pit as that. But there were other dangers; and those friends of hers would indeed be dangerous if they brought her into any society that made her husband jealous. Therefore, though she

343

liked Mrs. Montacute Jones very much, she had avoided the old lady lately, knowing that something would be said about Jack de Baron, and not quite confident as to her own answers.

And now Mrs. Montacute Jones had come to her. "My dear Lady George," she said, "where on earth have you been? Are you going to cut me? If so, tell me at once."

"Oh, Mrs. Jones," said Lady George, kissing her, "how can you ask such a question?"

"Because, you know, it requires two to play at that game, and I'm not going to be cut." Mrs. Montacute Jones was a stout-built but very short old lady, with gray hair curled in precise rolls down her face, with streaky cheeks, giving her a look of extreme good health, and very bright grey eyes. She was always admirably dressed, so well dressed that her enemies accused her of spending enormous sums on her toilet. She was very old—some people said eighty, adding probably not more than ten years to her age —very enthusiastic, particularly in reference to her friends; very fond of gaiety, and very charitable. "Why didn't you come to my ball?"

"Lord George doesn't care about balls," said Mary, laughing.

"Come, come! Don't try and humbug me. It had been all arranged that you should come when he went to bed. Hadn't it now?"

"Something had been said about it."

"A good deal had been said about it, and he had agreed. Are you going to tell me that he won't· go out with you, and yet dislikes your going out without him? Is he such a Bluebeard as that?"

"He's not a Bluebeard at all, Mrs. Jones."

"I hope not. There has been something about that German Baroness—hasn't there?"

"Oh dear no."

"I heard that there was. She came and took you and the brougham all about London. And there was a row with Lady Selina. I heard of it."

"But that had nothing to do with my going to your party."

"Well, no; why should it? She's a nasty woman, that Baroness Banmann. If we can't get on here in England without German baronesses and American she-doctors, we are in a bad way. You shouldn't have let them drag you into that lot. Women's Rights! Women are quite able to hold their own without such trash as that. I'm told she's in debt everywhere, and can't pay a shilling. I hope they'll lock her up."

"She is nothing to me, Mrs. Jones."

"I hope not. What was it then? I know there was something. He doesn't object to Captain de Baron, does he?"

"Object to him! Why should he object to Captain de Baron?"

"I don't know why. Men do take such fancies into their heads. You are not going to give up dancing —are you?"

"Not altogether. I'm not sure that I care for it very much."

"Oh, Lady George! where do you expect to go to?" Mary could not keep herself from laughing, though she was at the same time almost inclined to be angry with the old lady's interference. "I should have said that I didn't know a young person in the world fonder of dancing than you are. Perhaps he objects to it."

"He doesn't like my waltzing," said Mary, with
a blush. On former occasions she had almost made
up her mind to confide her troubles to this old woman,
and now the occasion seemed so suitable that she could
not keep herself from telling so much as that.

"Oh!" said Mrs. Montacute Jones. "That's it!
I knew there was something. My dear, he's a goose,
and you ought to tell him so."

"Couldn't you tell him?" said Mary, laughing.

"I would do it in half a minute, and think nothing
of it!"

"Pray don't. He wouldn't like it at all."

"My dear, you shouldn't be afraid of him. I'm
not going to preach up rebellion against husbands.
I'm the last woman in London to do that. I know
the comfort of a quiet house as well as anyone, and
that two people can't get along easy together unless
there is a good deal of give and take. But it doesn't
do to give up everything. What does he say about
it?"

"He says he doesn't like it."

"What would he say if you told him you didn't
like his going to his club?"

"He wouldn't go."

"Nonsense! It's being a dog in the manger, because he doesn't care for it himself. I should have
it out with him—nicely and pleasantly. Just tell
him that you're fond of it, and ask him to change
his mind. I can't bear anybody interfering to put
down the innocent pleasures of young people. A man
like that just opens his mouth and speaks a word,
and takes away the whole pleasure of a young woman's
season! You've got my card for the 10th of
June?"

"Oh, yes—I've got it."

"And I shall expect you to come. It's only going to be a small affair. Get him to bring you if you can, and you do as I bid you. Just have it out with him—nicely and quietly. Nobody hates a row so much as I do, but people oughtn't to be trampled on."

All this had considerable effect upon Lady George. She quite agreed with Mrs. Jones that people ought not to be trampled on. Her father had never trampled on her. From him there had been very little positive ordering as to what she might and what she might not do. And yet she had been only a child when living with her father. Now she was a married woman, and the mistress of her own house. She was quite sure that were she to ask her father, the Dean would say that such a prohibition as this was absurd. Of course she could not ask her father. She would not appeal from her husband to him. But it was a hardship, and she almost made up her mind that she would request him to revoke the order.

Then she was very much troubled by a long letter from the Baroness Banmann. The Baroness was going to bring an action jointly against Lady Selina Protest and Miss Mildmay, whom the reader will know as Aunt Ju; and informed Lady George that she was to be summoned as a witness. This was for a while a grievous affliction to her. "I know nothing about it," she said to her husband; "I only just went there once because Miss Mildmay asked me."

"It was a very foolish thing for her to do."

"And I was foolish, perhaps; but what can I say about it? I don't know anything."

"You shouldn't have bought those other tickets."

"How could I refuse when the woman asked for such a trifle?"

"Then you took her to Miss Mildmay's."

"She would get into the brougham, and I couldn't get rid of her. Hadn't I better write and tell her that I know nothing about it?" But to this Lord George objected, requesting her altogether to hold her peace on the subject, and never even to speak about it to anyone. He was not good-humoured with her, and this was clearly no occasion for asking him about the waltzing. Indeed, just at present he rarely was in a good humour, being much troubled in his mind on the great Popenjoy question.

At this time the Dean was constantly up in town, running backwards and forwards between London and Brotherton, prosecuting his inquiry, and spending a good deal of his time at Mr. Battle's offices. In doing all this he by no means acted in perfect concert with Lord George, nor did he often stay or even dine at the house in Munster Court. There had been no quarrel, but he found that Lord George was not cordial with him, and therefore placed himself at the hotel in Suffolk Street. "Why doesn't papa come here, as he is in town?" Mary said to her husband.

"I don't know why he comes to town at all," replied her husband.

"I suppose he comes because he has business, or because he likes it. I shouldn't think of asking why he comes; but, as he is here, I wish he wouldn't stay at a nasty dull hotel, after all that was arranged."

"You may be sure he knows what he likes best," said Lord George sulkily. That allusion to "an arrangement" had not served to put him in a good humour.

Mary had known well why her father was so much in London, and had in truth known also why he did not come to Munster Court. She could perceive that her father and husband were drifting into unfriendly relations, and greatly regretted it. In her heart she took her father's part. She was not as keen as he was in this matter of the little Popenjoy, being restrained by a feeling that it would not become her to be over anxious for her own elevation or for the fall of others; but she had always sympathised with her father in everything, and therefore she sympathised with him in this. And then there was gradually growing upon her a conviction that her father was the stronger man of the two, the more reasonable, and certainly the kinder. She had thoroughly understood when the house was furnished, very much at the Dean's expense, that he was to be a joint occupant in it when it might suit him to be in London. He himself had thought less about this, having rather submitted to the suggestion as an excuse for his own liberality than contemplated any such final arrangement. But Lord George remembered it. The house would certainly be open to him should he choose to come; but Lord George would not press it.

Mr. Stokes had thought it proper to go in person to Manor Cross, in order that he might receive instructions from the Marquis.

"Upon my word, Mr. Stokes," said the Marquis, "only that I would not seem to be uncourteous to you, I should feel disposed to say that this interview can do no good."

"It is a very serious matter, my lord."

"It is a very serious annoyance, certainly, that my own brothers and sisters should turn against me, and give me all this trouble because I have chosen to marry a foreigner. It is simply an instance of that pigheaded English blindness which makes us think that everything outside our own country is or ought to be given up to the devil. My sisters are very religious, and, I daresay, very good women. But they are quite willing to think that I and my wife ought to be damned because we talk Italian, and that my son ought to be disinherited because he was not baptised in an English church. They have got this stupid story into their heads, and they must do as they please about it. I will have no hand in it. I will take care that there shall be no difficulty in my son's way when I die."

"That will be right, of course, my lord."

"I know where all this comes from. My brother, who is an idiot, has married the daughter of a vulgar clergyman, who thinks in his ignorance that he can make his grandson, if he has one, an English nobleman. He'll spend his money and he'll burn his fingers, and I don't care how much money he spends or how much he burns his hands. I don't suppose his purse is so very long but that he may come to the bottom of it."

This was nearly all that passed between Mr. Stokes and the Marquis. Mr. Stokes then went back to town and gave Mr. Battle to understand that nothing was to be done on their side.

The Dean was very anxious that the confidential clerk should be despatched, and at one time almost thought that he would go himself.

"Better not, Mr. Dean. Everybody would know," said Mr. Battle.

"And I should intend everybody to know," said

the Dean. "Do you suppose that I am doing anything that I'm ashamed of?"

"But being a dignitary——" began Mr. Battle.

"What has that to do with it? A dignitary, as you call it, is not to see a child robbed of her rights. I only want to find the truth, and I should never take shame to myself in looking for that by honest means."

But Mr. Battle prevailed, persuading the Dean that the confidential clerk, even though he confined himself to honest means, would reach his point more certainly than a dean of the Church of England.

But still there was delay. Mr. Stokes did not take his journey down to Brotherton quite as quickly as he perhaps might have done, and then there was a prolonged correspondence carried on through an English lawyer settled at Leghorn. But at last the man was sent.

"I think we know this," said Mr. Battle to the Dean, on the day before the man started, "there were certainly two marriages. One of them took place as much as five years ago, and the other after his lordship had written to his brother."

"Then the first marriage must have been nothing," said the Dean.

"It does not follow. It may have been a legal marriage, although the parties chose to confirm it by a second ceremony."

"But when did the man Luigi die?"

"And where and how? This is what we have got to find out. I shouldn't wonder if we found that he had been for years a lunatic."

Almost all this the Dean communicated to Lord George, being determined that his son-in-law should be seen to act in co-operation with him. They met occasionally in Mr. Battle's chambers, and sometimes by appointment in Munster Court.

"It is essentially necessary that you should know what is being done," said the Dean to his son-in-law.

Lord George fretted and fumed, and expressed an opinion that as the matter had been put into a lawyer's hands it had better be left there. But the Dean had very much his own way.

CHAPTER XXXI

SOON after Mr. Stokes's visit there was a great disturbance at Manor Cross, whether caused or not by that event no one was able to say. The Marquis and all the family were about to proceed to London. The news first reached Cross Hall through Mrs. Toff, who still kept up friendly relations with a portion of the English establishment at the great house. There probably was no idea of maintaining a secret on the subject. The Marquis and his wife, with Lord Popenjoy and the servants, could not have had themselves carried up to town without the knowledge of all Brotherton, nor was there any adequate reason for supposing that secrecy was desired. Nevertheless Mrs. Toff made a great deal of the matter, and the ladies at Cross Hall were not without a certain perturbed interest as though in a mystery. It was first told to Lady Sarah, for Mrs. Toff was quite aware of the position of things, and knew that the old Marchioness herself was not to be regarded as being on their side.

"Yes, my lady, it's quite true," said Mrs. Toff. "The horses is ordered for next Friday." This was said on the previous Saturday, so that considerable time was allowed for the elucidation of the mystery. "And the things is already being packed, and her ladyship—that is if she is her ladyship—is taking every dress and every rag as she brought with her."

"Where are they going to, Toff? Not to the square?" Now the Marquis of Brotherton had an old family house in Cavendish Square, which, however, had been shut up for the last ten or fifteen years, but was still known as the family house by all the adherents of the family.

"No, my lady. I did hear from one of the servants that they are going to Scumberg's Hotel, in Albemarle Street."

Then Lady Sarah told the news to her mother. The poor old lady felt that she was ill-used. She had been at any rate true to her eldest son, had always taken his part during his absence by scolding her daughters whenever an allusion was made to the family at Manor Cross, and had almost worshipped him when he would come to her on Sunday. And now he was going off to London without saying a word of the journey. "I don't believe that Toff knows anything about it," she said. "Toff is a nasty, meddling creature, and I wish she had not come here at all." The management of the Marchioness under these circumstances was very difficult, but Lady Sarah was a woman who allowed no difficulty to crush her. She did not expect the world to be very easy. She went on with her constant needle, trying to comfort her mother as she worked. At this time the Marchioness had almost brought herself to quarrel with her younger son, and would say very hard things about him and about the Dean. She had more than once said that Mary was a "nasty sly thing," and had expressed herself as greatly aggrieved by that marriage. All this came of course from the Marquis, and was known by her daughters to come from the Marquis; and yet the Marchioness had never as yet been allowed to see either her daughter-in-law or Popenjoy.

On the following day her son came to her when the three sisters were at church in the afternoon. On these occasions he would stay for a quarter of an hour, and would occupy the greater part of the time in abusing the Dean and Lord George. But on this day she could not refrain from asking him a question. "Are you going up to London, Brotherton?"

"What makes you ask?"

"Because they tell me so. Sarah says that the servants are talking about it."

"I wish Sarah had something to do better than listening to the servants."

"But you are going?"

"If you want to know, I believe we shall go up to town for a few days. Popenjoy ought to see a dentist, and I want to do a few things. Why the deuce shouldn't I go up to London as well as anyone else?"

"Of course, if you wish it."

"To tell you the truth, I don't much wish anything, except to get out of this cursed country again."

"Don't say that, Brotherton. You are an Englishman."

"I am ashamed to say I am. I wish with all my heart that I had been born a Chinese or a Red Indian." This he said, not in furtherance of any peculiar cosmopolitan proclivities, but because the saying of it would vex his mother. "What am I to think of the country, when the moment I get here I am hounded by all my own family because I choose to live after my own fashion and not after theirs?"

" I haven't hounded you."

"No. You might possibly get more by being on good terms with me than bad. And so might they if they knew it. I'll be even with Master George before I've done with him; and I'll be even with that parson, too, who still smells of the stables. I'll lead him a dance that will about ruin him. And as for his daughter——"

"It wasn't I got up the marriage, Brotherton."

"I don't care who got it up. But I can have inquiries made as well as another person. I am not very fond of spies; but if other people use spies, so can I, too. That young woman is no better than she ought to be. The Dean, I daresay, knows it; but he shall know that I know it. And Master George shall know what I think about it. As there is to be war, he shall know what it is to have war. She has got a lover of her own already, and everybody who knows them is talking about it."

"Oh, Brotherton!"

"And she is going in for women's rights! George has made a nice thing of it for himself. He has to live on the Dean's money, so that he doesn't dare to call his soul his own. And yet he's fool enough to send a lawyer to me to tell me that my wife is a ——, and my son a ——!" He made use of very plain language, so that the poor old woman was horrified and aghast and dumbfounded. And as he spoke the words there was a rage in his eyes worse than anything she had seen before. He was standing with his back to the fire, which was burning though the weather was warm, and the tails of his coat were hanging over his arms as he kept his hands in his pockets. He was generally quiescent in his moods, and apt to express his anger in sarcasm rather than in outspoken language; but now he was so much moved that he was unable not to give vent to his feelings. As the Marchioness looked at him, shaking with fear, there came into her distracted mind some vague idea of Cain and Abel, though, had she collected her thoughts, she would have been far from telling herself that her eldest son was Cain. "He thinks," continued the Marquis, "that because I have lived abroad I shan't mind that sort of thing. I wonder how he'll feel when I tell him the truth about his wife—I mean to do it—and what the Dean will think when I use a little plain language about his daughter? I mean to do that, too, I shan't mince matters. I suppose you have heard of Captain de Baron, mother?"

Now the Marchioness unfortunately had heard of Captain de Baron. Lady Susanna had brought the tidings down to Cross Hall. Had Lady Susanna really believed that her sister-in-law was wickedly entertaining a lover, there would have been some reticence in her mode of alluding to so dreadful a subject. The secret would have been confided to Lady Sarah in awful conclave, and some solemn warning would have been conveyed to Lord George, with a prayer that he would lose no time in withdrawing the unfortunate young woman from evil influences. But Lady Susanna had entertained no such fear. Mary was young, and foolish, and fond of pleasure. Hard as was this woman in her manner, and disagreeable as she made herself, yet she could, after a fashion, sympathise with the young wife. She had spoken of Captain de Baron with disapprobation certainly, but had not spoken of him as a fatal danger. And she had also spoken of the Baroness Banmann and Mary's folly in going to the Institute. The old Marchioness had heard of these things, and now, when she heard further of them from her son, she almost believed all that he told her. " Don't be hard upon poor George," she said.

" I give as I get, mother. I'm not one of those who return good for evil. Had he left me alone I should have left him alone. As it is, I rather think I shall be hard upon poor George. Do you suppose that all Brotherton hasn't heard already what they are doing—that there is a man or a woman in the county who doesn't know that my own brother is questioning the legitimacy of my own son? And then you ask me not to be hard."

" It isn't my doing, Brotherton."

" But those three girls have their hand in it. That's what they call charity! That's what they go to church for ! "

All this made the poor old Marchioness very ill. Before her son left her she was almost prostrate; and yet, to the end, he did not spare her. But as he left he said one word which apparently was intended to comfort her. " Perhaps Popenjoy had better be brought here for you to see before he is taken up to town." There had been a promise made before that the child should be brought to the Hall to bless his grandmother. On this occasion she had been too much horrified and overcome by what had been said to urge her request; but when the proposition was renewed by him of course she assented.

Popenjoy's visit to Cross Hall was arranged with a good deal of state, and was made on the following

Tuesday. On the Monday there came a message to say that the child should be brought up at twelve on the following day. The Marquis was not coming himself, and the child would of course be inspected by all the ladies. At noon they were assembled in the drawing-room; but they were kept there waiting for half an hour, during which the Marchioness repeatedly expressed her conviction that now, at the last moment, she was to be robbed of the one great desire of her heart. "He won't let him come because he's so angry with George," she said, sobbing.

"He wouldn't have sent a message yesterday, mother," said Lady Amelia, "if he hadn't meant to send him."

"You are all so very unkind to him," ejaculated the Marchioness.

But at half-past twelve the *cortège* appeared. The child was brought up in a perambulator which had at first been pushed by the under-nurse, an Italian, and accompanied by the upper-nurse, who was of course an Italian also. With them had been sent one of the Englishmen to show the way. Perhaps the two women had been somewhat ill-treated, as no true idea of the distance had been conveyed to them; and, though they had now been some weeks at Manor Cross, they had never been half so far from the house. Of course the labour of the perambulator had soon fallen to the man; but the two nurses, who had been forced to walk a mile, had thought that they would never come to the end of their journey. When they did arrive they were full of plaints, which, however, no one could understand. But Popenjoy was at last brought to the Hall.

"My darling!" said the Marchioness, putting out

both her arms. But Popenjoy, though a darling, screamed frightfully beneath his heap of clothes.

"You had better let him come into the room, mamma," said Lady Susanna. Then the nurse carried him in, and one or two of his outer garemnts were taken from him.

"Dear me, how black he is!" said Lady Susanna. The Marchioness turned upon her daughter in great anger. "The Germains were always dark," she said. "You're dark yourself—quite as black as he is. My darling!"

She made another attempt to take the boy; but the nurse with voluble eloquence explained something which of course none of them understood. The purport of her speech was an assurance that "Tavo," as she most unceremoniously called the child whom no Germain thought of naming otherwise than as Popenjoy, never would go to any "foreigner." The nurse therefore held him up to be looked at for two minutes, while he still screamed, and then put him back into his covering raiments. "He is very black," said Lady Sarah, severely.

"So are some peoples' hearts," said the Marchioness, with a vigour for which her daughters had hardly given her credit. This, however, was borne without a murmur by the three sisters.

On the Friday the whole family, including all the Italian servants, migrated to London, and it certainly was the case that the lady took with her all her clothes and everything that she had brought with her. Toff had been quite right there. And when it came to be known by the younger ladies at Cross Hall that Toff had been right, they argued from the fact that their brother had concealed something of the truth when saying that he intended to go up to London only for a few days. There had been three separate carriages, and Toff was almost sure that the Italian lady had carried off more than she had brought with her, so exuberant had been the luggage. It was not long before Toff effected an entrance into the house, and brought away a report that very many things were missing. "The two little gilt cream-jugs is gone," she said to Lady Sarah, "and the minitshur with the pearl settings out of the yellow drawing-room!" Lady Sarah explained that as these things were the property of her brother, he or his wife might of course take them away if so pleased. "She's got 'em unbeknownst to my lord, my lady," said Toff, shaking her head. "I could only just scurry through with half an eye; but when I comes to look there will be more, I warrant you, my lady."

The Marquis had expressed so much vehement dislike of everything about his English home, and it had become so generally understood that his Italian wife hated the place, that everybody agreed that they would not come back. Why should they? What did they get by living there? The lady had not been outside the house a dozen times, and only twice beyond the park-gate. The Marquis took no share in any county or any country pursuit. He went to no man's house and received no visitors. He would not see the tenants when they came to him, and had not even returned a visit except Mr. de Baron's. Why had he come there at all? That was the question which all the Brothershire people asked of each other, and which no one could answer. Mr. Price suggested that it was just devilry—to make everybody unhappy. Mrs. Toff thought that it was the woman's

doing, because she wanted to steal silver mugs, minia-
tures, and such-like treasures. Mr. Waddy, the vicar
of the parish, said that it was "a trial," having probably some idea in his own mind that the Marquis
had been sent home by Providence as a sort of precious blister which would purify all concerned in him
by counter-irritation. The old Marchioness still conceived that it had been brought about that a grandmother might take delight in the presence of her
grandchild. Dr. Pountner said that it was impudence.
But the Dean was of opinion that it had been delib-
erately planned with the view of passing off a sup-
posititious child upon the property and title. The
Dean, however, kept his opinion very much to himself.

Of course the tidings of the migration were sent to
Munster Court. Lady Sarah wrote to her brother,
and the Dean wrote to his daughter.

"What shall you do, George? Shall you go and
see him?"

"I don't know what I shall do?"

"Ought I to go?"

"Certainly not. You could only call on her, and
she has not even seen my mother and sisters. When
I was there he would not introduce me to her, though
he sent for the child. I suppose I had better go.
I do not want to quarrel with him if I can help it."

"You have offered to do everything together with
him, if only he would let you."

"I must say that your father has driven me on in
a manner which Brotherton would be sure to resent."

"Papa has done everything from a sense of duty,
George."

"Perhaps so. I don't know how that is. It is
very hard sometimes to divide a sense of duty from

one's own interest. But it has made me very miserable—very wretched indeed."

"Oh, George, is it my fault?"

"No, not your fault. If there is one thing worse to me than another, it is the feeling of being divided from my own family. Brotherton has behaved badly to me."

"Very badly."

"And yet I would give anything to be on good terms with him. I think I shall go and call. He is at an hotel in Albemarle Street. I have done nothing to deserve ill of him, if he knew all."

It should, of course, be understood that Lord George did not at all know the state of his brother's mind towards him, except as it had been exhibited at that one interview which had taken place between them at Manor Cross. He was aware that in every conversation which he had had with the lawyers—both with Mr. Battle and Mr. Stokes—he had invariably expressed himself as desirous of establishing the legitimacy of the boy's birth. If Mr. Stokes had repeated to his brother what he had said, and had done him the justice of explaining that in all that he did he was simply desirous of performing his duty to the family, surely his brother would not be angry with him! At any rate it would not suit him to be afraid of his brother, and he went to the hotel. After being kept waiting in the hall for about ten minutes, the Italian courier came down to him. The Marquis at the present moment was not dressed, and Lord George did not like being kept waiting. Would Lord George call at three o'clock on the following day? Lord George said that he would, and was again at Scumberg's Hotel at three o'clock on the next afternoon.

CHAPTER XXXII

THIS was a day of no little importance to Lord George; so much so, that one or two circumstances which occurred before he saw his brother at the hotel must be explained. On that day there had come to him from the Dean a letter written in the Dean's best humour. When the house had been taken in Munster Court there had been a certain understanding, hardly quite a fixed assurance, that it was to be occupied up to the end of June, and that then Lord George and his wife should go into Brotherton. There had been a feeling ever since the marriage that, while Mary preferred London, Lord George was wedded to the country. They had on the whole behaved well to each other in the matter. The husband, though he feared that his wife was surrounded by dangers, and was well aware that he himself was dallying on the brink of a terrible pitfall, would not urge a retreat before the time that had been named. And she, though she had ever before her eyes the fear of the dulness of Cross Hall, would not ask to have the time postponed. It was now the end of May, and a certain early day in July had been fixed for their retreat from London. Lord George had, with a good grace, promised to spend a few days at the Deanery before he went to Cross Hall, and had given Mary permission to remain there for some little time after-

wards. Now there had come a letter from the Dean
full of smiles and pleasantness about this visit. There
were tidings in it about Mary's horse, which was
still kept at the Deanery, and comfortable assurances
of sweetest welcome. Not a word had been said in
this letter about the terrible family matter. Lord
George, though he was at the present moment not
disposed to think in the most kindly manner of his
father-in-law, appreciated this, and had read the letter aloud to his wife at the breakfast-table with
pleasant approbation. As he left the house to go
to his brother, he told her that she had better answer
her father's letter, and had explained to her where
she would find it in his dressing-room.

But on the previous afternoon he had received at
his club another letter, the nature of which was not
so agreeable. This letter had not been pleasant even
to himself, and certainly was not adapted to give
pleasure to his wife. After receiving it he had kept
it in the close custody of his breast-pocket; and
when, as he left the house, he sent his wife to find
that which had come from her father, he certainly
thought that this prior letter was at the moment
secure from all eyes within the sanctuary of his coat.
But it was otherwise. With that negligence to which
husbands are so specially subject, he had made the
Dean's letter safe next to his bosom, but had left
the other epistle unguarded. He had not only left
it unguarded, but had absolutely so put his wife on
the track of it that it was impossible that she should
not read it.

Mary found the letter and did read it before she
left her husband's dressing-room—and the letter was
as follows:

"Dearest George." When she read the epithet, which she and she only was entitled to use, she paused for a moment, and all the blood rushed up into her face. She had known the handwriting instantly, and at the first shock she put the paper down upon the table. For a second there was a feeling prompting her to read no further. But it was only for a second. Of course she would read it. It certainly never would have occurred to her to search her husband's clothes for letters. Up to this moment she had never examined a document of his except at his bidding or in compliance with his wish. She had suspected nothing, found nothing, had entertained not even any curiosity about her husband's affairs. But now must she not read this letter to which he himself had directed her? Dearest George! And that in the handwriting of her friend—her friend!—Adelaide Houghton—in the handwriting of the woman to whom her husband had been attached before he had known herself! Of course she read the letter.

"Dearest George,—I break my heart when you don't come to me; for heaven's sake be here to-morrow. Two, three, four, five, six, seven—I shall be here any hour till you come. I don't dare to tell the man that I am not at home to anybody else, but you must take your chance. Nobody ever does come till after three or after six. He never comes home till half-past seven. Oh, me! what is to become of me when you go out of town? There is nothing to live for, nothing—only you. Anything that you write is quite safe. Say that you love me."

"A."

The letter had grieved him when he got it—as had other letters before that. And yet it flattered him, and the assurance of the woman's love had in it a certain candied sweetness which prevented him from destroying the paper instantly, as he ought to have done. Could his wife have read all his mind in the matter her anger would have been somewhat mollified. In spite of the candied sweetness he hated the correspondence. It had been the woman's doing and not his. It is so hard for a man to be a Joseph! The Potiphar's wife of the moment has probably had some encouragement—and after that Joseph can hardly flee unless he be very stout indeed. This Joseph would have fled, though after a certain fashion he liked the woman, had he been able to assure himself that the fault had in no degree been his. But, looking back, he thought that he had encouraged her, and did not know how to fly. Of all this Mary knew nothing. She only knew that old Mr. Houghton's wife, who professed to be her dear friend, had written a most foul love-letter to her husband, and that her husband had preserved it carefully, and had then, through manifest mistake, delivered it over into her hands.

She read it twice, and then stood motionless for a few minutes thinking what she would do. Her first idea was that she would tell her father. But that she soon abandoned. She was grievously offended with her husband; but, as she thought of it, she became aware that she did not wish to bring on him any anger but her own. Then she thought that she would start immediately for Berkeley Square, and say what she had to say to Mrs. Houghton. As this idea presented itself to her, she felt that she could say a

good deal. But how would that serve her? Intense
as was her hatred at present against Adelaide, Adelaide was nothing to her in comparison with her husband. For a moment she almost thought that she
would fly after him, knowing, as she did, that he had
gone to see his brother at Scumberg's Hotel. But
at last she resolved that she would do nothing and
say nothing till he should have perceived that she
had read the letter. She would leave it open on his
dressing-table, so that he might know immediately on
his return what had been done. Then it occurred to
her that the servants might see the letter if she ex-
posed it. So she kept it in her pocket, and determined that when she heard his knock at the door she
would step into his room, and place the letter ready
for his eyes. After that she spent the whole day in
thinking of it, and read the odious words over and
over again till they were fixed in her memory. " Say
that you love me ! " Wretched viper ! ill-conditioned
traitor ! Could it be that he, her husband, loved this
woman better than her? Did not all the world know
that the woman was plain, and affected, and vulgar,
and odious? " Dearest George ! " The woman could
not have used such language without his sanction.
Oh—what should she do? Would it not be necessary
that she should go back and live with her father?
Then she thought of Jack de Baron. They called
Jack de Baron wild; but he would not have been
guilty of wickedness such as this. She clung, however, to the resolution of putting the letter ready for
her husband, so that he should know that she had
read it before they met.

In the meantime Lord George, ignorant as yet of
the storm which was brewing at home, was shown

into his brother's sitting-room. When he entered he found there, with his brother, a lady whom he could recognise without difficulty as his sister-in-law. She was a tall, dark woman, as he thought very plain, but with large bright eyes and very black hair. She was ill-dressed, in a morning wrapper, and looked to him to be at least as old as her husband. The Marquis said something to her in Italian which served as an introduction, but of which Lord George could not understand a word. She curtseyed and Lord George put out his hand. "It is perhaps as well that you should make her acquaintance," said the Marquis. Then he again spoke in Italian, and after a minute or two the lady withdrew. It occurred to Lord George afterwards that the interview had certainly been arranged. Had his brother not wished him to see the lady, the lady could have been kept in the background here as well as at Manor Cross. "It's uncommon civil of you to come," said the Marquis, as soon as the door was closed. "What can I do for you?"

"I did not like that you should be in London without my seeing you."

"I daresay not. I daresay not. I was very much obliged to you, you know, for sending that lawyer down to me."

"I did not send him."

"And particularly obliged to you for introducing that other lawyer into our family affairs."

"I would have done nothing of the kind if I could have helped it. If you will believe me, Brotherton, my only object is to have all this so firmly settled that there may not be need of further inquiry at a future time."

"When I am dead?"

"When we may both be dead."

"You have ten years advantage of me. Your own chance isn't bad."

"If you will believe me——"

"But suppose I don't believe you! Suppose I think that in saying all that, you are lying like the very devil!" Lord George jumped in his chair, almost as though he had been shot. "My dear fellow, what's the good of this humbug? You think you've got a chance. I don't believe you were quick enough to see it yourself, but your father-in-law has put you up to it. He is not quite such an ass as you are; but even he is ass enough to fancy that because I, an Englishman, have married an Italian lady, therefore, the marriage may, very likely, be good for nothing."

"We only want proof."

"Does anybody ever come to you and ask you for proofs of your marriage with that very nice young woman, the Dean's daughter?"

"Anybody may find them at Brotherton."

"No doubt. And I can put my hand on the proofs of my marriage when I want to do so. In the meantime I doubt whether you can learn anything to your own advantage by coming here."

"I didn't want to learn anything."

"If you would look after your own wife a little closer, I fancy it would be a better employment for you. She is at present probably amusing herself with Captain de Baron."

"That is calumny," said Lord George, rising from his chair.

"No doubt. Any imputation coming from me is calumny. But you can make imputations as heavy and as hard as you please—and all in the way of honour. I've no doubt you'll find her with Captain de Baron, if you'll go and look."

"I should find her doing nothing that she ought not to do," said the husband, turning round for his hat and gloves.

"Or perhaps making a speech at the Rights of Women Institute on behalf of that German Baroness, who, I'm told, is in gaol. But, George, don't you take it too much to heart. You've got the money. When a man goes into a stable for his wife, he can't expect much in the way of conduct or manners. If he gets the money he ought to be contented." He had to hear it all to the last bitter word before he could escape from the room and make his way out into the street.

It was at this time about four o'clock, and in his agony of mind he had turned down towards Piccadilly before he could think what he would do with himself for the moment. Then he remembered that Berkeley Square was close to him on the other side, and that he had been summoned there about this hour. To give him his due, it should be owned that he had no great desire to visit Berkeley Square in his present condition of feeling. Since the receipt of that letter, which was now awaiting him at home, he had told himself half-a-dozen times that he must and would play the part of Joseph. He had so resolved when she had first spoken to him of her passion, now some months ago; and then his resolution had broken down merely because he had not at the moment thought any great step to be necessary. But now it was clear that some great step was necessary. He must make her know that it did not suit him

to be called "dearest George" by her, or to be told
to declare that he loved her. And this accusation
against his wife, made in such coarse and brutal
language by his brother, softened his heart to her.
Why, oh, why, had he allowed himself to be brought
up to a place he hated as he had always hated London!
Of course Jack de Baron made him unhappy, though
he was at the present moment prepared to swear
that his wife was as innocent as any woman in
London.

But now, as he was so near, and as his decision
must be declared in person, he might as well go to
Berkeley Square. As he descended Hay Hill he put
his hand into his pocket for the lady's letter, and
pulled out that from the Dean, which he had intended
to leave with his wife. In an instant he knew what
he had done. He remembered it all, even to the way
in which he had made the mistake with the two letters. There could be no doubt but that he had given
Adelaide Houghton's letter into his wife's hands, and
that she had read it. At the bottom of Hill Street,
near the stables, he stopped suddenly and put his hand
up to his head. What should he do now? He certainly
could not pay his visit in Berkeley Square. He could
not go and tell Mrs. Houghton that he loved her, and
certainly would not have strength to tell her that he.
did not love her, while suffering such agony as this.
Of course he must see his wife. Of course he must
—if I may use the slang phrase—of course he must
"have it out with her," after some fashion, and the
sooner the better. So he turned his steps homewards
across the Green Park. But, in going homewards, he
did not walk very fast.

What would she do? How would she take it?

Of course women daily forgive such offences; and he might probably, after a burst of the storm was over, succeed in making her believe that he did in truth love her, and did not love the other woman. In his present mood he was able to assure himself most confidently that such was the truth. He could tell himself now that he never wished to see Adelaide Houghton again. But, before anything of this could be achieved, he would have to own himself a sinner before her. He would have, as it were, to grovel at her feet. Hitherto, in all his intercourse with her, he had been masterful and marital. He had managed up to this point so to live as to have kept in all respects the upper hand. He had never yet been found out even in a mistake or an indiscretion. He had never given her an opening for the mildest finding of fault. She, no doubt, was young, and practice had not come to her. But, as a natural consequence of this, Lord George had hitherto felt that an almost divine superiority was demanded from him. That sense of divine superiority must now pass away.

I do not know whether a husband's comfort is ever perfect till some family peccadilloes have been conclusively proved against him. I am sure that a wife's temper to him is sweetened by such evidence of human imperfection. A woman will often take delight in being angry; will sometimes wrap herself warm in prolonged sullenness; will frequently revel in complaint; but she enjoys forgiving better than aught else. She never feels that all the due privileges of her life have been accorded to her, till her husband shall have laid himself open to the caresses of a pardon. Then, and not till then, he is her equal; and equality is necessary for comfortable love. But the man, till he be well used to it, does not like to be pardoned. He has assumed divine superiority, and is bound to maintain it. Then, at last, he comes home some night with a little too much wine, or he cannot pay the weekly bills because he has lost too much money at cards, or he has got into trouble at his office, and is in doubt for a fortnight about his place, or perhaps a letter from a lady falls into wrong hands. Then he has to tell himself that he has been " found out." The feeling is at first very uncomfortable; but it is, I think, a step almost necessary in reaching true matrimonial comfort. Hunting men say that hard rain settles the ground. A good scold with a "kiss and be friends" after it, perhaps, does the same.

Now Lord George had been found out. He was quite sure of that. And he had to undergo all that was unpleasant without sufficient experience to tell him that those clouds too would pass away quickly. He still walked homewards across St. James's Park, never stopping, but dragging himself along slowly, and when he came to his own door he let himself in very silently. She did not expect him so soon, and when he entered the drawing-room was startled to see him. She had not as yet put the letter, as she had intended, on his dressing-table, but still had it in her pocket; nor had it occurred to her that he would as yet have known the truth. She looked at him when he entered, but did not at first utter a word.

" Mary," he said.

" Well, is anything the matter? "

It was possible that she had not found the letter—possible, though very improbable. But he had brought his mind so firmly to the point of owning what was to be owned and defending what might be defended, that he hardly wished for escape in that direction. At any rate, he was not prepared to avail himself of it. "Did you find the letter?" he asked.

"I found a letter."

"Well!"

"Of course I am sorry to have intruded upon so private a correspondence. There it is." And she threw the letter to him. "Oh, George!"

He picked up the letter, which had fallen to the ground, and, tearing it into bits, threw the fragments into the grate. "What do you believe about it, Mary?"

"Believe!"

"Do you think that I love anyone as I love you?"

"You cannot love me at all—unless that wicked wretched creature is a liar."

"Have I ever lied to you? You will believe me?"

"I do not know."

"I love no one in the world but you."

Even that almost sufficed for her. She already longed to have her arms round his neck and to tell him that it was all forgiven—that he at least was forgiven. During the whole morning she had been thinking of the angry words she would say to him, and of the still more angry words which she would speak of that wicked, wicked viper. The former were already forgotten; but she was not as yet inclined to refrain as to Mrs. Houghton. "Oh, George, how could you bear such a woman as that—that you should let her write to you in such language? Have you been to her?"

"What, to-day?"

"Yes, to-day."

"Certainly not. I have just come from my brother."

"You will never go into the house again! You will promise that!"

Here was made the first direct attack upon his divine superiority! Was he, at his wife's instance, to give a pledge that he would not go into a certain house under any circumstances? This was the process of bringing his nose down to the ground which he had feared. Here was the first attempt made by his wife to put her foot on his neck. "I think that I had better tell you all that I can tell," he said.

"I only want to know that you hate her," said Mary.

"I neither hate nor love her. I did—love her —once. You knew that."

"I never could understand it. I never did believe that you really could have loved her." Then she began to sob. "I shouldn't—ever—have taken you —if—I had."

"But from the moment when I first knew you it was all changed with me." As he said this he put out his arm to her, and she came to him. "There has never been a moment since in which you have not had all my heart."

"But why—why—why——" she sobbed, meaning to ask how it could have come to pass that the wicked viper could, in those circumstances, have written such a letter as that which had fallen into her hands.

The question certainly was not unnatural. But it was a question very difficult to answer. No man likes to say that a woman has pestered him with unwelcome love, and certainly Lord George was not the man to make such a boast. "Dearest Mary," he said, "on my honour as a gentleman I am true to you."

Then she was satisfied and turned her face to him and covered him with kisses. I think that morning did more than any day had done since their marriage to bring about the completion of her desire to be in love with her husband. Her heart was so softened towards him that she would not even press a question that would pain him. She had intended sternly to exact from him a pledge that he would not again enter the house in Berkeley Square, but she let even that pass by, because she would not annoy him. She gathered herself up close to him on the sofa, and, drawing his arm over her shoulder, sobbed and laughed, stroking him with her hands as she crouched against his shoulder. But yet, every now and then, there came forth from her some violent ebullition against Mrs. Houghton. " Nasty creature! wicked, wicked beast! Oh, George, she is so ugly! " And yet, before this little affair, she had been quite content that Adelaide Houghton should be her intimate friend.

It had been nearly five when Lord George reached the house, and he had to sit enduring his wife's caresses, and listening to devotion to himself and her abuses of Mrs. Houghton till past six. Then it struck him that a walk .by himself would be good for him. They were to dine out, but not till eight, and there would still be time. When he proposed it, she acceded at once. Of course she must go and dress, and equally of course he would not, could not go to Berkeley Square now. She thoroughly believed that he was true to her, but yet she feared the wiles of that nasty woman. They would go to the country soon, and then the wicked viper would not be near them.

Lord George walked across to Pall Mall, looked
at an evening paper at his club, and then walked
back again. Of course it had been his object to have
a cool half-hour in which to think it all over—all
that had passed between him and his wife, and also
what had passed between him and his brother. That
his wife was the dearest, sweetest woman in the
world, he was quite sure. He was more than satisfied with her conduct to him. She had exacted from
him very little penitence; had not required to put
her foot in any disagreeable way upon his neck. No
doubt she felt that his divine superiority had been
vanquished, but she had uttered no word of triumph.
With all that he was content. But what was he to
do with Mrs. Houghton, as to whom he had sworn
a dozen times within the last hour that she was quite
indifferent to him. He now repeated the assertion
to himself, and felt himself to be sure of the fact.
But still he was her lover. He had allowed her so
to regard him, and something must be done. She
would write to him letters daily if he did not stop
it; and every such letter not shown to his wife
would be a new treason against her. This was a
great trouble. And then, through it all, those terrible
words which his brother had spoken to him about
Captain de Baron rang in his ears. This afternoon
had certainly afforded no occasion to him to say a
word about Captain de Baron to his wife. When
detected in his own sin he could not allude to possible
delinquencies on the other side. Nor did he think
that there was any delinquency. But Cæsar said
that Cæsar's wife should be above suspicion, and in
that matter every man is a Cæsar to himself. Lady
Susanna had spoken about this Captain, and Adelaide

Houghton had said an ill-natured word or two, and he himself had seen them walking together. Now his brother had told him that Captain de Baron was his wife's lover. He did not at all like Captain de Baron.

END OF VOL. I

WS - #0051 - 061223 - C0 - 229/152/21 - PB - 9781331717348 - Gloss Lamination